The Cabo Contract

A Colin Pearce Adventure

Chris Broyhill

SECOND EDITION

Published by
Citadel Publishing LLC
Dover, Delaware, USA
2017

ISBN-13: 978-0-9988250-5-2
ISBN-10: 0-9988250-5-0

Paperback

Cover Design By: Robin E. Vuchnich

Preface for the Second Edition

The Cabo Contract is Colin Pearce's second adventure and came shortly after the first. In fact, the ideas for *Cabo* began coming to me as I was in the final stages of editing *The Viper Contract*. Thoughts about Colin Pearce and Sarah Morton, who is mentioned in *Viper*, began occurring to me. What would happen if Sarah was in trouble and called Colin for help? What would that look like? How would she know that his array of talents had expanded?

Viper was a relatively straightforward story to write and was more a function of time than of thought about the plot. *Cabo* was much different. I'm not the sort of writer who has a detailed plan for a book when he sits down to compose. While I start with a sketch, as I write, the characters become real and sometimes do things I can't control and elements of the story can go in directions that I can't predict. In many ways, writing is a journey of discovery for me and I am often surprised by the way the story turns out. Cabo developed exactly in that way. It took me awhile to get through the first 30-50% of the book. Once the plot started to "break," I couldn't write it fast enough. Surprisingly, the character of Miguel Hidalgo was almost an afterthought. Initially, he was just a background character but he soon assumed a much greater presence in the story and became a formidable co-villain in his own right as the story developed to its suspenseful conclusion.

Acknowledgements for the Second Edition

Once again, I'd like to thank you, my readers, for supporting Colin Pearce and my writing "habit." Without you, there would be no Colin. I am grateful for each of you. I'd also like to thank my friends and loved ones for their continued support. Without the encouragement and understanding all of you have provided, I would have never gotten this far.

This second edition of *The Cabo Contract* is published by Citadel Publishing LLC. The move to Citadel from my previous publisher was difficult but worth the trouble as Cabo is now offered in more versions than it was before, including an audiobook! Like its predecessor, this second edition of Cabo has been reformatted, proofread and has had minor changes to correct errors and improve readability.

Thanks again to everyone who has supported Colin Pearce and me through our literary journey into the sky and pages and beyond, together.

Check six!

Chris Broyhill
Irving, TX
December, 2017

To those who encouraged.

You were more important than you know.

PROLOGUE

Didn't I just do this?

The question races through my mind as I pull the T-38's control stick into my lap and watch the sleek nose rotate skyward in response. The supersonic jet roars off the pavement of runway 16 Right at Van Nuys airport and into the clear Southern California sky. I can feel the brisk thrust from the twin afterburning J-85 engines rapidly accelerating the aircraft through 300 knots as the altimeter winds upward.

Again, I'm airborne in a high-performance jet. And again, I have to do the impossible.

Moments ago, a commandeered Gulfstream G-IV lifted off for the Bay Area of California, carrying a gruesome biological weapon and piloted by a madman and his hostage - the woman I love.

"Van Nuys, this is Talon 5494 Delta, I'm in the turn to the north and maintaining VFR at low altitude. Did you receive verification of the air defense fighter launch?"

"Talon 5494, Van Nuys tower, affirmative. F-16s from March have been scrambled. Contact AWACS, call sign Dragnet, on 346.5 for details."

The mention of the AWACS stuns me momentarily and stirs the pieces of the mental puzzle swimming around in my head. As the madman heads north, a platoon-sized unit of heavily-armed men on a high-speed yacht is headed for

Santa Catalina Island to the south.

And the damned Secret Service won't tell us if the President is there or not.

So now I'm going to have to be in two places at once. I've got two bullets in my already wounded leg and I'm flying an airplane with no gun, no missiles, and no radar.

Luck won't be enough this time.

I'm going to need a goddamned miracle.

CHAPTER ONE

Monday, 16 November
1100 Hours Local Time
My Townhouse
Wilmington, Delaware, United States

I guess I was lonely on that fateful Monday. Maybe that was why I was so damn eager to answer the phone. But once I saw the caller ID, and felt the corresponding leap in my chest, I would have picked up anyway.

The installation team from Lowe's was tacking down the new carpet in my dining room and I was comfortable on my sofa, surrounded by the familiar accoutrements of my study/living room, watching the day go by. The LCD TV over my fireplace was tuned to a news channel and muted. My peripheral vision detected a man standing in front of the White House as the crawler on the bottom of the screen flashed, "News Alert! Presidents Agree on Border Treaty!"

The image barely registered in my brain.

I was watching the BlackBerry vibrate on the wooden surface of the coffee table next to me as the first notes of AC/DC's "Back in Black" cut through the air. But it was the number and the name flashing on the screen which had me riveted.

Sarah Morton was calling.

Sarah was the chief pilot for Bachelor Magazine's flight

department and a former Monthly Mistress, with shimmering hazel eyes, red hair like silk, and a body to die for. A few years ago, she had come across my name, hired me to perform contract pilot services in Bachelor's new Gulfstream G-IV, and had retained me to teach her the nuances of flying it after her recent qualification training. We were together for less than a month, but the connection we shared still haunted me today. Even after all that had happened over the last several weeks.

Hell, maybe because of what had happened over the last several weeks.

The insistent strains of Angus Young's classic guitar reached out to me. I grabbed the phone. "Colin Pearce," I said.

"Colin!" A very excited female voice came over the receiver. "It's Sarah!"

The sound of her voice stunned and delighted me. I paused, reveling in the sound of it and the corresponding gyrations that were going on inside me. "Well, hello there," I said after a moment. "It's been a long time. How are you?"

"You better remember me," she said in a tone that was mostly playful, but not entirely so. Women are funny about that sort of thing.

"Of course, I remember you," I replied. "It may have been three years ago but it was still *the* best contract assignment of my life." *More like the best three weeks of my life.*

It was an unexplainable miracle. Like something you only read about. She could have had anyone in the world and for a few blissful weeks, that person had been me. I was at least fifteen years older than she was and nowhere near her equal in looks or poise. But somehow, we clicked. Maybe it was the hours spent at high altitude with nothing else to do but monitor systems and talk. Perhaps it was the lingering conversation over and after our many dinners together on the road. One night, after revealing some particularly intimate details of our lives, we found ourselves in each other's arms, and then in bed shortly after that. But what had transpired had been deeper than mere physical satisfaction. And once we had experienced it, we couldn't get enough of each other.

For the first time in my life, I understood why people did stupid things when they cared about someone else. She had even managed to persuade me to participate in a drive to donate sperm for a local fertility clinic where one of her friends, also a former Monthly Mistress, worked as a fertility specialist - quite literally the last thing I ever saw myself doing. Of course, the fact that Sarah had volunteered to assist in the donation process was no small enticement.

My thoughts were drawn to the night when the two of us had realized exactly what was happening. As we lay in each other's arms after a particularly passionate interlude, she raised her face to mine and looked deeply into my eyes while she lightly toyed with the hair on the side of my head. I could see her eyes were glistening.

"This scares the shit out me," she whispered. "It's almost too perfect."

I remembered swallowing hard and nodding as my own eyes welled up. I didn't trust my voice to speak.

She smiled tenderly when she saw my reaction and put her fingers to my lips.

"You don't need to say anything," she said as she brought her lips to mine. "I can see everything I need to see in your eyes."

The kiss led to another, longer, and even more intimate encounter. Then we fell asleep in each other's embrace afterward.

And we didn't speak of that moment again.

When the contract ended a few days later, she took me to the Burbank airport to put me on a plane back to Philadelphia and on the sidewalk there, in front of God and everyone, she kissed me passionately under the clear, blue, California sky. Then she quickly got back into her little sports car and shot off into traffic, leaving me standing on the sidewalk watching her go. Part of me had longed for her to come back and another part of me was terrified at what I might do if she did.

Neither of us had initiated contact since then. It was like there had been an unspoken pact between us.

Until now.

"You'll have to excuse me for taking a second," I said as I returned to the moment. "My mind is a little slow these days. I've been through some... stuff recently."

"I know," she said sweetly. "I saw your picture in the paper."

Okay, so there was this front-page picture of me in a lot of national newspapers after my last escapade several weeks ago, but it was taken from a distance and my name was never attached to it. Not formally anyway.

"Uh," I responded eloquently, "I'm afraid I don't know what you're talking about there."

"You can play hard to get all you want, mister, but I spent enough time with you to know you when I see you."

There were lots of politically correct thoughts which ran through my head and lots of official blather I could have uttered in response. Working with the CIA tends to bring that out in you, but at the moment, I was at a loss for words.

"It doesn't matter," she continued, "the photo reminded me of you and that's why I'm calling. I have a situation here..." She paused as if she was trying to find the right words to continue and when she spoke there was a hint of desperation in her voice. "I *need* you. I need *help*." And as the word help escaped her lips, her voice cracked. Ever so slightly.

And then the oddest thing happened. I heard the sound of a door closing in the background and she fought to rein her voice into a businesslike tone.

"So, Mr. Pearce, I understand you are current and qualified on the Gulfstream Four SP?"

Goddamn my curiosity and goddamn all the other shit that was tumbling around inside of me. A smart man would have said "no" and hung up just then.

But, of course, I did neither of those things.

"Yes, ma'am," I answered dutifully. "My last recurrent training in the jet was about four months ago and I've been... flying since." I wasn't going to tell her exactly what I'd been flying because she would have never believed me, but I got the feeling it didn't matter.

"Is your schedule free for the next two weeks?"

"Yes, it is." The truth was, it was free for the next several months, but that was beside the point.

"I'll need you in Burbank by tomorrow evening. Can you do that?"

"I sure can."

"I understand your daily rate is twelve-hundred dollars per day?" Now she was being generous. A G-IV guy typically makes about a grand a day but I wasn't going to object. Two hundred dollars was two hundred dollars.

"That's correct," I replied, "with all expenses paid by the client. I'll send you my standard contactor's agreement along with copies of my FAA certificates, training certificates, and insurance certificate. Would you like that by fax or e-mail?"

"E-mail is fine," she said. "Send it to sarah at bachelormag dot com."

"I'll have it on the wire to you momentarily, Miss Morton."

"The name is Marciano now," she said in an odd tone of voice. "I got married about a year ago."

I felt like I had been slapped in the face. "Great," I said with a laudable attempt at sincerity. "Will I get to meet the lucky bastard?"

"It depends on when he gets back from... where he is," she said with the same odd tone. "Looking forward to working with you, Mr. Pearce." She was now anxious to get off the phone.

"Likewise," I said as she broke the connection.

What a fucking idiot.

The throbbing pain in my left leg brought me back to myself

and reminded me that the reposed posture I maintained was in begrudging compliance to the CIA doctor's orders.

"Well, shit," I said to no one in particular. "The doc's not going to like this."

"Too much activity, Mr. Pearce," the doctor had said. "I treat a lot of gunshot wounds in this job and guys like you always want to push things too hard too early. If you don't spend at least two weeks and maybe even more on your butt and let your body mend, it won't work for you when you need it to. Trust me on this."

I hadn't been a model patient. A week after sustaining three 9mm gunshot wounds in the leg and one in the left shoulder, I had buried my best friend and then flown to England for interrogation at the hands of British Intelligence and one Kim Page, a gorgeous brunette agent with whom I had shared some quality time during my last escapade. Between the questioning and the sex, it had been a busy week and not one spent in restful recuperation. While that time had been fun and light, it had left me empty, somehow, especially in view of the emotional roller coaster of the previous weeks. Then I had flown to Florida to spend a few days with my best friend's widow and her kids, and that time had been platonic, deep, and fulfilling. Mandy Magnusson had been her name, and we had spent the evenings talking late into the night about Burt, her murdered husband, our history together, and life in general. I left there for another debriefing at a CIA safe house near DC and a royal ass-chewing from the doctor assigned to my case.

And now I was on my sofa, trying to obey his instructions and make it through the day without another dose of Vicodin. Fortunately, I was still permitted to take the CIA's version of the performance-enhancing drugs I had been fed during my last mission. A mixture of vitamins, thermogenic compounds, a host of natural minerals and herbs, and a lot of stuff they wouldn't tell me about. The resulting energy boost was the only thing that made life bearable sometimes, although it added to my frustration at being forced to sit around continually.

The head of the Lowe's work crew brought me a clipboard with a work order on it for my signature. He was an average-looking guy in his late twenties or early thirties with shortly-cropped blond hair, a pockmarked face and, of course, the ever-present series of tattoos on his forearms. He sported the beginning of what promised to be an admirable potbelly by the time he reached middle age.

"Hell of thing about that treaty, huh?" he said, motioning to the TV with his clipboard before handing it to me.

"What treaty?" I replied absentmindedly as I searched the document for a signature block.

"That US-Mexican thing," he said, clearly impressed. "I mean, if the US and Mexico are going to combine forces to close the border and deal with those damn drug cartels, that might really do it!"

"Wouldn't tightening the borders mess with your..." I motioned in the direction of his crewmembers who were still cleaning up in the background.

"Oh no," he said. "We only hired fully documented folks. We fill out the I-9s and everything. The company is real strict about that."

"That's good," I replied, scratching my signature on the paper and handing the clipboard back to him. "It's good that somebody is."

The repair process on my house was finished. The repair process on my body still needed quite a bit of time. My bank account was fat. There was no reason at all for me to go to California and get mired in Sarah's problems.

I should have called her back and made an excuse. But I couldn't have said no to her, even if I wanted to. She was one of two women in the world who had ever meant anything to me. One of them had died in my arms a few weeks ago, just a few feet from where I was standing. And there was no way in hell I was going to allow Sarah to meet a similar fate.

CHAPTER TWO

Contract Day One
Tuesday, 17 November
1530 Hours Local Time
Bob Hope Airport (KBUR)
Burbank, California, United States

The flights from Philadelphia International Airport to Burbank's Bob Hope airport connecting through Las Vegas had been typically uneventful. As usual, Southwest Airlines' 737s had run like clockwork; more like trains than airliners. After I practically killed myself getting down the air stairs since they use stairs to get in and out of the airplanes at Burbank, I half-walked and half-hobbled down the airport's small concourse, trailing my computer bag. My cane was with my checked baggage and I couldn't wait to get it. My left leg was on fire.

Walking through the Burbank airport was always an experience. This was true Southern California and the people and the environment here were like nowhere else in the world. You could always count on seeing a haircut or outfit that turned your head. Today was no exception. I was following a young blonde girl and her significant other as I made my way to the outdoor baggage claim. The man was wearing cargo shorts and a tank top and the girl was wearing a lime-green floor-length dress made of very flimsy cotton. It was obvious that they were very much in love and had just come back from a place in the southern latitudes where it was warm and sunny. It was also obvious that the girl didn't have a damn thing on under the nearly diaphanous material. Her ass was simply magnificent.

"I love this place," I said under my breath.

News of the impending border treaty was everywhere. It was on the front page of every newspaper and on the crawler line of every news monitor. Even as I waited for my baggage at the outdoor baggage claim, one of the omnipresent TV monitors relayed the latest from the news networks about the story and I found myself remembering yesterday's conversation with the carpet installer from Lowe's as I listened.

"The treaty talks," the female reporter said in the standard monotone, "had been underway for over two months and focused on the formation of a US-Mexican agency which would assume control of the border and an associated combined police force, composed of officers from both nations, to provide border security. The basic provisions of the agreement enjoy widespread support in both houses of the US Congress and in the Mexican government as well. If signed, swift ratification by the Senate is expected. After yesterday's agreement on terms, the only issue appears to be fierce opposition to the treaty inside of Mexico, particularly from the powerful Drug Lord who calls himself Miguel Hidalgo."

The name caused me to glance up at the screen. A post-graduate international affairs class many years ago had provided me with a rudimentary knowledge of Mexican history. Miguel Hidalgo was the name of a Mexican priest who was largely regarded as the father of Mexican independence. A modern-day drug lord who assumed that name must have an ulterior motive. The picture of Hidalgo on the screen didn't look like that of a priest at all, though. It showed a suave-looking man with dark hair, a European complexion, piercing brown eyes, and distinctly aristocratic features. He looked like he'd be more at home in a palace somewhere than leading a drug cartel.

"Hidalgo, whose influence inside Mexico rivals that of the president's, has vowed he will stop the treaty by all means necessary. White House sources have revealed that a secret meeting between the two presidents for the formal signing ceremony has been under consideration since the negotiations began."

I was glad for the distraction. I had forgotten about the pain in my leg until I heard the clunking sound of bags sliding down the metal chute behind me. I turned from the monitor to find that my bag had reached the bottom with my newly-acquired cane securely strapped to it. Both the black roller bag and the shiny, black cane looked none the worse for wear. I placed my computer bag on top of the roller bag, released the cane, and then transferred some of my weight off my leg and onto the cane. A great deal of pain immediately subsided.

"Damn," I whispered in relief.

It was remarkable that my leg was in such pain when my shoulder was not. It might have had something to do with the fact that the shoulder wound was a "through and through," while the bullets fired into my thigh had lodged there. Of course, it might have also had to do with the damage inflicted by one bullet versus three.

I sighed and took in the typically pleasant Southern California climate. Even in November the temperature was no lower than the mid-seventies. There were a few wispy clouds up in the terrific blue sky above me and they seemed to lazily float by with no agenda at all. The slight breeze felt good on my skin. I smiled to myself. I had missed this place.

And I had missed Sarah. I felt my heart picking up a bit. Now it was time to find her.

She'd told me that she'd be sending a limousine for me and I supposed that at a small airport like this one, a limo would be relatively easy to spot. I assumed the awkward three-legged gait I had adopted for the last several weeks and made it to the curb quickly. The small airport was teeming with activity on this weekday afternoon and the crowd was a mix of people clad in business attire and more casual wear. Because we weren't far from Beverly Hills or studio country, there were plenty of expensive cars vying for positions at the curb. But even with all this, the long, black limo was easy to spot. Any questions about whether it was the right limo were eliminated by a glance at the license plate, which read: BACHLR-1.

Nothing like making an entrance, I thought to myself.

My eyes scanned the crowd for Sarah; and for a moment, I almost didn't recognize her. She was standing on the curb a few feet from the limo with her back to me and while I could see the curve of her face as she scanned the crowd, the red hair I remembered was now blonde. I cocked my head for a moment as I regarded her. The blonde hair fluttered very slightly in the breeze and sparkled in the sunlight. I nodded unconsciously. The color seemed to suit her. Her clothes however, were a different story. She wore some sort of long, flowing, blue dress that seemed a little big for her. Definitely not the style I remembered and one that didn't highlight a physique which had sold over a million magazines.

Immediately to her side was a tall man with black hair and a dark-olive complexion. He was dressed in khaki slacks and a blue blazer, and his posture indicated that he was impatient about something. I felt a stir of recognition, not personal, but general.

As I neared them, they turned around and we made eye contact at the same time. Sarah's eyes lit up when she saw me and then they looked down at my cane, and her perfect lips turned downward into a small frown. My eyes probably lit up in return and I'm not sure what my face did when I looked at her belly and took in the fact that she was several months pregnant. The man's dark eyes narrowed. That wasn't a good sign.

I extended my right hand to maintain appearances.

"Colin Pearce," I said. "I don't know how well you remember me, Sarah. We flew together once a few years ago."

She played along. "Of course, I remember you, Colin. You did some great work for us. That's why I called you before I called anyone else." She turned toward the man.

"Allow me to introduce you to our new Director of Aviation, Adam Archmere. He's also qualified in the G-IV."

If his real name is Adam, then mine is Ching Su, I thought to myself. After the amount of time I had spent in the Middle East, I knew a Saudi when I saw one.

Adam was at least two inches taller than my six feet two-inch height and undoubtedly weighed less than my 225. He was thin in a fit sort of way with the veins in his arms clearly visible between his skin and the underlying muscle. At this distance, I could just make out a thin scar down the right side of his face, nearly on his jawline. It looked like it might have been made by the point of a blade of some sort. He offered his hand reluctantly, which of course inspired me to grab it firmly and pump it several times.

"Glad to meet you, sir," I said along with my best 'client introduction smile.'

He didn't answer at first but looked down at my leg and the cane. Then he made eye contact. "We didn't know you were... damaged," he said skeptically. He pronounced his "a's" with just a hint of a Boston accent in his voice.

"Oh, this?" I gestured to my leg. "It's no big deal," I replied lightly. "I had a little accident a few weeks back and the doctor insisted I use this thing," I lifted the cane and shook it, "until I was completely healed. I can fly an airplane and load baggage just fine, sir."

He nodded slowly.

I actually didn't know if I could do either of those things.

He motioned toward the limo. A driver appeared at my side to take my bags and I absentmindedly handed them over to him, subconsciously noting that he had the same complexion and hair color as Adam did.

Sarah entered the limo first and sat on the bench seat at the back end of the compartment. I entered next and sat across from her on the end of a long sofa that ran nearly the entire length of the vehicle's interior along the left side. Adam got in last and sat on the bench with Sarah, next to her, but with a discrete distance between them. I noticed then that Sarah's attire was extremely modest. The blue dress went from below her knees to her neck and she wore it over a white cotton shirt. When I had last spent time with her, she had loved wearing as little as possible when she wasn't flying and shorts and tank tops had been the rule. Marriage does strange things to people though. Maybe her husband had a jealous streak. It'd be hard having a wife who looked like Sarah and who had been a Monthly Mistress for Bachelor Magazine. I wasn't sure I could have dealt with it.

I should have stayed here three years ago.

The thought came out of nowhere and then, completely unbidden, a kaleidoscope of images ran through my mind: Sarah and I laughing together as we cruised along at altitude, her face smiling at me across the table at a restaurant, her eyes looking dreamily at me across the pillow before we fell asleep together; drinking together at a small Tiki bar in the Islands; her sensual grin as she put her panties into my hand under the table; us splashing each other like kids in the warm Caribbean before laying side-by-side under the tropical sun, our hands clasped.

And I was completely unprepared for the wave of emotion that came with those images. It was like a curtain inside of me had been ripped away and I could see the time we spent together in a new, more intense light.

But why now? The time we had three years ago had been incredibly special but why was it triggering this new revelation?

And then I knew.

Sammy.

Samantha, the woman who had died in my arms mere weeks ago, my time with her, caring for her, being with her, had created an emotional earthquake in my carefully compartmentalized world. And now the feelings I had for Sarah, stored carefully behind the rocks inside of me for three years, had been freed and were rushing toward me like a tsunami. And I was just standing on the beach, mesmerized by the sight of the approaching wave and waiting for it to hit me.

Jesus, I thought.

"We're just going to drop you at the Marriott here at the airport for tonight. Is that ok?" she asked.

The sound of Sarah's voice startled me out of my reverie and I nodded slowly, returning to the moment.

"Our first trip will be tomorrow morning. You, Adam, and I will fly to Cabo, pick up Bill and two passengers and then return."

"Sounds good," I said, although I didn't understand why it took three pilots on a two-hour flight.

She answered my unspoken question. "I'm getting to the point where I can't get to everything in the cockpit so well," she said, gesturing at her stomach. "I'm going to pull right seat duty and Adam will observe you from the jump seat. Assuming all goes well, it will just be you and Adam after that."

"I see," I replied. "You must be very excited," I continued, looking at her. "I'm assuming this is your first child."

Sarah's eyes sparkled, but there something incongruous about her expression. "*I* am very excited," she said. Her emphasis on the singular pronoun was unmistakable. "I can't wait."

Hmmmm. What does that mean?

"That's awesome," I said, as I stole a glance at Adam, who was looking idly out the limo's side window. He appeared to be bored.

"So," Sarah continued, anxious to change the subject, "have you been busy?"

I nodded. "Very much so. I completed a month-long contract before my accident and had plenty of work before then. I fly about as much as I like."

"How'd you get hurt?" she asked innocently.

Fortunately, I had a story ready for this. "I was replacing some siding on my house, fell off the ladder, and fractured my left femur," I answered in a self-deprecating tone. "The next time I'll leave that sort of thing to the experts."

She smiled at me. It was the first genuine smile I had seen since I arrived and it lit up the limo's interior. "Has it cost you much work?" she asked, genuinely concerned.

"Well, I spent a few weeks taking it easy," I replied. "But I was due for a vacation anyway. You should feel honored," I teased. "This is the first job I've taken since my accident."

"I'm glad," she said sincerely. "We'll take good care of you. I promise."

"I'm here to serve," I said.

She smiled at me again. I could tell she wanted to reach out and touch me - she had been a "touchy" talker when I had spent time with her before. But she restrained herself.

We arrived at the Marriott a few moments later.

"We have an account here," she said as the limo pulled up to the hotel's grand entrance and lobby, a one-story structure that connected the two eight-floor towers. "I'm going to go inside with you and make sure they get the billing straight."

The driver opened the door on her side and she exited.

I nodded toward Adam.

"Nice meeting you, Adam. Looking forward to flying with you."

He just looked at me and nodded slightly.

Not just a Saudi, I found myself thinking. *A Saudi with some status.*

I exited to find my computer bag stacked on top of my

roller bag next to Sarah. She had her hand on the handle. The driver stood next to her in a posture that indicated he felt he had completed his duties.

I assumed my three-legged gait and placed my hand on the pull handle next to hers.

"I may be crippled," I said, "but I can't let a pregnant woman haul my bags. I'd never be able to look myself in the mirror again."

She nodded with a smile and I took the handle. We walked into the hotel's main doors.

The lobby had been redone in the last few years. There was a long registration desk made of some sort of rich-looking wood with artistic lighting complementing it. The room was large, open and airy, with several areas where chairs and sofas were grouped together in separate, conversational arrangements.

We walked to the reception desk and Sarah spoke briefly to the girl behind it. Sarah provided her credit card for the room charges and I provided my Marriott frequent guest number. After the appropriate fuss was made about my platinum guest status, I was presented with my keycard. From there, Sarah led me across the lobby to a seating area that was out of the main flow of people and also not directly visible from the limo idling outside. She motioned me to the nearest of two chairs arranged around a magazine table and took the chair facing the main lobby door. We had no sooner sat down when she reached out and grabbed my hands with both of hers. Her skin felt warm and soft on mine, and the imagery of the approaching wave appeared in my mind again. And yet even as the emotion surged, I recognized the futility of it. This was a married woman and whatever claim I might have had on her was ancient history.

"Thank you so much for coming," she whispered, looking down at our hands. "I didn't know if you would." She clenched her jaw and I could tell she was searching for the right words. "Especially after I told you I was... I was married."

"Well, you offered me twelve-hundred dollars a day," I responded, playfully. "How could I refuse?"

She raised her eyes to mine and fixed her gaze on my eyes and my face. Her expression was one of intense concentration. Suddenly, I felt her looking inside of me - something she had been able to do when we were together before. I looked back at her with the same conflicting sensations of tranquility and terror I had felt then. After three years the sensations had not changed.

"Sarah, you called and I came," I sighed, answering her unspoken question. "That's all it took."

She looked away quickly. "You don't know how many times I almost called you before now, Colin," she whispered, her voice on the edge of cracking. "I missed you so much."

I swallowed hard and rubbed her hands with mine.

"Well, if you had called before, the result would have been the same," I said, softly. "I would have come."

"I know," she said, shaking her head. "I know. I guess I just didn't want you to feel like I was weak or something."

I laughed. "You, weak? There are a lot of adjectives I'd use to describe you, Sarah. But weak isn't on the list."

"Why did I ever let you go?" she said, barely audibly. "I was such a fool."

I extracted one of my hands from hers and reassuringly stroked her shoulder.

"Everyone makes the best decisions they can with the information they have available at the time. If you get them right half the time, you're doing well. Besides, I'm sure your husband..."

I felt her body stiffen and I could see her jaw working as if there was something she wanted to say in response.

"Marrying him was probably the biggest mistake I've ever made in my life for so many reasons, but we can't talk about that right now. We don't have the time."

She looked over at me.

"Adam and his people have taken over our flight department and I don't have a clue what they're doing. They've got my husband, Damian," she said, almost spitting the name out. "But more importantly, they've got Bill's daughter, Shelly. They both were taken when we were in Dubai about eight weeks ago." Bill was William Spratt, the owner and publisher of Bachelor Magazine. He was Sarah's boss and, to some degree, her mentor. I knew she cared very deeply for him.

"Adam is forcing us to make these flights back and forth to Cabo," she continued, the frustration in her voice evident, "and he won't tell me a goddamned thing! He's got this greasy bodyguard named Felix who gives me the creeps and is always watching me or Bill or both of us. And to top it off, every time we've gone to Cabo they've been meeting with these guys that I'm sure are Mexican gangsters. There is something going on that can't be good and I don't have the slightest idea what to do about it."

She looked at me intently. "Colin, I need you to help me figure this out. I needed a contractor and apparently you not only can fly a jet, but also you can do... other stuff. After what you did a few weeks ago, I'm thinking that if anyone can help me do something about this, you can."

"What if that wasn't me?" I asked, quietly.

A tender expression ran across her features. "I never forgot your face," she said, as she unconsciously raised a hand to my cheek and ran her fingers back through my hair. "I knew it was you as soon as I saw the photo in the newspaper. The brown hair, the build, wide shoulders, narrow waist, and above all the way you stood there with your 'don't fuck with me' attitude." She paused a moment and looked directly into my eyes. Then she seemed to remember herself and her hand dropped down to mine again and she looked away. "Besides, I have a friend who works in the tower cab at Edwards Air Force Base."

"I see." I was amazed that she even remembered what

I look like. I'm not memorable in appearance. I'm six feet two inches tall and weigh about two-hundred and twenty-five pounds - more than I should. Every time I look in the mirror, all I see there is an average-looking, middle-aged guy.

"Look, there isn't time for me to explain the rest of it now. Our jet is at Atlantic Aviation on the other side of the field," she continued, now speaking more rapidly.

I looked at her questioningly.

"We moved it from Van Nuys because we got a better deal on fuel here," she said in answer. "You know me, always trying to save Bill money."

"I'm familiar with the Atlantic location here," I said. "I've flown in here a few times."

"Good," she nodded. "Try to get there about 10 A.M. tomorrow morning. I've left an envelope for you at the front desk. It has a temporary airport ID, keys to the jet, our flight planning account information, and the Jeppesen subscription codes." She looked at me apologetically. "I'll need you to update the EFBs. Sorry about that."

EFBs were electronic flight bags, tablet computers which displayed the terminal airport charts. Jeppesen was the company that published the charts and had a virtual monopoly on providing aeronautical information worldwide. Typically, the computers are Apple iPads, which irks me to no end because I hate to think of Steve Jobs' company taking over the world.

"No big deal," I said, smiling at her. "Updating EFBs comes with the daily rate. Now if you needed me to update paper charts, I'd have to charge you extra." I was kidding her, but updating paper charts could take hours. The online updates took just a few minutes.

She smiled back at me and pressed my hands.

"I also left a few notes in the envelope, what I felt I could say about what we're doing in a format that sounded relatively generic."

I nodded. "Do you want me to get the jet pulled out and fueled? Get it ready for passengers?"

"That'd be great," she said. "Adam and I will get there at about 1130 and then we can depart shortly thereafter. Can you file us down to Los Cabos International with a 1200 departure with three people aboard and then back here with a 1700 departure and six people?"

"No... company?" I asked her. My previous flights with Mr. Spratt and Sarah had always included a bevy of beautiful women.

"No," she said. "Adam put a stop to that."

That's not a surprise, I thought. "Who will the other three people be?"

"One of them will be Bill. The other one is Felix, Adam's... bodyguard." She shivered involuntarily. "And one of them is unknown."

"What about the paperwork? The Private Aircraft Enforcement System Arrival Report?" I asked. It was the form for the Customs and Border Protection agency that detailed passengers and aircraft information for non-commercial aircraft.

Sarah shook her head.

"Adam takes care of that."

I just looked at her, trying to keep my expression as neutral as possible.

"Any catering?" I asked.

She shook her head.

"I'll have everything ready," I said, mustering a brightness that I didn't feel.

She clasped my hands again and but I could feel a difference in her grip. Before it had been tense, frantic. Now it felt purposeful and determined.

"God, I'm glad you're here," she said.

She was looking over my shoulder toward the entrance and suddenly she rose very quickly, turning her grip into a business-like handshake in an instant. I rose with her.

"Great, Captain Pearce," she said. "We'll see you at Atlantic tomorrow. The tail number is November three six whiskey mike sierra. We'll get there about eleven thirty or so."

"Sounds good," I replied. I lowered my voice. "Do you have any pictures of Adam and or Felix?"

She cocked her head slightly and nodded.

"I might have some of Adam," she said.

"E-mail or text them to me as soon as you can," I said. Then I raised my voice to a normal level. "See you tomorrow, Sarah. I'll have the jet ready for you."

She nodded perfunctorily and then walked around me toward the entrance. I turned and watched her leave. The driver was standing there waiting for her, looking back and forth between the two of us.

His eyes were narrow and suspicious.

A few hours later, the BlackBerry buzzed as it sat on the solid wood surface of the Marriott's bar. I glanced down at it. The number was familiar.

"That was fast," I said as I answered. "You must have gotten the e-mail I just sent you."

"Where are you?" CIA Operations Officer Dave Smith's voice came clearly over the phone.

"Sitting at the bar here at the Daily Grill in the lovely Marriott Hotel at the Burbank Airport, enjoying a nice glass of Bowmore."

"Well, that fits with the GPS plot. It would have been nice to get a phone call from you instead of a GPS movement alert. If you hadn't sent the e-mail I would have had to call you anyway."

The BlackBerry I carried was the one the CIA gave me for my last gig. It had a built-in GPS transmitter which couldn't be tracked by anyone other than the CIA and lots of other little tricks. They had programmed all my data into it and I had never transitioned back to my old one. It never occurred to me that they'd still be interested in tracking me.

"I thought you'd enjoy the photos," I replied. "But honestly, I wasn't aware that I had to file movement reports with you guys."

"You're an asset now, Colin," Smith said tiredly. "We made you one. And you know stuff. That means we sort of need to keep track of you. I guess I should have made that clearer in the briefing."

"Apparently," I said. "But now that you know where I am, let me tell you why I'm here. I've been hired for a contract job with Bachelor Magazine's flight department. They needed some extra help for a few weeks. The chief pilot is a friend and asked for me personally."

"This would be the same chief pilot who was Miss November a few years ago? The same one you have some history with? I can see why you took the job."

Goddamn feds. I had never told Smith or his partner, Amrine, anything about Sarah Morton. But they knew. *Bastards.* "Ironically, she's married now," I replied, taking a sip of the very complex Islay malt and relishing the peaty flavor of the whiskey, "and apparently not very happy about it. But she's in a little bit of trouble, hence the reason for my e-mail."

"Pearce to the rescue," Smith said with a hint of irony in his voice.

I ignored him. "Evidently, Sarah's husband and the daughter of Bill Spratt, the publisher, were both snatched recently during a trip to Dubai. And as a side note, the guy who has taken control of their flight department is a Saudi or I'm a drag queen."

"We never did any background investigation into your fetish preferences," Smith teased.

"You're a funny guy, but don't give up your day job," I

continued. "Anyway, this guy goes by the name Adam Archmere and has just a hint of Bostonian accent in his English. He's the photo I sent you."

"Harvard or MIT," Smith said, thinking out loud. "That means he's somebody. We're having the photos analyzed now."

"And evidently he has this bodyguard whom he travels with named Felix. I don't know his last name. Sarah described him as greasy. She didn't have a photo of him."

There was a profound silence on the other end of the line.

"You know who this guy is, don't you?" I asked after a long moment.

"What will you be flying and where will you be going?" Smith replied, neatly avoiding my question.

"They have a nice G-IVSP, registration November three six whiskey mike sierra," I answered, "and the only trip I know about so far is an out and back to Cabo San Lucas tomorrow. We depart Burbank with just us crew and return with Bill Spratt, the owner of the jet, Archmere's bodyguard, and an unnamed passenger tomorrow evening."

"Any idea what the trips to Cabo are all about?"

"Sarah said something about Adam and company meeting with people she thought were 'Mexican gangsters,'" I said. "She didn't have any time to provide additional details."

For the second time in as many minutes, there was silence from the other end of the line. I could almost hear the gears inside Smith's head turning.

"Something else," I said. "They don't seem to let Sarah out of their sight. Once I get into this, I'm guessing they'll keep me close aboard as well."

"Makes sense."

"If we're going to meet in person to discuss this, tomorrow night after we return may be the only time to do it without attracting attention."

"I'll put it together."

"You know I've heard that the Daily Grill here has fantastic prime rib."

"It's been awhile since I've had a good cut of prime rib," Smith said.

"You're overdue."

"Okay, Colin, we'll be in touch." There was a pause. "By the way, did you happen to bring the package we gave you to California?"

The "package" was a Glock Model 23, .40 caliber pistol Smith had given me for self-protection a few weeks ago when there had been a possibility that some bad guys might come after me. Ironically, when the bad guys had shown up, I totally forgot about the gun, and fought them hand-to-hand. This had resulted in me getting shot, of course.

"Nope," I said a little ruefully. "I left it locked up in my house in Delaware. I assumed because I was on a personal engagement, I wasn't allowed to bring it."

"You're a pseudo-federal officer now with a federal carry permit. You can take that thing anywhere," Smith said.

"I'll remember for that for next time."

"I hope you don't regret it this time."

"That makes two of us," I replied, feeling the smooth Scotch turn harsh on my tongue.

From: Special Projects Group [NCS]
Sent: Tuesday, 17 November 2009, 2217 EST (18 November 2009, 0317Z)
To: Director, NCS
Cc: Special Projects Group [NCS]; damrine@cmail.cia.gov; dsmith3@cmail.cia.gov

SUBJECT: Watch List Subject Identified In Country

(TS) Narrative:

Information gleaned from routine contact to confirm the movements of Contractor 09-017 (Pearce, Colin M.). Pearce is currently in Burbank, California performing contract pilot services for Bachelor Magazine's flight department at the request of Bachelor's Chief Pilot, Sarah Morton Marciano. A conversation between Pearce and Marciano revealed that Shelly Spratt, the daughter of Bachelor's publisher, William Spratt, and Marciano's husband, Damian Marciano, may have been kidnapped. Also, the flight department's director is a Saudi whose photo is attached to this e-mail. Facial recognition analysis has confirmed his identity as Abdullah bin Rashid al Qudamah, a member of the Saudi royal family and currently on our watch list of potential hostile actors. He is currently using the alias Adam Archmere. Additional information leads us to believe al Qudamah's enforcer, Saif-al Din, is in country as well. Marciano informed Pearce that they have been making regular trips to Cabo San Lucas, Mexico and she believes al Qudamah is regularly meeting with "Mexican gangsters."

(TS) CONCLUSION:

While the efforts of both the al Qudamah brothers, Abdullah and his younger brother Mohammed, to initiate hostile operations against the United States in the past have been somewhat dubious, the fact that Abdullah may be meeting with members of the Mexican underworld could be significant, especially considering the suspected contact between him and known associates of Mexican drug lord Miguel Hidalgo in March of this year in Oman. If you recall, this contact involved a large shipment of hijacked arms (See Operations File 09-03-462). DI analysts have long warned of the probability of an attack on US soil by an alliance of Muslim terrorist organizations and Mexican criminal elements. It is possible that al Qudamah may be assembling an operation that is a plausible threat to the United States. We believe the situation deserves further scrutiny.

(TS) ACTIONS:

1. We will assemble a small operations team to begin monitoring this situation, including an agent who has met al Qudamah previously under an assumed name in a previous covert operation.

2. We will also contact our counterparts in other directorates, in the FBI and the DHS and prepare to convene a cross-functional/cross-agency team to deal with this situation.

(TS) RECOMMENDATIONS:

1. Authorize cross-directorate/cross-agency team to analyze data and develop action plans.

2. Implement aircraft movement alerts for N36WMS.

TOP SECRET / SPECIAL
COMPARTMENTALIZED INFORMATION
CLASSIFIED BY: US Central Intelligence Agency
DECLASSIFY ON: OADR

CHAPTER THREE

Contract Day Two
Wednesday, 18 November
1000 Hours Local Time
Bob Hope Airport (KBUR)
Burbank, California, United States

The van from the Marriott dropped me off in front of the Atlantic FBO at 10 A.M. sharp the next morning. Atlantic Aviation was one of the largest chains of fixed-based operators or FBO's in the general aviation industry. FBOs were a pillar of the business jet world. They're typically a combination of executive terminal and fuel station, but can also feature full aircraft maintenance facilities, conference rooms, crew rest areas and a host of other amenities.

I let the van driver unload my bags, slipped him a five-dollar tip, and hobbled my way through the glass doors and into the FBO, rolling my two bags behind me. Even though we were scheduled to return to Burbank tonight, I had checked out of my room and brought my baggage with me. In business aviation, the crew never goes anywhere without baggage because between passenger whims and maintenance issues, the day's final destination can change without warning.

As my eyes adjusted to the interior light, I glanced around. This Atlantic location, which I had visited several times before, was a fine example of the chain. It featured an airy lobby with an arched roof, wood-paneled walls, and a floor of rich ceramic tile. The staff was attentive. I had barely made it through the doors before a young Hispanic man in an Atlantic uniform appeared at my side and asked if he could help me with my bags. I thanked him and told him I needed to get out to N36WMS. He nodded and motioned me toward the desk to sign in.

"Hello there," I said brightly to the cute thirty-something brunette behind the counter, "I'm the contract guy for November three six whiskey mike sierra. I was told you'd have a package for me?"

She nodded. "Sarah told us about you. Do you have any identification?"

I produced my driver's license and placed it on the counter in front of her. She looked down at it purposefully and then raised her eyes to me.

"Delaware, huh?" she said. "I don't think I've actually met anyone from Delaware. What's it like there?"

I shrugged. "Boring. Unsophisticated. Generic. And I'm not from there. When I retired from the Air Force, I needed to live someplace in the northeast where the taxes were low."

"The tax thing gives it an advantage over California."

"Let me tell you something," I countered. "You get what you pay for. We have had the dubious distinction of having had the only governor in the US who did not graduate from high school."

Her jaw dropped.

"It's true. The whole state is run like a trailer park."

She smiled.

"All we need is Jerry Springer to officiate the legislative sessions and then we could televise them and make money. And don't forget, we're the state that gave you Joe Biden, the only man capable of the physically-impossible act of speaking with both feet in his mouth."

She laughed and pushed the license back across the counter at me. "I have an envelope around here for you. Sarah dropped it off yesterday." She turned around to a shelving unit behind her where the several partitions were labeled with the tail numbers of various aircraft.

"How long has the jet been based with you?" I asked.

"About two years," she answered, now looking through the partitioned compartments in the unit. "Ah, here it is."

She handed me a manila envelope.

"Thanks," I said.

"How long has she hired you to help out?"

I looked back at her. According to the tag above her left breast, her name was Fran, and now, she was crossing the line. Even through many facets of the business aviation industry are steeped in confidentiality, gossip runs rampant. Anything you utter in the FBO on one side of the field can easily make its way to every other place on the field in a matter of hours, sometimes in mere minutes.

But Fran's light blue eyes weren't radiating keen curiosity. Instead they showed concern. She must have sensed my hesitation. "We just love her," Fran blurted out. "Since she brought that jet here from Van Nuys she's been like a little slice of sunshine."

"And let me guess, not so much sunshine recently."

Fran cocked her head at me and nodded slowly.

"And let me also guess, the sunshine started subsiding when a certain gentleman showed up?"

I had her then. Her face transitioned between curiosity and concern. "Well, now that you mention it.... " Her voice trailed off.

"How long has he been around?"

"He came back with them on a trip they flew to Dubai, about six weeks ago. I was here when they returned."

The information was coming hot and heavy now.

"Was her husband, Damian, with them when they came

back?"

She thought for few moments.

"I didn't see him," she said at last. Then she frowned.

"What?" I asked softly.

"It's funny, I don't remember seeing Shelly either." She looked at me. "Shelly is Bill Spratt's daughter."

Bingo. Okay, time to change the subject. People remember if someone has tried to ask too many questions. "Well, just so you know, I've been told that I'll be around about two weeks," I said. "Sarah hired me once a few years ago when they first got the airplane so we have a little history."

It was her turn to nod. "Maybe you can help get Sarah back to her normal self," she said hopefully.

"I'll do my best," I said to her evenly.

She smiled warmly at me. "I think you will," she said. Then she looked closely at my face. "God," she said. "You look really familiar."

"I get that a lot," I said hurriedly. "Hey, can you have the line guys pull November three six whiskey mike sierra out here and have a fuel truck standing by? I'm going to file a quick flight plan and then go outside and wake the jet up."

"Can do," she said.

She picked up a microphone to call the line service crew as I stepped away from the desk. My cane and I made our way down the hall and around the corner to the flight planning room. Sitting down at a computer, I opened the manila envelope, located the flight planning account information, and opened a browser window. ARINC Direct's website came up quickly and I smiled when it did. ARINC had been my suggestion when I had flown with Sarah and it looked like she had followed my advice. A check of the weather and the notices to airmen (NOTAMS) at Burbank and Cabo showed great conditions and nothing to affect the flight.

A few quick minutes on the site and I had filed us from Burbank (KBUR) to Los Cabos International (MMSD) at flight level 450 and back at flight level 430, typical Gulfstream altitudes. The flight each way was going to take about an hour and three quarters to two hours depending on air traffic delays. That meant about seven thousand pounds of fuel each way and four thousand pounds in reserve. I needed to bring the fuel level on the jet up to about eighteen thousand pounds. Probably a little conservative; but where fuel was concerned, I tended to be that way. I input that fuel load into the flight planning engine, ensured I selected an ATC preferred route, and ran both flight plans, filing them as I ran them. Then I told ARINC to fax the flight logs, weather data, and NOTAMs to me here at Atlantic and I was done.

By the time I hobbled my way back into the lobby, the jet was being tugged into position outside the doors.

"There's a fax coming in for you," Fran said to me as I watched the line crew put wheel chocks in front of the nose and main gear tires. "Do you have any idea how much fuel you want?"

"I don't know how much is onboard," I said, "but I can't imagine needing any more than about twenty-five hundred gallons."

She nodded at me. "I won't need to get the truck refilled then."

The line crew had disconnected the tug from the jet and was in the process of reconnecting the steering assembly on the nose gear.

"Looks like I'm on," I said.

"Here's your fax." Fran handed me a stack of paper. "Do you want ice, coffee, and newspapers?"

Sarah hadn't specified any catering arrangements but ice, coffee, and newspapers were pretty much universal.

"Sure," I said. "Let me get in and wake the jet up first."

"Will do. Please let me know if you need anything else."

"I will, Fran. Thanks for your help."

I walked toward the door to the flight line and paused while

Fran punched a button under her counter which unlocked the door and allowed me access to the ramp. The door buzzed and I walked through into the mild Southern California morning. The whine of jet engines suddenly assaulted my eardrums and I walked around the nose of my jet to see another Gulfstream becoming airborne on runway 26, almost directly in front of me. The jet was a G-V, white with red and blue stripes, and it gracefully climbed into the relatively clear sky of the San Fernando Valley on a westerly heading.

As the noise of the engines faded, I turned my attention toward the jet I had been hired to fly. Bachelor Magazine's G-IVSP, registration N36WMS, sported a brilliant tri-color paint job based on the color scheme of the magazine. The underside of the jet was a deep hunter green and the top half of it was a dark tan with a broad maroon stripe joining the two colors. It was unlike any paint pattern I'd seen, and I'd seen a lot of them.

I removed the key Sarah had given me from my pocket and unlocked the pull handle on the main entry door. Then I stuck my hand into the recess in lower section of the pull handle and pulled it toward me. This unlocked the door and I stood clear as gravity and residual hydraulic pressure, working together, slowly lowered the door to the ramp. About that time, the same Hispanic gentleman who had taken my luggage earlier wheeled it around the nose of the jet and brought it to the door of the airplane. "Manny" was what the nametag said.

"Carry it inside for you, sir?"

"No thanks," I said. "I'll get it."

"How soon do you need the fuel truck?"

"In about fifteen minutes," I replied.

"I'll have it here for you."

I gave him a ten-dollar bill for his trouble. Then I disconnected my computer bag from my roller bag and awkwardly climbed the stairs into the jet's dark interior, bags in hand. I set them down in the main cabin, went into the cockpit to get a Maglight, and then began my preflight inspection.

It had been several months since I had performed this chore on a G-IV and since I had some extra time I was determined to go through the process slowly and methodically. I did a quick inspection of the cockpit and power distribution panel. Then, I went outside and worked my way around the aircraft, opening every service door and peering into every dark nook and cranny that I had access to. I even climbed into the rear equipment bay or "hell-hole" and ensured everything was in order there as well. As I completed the inspection, I breathed a small sigh of relief. While the pain was ever-present, my leg injuries hadn't proven to be terribly limiting.

I arrived back at the entry door as Manny returned with the fuel truck. I laid the three landing gear safety pins on the second step of the entry door and climbed back up to the cockpit. After a few quick checks, I started the auxiliary power unit, or APU, brought the APU alternator online along with the associated power busses, and finally powered up the display units. Then I set the fuel panel and peered through the cockpit windows to give Manny the "thumbs-up sign." The fuel counters began increasing immediately.

Thirty minutes later, my bags were stowed, the jet was fueled, iced, coffeed, and the checklist was completed through the "before engine start" section. I had downloaded the flight plan into the jet's flight management system and updated the EFBs. We were ready to go.

As promised, Sarah had left me a few notes about the "goings on." They took the form of trip notes—notes pilots take so that they don't have to relearn the same lessons over and over.

Today's trip would evidently be the fourth trip Adam and Sarah had made to Cabo in about three weeks. The first trip had been from the 30th of October to the 2nd of November—four days. The second trip had been from the 4th of November to the 9th of November—6 days. For the latest trip, they had initially gone to Cabo on the 12th and come back on the 15th. But it was an anomaly because Spratt was still there. It suddenly occurred to me that they had returned to Burbank specifically to pick me up. Sarah's condition was going to make her unusable in the cockpit and they wanted to ensure that they had someone in place to fly for her. They had a timetable.

But for what?

They stayed at the same hotel in Cabo each time, the Hotel Imperial del Cabo, probably the most upscale resort in the area. I wondered if there was a reason behind that other than the amenities involved. While I had heard of the place, I wasn't familiar enough with the geography of the area to know exactly where the hotel was; but since the crew had stayed at the same hotel as the passengers, it seemed as if I would find out soon enough. The fact that the crew was staying at the same hotel was curious as well. Crew and passengers in the same hotel was one of the 'thou shalt nots' of business aviation.

In the note, Sarah also included the name of the handling agency they used at the Los Cabos International Airport. Handling agencies typically dealt with all the customs and immigration issues when business jets make international stops, as well as provide parking and aircraft servicing. If there was something odd about the passengers being brought into the US, there was a good chance that the handling agency was in on it. A little payola went a long way in Mexico.

I sent a quick e-mail to Smith and Amrine from my BlackBerry, via the special *Phil.Collins@goldmail.com* e-mail address which activated an encrypted datalink and deleted the e-mail after it was transmitted. I shared all the information I had accumulated thus far and hoped that they could make some sense of it.

I looked at my watch. It was 11:15. I tuned one of the aircraft radios to the frequency for clearance delivery, and then asked for and received our flight plan clearance to San Jose Del Cabo airport. We were cleared via radar vectors to our flight planned route with an initial climb to 5,000 feet. Our final altitude would be flight level 450, about 45,000 feet. I ensured the flight management system was updated and that 5,000 feet was set into the altitude alert window, and then decided to have a quick look through the cabin.

Thanks to my contract work, I'd flown several different G-IV's and the layout of this one seemed pretty standard. In the vestibule, a hallway area just behind the cockpit and forward of the main cabin, was a lavatory for the crew and few small closets where aircraft manuals and a few other books were stored. The main cabin area was arrayed in three subsections. Four chairs up front in "club" fashion, two seats facing aft, two seats facing forward. In the center were two divans, one on either side; and in the aft portion of the cabin was a four-place table on one side, opposite a credenza with a large LCD TV. Aft of the table area was a galley, and beyond that the aft lavatory and baggage storage area.

The wood, and there was a lot of it, was highly-polished light oak. The four chairs in the front and the four in the back were all covered in light brown leather, while the two divans were covered in fabric that was hunter green and maroon. The sidewalls and headliner were lightly colored as well, and I realized the decorators had done the best they could to import the magazine's color scheme into the jet without making it too dark on the inside.

I made my way through the rest of the interior and noted that there was nothing unusual. I did take the time to acquaint myself with the location of all the fire extinguishers, first-aid kits, walk-around oxygen bottle, automatic electronic defibrillator, and the other safety gear aboard the aircraft. I also ensured that the newspapers which Manny brought were neatly lined up on one of the aft-facing seats up front.

I worked my way back to the front of the jet just in time to meet Adam and Sarah as they came up the stairs. I backed myself into the opening to the cockpit to make room for them to get by. Adam was impeccably dressed in a black Armani suit with a white shirt and no tie. Sarah was behind him, of course, dressed in navy blue slacks and a white maternity top. Her shiny blonde hair was pulled back in a businesslike pony tail. Both she and Adam looked my attire over briefly, but thoroughly. I was wearing my typical navy-blue Brooks Brother's suit, white shirt, and maroon tie, the closest thing I had to a uniform in my wardrobe. I received a grunt of approval out of Adam and a winning smile from Sarah.

Adam had a small briefcase with him which he seemed to carry very close to his person. I'd flown bonded couriers before as well as corporate heavy hitters with confidential documents and the grip on the briefcase was always the same. I deliberately ignored it.

"We're all ready to go," I said. "I've got the clearance and the ice, coffee, and the newspapers are in the back. I didn't know what sort of catering arrangements you had made."

Adam didn't answer. He just continued past me and into the cabin.

Sarah stopped as she reached the top of the stairs.

"Did you see the gear pins I left you on the steps?" I asked her.

She nodded. "Three of them."

"Why don't you get seated? I'll get the chocks pulled and give the jet another quick look. I've got all the checklists done through the 'Before Starting Engines,' but you're welcome to check my work." I smiled at her.

"Thanks," she said gratefully. "I'm sure everything is fine."

"Do I need to sign anything with Atlantic or is everything on account?"

"It's on account."

I squeezed by her and made my way down the air-stair, cane in hand, reminded again how difficult it was to get down stairs when one of your legs doesn't work properly.

I did my normal "before shutting the door" walk-around

inspection, which includes verifying that the wheel chocks are not in front of any of the tires, the landing gear safety pins are pulled and stowed, the steering assembly or "scissors" is properly connected to the nose gear strut, and checking the general condition of the aircraft. I made a point of walking as quickly as I could in case Adam was watching. I wanted to convince him that the cane was not something I needed. Even though it was.

I arrived back at the door of the airplane in time to meet Manny once again.

"Leaving now, sir?" he asked.

"Yes, we are, Manny," I answered. "But we'll be back tonight about seven o'clock."

He nodded.

"You'll probably be long out of here by then."

"Depends," he said. "If we get a lot of traffic, I'll stick around and work the extra hours. Overtime is overtime, man."

"Can't fault you there," I said, climbing the stairs.

I reached the top and turned around and gave him a "thumbs-up." He returned it enthusiastically. By this time, I noticed that Sarah was ensconced in the right seat, strapped in, headset on, EFB powered up, and en route charts on the console next to her.

"Ready for me to shut the door?" I asked.

She nodded.

I activated the door switch, located in a niche on the bulkhead between the cockpit and the vestibule. The G-IV's auxiliary hydraulic pump activated with its usual whine and powered the door upward. The bottom half of it pivoted on hinges and swung on top of the upper half so that the assembly would fit through the aperture. The assembly came through the door opening and I waited until it was nearly completely shut. Then I pulled it toward me and latched the locking handle. The hydraulic pump automatically shut down and I could hear the pressurization seal in the door begin to inflate.

I glanced at the warning display in the cockpit. The red MAIN DOOR light had extinguished. The door was closed and locked.

"Door's closed," I said.

"And verified," Sarah replied in her typical bright, businesslike fashion. "As soon as you're strapped in we'll run the starting engines checklist."

"When do you suppose Adam will join us?" I whispered, as I initiated the awkward process of getting myself through the narrow entrance to the cockpit and into my seat without bumping anything or accidentally kissing Sarah. To get into the either seat in the G-IV cockpit, I had to get my outside foot on the far side of the yoke column, then bend at my waist and turn toward the center of the cockpit, which typically placed my head within inches of the other pilot's. Then, I slid my near foot into place and slid my butt down into the seat.

"In a few minutes," she responded, her voice lowered to match mine. "Sometimes we come aboard and he spends awhile back there."

"Let me guess, midday prayer time?"

She looked at me respectfully.

"Didn't take you long to figure him out. How did you know?"

"I'll tell you later," I said, glancing back again. "Do you think we need to wait for him or can we start engines and taxi?"

She recovered from her astonishment and looked at me with a sudden gleam in her eyes. "Let's live dangerously," she said.

"Roger that," I relied. "Do you mind if I run a flow for the before and after starting engines checklists and you can back me up when I'm done?"

"Not at all," she said.

A "flow," in cockpit terminology, meant accomplishing several checklist steps in a particular order without referencing the checklist. The steps were usually performed in an ergonomically efficient order vis-à-vis the layout of the applicable switches in the cockpit.

I ran my "Before Starting Engines" flow and then Sarah read the applicable checklist items and we ensured everything was done. The START MASTER SWITCH was activated.

"Clear right?" I asked.

Sarah looked in the small rear-view mirror bolted into the bottom part of the opening for the right-side window. She rotated it slightly on its stand so that she could clearly see the area around the right engine.

"Clear," she replied.

"Starting two," I said as I hit the START button for the right engine. I glanced down at the top center display unit where the engine instrumentation was located.

"Start valve and ignition," I said, verifying that the indicators for both were illuminated. The APU was now pumping air into the right engine to turn it for the start. The engine igniters were providing sparks so that fuel would be ignited when I added it. The high-pressure turbine, just aft of the combustion chamber of the engine, began turning immediately and building RPM. The low-pressure turbine, further aft, began turning a few seconds later.

"Positive LP," I said. The low-pressure turbine was what turned the "fan" which was the part of most modern jet engines that you'd see if you looked down the intake. The fan generated most of the engine thrust and was essentially a propeller encased in the engine housing. Because the fan was so large and exposed, it could be turned by the wind. On engine start, it was important to make sure that the fan was turning in the correct direction before adding fuel to the process. If the fan was turning the opposite direction, LP RPM would rapidly decrease, then increase in the proper direction.

"Fifteen percent HP," Sarah said. The high-pressure turbine had reached the minimum RPM for start. Your typical G-IV driver will wait until max RPM before adding fuel to keep the start cooler though.

The HP RPM topped out just over twenty percent.

"HP cock coming up," I said, moving a knob behind the right throttle in a vertical track. This opened high-pressure fuel flow to the engine. Almost immediately, the engine's internal temperature began to rise.

"There's the light off," Sarah mentioned.

The temperature climbed up to about six hundred degrees Celsius and then began to decrease. The high-pressure RPM moved up to idle power range and stabilized.

"Good start," I said.

I checked the combined and utility hydraulic system pressures, both powered by the pump connected to the right engine. They were both 3,000 psi, just as they should have been.

"Starting one," I said.

I started the left engine and performed my after starting engines flow. Sarah backed me up with the checklist.

"You ready to taxi?" I asked Sarah.

She smiled and nodded at me.

"Call 'em," I said, smiling back.

"Burbank Ground," Sarah said, keying her headset microphone. "Gulfstream November Three Six Whisky Mike Sierra, taxi from Atlantic with information delta and clearance."

"Gulfstream Whiskey Mike Sierra, Bob Hope Ground, taxi to runway two six via delta, hold short of runway one five."

"Gulfstream Whiskey Mike Sierra copies taxi to runway two six via delta and we will hold short of runway one five."

"Left turn out of the ramp here and delta's the parallel, right?" I verified the controller's taxi instructions with Sarah.

"Yes sir," she said.

"Here we go. Would you turn the taxi light on, please?"

Sarah reached up on the panel right in front of my face and turned the taxi light on. I have a rule when I'm taxiing or hand-flying an airplane - I don't touch any switches; that's the other pilot's job.

Manny was on the ramp in front of us and began giving us the standard ground marshaling hand signals to get us out to the ramp. I released the parking brake and advanced the throttles to about seventy percent RPM. Once the jet began to roll, I pulled the throttles back and used the "tiller" on the left console to turn the jet. The tiller in the G-IV was shaped like a small steering wheel about six inches in diameter and turned the nose wheel of the aircraft. Until the rudder was effective at about 80 knots, the tiller was the primary means of steering the aircraft. I turned us 90 degrees and headed east on taxiway delta, the taxiway which paralleled runway 8-26, the shorter of the two runways at KBUR.

I heard the sound of a door opening up in the cabinet behind us and I knew that Adam was extending the jump seat just behind the cockpit. In a G-IV, that seat placed the person sitting in it between and slightly aft of the two pilot seats.

"Flaps twenty, taxi checks please," I said just as Adam's Armani-clad knees slid into my peripheral vision. I could hear the seat belt and shoulder harness clicking into place.

Sarah began running the taxi checklist and we verified that the flaps were set at 20 degrees, the correct setting for takeoff. We also verified that the horizontal stabilizer had traveled to the correct position for the flap setting.

"Okay, Sarah," I said, "pretty much a standard briefing. We'll fly the radar vectors to five thousand feet. Prior to eighty knots if you see something you don't like, call the abort and I'll do the same. If we abort, back me up with the speed brakes. Between eighty knots and V one, our decision speed, we'll abort for a loss of thrust, thrust reverser, ground spoiler deployment, any sort of directional control issue or a runway incursion. After V one, if we lose an engine, we're going flying. We'll climb straight ahead to fifteen hundred feet AGL. I'll fly and talk on the radios while you run the checklist. After the appropriate checklists are complete, we'll come back here to land unless we have a hydraulic failure or a braking issue, in that case we'll go down to LAX or over to Ontario where the runways are longer. Do you have any questions?"

"None," she said.

We rolled up to the intersection of our taxiway and the crossing runway. I began to apply brakes to stop us. "I will be holding short of runway one five," I informed her. I always made sure the other pilot in the cockpit knew exactly what I was doing. It was a reflexive mechanism for me and one to ensure that the other pilot could correct me if I screwed something up.

"Copy that," she said.

"Gulfstream Whiskey Mike Sierra, Bob Hope Ground, cross runway one five and monitor tower."

"Whiskey Mike Sierra, Wilco," Sarah replied.

In a two-person crew, usually the pilot not flying, or in our present case, not driving, the airplane spoke on the radio.

"How do you hear me?" Adam said, as he plugged a headset into the intercom system.

"Loud and clear," I replied.

"Me too," Sarah said. She was tuning one of the aircraft radios to the tower frequency. As soon as the radio tuned, our headsets filled up with chatter from the aircraft to the tower and vice-versa. At busier airports, pilots don't contact the tower for takeoff clearance because it generates an extra radio call.

I looked over at Adam briefly. "Are you all strapped in?"

He nodded without looking at me and I had the opportunity to catch his face in profile for a few seconds. The olive hue to his skin was so lustrous it looked like it could have been painted on and his complexion was flawless. His hair was impeccably styled, short enough to be professional but long enough to be fashionable. As he sat there with his head propped up with his left hand I could also see that his nails were manicured. He seemed to take good care of himself. Or maybe he was taken care of.

"Gulfstream Whiskey Mike Sierra, Bob Hope tower, runway two-six, taxi into position and hold."

Sarah repeated the instructions back to the controller as a Hawker business jet flew past us and landed several hundred feet down the runway.

"Are you ready?" I asked Sarah. I asked this question a lot. I'd seen too many captains who just do what they wanted to do without making sure their crew was prepared.

She nodded.

"Line up checks," I said. "I have one up." This meant that I had one throttle above the idle position and that Sarah was free to arm the ground spoilers. With one throttle out of the idle position, the spoilers wouldn't deploy.

Sarah's hands swept over the cockpit and I had a small twinge of pride. She was using the same flow pattern I had taught her long ago. I guided the big jet out onto the runway and lined it up on the centerline stripe. Down toward midfield, the Hawker that had landed earlier was taxiing clear of the runway.

"Gulfstream Whiskey Mike Sierra," the tower controller intoned, "fly runway heading, maintain five thousand, cleared for takeoff."

"Gulfstream Whiskey Mike Sierra, runway heading to five-thousand, cleared for takeoff," Sarah replied as she turned the landing lights on, the universal symbol for acknowledging the takeoff clearance.

"My yoke," she said to me, placing her right hand on the yoke. For the initial part of the takeoff roll, the pilot who flew in the left seat had to keep his or her left hand guarding the tiller and his right hand on the throttles.

"Your yoke," I acknowledged. Here we go."

I released the brakes, evened the throttles up and advanced them slowly. The exhaust pressure ratio or EPR passed about 1.2 and I engaged the auto-throttles. The throttles then advanced themselves to take-off power as I rested my hands on them. We began to accelerate rapidly. I smiled to myself. The G-IV had a lot of power, but it didn't have nearly the thrust of the last jet I flew.

"Power set," Sarah said a moment later.

"Airspeed's alive, once, twice, three times," she continued, as she checked the three airspeed indicators in the cockpit and verified that they were all operative and in agreement.

"Sixty knots and hold," she said. In the flight display on each side, the word HOLD came up with a rectangle around it. This meant that the auto-throttles had latched into place.

"Eighty knots," she said.

"My yoke," I said, lifting my left hand from the tiller to the control yoke.

We continued to accelerate down the runway.

"V one," Sarah said. V1 was the maximum speed at which we could abort the takeoff. At this point, no matter what happened, we were committed to fly. I took my right hand off the throttles and placed it on the yoke.

"Rotate," she said. We had reached flying speed.

I smoothly pulled the yoke toward me and the nose of the G-IV gracefully lifted off the runway. I set the climb angle at ten to twelve degrees of pitch and the main gear lifted off a moment or two later.

"Positive rate," Sarah said, after confirming that we were definitely climbing.

"Gear up," I commanded in response.

Sarah raised the landing gear handle and the handle itself turned red until all three gears were fully retracted and the doors were closed. The red light then extinguished.

"Four hundred feet," Sarah intoned with her hand on the flap handle.

"Flaps up," I said, "manual speed two hundred, flight level change."

She raised the flaps and then her hands flew over the

guidance panel, setting the airspeed control for the autothrottles at two hundred knots and selecting the flight level change mode or FLCH for the climb. FLCH automatically adjusted the climb angle of the aircraft to maintain the selected airspeed.

"Gulfstream Whiskey Mike Sierra, Bob Hope Tower, contact SOCAL departure."

"SOCAL departure, Gulfstream Three Six Whiskey Mike Sierra," Sarah repeated dutifully as she typed the pre-assigned frequency into the entry line of the flight guidance computer. She hit the entry button.

"Autospeed," I said.

She reached over to my guidance panel and selected the automatic speed mode for the FLCH mode. The indexed speed increased to two hundred forty knots.

"SOCAL, Gulfstream November Three Six Whiskey Mike Sierra passing four thousand, runway heading."

"Gulfstream November Three Six Whiskey Mike Sierra, SOCAL, radar contact, climb and maintain one six thousand, turn left to one four zero degrees. When able, proceed direct Seal Beach."

Sarah repeated the altitude, heading, and the name of the navigational fix on the departure and entered the data into the guidance panel. The navigation system directed me to begin a turn toward the Seal Beach fix and the jet settled into its climb.

"Autopilot," I commanded.

Sarah nodded and punched the button. I kept my hands on the yoke until I was sure the autopilot had engaged. Then I released the controls and slid my seat back on its rails.

"On the way," I said into the intercom.

"Yes, we are," Sarah said.

The blue Southern California sky beckoned the jet upward and we crossed the mountains and left the San Fernando Valley behind. The green Los Angeles basin lay in front of us, buried under the usual layer of smog, bordered by the deep azure Pacific Ocean to the right.

It felt good to be at the controls of an airplane again. I stole a glance across the cockpit at Sarah and she had a pleasant smile on her face as she stared through the windscreen and into the sky beyond.

Between us, Adam sat back, sighed, and crossed his arms. He seemed to be disinterestedly eyeing the overhead panel in the cockpit, while drumming his fingers on his sleeve, obviously pre-occupied with something. I could sense the impatience emanating from him.

This whole process of hiring me and coming to pick me up had delayed them, I realized. But delayed them from what?

In front of us, some eight-hundred odd-miles away, San Jose Del Cabo International Airport awaited us. I stared out the windscreen as I felt my guts begin to churn. Once again, in typical Pearce style, I had said yes to something before I knew what it was about. And once again, I was into some deep shit that I didn't understand.

From: Special Projects Group [NCS]
Sent: Wednesday, 18 November 2009, 1200 PST (18 November 2009, 2000Z)
To: Director, NCS
Cc: Special Projects Group [NCS]; damrine@cmail.cia.gov; dsmith3@cmail.cia.gov

SUBJECT: Aircraft Movement Alert – Gulfstream G-IVSP N36WMS

(TS) Narrative:

1. N36WMS departed KBUR (Burbank/Bob Hope Airport) at 1147 PST / 1947Z. Flight planned destination is MMSD (Los Cabos International Airport) with ETA of 1345 PST / 2145Z.

2. Ground surveillance of KBUR airport confirms Contractor 09-017, (Pearce, Colin M.), Sarah Morton Marciano and Abdullah bin Rashid al Qudamah, aka Adam Archmere, are aboard the aircraft.

3. We are attempting to position ground assets at MMSD to tail Archmere in the event he leaves the airport after arrival. We will present further updates as required.

(U) CONCLUSION: None. Information only.

(U) ACTION: None. Information only.

(U) RECOMMENDATIONS: None. Information only.

TOP SECRET / SPECIAL
COMPARTMENTALIZED INFORMATION
CLASSIFIED BY: US Central Intelligence Agency
DECLASSIFY ON: OADR

CHAPTER FOUR

Contract Day Two
Wednesday, 18 November
1630 Hours Local Time
Los Cabos International Airport (MMSD)
San Jose Del Cabo, Mexico

Sarah looked comfortable lying there on the divan and I didn't really want to wake her. But the passengers were due to show in about thirty minutes and I knew enough about corporate aviation to know that they were as likely to arrive early as late.

##

The flight down had been uneventful and my landing had been fairly good considering I hadn't flown the G-IV in a few months. I'd like to say that was a testament to my skills as an aviator—and that was certainly part of it, but it was also a lot about the technology of the aircraft. When you hold a three-degree glide path, cross the threshold of the runway at the right airspeed, pull the power to idle shortly thereafter, and flare the jet when the ground proximity warning says "ten feet," it becomes a somewhat mechanical process.

We had no sooner shut down the engines and opened the door, and Adam was on his way.

"I'll take care of all the paperwork," he said as he went down the stairs. "We'll be back precisely at five. We won't need any catering. Don't leave the aircraft, please."

Sarah and I retreated to the main cabin after he left and she retrieved some soft drinks and snacks for us from the jet's onboard stores. We sat down at the table to consume them.

"Somebody's connected," I said as I opened some packaged crackers. "I've never been able to get out of here without at least an hour of running around with a lot of paperwork and dropping a lot of twenty dollar bills on the inside of the terminal."

Sarah nodded. "Adam has influence here," she said between chews. "From the first trip we made here it's been like this. I've never actually seen what he does when he's on the inside, but it's like magic." She took a drink of full-strength Coca-Cola. "What are you smiling at?"

"You," I said. "You have this amazing bod and you don't watch what you eat at all. I'm just wondering when the spell is going to wear off."

"It's gotten worse since I got pregnant," she said, smiling back at me. "I'm always hungry now, as opposed to before when it was just most of the time."

"Particularly after a certain activity had occurred, as I recall."

"That hasn't changed either," she said wistfully. She seemed to clear her head and she leaned across the table toward me, whispering conspiratorially. "So, talk to me," she said, those damn eyes of hers sparkling mischievously, "what got you into the newspapers?"

I looked back at her. In spite of whatever angst she might be feeling about her marriage, pregnancy had made her even more beautiful. I had heard about that before but I had never seen it demonstrated.

"There's a tired phrase from the movie 'Top Gun' that people throw around all the time, something like 'I could tell you but I'd have to kill you,'" I said as I cleared my throat and my mind. "In this case, though, the information involved is for real. I don't know at what level it's classified, but it's up there."

She frowned at me. "Well, you're no fun."

"Story of my life," I responded. "The short answer, suitable for semi-public consumption, is that I did some contract work for the US Government in September."

"Wow," she whistled. "A government contractor. That's a big deal. What were you flying?"

I looked at her across the table and raised my eyebrows. "What did you hear in the news?"

"There was this huge dogfight above the high desert and all these rogue fighters were shot down and that the Air Force sent in fighters from March Air Reserve Base."

"That is what the news said," I echoed. "Do you remember what kind of jets the bad guys were flying?"

"F-16s!" she said. Then her eyes nearly popped out of her head. "That's what you used to fly, right? You were flying one of their jets!"

I just looked at her and smiled. "You never heard me say that."

"So, the government hired you to get inside their organization?"

"This contract job I did for the government paid an obscene amount of money," I said in response.

"Wow," she sat back in her chair. "The news story directly attributed the 'unnamed pilot' as being the guy that stopped the attack. Did you have to fight any of them?"

"Did your friend tell you why that jet had to land at Edwards?"

"Yeah, she did. She said it ran out of fuel and glided in. It was a big deal because of the hydrazine system on the F-16 and all the hazmat implications."

"Dogfights burn a lot of gas," I said, looking at the ceiling. "A lot of gas."

"Wow," she said, sitting back in her seat. Every pilot with an ounce of competitiveness dreams about being a fighter pilot. The ones who say they don't are liars.

She leaned forward again with a concerned look on her face and took my hands in hers.

"Now cut the bullshit. What's really with the leg?"

I looked down at her hands.

"All of the bad guys might not have been killed over the high desert," I replied. "And some of them might have paid this pilot guy a visit a few days later."

Her eyes widened.

"This guy successfully defended himself but he may have gotten shot a couple times in the process. And someone he cared about might have actually been killed."

I looked back up at her. Her eyes were suddenly very shiny and tears had welled up in them. I found myself astounded at the depth of feelings she apparently still had for me. She removed one of her hands from mine, unabashedly snagged a tissue from a nearby dispenser, and wiped her eyes, holding my gaze throughout. "You're amazing," she said quietly.

"No," I said firmly, "I am not. Some people have a knack for being in the wrong place at the wrong time and I'm one of them." She started to protest but I cut her off. "Here's what you need to take away from this. I know... people."

She took this in for a moment. "Have you spoken to them since you got here?"

I nodded.

"What did they say?"

"They are very interested," I responded.

Her eyes widened again and a wry smile found its way onto her lips.

The aircraft vibrated a little and I could tell someone was walking up the air-stair. I rose from my seat and went to the front of the cabin. A very attractive Latina entered the vestibule and was looking aft into the cabin. Her eyes obviously hadn't adjusted from the bright Baja sun outside.

"May I help you?" I asked.

"Ay!" she cried, nearly jumping out of her skin.

"I'm sorry," I said.

"Es no probleem," she said in heavily-accented English. "Buenos Tardes, Cap-i-tan. I haff your flight plan and papperwork heere." She extended her arm and handed me a brown file folder. She was wearing a uniform that identified her as belonging to the handling agency we were using and also revealed quite a lot of her superb body.

"Gracias," I said.

"De nada," she replied with smile. "Weel you need any serveeces?"

"No," I replied.

She nodded. "Call on radio if you need sometheeng."

"I will."

"Adios, Capitan."

"Adios, Señorita."

She turned and went down the stairs quickly, trying not to trip as she negotiated the steps in a pair of ridiculously high heels.

I took the folder and went back into the cabin. Sarah eyed me with a smirk on her face as I sat down.

"Now how do you think she got that job?" she asked me.

"It wasn't for her English," I replied, opening the folder and going through the papers inside. It was the standard stuff. Confirmation that our flight plan had been filed, updated weather and NOTAMS, and an itemized receipt for "services."

"What a racket," I said as read the receipt. "Five-thousand dollars for a quick turn. Welcome to Mexico."

"It wasn't that expensive before Adam joined us," Sarah said.

I nodded. "That helps to explain why the turn is so smooth."

"Hey, listen," Sarah said, "would you mind doing the preflight and getting us set up for the return? I'd like to lie down for a little while."

"I'm a contractor," I said. "It's part of the service."

She smiled and started to try to slide out of her chair. I quickly rose and offered her my hand. She took it gratefully and I helped her to her feet. Her arms went naturally around me and mine around her. With the size of her stomach, she had to turn sideways to get completely next to me. She rested her head on my chest.

"You know," she said after a few moments, "I never forgot how you felt."

"That's nice to know," I answered, "considering that I'm sure I'm one of the lesser examples of the male species you've run into."

"You'd be surprised."

She released me and patted me twice on the chest, not making eye contact. Her mind was in the same place mine was.

She lay down on the divan located on the right side of the airplane and pulled one of the throw pillows under her head.

There was a light blanket on the divan across the aisle from her. I unfolded it and put it on top of her, making sure it completely covered her from her neck to her feet.

"Come here," she said, lifting her head off the pillow.

I lowered my face to hers and she kissed me, letting her lips rest on mine for just a second longer than a married woman probably should have. But while there was an air of what could have been, there was much more an air of gratitude.

"Don't let me sleep past four, please," she said, as our lips parted. She smiled at me and lay back on her pillow. She was asleep in seconds.

##

"Time to wake up, Sarah." I knelt on the carpeted floor of the jet and shook her shoulder gently.

Her eyes opened slowly and she seemed to take a second or two to get them into focus. She finally fixated on my face and smiled sleepily.

"I had a dream about you," she said.

"Oh really?"

"What was it about?"

"Something it shouldn't have been for a married, pregnant woman."

"That's why they're dreams."

"What time is it?"

"Four thirty."

She sat up quickly, a look of mild panic on her face.

"Relax," I said calmly. "We're completely ready to go. Everything is done."

I helped her to her feet. She slid into my arms and we held each other again for a few minutes.

"I need this," she said simply, looking up at me, "but obviously we can't do it when Adam's around." She gently extracted herself. "I guess we need to get down to business. First things first though. I need to pee."

She made her way to the aft lavatory and shut the door behind her.

I went to the front of the aircraft, down the stairs, and out into the dry, temperate air of the Cabo November. October to April is tourist high season here. The temperature is typically 80 degrees Fahrenheit during the day and cools to the 60s at night. From May to September though, it's a different story. The temperature increases to over 100 Fahrenheit during the day and will stay in the upper 70s and low 80s in the evening. While there were those who would consider this warm, compared to Phoenix, Arizona and Saudi Arabia, where I had spent considerable portions of my life, it was positively heavenly.

Unlike most other airports, where the general aviation terminal is relegated to some far corner of the field, here at

Los Cabos, it was right in the center of the ramp area between the two major airline terminals. The airport was served by several US major airlines and was busy on a daily basis. There was another smaller airport closer to the town of Cabo San Lucas which could have easily handled an aircraft of this size but for some reason, Adam didn't want to go there. I looked around the ramp and saw that we were amidst at least thirty or forty business jets and I nodded my head.

"He wants to blend in," I said to the air around me.

The airport was surrounded by the arid desert landscape with some craggy mountains to the west and a dry riverbed to the east. As I looked around, I had a brief flashback to my last job, the one Sarah and I had just talked about inside the jet. The locations had been diverse during the several weeks I had worked there, a desert island in the south Pacific Ocean, eastern Oman and Southern California to be precise. But deserts look a lot alike and I found some thoughts triggered in my mind, about events and people - particularly one person, whom I had cared for and who had subsequently died in my arms on the floor of my townhouse in Wilmington. It occurred to me that getting out of there was probably the best thing that could have happened to me. Sitting there, moping in self-pity while I lived on the considerable funds stored in my Bermuda bank account was no way to exist.

I smiled up at the sky, cleared my mind, and hobbled around as I did a quick external preflight of the aircraft, once again enjoying the touch of the cold metal and machinery. I climbed back up the ladder to find Sarah waiting for me in the vestibule at the top of the stairs. Her face looked a little pale.

"I threw up while I was back there," she said. "Came out of nowhere. One of the downsides of being pregnant."

"Will you be okay to fly back?"

"It's up to you," she said with a hopeful look on her face. "I may manage the airplane but you're the pilot-in-command on this flight and I'm not going to make you fly with someone you don't want to fly with."

I looked at her softly. "No problems here, ma'am."

She nodded. "What would you like me to do?"

"Why don't you sit up front, look over the flight plan and the clearance, and let me play the gallant contract guy. I'll help Adam and his passengers get situated."

She looked at me questioningly as I unholstered my BlackBerry and turned it around to show the camera aperture on the back.

"I need to get some pictures for my friends."

She gave me a crooked smile. "That's a good idea."

"I have them occasionally."

She climbed back into the cockpit and seated herself. I leaned back against the avionics cabinet on the right side of the vestibule and peered out the door toward the terminal. Our G-IV, like all the other jets on the ramp, was parked facing south with the terminal on the left side of the aircraft. This made it easy for me to keep my eyes on the double doors at the near end of the white-roofed, glass-walled building while remaining comfortable in the vestibule. I looked at my watch. It was almost exactly five o'clock in the afternoon. As I glanced up, the doors of the ramp side of the building opened and Adam walked out of them with a veritable parade of people accompanying him. There was a shorter olive-complexioned man at his side who walked with a supremely confident stride. Bill Spratt and a uniformed airport official followed. Behind them was a man in a dark suit wearing thick glasses who was pulling a large suitcase on wheels. Two large men in dark suits walked just behind the suitcase, apparently guarding it. A discrete distance behind all of them, a line service technician pushed a baggage cart.

"And they didn't want the one bag on the cart," I said out loud. "Makes you wonder what the heck they have in there."

"Yes, it does," Sarah said from the cockpit. She was watching them approach as well.

We were the third of four jets parked in a row from the edge of the ramp to the parallel taxiway, and once Adam and his party negotiated the long concrete walkway from the terminal and made it out onto the ramp, they still had about fifty yards or so to go. I was hoping that I'd be able to snap a few unobtrusive photos with the BlackBerry before they got too close to the airplane.

Then, an idea popped into my head.

"Can you hand me the clipboard with the flight plan and weather on it?" I asked Sarah.

She looked back at me quizzically and handed me the clipboard over her left shoulder.

I called up the application on the BlackBerry which reported airport weather and punched in KBUR. Then, I called up the video camera mode and placed it "casually" on top of the clipboard.

They reached the end of the walkway and Adam turned toward the uniformed official. The man shook Adam's hand and then bowed slightly, clearly as a sign of respect. I felt my jaw drop. The man then departed, ignoring Spratt and the other men in the party. The six of them continued toward the airplane. As they rounded the nose of the jet next to us, I began to make a production of checking the weather and NOTAMS on the clipboard and checking it against my BlackBerry. I then looked up and "noticed them." Hurriedly, I activated the video camera, placed the BlackBerry casually on top of the clipboard and held it there with my thumb.

"When the three of us are seated in the cockpit," I whispered to Sarah, "ask me how I use my BlackBerry to check the weather."

"Okay," she said with a questioning tone in her voice.

I walked to the bottom of the stairs and awaited my passengers. Adam arrived first and I reversed the way I was holding the clipboard so that the paper and BlackBerry were facing out, away from my chest, and toward the passengers. I just hoped the angle was adequate for the lens to catch a few faces as they came by.

"Hello, Adam," I said as he neared the top of the stairs, "welcome back."

"I will load the baggage," he said flatly. "You will remain in the front of the aircraft."

I nodded as he went up the stairs.

Very interesting.

"Colin Pearce," I said as I offered my hand to the unknown, shorter gentleman next in line.

"Felix Lopez," he replied in mildly accented English. He was short, about five feet eight with black hair and dark eyes. His hair, what little there was of it, was combed back across his head in strands and his scalp was spotted and freckled. This man spent a lot of time outside. He had to have been middle aged, but he seemed "used up." There were deep wrinkles and age marks on his face. He wore a non-descript green suit that reeked of cigarette smoke. I wondered if he'd be able to last the two hours back to Burbank without a cigarette.

But there was something else. As I released his hand and looked into his eyes, I felt a familiar sensation go through me. I may not have known who this man was, but I knew what he was. The adage "it takes one to know one" ran through my mind.

I thought I saw the hint of a flash of recognition in his eyes.

Bill Spratt came up to the stairs next.

"Hi Mr. Spratt," I said, "I don't know if you remember me or not. Colin Pearce. I got Sarah checked out in this jet right after you bought it."

He looked at me for a second and his eyes seemed to focus for the first time. It was apparent that his mind had been elsewhere.

"Of course, I remember you, Colin," he said with a forced joviality I could tell he didn't feel. "That was a great couple of weeks."

Spratt was five feet ten inches and probably weighed an athletic 170 pounds. He had a full head of thick, gray hair and dark brown eyes. When I had flown him before, he had just turned sixty years old and the G-IV had been a birthday present to himself. At the time, I had been envious of his apparent energy and vigor for his age. He didn't look like a man approaching eligibility for social security.

But today he was a few years past sixty and looked every day of it. He moved slowly, almost aimlessly, and it was easy to tell that he was having difficulty staying mentally present.

"Yes sir, it was," I replied without missing a beat. "And I'm here to take good care of you again."

He looked hard at me and I could tell his mind had focused on what I had said. He looked at my face and I saw a flash of hope go through his expression. Then he nodded and went up the stairs.

The last guy was average height, average build, with black hair and dark eyes. He wore heavy, metal-framed glasses. The suitcase he rolled behind him seemed to be larger in both width and height than a normal bag. As he approached, he eyed the door, and then looked down the fuselage of the aircraft.

"Baggage?" he asked with a heavy middle-eastern accent.

"You want to stow this in the baggage compartment?" I asked him.

He cocked his head for a moment; and then, as I pointed to the rear of the aircraft, I saw the baggage door open on the fuselage under the left engine. Adam's face appeared in the opening and he motioned to the three men impatiently. The line technician was already waiting under the engine and he began handing Adam the few bags on the cart which Adam quickly took from him and stowed. Meanwhile, the man wearing glasses rolled the large suitcase around the left wing and to the baggage opening. Once the line technician had left, the two large men accompanying him lifted the case to the height of the door while the man with glasses carefully supervised. The look on his face made it very apparent that he was very concerned that the case was not dropped or mishandled. Adam reached out for the case's handle and with considerable help from the guys on the ground, he rolled it inside the compartment. Once it was in, he sealed the door. The man with the glasses returned to the stairs without looking at me and boarded the aircraft. The two large men returned to the terminal.

"Well, I wonder what the hell is in that," I said to myself as I hobbled up the stairs.

"Gentlemen," I said after I entered the cabin, "about two hours to Burbank. Weather's good, should be a smooth flight. Tell me if you need anything." I looked at Adam. "Am I to understand that you have all the appropriate paperwork accomplished so there will be no issues with customs when we arrive?"

Adam's eyes locked onto me with a hostile glare and he nodded solemnly. Then he seemed to notice the clipboard and BlackBerry on it for the first time. Before he could say anything, I turned and retreated down the vestibule toward the cockpit.

"Are we ready to go?" I asked Sarah as I handed her the clipboard.

"Yep," she replied.

"I'm going to take a last look around the jet and we'll blast," I said. When I was shielded from the view of the main cabin, I stopped the video capture mode on the BlackBerry and called up the e-mail mode. I fired a quick e-mail to Smith and Amrine with the video clip attached. Then I re-holstered the BlackBerry and went down the stairs.

I walked around the jet and gave it a quick once-over, signaling the Mexican ground crew to pull the wheel chocks as I did so. Everything seemed to be in order. I climbed the stairs.

"Ready to shut the door?" I asked Sarah.

"Yes," she said.

I shut the door, locked it down and then climbed into the cockpit.

I felt a presence just aft of the cockpit. Adam was coming forward.

"When are you going to show me how you check weather on that thing?" Sarah asked quickly.

I pulled the BlackBerry from its holster, ignoring Adam as he glowered from behind us.

"It's a service I subscribe to," I said, as I showed her the screen. "I just click on the icon and then input the ICAO four letter identifier. Here's Burbank since I just used it."

I clicked and the terminal observations and forecasts for Burbank came up a few seconds later.

"Wow," she said. "That's useful."

"I always use this to cross check the printed weather we get from the FBO or from a flight planner, just to be sure."

"Good idea," Sarah said, as I re-holstered the BlackBerry and finished strapping in. "You can never be too careful."

Adam returned to the cabin without saying a word.

"Nice job," I whispered to Sarah.

She looked over at me and flashed me the brilliant smile that had remained permanently imprinted on my brain for the last few years.

We were established at flight level 430 on our way back to Van Nuys about thirty minutes later. Adam had stayed in the back of the aircraft for the entire taxi, take-off, and climb-out which I found unusual given the fact that he was theoretically supposed to evaluate me.

Once the G-IV had settled into cruise, I looked over at Sarah. "So, you're really thirsty and you need something to drink. What will it be?" I asked.

She looked at me quizzically for a fraction of a second and then her eyes registered understanding. "A Fiji Water. I've had my one shot of caffeine for the day."

"Of course."

I unstrapped and gingerly climbed out of the cockpit, using the usual series of contortions to do so, only taking infinitely more care since jarring the flight controls in flight would make for a severe lack of form. Of course, during the process, my face came within inches of Sarah's, and while she didn't turn her head, she smiled and winked at me with her left eye.

I stood up in the vestibule and found that the door to the main cabin was closed. I turned around to Sarah. "I guess they don't like us. They shut the cabin door."

"Not surprising," she said dryly. "That's what's happened on our previous trips. We'd no sooner get airborne and Adam would excuse himself and make his way back to the cabin and stay there for the whole flight."

I nodded. "Back in a few," I said.

I walked to the door of the main cabin and opened it as silently as I could.

I found Bill sitting in the "power chair," the first forward facing chair on the right side of the aircraft, which in most G-IVs, is where the principal passenger always sits. It's also where nearly all the audio, video and lighting controls are located. Bill had a magazine in his lap and was staring out the window. He didn't even turn his head as I walked by.

Adam and "Felix" were seated across from one another at the table in the aft of the cabin, in the same two seats Sarah and I had occupied earlier. They were engaged in a heated conversation - in Arabic. I don't speak the language, but I've been around those who do enough to know it when I hear it. Adam was facing me and Felix was across from him. As I approached, Adam looked up at me disinterestedly.

"Sorry, gentlemen," I said, "I'll just be second."

The door to the lavatory, aft of the galley, was closed and locked and I assumed, occupied by the guy with the glasses. Considering that someone would have to go through the lavatory to get to the baggage compartment, I couldn't decide whether he was using the facilities or performing guard duty.

I found the ice drawer in the galley, retrieved a Diet Coke and a square bottle of Fiji, and started to make my way forward. I kept my eyes fixed on the front of the airplane, but I could feel Felix's gaze on me as I passed. I handed Sarah the drinks and contorted my way back into the cockpit a few moments later.

"Adam and Felix or whatever his name really is, have a lot to talk about," I said over the intercom, once I had gotten my headset back on. "And they're speaking fluent Arabic."

"How do you know that? And I meant to ask you before, how did you know Adam was a Muslim?"

"I knew he was a Saudi," I said. "The Muslim thing is just a natural extension. After spending time around them, you just know. I knew he was a Saudi from the moment I met him and I guarantee you that he's not an average Saudi, he's way up in the food chain." I took a sip of my Diet Coke and let my thoughts settle for a moment or two. "Tell me about Dubai," I said.

"Damian got Bill invited to this special VIP yacht show there," Sarah said resignedly. "That was the whole reason we flew over there. It was amazing. You wouldn't believe the boats. For the first few days, all of us went, Bill and Shelly and Damian and me. On the final day, I stayed at the hotel because I wasn't feeling well. That's the day Bill bought the boat. It was a special prototype of a new yacht this Palmer Johnson Company was coming out with."

"And that's the day they didn't come back."

She nodded as she looked straight ahead.

"How did you find out?"

"I went down to meet everyone for dinner at the hotel restaurant that night and found Adam sitting with Bill at the bar. Bill introduced Adam and Adam flashed that smile of his and very politely told us Damian and Shelly were in his custody and if we wanted to see them alive, we had to do exactly as he said."

The questions were flying around in my head. The timing of all of this seemed way too coincidental.

"I have to ask you about some things and if the answers are too personal, you certainly don't have to respond. But believe it or not, it might help."

She turned her head and looked at me.

"I can use all the help I can get," she said. "Ask away."

"You obviously aren't too happy about being married," I said. "Why'd you do it?"

She slumped back in her seat. "Wow," she said. "You don't waste any time, do you?" She paused a moment to gather her thoughts. "That's a damn good question," she said at last. "Do the words 'it seemed like the thing to do at the time' sound too trite?"

"Not at all," I said. "Been there, done that, just not in this context."

She turned her head to look out the side window as she continued speaking, as if she was ashamed to look me in the eye as she explained, "I met Damian about eighteen months ago at a party at the Bachelor Mansion. He seemed to be perfect. He was good looking, charming, and he was very unpretentious." She tilted her head toward me without looking at me. "He reminded me of you."

I allowed my heart to be warmed by that comment and kept my mouth shut.

"He was typed in the G-IV so we started flying him and before long he and I were spending a lot of time together... like you and I did... I guess I wanted to believe it was the same thing."

I didn't know what to think about that. Despite the extended hours at close quarters, relationships between cockpit crew members of the opposite sex were rare, even if both crew members were single. This was mostly due to the nature of the relationship itself which involved a lot of forced intimacy and exposure to the other person on a twenty-four-hour basis with no break-in period. It didn't allow for the foundation of gradual exposure, adaptation, and acceptance that was the basis of most romantic relationships. A cockpit relationship also involved a degree of authority and submission and a requirement to be brutally honest when mistakes were made. The character of the environment basically ensured that romantic relationships didn't form. Except on rare occasions. Like what happened to Sarah and me. Or so I wanted to believe.

"After about three months he started to talk about marriage and after six months he just sort of wore me down," she continued. "But after the wedding, he started to change. He became very domineering. First, he tried to run my personal life, and as you may remember, I don't deal well with that."

I grinned at her.

"I do remember. Let me guess, the blonde hair was your way of telling him he wasn't going to get everything his way."

She smiled back at me.

"Very good," she said lightly. "He really liked my natural color but I decided I wanted to be a blonde for a while and there was nothing he could do about it." Then her face turned serious again. "The next thing he tried to do was take over all of the day-to-day operations of the flight department, like he was entitled to do it since he was my husband. I stood my ground there as well and he didn't like it. Then he started going behind my back to talk to Bill directly, particularly after I became pregnant, like my 'delicate condition' was affecting my judgment. Probably the biggest deal was the whole trip to Dubai for the yacht show. I didn't know about it until about two days before we left. He had talked Bill into it and planned the whole thing. I didn't have a chance to consider security or customs or anything. I had to completely trust what he had done."

I nodded my head. I was beginning to understand now.

"Do you have pictures of him? Damian, I mean."

69

She shook her head.

"No. He hated having his picture taken. We didn't even have a photographer at the wedding. It really pissed my parents off."

"Describe him for me."

"Well he's Italian and has a Mediterranean complexion and dark hair. He has dark eyes and he's built lean, more like Adam than you."

She was staring at me now.

"What are you thinking, Colin?" she asked.

I ignored her question and asked her one of my own.

"Just to reiterate, before you married him, did he seem to know most, if not all of the things you liked? Did he insist on doing only things you wanted to do?"

She was nodding slowly. "Yes," she said in slow realization. "It was like he was made for me." She looked at me and I could see the realization emerge in her eyes. She sighed deeply and sank back against her seat again. "No way," she said. "I can't believe what an idiot I am."

"He was a plant, Sarah," I said, stating the obvious. "Don't be too hard on yourself. I'm betting he's had some practice at this. Seduction is an art. If a man or a woman is good at it, they can get under the defenses of the person they're targeting every time. It's just a question of what buttons they need to push."

She sat there, looking out the windscreen and shaking her head.

"By the way," I continued, "Not to put too fine a point on it but I'm betting that it was his idea for you to get pregnant as soon as possible. Wasn't it?"

"I wanted to wait," she said, still shaking her head. "Hell, for a while I didn't even want to have sex with him. I put it off as long as I could but he just wouldn't let it go. Finally, I had to take measures. He had to learn there were things he couldn't control there as well."

She looked at me with an expression I couldn't discern but I ignored her.

"Do you know what type of person is typically considered the least threatening human being on the earth?" I asked her.

She didn't answer.

"A pregnant woman, for obvious reasons."

She turned her head away and looked out of her windscreen, shaking her head. "Son of a bitch," she said after a moment. "How did I not see this?"

I reached out and gently rubbed her shoulder. "Sometimes it's tough to see things clearly when you're caught up in the middle of them. In my last job..." I paused as I remembered and tried to search for the right words. "I actually thought somebody I cared about was trying to kill me when in actuality, she was trying to save me. It was all a matter of perspective."

She looked at me questioningly.

"My point is it's easy for me to come here with fresh eyes and see all this because I can look backwards and see the timeline without anything clouding my perspective. It's obvious they wanted access to this jet and that as their plans progressed they wanted you out of the way."

I held up fingers to illustrate the events in sequence.

"One, Damian meets you and courts you. Two, he marries you, tries to take over the department and subvert you. Three, he gets you pregnant. Four, Damian pushes Bill to the yacht show, Bill buys the boat and then he disappears with Shelly. Five, Adam comes aboard and takes over. Six, you return to the US and these trips to Cabo begin with Adam talking to the gangsters." I looked at her. "Is that damn boat that Bill bought in Cabo?"

She nodded.

"Seven," I said.

"Wow," she said. "What in the hell do you think they're up to?

"No idea," I said. "But you can bet your ass I'm going to

find out." I looked over at her. "And by the way," I added, "about your husband, I guarantee you he isn't Italian. I'd be shocked if he isn't Saudi and someone Adam knows very well. In fact, Shelly is probably his prisoner."

From: Special Projects Group [NCS]
Sent: Wednesday, 18 November 2009, 1715 PST (19 November 2009, 0115Z)
To: Director, NCS
Cc: Special Projects Group [NCS]; damrine@cmail.cia.gov; dsmith3@cmail.cia.gov

SUBJECT: Aircraft Movement Alert – Gulfstream G-IVSP N36WMS

(TS) Narrative:

1. N36WMS departed MMSD (Los Cabos International Airport) at 1702 PST / 0102 Z. Flight planned destination is KBUR (Burbank/Bob Hope Airport) with ETA of 1913 PST / 0313 Z.

2. Abdullah bin Rashid al Qudamah, aka Adam Archmere left the aircraft while it was on the ground in MMSD and was driven away from the airport. Limited ground surveillance assets available prevented following al Qudamah to his destination. Contractor 09-017, (Pearce, Colin M.), and Sarah Morton Marciano remained aboard the aircraft.

3. Upon his return to the airport, al Qudamah was accompanied by William Spratt, publisher of Bachelor Magazine, a man matching the description of Saif al Din and an unidentified third man. Facial recognition analysis of photographs taken by ground surveillance and of a video clip provided by Pearce

confirm al Din's identity. The third man brought an oversized suitcase, which appeared to be quite heavy, along with him. This suitcase was loaded on the aircraft as well. Photos of the suitcase have been submitted for analysis. Unfortunately, infrared surveillance was not available.

(TS) CONCLUSIONS:

1. Al Qudamah's involvement in a feasible operation which presents a credible threat against the US in unknown, but his actions remain suspicious.

2. We have learned that William Spratt bought a yacht at the Dubai boat show which took place the last week of September, the same show in which Shelly Spratt and Damian Marciano went missing. The yacht is a prototype Palmer Johnson P2J10, an ocean-going sports yacht with a top speed of 30 knots. The yacht is currently docked in the harbor at Cabo San Lucas.

3. If al Qudamah's intent were to bring weapons or personnel ashore, Cabo San Lucas and the associated area would be an ideal place to do so due to the geographical location, ineffectual efforts of the Mexican Navy and the significant influence of Miguel Hidalgo in the region. Of additional concern is the previous possible interaction between al Qudamah and representatives of Hidalgo earlier this year in Oman and the associated hijacked weapons shipment.

(TS) ACTION: Cross agency team is being formed. We will meet Pearce tonight at the Burbank Airport Marriott with the officer on our team who has met al Qudamah in a past operation. We are also preparing a briefing for you to present to the DCI at the next staff meeting tomorrow.

(U) RECOMMENDATIONS: None. Information only.

TOP SECRET / SPECIAL
COMPARTMENTALIZED INFORMATION
CLASSIFIED BY: US Central Intelligence Agency
DECLASSIFY ON: OADR

CHAPTER FIVE

Contract Day Two
Wednesday, 18 November
1915 Hours Local Time
Bob Hope Airport (KBUR)
Burbank, California, United States

We touched down on Runway 08 at Burbank about an hour and a half later. After clearing the runway, I taxied the jet to the area on the ramp where the US Customs and Border Patrol inspected international arrivals and shut down the engines. One agent, a short, unimpressive-looking, dark-haired officer with a thin mustache, boarded the aircraft and checked my paperwork, and Sarah's, almost perfunctorily. His nametag said "Bjellos."

After returning our passports, he went into the back of the aircraft where Adam, Bill, "Felix," and the guy with glasses were seated and took the highly unusual step of shutting the cabin door behind him. No sounds were audible. After a few minutes he emerged, waived to us as he passed the cockpit, and then went down the stairs. It might have been my imagination, but there seemed to be a large bulge in his right pants pocket that wasn't there before.

"That's interesting," I said, more to myself than to Sarah. "Very interesting indeed."

"What?" Sarah asked, obviously intrigued.

"Do you see the same CBP agent every time you come through here? Officer Bjellos?" I asked, motioning with my head toward the customs guy as he walked across the ramp back into his building.

I looked over at her and I could see the light of realization come on behind her eyes. "As a matter of fact, we do," she said.

"I'd wager he leaves the jet just a little heavier than when he boards it."

She sat there and shook her head slowly. "Unbelievable," she whispered.

I rose from my seat to close the air stair. The cabin door was open and two sets of eyes, Adam's and Felix's, watched me closely.

"We'll just reposition to Atlantic now. Should just be a few minutes."

Adam nodded, his eyes never leaving mine. Felix looked at me with a half-smile on his face, with an expression like he was regarding the entrees in a buffet line. It gave me an odd feeling.

We started the engines and taxied to Atlantic's ramp.

Manny was waiting for us on the tarmac in front of the FBO. He marshaled us onto the ramp and I shut down the engines. The limousine pulled up to the base of the ladder while the fan blades were still turning and the driver and another large man got out and walked to the baggage door on the rear of the aircraft.

"I'm going to let you get the door while I get the post shutdown checks and fill out the paperwork," I said to Sarah in a soft voice. "And this probably goes without saying, but obviously Adam can't learn about anything we've discussed. I'm not talking about you telling him anything, I'm just afraid he'll figure it out, somehow. He's not stupid. You're going to have to play along."

"No problem," she said as she unstrapped. "I've sort of

been doing that for the last six weeks anyway." Then she paused for a moment. "As a matter of fact, I've probably been doing that for the last year."

Her hair brushed my face as she leaned over to position herself to exit the cockpit. I closed my eyes and inhaled her scent as she passed me on her way out. Then I busied myself with the post shutdown checklist. In my peripheral vision, I saw Bill and Felix go by the cockpit door and felt them go down the stairs. A few moments later, the luggage, including the oversized suitcase, was delicately placed in the limo's spacious trunk while Bill and Felix entered the limo. Finally, Adam and the guy with glasses went through the vestibule and down the stairs behind me.

Then I felt a hand on my shoulder.

"Everyone's out," Sarah said. "I've got you set up in the Marriott again tonight. Is that okay?"

"Perfect," I said. "Will you be going to Cabo with us tomorrow?"

She shook her head and the blonde hair floated around her. "No," she said sadly. "Today was it. I'm going back to the mansion in the limo and I don't think I'll get to leave there until this business is over."

"Tell Adam I said something about staying at the mansion during the next layover," I said. "Maybe I can look in on you and keep you company."

She smiled at me gratefully. "I'd like that." She leaned into the cockpit and brushed my lips lightly with hers. "Thanks for being here," she said.

"I wouldn't miss it."

"Do you still kiss as well as you used to?" she asked softly.

I nodded. "But I might be a little out of practice."

"Okay, Colin," she said, her voice assuming a businesslike tone. "I'll take care of your room at the Marriott tonight. Please have the jet ready for a noon departure tomorrow. One way to Cabo."

I looked through my side window to see Adam gazing up the air-stairs at her. *What was the deal with him?* I found myself wondering. *He's more than suspicious. He's actually a little possessive.*

"Sounds good, Sarah. I'll see you later."

She nodded and left the jet with a wistful expression on her beautiful features.

I finished putting the jet to bed and filled out the flight log with the data from our two trips. Then I cleaned up the little trash the passengers had left behind, put it into a trash bag, and tossed it out the front door. Finally, I emptied the coffee pots and retrieved my luggage from the forward storage closet. Manny appeared at the top of the stairs as I placed the two bags on the floor of the vestibule.

"Can I help you with those?" he asked.

"That'd be great, Manny. Just take them inside the lobby. I'm going to have to call the shuttle bus for the Marriott."

"You don't have to do that, sir. I'll take you over in one of our vans."

"That'd be awesome. Thanks."

He smiled at me, picked up the bags, and quickly scampered down the ladder. As I was looking around the cabin ensuring I didn't miss anything, I saw a sheet of paper had fallen between the one of the seats at the table and the cabin wall. I pulled it gently, freed it, and began to look it over.

"Wow," I said aloud, "what could this be about?"

I took a picture of the paper with my BlackBerry and then returned it to where I found it, pushing it back into its niche so that it was even a little more concealed than before.

I hobbled down the stairs a few moments later to find Manny sitting in the driver's seat of a van with the Atlantic logo painted on the side. My bags were visible on the middle row of seats. I nodded, and then closed and locked the aircraft door.

"Did you leave the aircraft parking brake off?" he asked

as I struggled into the front passenger seat.

"Yep," I said. "I re-checked it on the way out. You're free to tow it. I'll need it ramped by eleven in the morning, though. Evidently we're going back to Cabo tomorrow at noon."

He nodded as he put the van in gear and headed for the ramp's exit gate. As I settled into my seat, the BlackBerry on my hip vibrated with notice of an arriving e-mail. I unholstered it and regarded the new message.

Daily Grill Bar. Burbank Airport Marriott. 9 PM. You need to ask your server: "What Shirazes are you pouring by the glass tonight?"

I closed the mail and it was deleted automatically. As always.

I walked into the bar attached to the Daily Grill restaurant at the Marriott about an hour later after checking into my room and showering off the day's sweat. The bar featured a luxurious interior with wood paneling, brass rails, and large windows with frosted edges. I found a high-top table on the window side of bar all the way in the corner, from which I could watch the door.

My left leg was positively killing me. I had walked on it more in the last twenty-four hours than I had in nearly the last two weeks, and it obviously wasn't ready for that sort of use. I unconsciously rubbed my left thigh as sat down at the table with my cane and waited for a server to take my drink order. I longed for the bottle of Vicodin I'd left up in my room. I had brought it with me to California in a moment of weakness and I was now sorry I had. When the pain flared up, the temptation to pop one or two of the little caplets was nearly overwhelming. I understood how people slipped into prescription drug abuse.

I glanced around. The lounge was doing a decent business tonight. It was about half full of people, scattered about the bar itself and the tables which surrounded it. The clientele appeared to be nearly all businessmen and women. Suits, ties, and business-casual clothing abounded, and the snippets of conversation I overheard were business-related or the safe subjects that business people discuss when they aren't discussing business.

I love bars. I'd spent a large portion of my post-USAF life in them when I hadn't been flying, and they felt like a second home to me. I could nurse glasses of wine or Scotch for hours and watch the world go by; I needed no other entertainment. As my eyes floated from table-to-table and face-to-face, I saw one set of eyes which looked quickly away when my gaze reached them. The eyes belonged to a swarthy, olive-complexioned man who had seated himself at another high-top table opposite me on the other side of the bar.

Adam had assigned me a baby-sitter. That was ever so thoughtful.

A striking African-American woman glided over to my table, clad in the standard black and white server's apparel. She had skin the color of cappuccino, and hair done in fine braids which went over her shoulders and well down her back. She carried herself with a degree of poise which belonged more on a fashion runway than a bar. I wondered if she was yet another service person who was trying to get through the doors of Hollywood.

She saw me regard her approach and flashed me a brilliant smile as she stopped in front of me. "May I get you something, sir?" she said in very precise English.

"What shirazes are you pouring by the glass this evening?" I asked.

"You mean what shirazes are we pouring by the glass tonight, don't you?" she asked with a bemused smile on her face.

I looked at her quizzically for a moment and then the exact words from the e-mail appeared in my mind's eye. "You know what," I said, "that's exactly what I meant to say."

She smiled again and her eyes positively lit up.

"I'm new at this sort of thing," I whispered conspiratorially.

"Well, you made quite an impression with your initial efforts," she said lowering her voice and looking at me respectfully. "So, may I offer you a recommendation?"

"Certainly," I replied. "I'm always in the mood to try something different."

"There's a private wine-tasting in a suite on the tenth floor of the eastern tower. They'll have quite a selection of shirazes there."

"Well," I said, "now that you mention it. Maybe a little tasting would be just the thing."

She took a card key from her tray and slid it across the table to me. "Wait a few moments before you go up there. The gentleman on the other side of the bar watching you is about to make an inappropriate comment to me and get thrown out of here. Once that happens, you can make your way across the lobby and up to room 1022 in the eastern tower."

"Is he the only one?" I asked. "Or is he the one we're supposed to see?"

She nodded toward me slightly as if to congratulate my powers of deduction. "He's the only one," she said.

"I'm going to go out on a limb. I bet the waitressing thing isn't your day job, is it?"

She smiled back at me and raised and lowered her eyebrows in answer. Then she left my table and made her way to the bar. I pulled my BlackBerry from its holster and made a show of checking my e-mail as I watched her in my peripheral vision. She stopped at the order station at the bar, ostensibly to place my order with the bartender, and then she rounded the bar to take orders at the high-top tables on the other side. After a few minutes, she arrived at the table where my observer was ensconced and stood directly in front of him, blocking his view of me. I suppressed a smile as I could see him squirming to see me around her.

Soon, I could hear voices as the two of them argued about

something. The voices increased in volume and then the restaurant manager arrived at the table. The manager was more solidly-built than a lot of other men I had seen in that same position. After some more heated conversation, the manager escorted the observer, who was now nearly red-faced with anger, out of the bar. I continued to look down at my BlackBerry and tried to keep the inevitable grin from forming on my lips.

I rose from the table a few minutes later, gathered my cane and hobbled out the door of the bar, across the beautifully tiled main lobby, through the attached breezeway, and into the elevator lobby of the eastern tower. I pressed the call button and the doors to the elevator on the left immediately opened. I entered the car, swiped my keycard in the slot on the panel and pressed 10. The doors closed and the elevator ascended. The ride to the tenth floor took less than a minute. I walked down the hallway only a few steps before I came to room 1022. Feeling adventurous, I swiped the keycard and opened the door.

The room was an executive suite. There was a small foyer, a king-sized bed directly in front of me, and a seating area to the right complete with a sofa, chairs, a TV credenza, and a meeting table. Seated at the table were two men I knew and a woman I didn't.

"Howdy, boys," I said, as the door clicked shut behind me. "I would have been here sooner, but I'm not moving so quickly these days."

"Hey, TC!" said the taller of the two of them, CIA Operations Officer Dave Smith. A few years younger than I was, he was lean and athletic with brown hair, jade-green eyes, and distinct dimple on his chin. He rose from the table and offered his right hand. I shook it firmly and resisted the impulse to give him a "man-hug."

"Good to see you again, Dave," I said and I meant it.

"Colin, how are you?" said the other man, Dave's partner,

John Amrine. He was shorter than me but broader and incredibly muscular. He had a mop of blond hair, brown eyes, and a dark tan. If you looked up "California Surfer Boy" in the dictionary, his picture could have been there.

I shook his offered hand warmly. "Hello, John. Glad you guys could make it out here."

"Well, you piqued our interest," he replied. He motioned to the third person at the table - a woman. She was about a head shorter than my six feet two and although she was dressed in a businesslike pantsuit, it was apparent that her body was incredibly toned. She had blonde hair a few shades darker than Amrine's, deep brown eyes, and a complexion that liked the sun. "May I present Operations Officer Susan Turner? We've worked together in the past. Ironically, she's actually met the guy you know as Adam Archmere in an operation we ran in Saudi not too long ago."

I extended my hand and she took it with a firm, warm grip. Our eyes met and I saw a degree of professional respect in them. But then I felt a strong vibe of something else from beneath her highly composed exterior. It was like an unexpected pleasant aftertaste.

"Agent Turner, very nice to meet you."

She smiled. "Call me Susan, please."

"Susan, Colin."

"Well, now that everyone knows each other let's get down to business," Amrine said.

We seated ourselves at the round, wooden table. There were several dossiers on the highly polished surface and a few wine glasses.

"Before we begin, lady and gentlemen," I said, "the young lady in the bar said there'd be some Shiraz around here somewhere."

"Hey, good call," Smith said. He rose from the table and retrieved a bottle from several on the credenza and brought it over. "This is one John and I like because its name reminds us of ourselves." He showed me the label.

"Two Hands Gnarly Dudes?" I read. I looked up at him. "Seriously?"

"From the Barossa Valley. We picked up several cases there... recently. Don't knock it until you've tried it."

Smith poured for all of us. I swirled the wine in the glass and buried my nose in the opening, closing my eyes as I did so. The black fruit aroma wafted into my nostrils. Although I first cut my wine-tasting teeth on the heavier stuff, like Cabernet and Chianti, Shiraz/Syrah was my favorite, followed closely by Pinot Noir. As I got older, I found that I liked my red a little lighter.

"Nice," I said, as I opened my eyes. Then I took a slow sip and saw all three of them looking at me with various expressions on their faces. "Hey, life is short," I said as I swallowed the grape nectar. It was long and juicy on my tongue, wonderfully rich with a light touch of oak. "It's stuff like this that makes it worthwhile." I nodded toward Dave Smith. "I sit corrected. Good selection, sir."

Smith nodded back and raised the glass to his lips. Amrine took a sip from his own glass and a contented expression crept on to his face.

"My boss doesn't like me to drink when I'm armed," Susan said carefully.

"Suit yourself, ma'am," I said. "Rules are rules."

She smiled at me wryly and reached under her jacket and behind her right hip. Her hand appeared on the table a moment later holding a Glock pistol in a pancake holster. She placed the weapon next to her stack of paperwork, and then took a long sip of the wine. "I've never been too good at the whole rules thing."

"Woman after my own heart," I said. I took another drink and felt the beginning of the relaxing sensation brought on by the day's first alcohol. I looked around the table, including all three of them in my glance. "Were you able to do anything with the video I sent you?"

"Oh yes," said Smith, "and it's not good."

Amrine had a half-smile on his face as he opened a folder in front of him. He pushed a photo across the table at me. It was a picture of several Arab men clad in the traditional white *dishdasha* and red and white headgear, the *keffiyeh*. "Do you recognize the guy in the middle? The one all the others are talking to?"

"Holy shit," I said involuntarily. "It's Adam!"

"Actually," Smith said, "his name is Abdullah bin Rashid al Qudamah."

"*Prince* Abdullah bin Rashid al Qudamah," Amrine added. I must not have reacted the way he expected. "You don't seem too surprised."

"He acted like he was somebody," I said. "Who are these guys around him?"

"No one of importance, except for this one," Amrine said, pointing to the man immediately to Adam/Abdullah's right. "This is his younger brother, Mohammed."

"How did you make the judgment that he was *somebody*?" Susan asked.

"I did a nine-month contract over there a year or two ago, flying a nice G-IVSP out of Jeddah," I answered. "The owner was a rich sheik who owned all the BMW dealerships in the Middle East. A real nice guy. As part of the gig, we carried members of the Saudi Royal Family on several occasions. I thought it was a big deal until I found out there are between four and five thousand of them depending on how you do the math. The 'vibe' they give off is unmistakable. All Saudis think they're better than we are, but the royals act like they *know* they're better."

She nodded at me knowingly. "I could barely get their security teams to talk to me when they liaised with us. I had to go undercover as a banking executive while we were over there on the op earlier this year and they treated me like dirt."

"Well, you're a woman," I said, looking at her, "and as you know, women in authority positions are difficult for Arab men to deal with, especially if they're fundamentalist Muslims."

"What was your overall impression of the people when you worked there?" Susan asked.

I took another sip of wine and felt it ooze its way down my throat as I considered her question. Then I twirled the stem of the glass slowly between my thumb and index finger while I contemplated the depths of the Shiraz.

"You know," I began, "I went over there with the usual ethno-centric views that most Americans have about Saudi Arabia and I learned some things. If you could take the Islam thing and put it aside, I think the people there are a lot like us in many ways. They want to earn a decent living, they love their families, and they want to enjoy their lives. But the problem is that you can't put the Islam thing aside. It is the dominating force in their lives. It rules everything; from the way they run their society to the way they treat outsiders. In the US, you meet people who claim to be religious but their degree of devotion runs the full gamut. Some are nearly fanatical about the way they submit to their faith, others are much more casual. But I don't think you get that option with Islam. It seems that if you're Muslim, you're Muslim all the way. And if you're not Muslim, you are unclean. Period. While I was in Saudi Arabia, everyone I dealt with was nice, polite, and respectful, but they kept their distance and they made it clear I wasn't one of them. It was very interesting and just a little disconcerting."

She nodded.

"So," I said, "that brings us to the big question: why is a Saudi Prince trying to commandeer a G-IV?"

Amrine held his hand up. "Let's begin at the beginning. Abdullah and his brother, Mohammed, are like the black sheep of their family. Their dad, Rasheed al Qudamah, has basically cut them off from anything but the most minimum allowance necessary to maintain appearances."

I interrupted him. "I gotta know. How much is the minimum necessary to maintain appearances?"

Amrine smiled. "Near as we can tell, about $10 million per year."

"That's a nice minimum," I quipped.

"Anyway," Amrine continued, "both of the al Qudamah brothers have ties to Wahhabi fundamentalist radicals inside the kingdom. Mohammed is an Imam in the Wahhabi sect. The two of them have tried repeatedly to put operations together to bring Allah's vengeance," he rolled his eyes, "down on the Great Satan. But for several reasons, mainly incompetence on their part, they haven't been able to make it happen."

"It's gotten so bad that nearly every counterterrorist organization in the US government calls a boned-up terrorist op a QC, short for Qudamah Caper," Smith added. "Even our allies don't take these guys seriously."

I chuckled involuntarily as I pictured Adam's arrogant face.

If he only knew.

"Okay, so that's funny and interesting but it begs the question: 'Why are you guys taking this seriously?' Or am I missing something?"

"It's the Mexican piece," Smith said quietly. "When you told us that al Qudamah the elder was meeting with 'Mexican gangsters,' that got our blood flowing. You see, we think al Qudamah met with Miguel Hidalgo in Oman earlier this year."

I leaned forward, suddenly remembering the TV news report I had watched yesterday.

"Miguel Hidalgo, the Mexican drug lord?" I asked incredulously.

He nodded.

"And the reason they were meeting involved a huge cache of weapons, small and large automatic weapons, cannons, surface-to-air missiles, etc. that was hijacked. The al Qudamah family owns a large fleet of merchant ships in addition to oil tankers. They've been known to ship arms from time-to-time. If Hidalgo was interested in a large quantity of arms, I'm sure the al Qudamah boys would have made him a good deal, assuming they could do it without their father finding out."

"Holy shit," I said.

"Exactly," Amrine chimed in. "So now, even though no one else seems to think the al Qudamah boys might be on to something, we have a different opinion. We think there's traction here, which is why we're here and why Susan's here."

I nodded.

"Well, they're up to something," I said. "They've been planning this for a while. I think this guy that Sarah's married to is part of it. I think the whole thing was a set up to get them access to the jet."

I recounted everything I told Sarah. They were silent but thoughtful when I finished.

"Pretty thin," Amrine said.

"But possible," Smith added.

"Definitely," Amrine concluded.

"So, I have a question out of left field for you. Who's Felix Lopez?"

"Not a guy you want to get on the wrong side of," Amrine said, sliding a folder across the table to me. There was a photo of Felix clipped inside the front cover, obviously taken when he wasn't aware a camera was on him. His small, dark eyes were narrow slits and he looked like was concentrating on something. "He goes by the name Saif-al Din. We don't think that's his real name. Do you know what it means in Arabic?"

I shook my head.

"Sword of the Faith," he replied.

"Nice," I said.

"He's a stone killer, about as bad as they come. Do you remember that line from the movie *Unforgiven* where Clint Eastwood's character says he's killed just about everything that's walked or crawled at one time or another? Well this guy has actually done that. We did a search on our classified database and his name comes up as either being involved or suspected in literally hundreds of deaths. And while he's proficient with all sorts of weapons, he likes to work close. He'll use a silenced .22 pistol if he has to hurry, but he prefers a traditional Arab knife known as a *jambiya*. Metal handle with a curved blade about seven inches or so in length. Typically honed to a razor's edge."

I gave Amrine a questioning look.

"Occasionally, he'll leave one behind after he does what he's sent to do. Sort of like a calling card."

I found myself nodding. "He had *those* eyes when I met him. Cold, lifeless eyes." I saw Amrine and Smith exchange a glance between them.

"He's been with the al Qudamah boys since they were little," Smith said. "Sort of like a live-in bodyguard who also gets to take out the garbage, so to speak, from time to time."

"Wow," I said after a long moment. I took a slow sip of wine as I considered all we had discussed. "So where do we go from here, gang?" I asked at last.

"We have to gather more intelligence and find out what the hell these guys are up to," Amrine said simply. "Fortunately, we have just the asset to do that."

He looked at Susan.

"Susan has an idea about how we can get close to him; but she's going to need your help."

I looked at her.

"What do you have in mind?" I asked.

It took her a few minutes to explain it. When she was finished, my cheeks were flushed. And I don't embarrass easily.

"How real does it have to be?" I asked quietly.

"Real enough to convince him," she answered. "And depending on how closely he's watching, it may need to be completely real."

I nodded slowly.

"Believe it or not," I said, "it won't be the first time I've been 'on stage' for this kind of thing."

It was her turn to nod.

"Good to know," she said. "Now, change of subject. I've got to know how reliable this Sarah Morton or Sarah Marciano is. How is it possible that a woman who does the centerfold thing winds up running the flight department for that magazine's publisher? That just strikes me as strange."

I smiled, grateful to talk about something else, and took another sip of the Shiraz to steady my nerves a little.

"It's certainly not your usual flight department accession plan. Sarah was a charter pilot, flying Learjets and Challengers, for an operator at the Van Nuys Airport called Fred Gracy Aviation. She had climbed the ranks like any pilot in that line of work, from flying as a first officer in the right seat of Barons and King Airs until she got into jets and was promoted to captain. Along the way, she'd attended leadership courses offered by the National Business Aviation Association and even completed a Master's Degree Program in Aviation Safety Management from Embry-Riddle Aeronautical University."

I saw questioning looks on their faces.

"Embry-Riddle is the preeminent aviation university. It is to aviation what Harvard and Wharton are to business schools."

There were nods around the table.

"Anyway," I continued, "after filling several junior leadership positions at Gracy, the chief pilot job came open and she applied for it, only to be told by the director of operations there, a clueless individual named Gary Brock, that there would be no women in leadership positions on *his* watch."

I saw Susan wince across the table at me.

"Exactly," I said, nodding in her direction. "But Sarah was not going to be put off. It seems that Bill Spratt, who didn't own an airplane at the time, was a high-time charter client with this company and it also seems that Sarah had flown him regularly. Furthermore, it seems that Spratt had regularly, and perhaps jokingly, asked Sarah that if she ever wanted to be in his magazine, all she had to do was ask."

I took a moment to take another sip of wine and watched the smiles form on Smith and Amrine's faces.

"So, she asked," I said. "A few months later she was the featured centerfold or 'Monthly Mistress' as the magazine calls it. While the photos were certainly awesome, the text of the article painted a picture of this all-American girl who always wanted to be a pilot and aviation leader and how this evil company dashed her career hopes."

Susan grinned at me across the table. "I'm beginning to like this woman," she said. "A girl's got to use the weapons God gave us. So, let me guess. The company fired her and she sued them."

I grinned back. "Bachelor Magazine's entire legal department sued Gracy on Sarah's behalf pro bono. It was a huge case, even made the national papers for a few days. The company settled out of court and paid Sarah two years' salary. The director of operations was fired and the company nearly went out of business. The magazine with Sarah in it sold over a million copies. At some point along the line, Spratt decided to buy a jet and put Sarah in charge of building the new flight department. When they took delivery of the jet, they needed an experienced G-IV guy to fly with her until she had enough experience to satisfy the insurance company. I was lucky enough to be that guy."

"Lucky indeed," Susan said.

"Well, as I've often said, 'I'd rather be lucky than good.'"

She smiled and nodded. "I get that about you," she said. "And that brings up another thing. It's obvious you have some feelings for this Sarah chick. You're going to have to put them somewhere if you and I are going to create the scenario we discussed."

I just looked at her. *If you looked up compartmentalization in the dictionary,* I thought, *my picture would be there.*

"No worries, there. Anything else, lady and gentlemen?" I said, struggling to my feet, cane in hand. "I have a date with a nice bottle of The Glengoyne back at the bar. The seventeen-year-old, of course."

Smith laughed and Amrine smirked at me. Susan just looked back and forth at all three of us. "It must be a guy thing," she said.

"I'll take my leave then," I said. "Oh, by the way, cover story for my little visit to the room here?"

"I wondered if you'd remember," Smith said. He produced an invitation to a "Manager's Special Reception for Platinum Members," and shoved it across the table to me. It was appropriately spindled and folded, like it had been in a pocket for a while. "You might drop that on the floor somewhere when you get back to your room in the other tower. Hopefully, the watcher they have on you will pick it up."

"Roger that," I said. "Well, gentlemen, a pleasure as always. Miss Susan, a pleasure to meet you as well. Looking forward to working with you."

"Gentlemen," I said, addressing Smith and Amrine. "May I assume the usual payment arrangements?"

Susan looked at me, surprised. "Aren't you already being paid by Bachelor magazine?"

"They're paying me to fly a jet, ma'am, not risk my ass. If we're talking about me playing along on behalf of the government, then the government owes me two-thousand dollars per day. If the government wants me to start kicking ass, we'll have to renegotiate."

"What about doing it for your country?"

I was turning to go, but looked back over my shoulder at her. "Those days are over, Susan. Helping a friend like Sarah, I'll do for nothing; but any work for the government has a price tag."

She rolled her eyes.

As I exited the room and the door slowly closed behind me, I could hear Susan's voice, barely above a whisper. "He's a piece of work," she said. "Is he worth it?"

"He can do some incredible things," Smith said.

"Do you think he can handle what we discussed earlier?"

"No doubt," Amrine said. "But you're just going to need to be careful with your end of the plan. One word of warning: Don't be around if he gets pissed off. He and al Din are two sides of the same coin."

TOP SECRET/SPECIAL
COMPARTMENTALIZED INFORMATION
CLASSIFIED BY: US Central Intelligence Agency
DECLASSIFY ON: OADR

From: Special Projects Group [NCS]
Sent: Thursday, 19 November 2009, 1315 PST (19 November 2009, 2115Z)
To: Director, NCS
Cc: Special Projects Group [NCS]

SUBJECT: Aircraft Movement Alert – Gulfstream G-IVSP N36WMS

(TS) Narrative:

1. (TS) N36WMS departed KBUR (Burbank/Bob Hope Airport) at 1207 PST / 1807 Z. Flight planned destination is MMSD (Los Cabos International Airport) with ETA of 1400 PST / 2200 Z. Contractor 09-017, (Pearce, Colin M), Abdullah bin Rashid al Qudamah, aka Adam Archmere, William Spratt and Saif al Din aka Felix Lopez, were aboard. Ground surveillance teams are in place at MMSD and Cabo San Lucas to monitor all ground movements. Operations Officer Susan Turner has been assigned to lead the covert operation on scene and to work with Pearce.

2. (TS) Based on information provided by Pearce, we worked with a team from the DS&T and asked them to target computers which might be online at the Bachelor Magazine mansion. After working through a network of proxy servers, discovering multiple computers logged into the Internet at that location and filtering the audio feeds for background noise and language, the DS&T team discovered one feed where Arabic was being spoken. Voice

print analysis confirmed the identity of the four participants.

    a. Prince Abdullah bin Rashid al Qudamah (aka Adam Archmere);
    b. Saif-al Din (aka Felix Lopez);
    c. Achmed Kattan; and
    d. Sarah Morton Marciano.

3. (TS) The following is a partial transcript of a conversation which took place last evening beginning at (18 November 2009) 2313 PST (19 November 2009 – 0713Z) Time sequence marks are provided for reference.

2313:45: BACKGROUND NOISE, DOOR SLAMMING
2313:53: UNINTELLIGIBLE SPEECH, FOLLOWED BY A SLAPPING SOUND
2314:02: AL QUDAMAH (Arabic): "You lost him?"
2314:05: KATTAN (Arabic): "Yes. I was chased out of the bar where I was watching him."
2314:10: SLAPPING SOUND, DULL THUD
2314:15: AL QUDAMAH (Arabic): "Dog! Did we not bring you with us to accomplish menial jobs like this?"
2314:25: KATTAN (Arabic): "Yes, my Prince, I am sorry."
2314:28: BACKGROUND NOISE, SCRAPING, LEATHER SHOE SOLES AGAINST LOW-PILE CARPETED FLOOR, SUGGEST KNEELING POSTURE?
2315:00: AL QUDAMAH (Arabic): "Get up."
2315:03: AL QUDAMAH (Arabic): "So where did he go?"
2315:07: KATTAN (Arabic): "I don't know. When I left the bar, he was still at a table."
2315:15: AL QUDAMAH (Arabic): "And when did you regain sight of him?"
2315:19: KATTAN (Arabic): "About an hour later, but he was in the breezeway coming from the East Tower. He couldn't have come from the bar. The bar is under the West Tower of

the hotel."

2315:27: BACKGROUND NOISE, FOOTSTEPS BACK AND FORTH ACROSS CARPETED FLOOR.

2316:02 AL DIN (Arabic): "He met someone there, my Prince. We must be cautious with and around Mr. Pearce. There is something (pause 2.5 seconds) unique about him."

2316: 28 AL QUDAMAH (Arabic): "Hardly. He's just another middle-aged American business jet pilot. To use the American phrase, they're (English) a dime a dozen (Arabic) these days."

2316:43: AL DIN (Arabic): "Did you ask the woman why she chose him?"

2316:49: AL QUDAMAH (Arabic): "I told her to find a replacement pilot. She knows many contract pilots."

2316:58: AL DIN (Arabic): "I understand that, my Lord. But we still need to ask her the question."

2317:05: AL QUDAMAH (English): "Fetch the Marciano woman."

2317:09: BACKGROUND NOISE, FOOTSTEPS, DOOR OPENING AND CLOSING.

2317:15: AL DIN (Arabic): "So she doesn't know?"

2317: 19: AL QUDAMAH (Arabic): "No one does except you and I, and my brother of course. He played his part perfectly. She doesn't suspect a thing."

2333:03: BACKGROUND NOISE, DOOR OPENING AND CLOSING.

2333:07: MARCIANO (English): "Adam, what's the meaning of this? I was getting ready to take a bath."

2333:12: AL QUDAMAH (English): "Why did you hire Colin Pearce?"

2333:22: MARCIANO (English): "Because I knew him. We had flown together before. I knew he was reliable and very discrete."

2333:41: AL QUDAMAH (English): "Are you sure that's the only reason?"

2333:54: MARCIANO (English): "Yes. Of course. You didn't give me much notice to pick someone anyway. Colin was, uh, the best I could do with short notice."

2334:07: AL QUDAMAH (English): "Take her back."

2334:13: BACKGROUND NOISE, DOOR OPENING AND CLOSING.

2334:22: AL DIN (Arabic): "There's something else there, of course."

2334:27: AL QUDAMAH (Arabic): (unintelligible) "But there is no time to replace him! Events are already in motion. We've been planning this for nearly two years."

2334:35: AL DIN (Arabic): "I'll deal with him when the time comes. It won't be an issue."

2334:42: AL QUDAMAH (Arabic): "It better not be. The day of Allah's vengeance on the Great Satan will soon be here."

2334:57: AL DIN (Arabic): "Is it still the original day you planned?"

2335:03: AL QUDAMAH (Arabic): "Yes and the other event we were looking for has been scheduled for that day as well so that Mexican dog will get what he wants from our arrangement."

*** INTERCEPT ENDS *** POSSIBLE DETECTION AND ELIMINATION OF LINK BY SECURITY SOFTWARE.

(TS) CONCLUSION: Al Qudamah is planning hostile action against the United States. While past attempts have been ineffective, we believe this attempt poses a definite threat due to the possible Mexican connection. Further intelligence gathering is underway to corroborate the feasibility and threat level.

(TS) ACTION: Cross agency team will brainstorm possible targets and counter action. Limited surveillance assets are enroute both to the Bachelor Magazine Mansion and to the Hotel Imperial del Cabo to collect intelligence.

(U) RECOMMENDATIONS: None. Information only.

TOP SECRET / SPECIAL
COMPARTMENTALIZED INFORMATION
CLASSIFIED BY: US Central Intelligence Agency
DECLASSIFY ON: OADR

CHAPTER SIX

Contract Day Three
Thursday, 19 November
1400 Hours Local Time
San Jose Del Cabo Airport (MMSD)
Cabo San Lucas, Mexico

Roughly eighteen hours later, I was in the back seat of an air-conditioned mini-van, pulling out of the FBO parking lot at the San Jose Del Cabo Airport. My driver's name was Juan and his English was *muy bueno*. He told me that "Mr. Adam" had instructed him to drive me to the Hotel Imperial del Cabo and that the trip would take about forty-five minutes to an hour. I leaned back into the worn and stained fabric seats and tried to tune the mariachi music from the van's radio out of my head as I watched the barren desert landscape go by.

I had flown the G-IV down here with Adam in the right seat, and Bill and Felix in the back. Adam was proficient and businesslike with the checklist, but apart from the take-off and landing portions of the flight, he had been absent from the cockpit. This hadn't bothered me at all. With several thousand hours of single-seat fighter time, the cockpit had long become a personal refuge. I had no sooner shut down the engines on the ramp when Adam had the door open and he had vanished down the stairs and into the FBO with a briefcase in one hand

and a small duffel bag in the other. Bill and Felix followed him shortly thereafter, each carrying their own suitcases.

After recovering from the surprise of their quick exit, I had finished the shutdown checklist and put the airplane to bed. Then after I walked into the FBO and went through the nonexistent immigration and customs, Juan had found me in the lobby.

The highway from the airport to Cabo San Lucas was a very modern, four-lane road which began inland, proceeded south to the sea, and then traced the coast of the Baja peninsula as it went west to the town. It was a testimony to the modern face Mexico was trying to show the world but it showcased the disparity in wealth typical in the resort areas of the country. Literally, on one side of the road were the elaborate resorts and hotels of the foreign wealthy and on the other, the shanties and squalor of the local poor.

I had been a conservative Republican and dedicated capitalist all my life, but I had made this drive many times and every time I did, there was something about the disproportionate gap that didn't seem right. I shut my eyes again as I rested my head against the back of the seat and forced my mind into other areas. I found my thoughts once again turning to last night's discussion about Felix Lopez and the rising hunger of the rage inside of me. There was an itch developing that would need to be scratched again soon.

I clenched my fists unconsciously as I recalled how I felt when the rage was last satisfied. A little over three weeks ago, I had brutally cut the throat of someone who had been responsible for taking thousands of lives and who was bent on killing millions more. But that wasn't why I had done it. She died because she killed someone I cared deeply about, my best friend and roommate from the Air Force Academy. The revenge aspect had been quite gratifying for me.

But what I had felt at that moment went far beyond mere emotional gratification. I trembled when I recalled the feeling of the knife cutting into her flesh and the wetness of the arterial spray landing on my skin. The rage had been sated and the high had been incredible. I remembered the exquisite sensation of my blood literally singing as it pulsed through my veins. The act had reawakened a hunger inside of me that I thought was long dormant. The hunger generated by similar episodes of euphoria I had felt when I slashed the throats of ten Iraqi guards as an escaping prisoner-of-war back in 1990 and when I blasted three Chicano burglars at close range with a shotgun in my home in Phoenix, Arizona in 2000.

There was absolutely nothing like it.

I had done everything I could to forget the hunger over these last nine years since Phoenix. Endless work had been one refuge. Alcohol in general and Scotch Whiskey in particular, another. Then there had been the occasional meaningless trysts thrown in for good measure.

But it all came rushing back when I blew four jets out of the air and ripped open the throat of a woman in my dining room. I wanted to feel the rage again. I wanted to feed the rage again. I wanted to kill Felix Lopez. Not because he was a bad man and not because he deserved to die. I wanted to kill him to feel that high again.

##

With a sudden lurch, the van stopped and my eyes snapped open.

"We are here, Señor."

Juan had stopped the van under the covered entryway to the Hotel Imperial del Cabo. I had only heard about the place from passengers I had brought here. It was the most upscale hotel on the Baja peninsula and in a place where the rich come to play, that's saying something. Words like gorgeous and elegant didn't do it justice. Built in the grand tradition of the great haciendas of the Southwest, it took that archetype to new heights and was often featured in magazines and television shows that tease mere mortals with views of how the very wealthy live.

I felt instantly out of place. It was the kind of beauty and class that was the realm of people I flew, not someone like me. But I knew why I was here. Adam wanted me close by - to watch me. Which, of course, was the whole basis for the plan I was supposed to implement with Susan, a plan I still didn't feel comfortable about.

Juan flashed around the back of the van, retrieved my roller bag and computer bag, and appeared at my side as I eased my weight onto my one good leg and the cane. I reached into my pocket for my wallet and had yet another shock. He shook his closely-cropped head rapidly back and forth and flashed me a huge smile, which surprisingly featured all of his teeth.

"There is no need for that, Señor. Mr. Adam, he tip me plenty."

A Mexican taxi-cab driver refusing a tip. I suppressed the urge to search the sky for flying pigs.

"Very well, Juan, thank..." He had already handed my bags to the immaculate doorman, who was clad in a khaki-colored uniform with creases so sharp they could have sliced tomatoes. Juan returned and handed me a very professional-looking card.

"If you need a ride somewhere, Mr. Adam say you call me."

"Muchas gracias, Juan." Nothing like having built-in surveillance if I wanted to go out on the town.

He nodded to me, pumped my right hand vigorously, and was back inside the van and on his way. I turned toward the doorman, at something of a loss. Things were happening just a little too quickly here.

"This way, sir," said the doorman with the mildest hint of an accent.

"Thank you," I replied automatically.

I walked slowly underneath the arch of the entryway and into one of the most luxurious hotel lobbies I had ever seen. Done in authentic southwestern style, it featured a high ceiling, wooden beams, and a vast, airy feel. The walls were decorated with pieces of elegant artwork that I was willing to bet were inscribed with original signatures. The furniture, arrayed in conversation groups throughout the structure, was the sort of stuff you couldn't even buy in a high-end store. I had stayed in a Ritz Carlton Hotel once and thought that was the top of the line. This place put the Ritz to shame.

George Goebel's famous quote from the Tonight Show popped into my head: "Did you ever feel like the whole world was a tuxedo and you were a pair of brown shoes?"

I walked up to the front desk, a richly-carved counter of dark wood that probably cost more than I made in a year. The two young Mexican women behind the counter were positively striking with matching raven-colored hair, warm dark eyes, and the usual olive complexion. Their outfits were tropical, like the doorman's, but their shirts were unbuttoned lower in the front and revealed splendid cleavage and the curve of ample breasts. I wondered if they moonlighted for one of the Spanish-speaking TV networks.

"Hello there," I said, trying to clear my throat. "I guess I have a reservation here, my name is..."

"You are Colin Pearce," the girl to my left said. "Welcome to the Hotel Imperial del Cabo." Her voice was positively musical, with just enough accent to be enchanting. "We've been expecting you."

Out of the corner of my eye, to my right, I saw someone sitting in the lobby stir at the mention of my name. I ignored the temptation to turn around and struggled to keep my eyes on the girl's face and not her cleavage.

"Thank you..." I responded as I glanced at the name tag perched atop her right breast, "Maria. I guess my client has decided to be very generous. I usually don't get to stay in places as nice as this."

Okay, I might have done more than glance. The truth is that I don't know where I was looking when I spoke, but it wasn't at her face.

She smiled at me, knowingly but with a mildly flattered look on her face. Then she looked over at her equally well-endowed co-worker. "Elena, do you have Señor Pearce's room folio?"

"Yes, certainly," Elena said, looking at me appraisingly. "Welcome to the Hotel Imperial del Cabo Señor Pearce. It's good to have you here."

I nodded stupidly, looking back at her. She was every bit as breathtaking as Maria was and the standard male-threesome fantasy quickly ran through my head. She handed me a richly-embossed folder.

"We've got you in one of our ocean-view suites on the fifth floor," she said looking into my eyes. "This folder contains some information about the hotel and your *benefits* as a guest."

A quizzical expression ran across my face and she smiled at me.

Maria stepped up and looked over the counter down at my cane. "Hector has already taken your luggage to your room," she said. "The elevators are down toward the middle of the lobby. Do you need help up to your suite?"

I opened the folder to find a key card placed in the slot, with "504" typed underneath the slot. "This is my room number, I presume?"

They nodded.

"Thank you, but no. I need all the exercise I can get."

"We hope you enjoy your stay, Señor Pearce," she said.

"Yes, and please, if there is anything we can do to make your stay more enjoyable, don't hesitate to ask," Elena chimed in.

"Well, ladies," I replied, "just speaking to the two of you has made my day. If your hospitality is what this hotel is about, I'm sure I'll love it here."

The two of them smiled warmly at me and I turned to walk to the elevators before I made myself sick.

While the floor was covered in rich ceramic tile, the surface was contoured so my cane did not slip on it while I hobbled to the elevators. As I walked, I searched the lobby for the person who had exhibited interest in my arrival as I pretended to take in the sights around me, but I detected nothing out of the ordinary.

I made it to the elevators and pressed the call button. The inlaid wooden doors opened a few seconds later and I stepped inside. As I turned around to press the button for my floor, a blonde woman rushed in with a bevy of shopping bags with names like Gucci, Versace, and Prada on them.

"Could you be a dear and press four please?" she cooed at me with a distinct southern accent.

"My pleasure, ma'am," I said, pressing her floor's button and my own.

The elevator doors closed and the woman turned and leaned her back against the opposite side of the elevator.

"What brings you here?" she asked brightly.

"Business," I replied, turning to face her. While obviously older than the two beauties behind the front desk, this woman was spectacular in her own right. She was tanned just enough to look radiant with long blonde hair that framed her face and deep brown eyes. I like women with a little mileage on them and I've always seen the lines on their faces as badges of a mature beauty. She wore a flowing, yellow sundress which hung from her shoulders, clung to her upper body, and was loose below her breasts. Her legs and arms were highly toned and her body looked promising beneath the dress. I couldn't help smiling at her. "Boring, I know," I continued.

"Better here than somewhere else," she said. Her voice was light and mellifluous. It fit the stereotype of the rich, pampered woman to a T.

"Very true."

"Do you like the beach?"

A tremble ran through me as I remembered the last beach I was on and what had happened there. "There was a time," I said.

"So why don't you make that time again?" she asked sweetly.

"Not much fun alone," I blurted out before I thought about what I was saying.

"Well, I'm headed out there in about ten minutes. You can join me if you want. The chaise lounges they have are really comfy, and the view is just marvelous."

"That sounds great," I said genuinely. "Here's the important question: can you get a drink out there?"

"Why, of course you can, sugar. I've even got a waiter of my very own!"

The chime rang indicating the elevator had stopped on her floor.

"See you out there," she said as she stepped through the doors, her dress flowing around her. She turned to face me as she exited. "I think we'll find we have a lot in common," she said, winking.

As the elevator doors closed, I realized I had been speaking to Susan Turner and that I had been completely played.

"What a disguise," I muttered in amazement.

I walked into my suite a few moments later, still in a daze. The accommodations didn't help to bring me back to reality. I felt like I was stepping into an episode of "Lifestyles of the Rich and Famous." The heavy wooden door opened into a small foyer area with a richly-marbled powder room immediately to the left. Beyond it was a great room complete with an adobe fireplace and floor-to-ceiling windows with an awe-inspiring view of the Pacific Ocean. A set of French doors opened onto a balcony from which I immediately planned to enjoy a single-malt or two this evening. As I walked across the ceramic tile floor, a kitchen was on my right and featured tiled counters and the full range of appliances. Names like *Wolf* and *Viking* leapt out at me. The cook top was located on an island with an elevated bar. An ornately-inlaid dining room table with eight chairs around it abutted the great room and looked out through more floor-to-ceiling windows.

A bedroom lay off each side of the central living area and I flipped a mental coin and entered the one immediately to my left. I found my suitcase neatly laid out on a piece of furniture obviously devoted to that purpose and my computer bag placed next to it. I unzipped the suitcase and examined the contents. Everything seemed exactly where I had placed it. Then I raised the lid and looked at the inside of the zipper about three quarters of the way down. The tiny dab of toothpaste I had placed there this morning was broken and crusted. My suitcase had been searched. Quickly, thoroughly, and professionally. I wondered if the doorman was on Adam's payroll or whether someone else had done the deed.

I nodded grimly. About the only "device" I had that was even slightly out of the ordinary was the CIA-issued BlackBerry. I kept it with me and it would have to be disassembled to reveal its secrets. I walked over to another wall of windows. My bedroom, like the great room, had a set of French doors which opened onto the balcony. I unlatched them and walked out into the Baja heat. The balconies were exceptionally private. A stucco wall isolated the balcony from the balconies on either side and extended far enough out from the wall to eliminate any prying eyes from peering around it. The side of the hotel facing the water was parallel with the beach so no other balconies were visible from mine.

I walked up to the wrought iron railing which faced the sea and placed my hands on the top of it as I gazed out over the placid Pacific. I took a second or two to collect my wits and then looked down and saw the tranquil blue waters of the hotel's pool with the infinity edge facing the ocean. Several tanned bodies lay around the pool in designer swimsuits, some that looked good in them and a few that didn't. I could see the walkway to the beach and the inviting golden sand beyond.

Where I needed to meet Susan Turner.

Resignedly, I walked back into my room and changed into a pair of board shorts, a tee shirt, and flip-flops as quickly as my crippled state would allow. Then I grabbed my wallet, BlackBerry, a pair of sunglasses, and a room key and got out of there. I elected to leave my cane behind and regretted the decision before I even made it to the elevator. I gritted my teeth, rode the elevator down on one foot and then limped out past the pool and to the beach walkway. The walkway meandered through some trees, past a bar, and spilled out onto the beach. The surface must have been treated with the same material pool decks are made from because I felt no heat through the rubber soles of my flip-flops. As I stepped out onto the sand, I noticed several rows of chaise lounges already set up in two groups of several rows each. Some of the chairs had umbrellas attached to them, ready to be deployed. There were enough people on the beach to make it seem lively, but not so many that it was crowded.

I scanned the rows of chairs looking for blonde heads, but none was the right size and shape. Finally, I spied a likely candidate lying on her stomach in the row of chairs nearest the waves on the right side. The sun was reflecting off her hair, making it look like fine strands of gold.

I gritted my teeth for another painful walk and negotiated the sand for about fifty yards or so up the aisle between the two groups of chairs. I made the right turn and walked down several chairs until I was standing next to the woman I saw from the walkway.

It was Susan Turner, all right. And she was lying on her stomach in nothing but a black thong bikini bottom. Her head was turned toward me and her eyes were closed. The ocean breeze was gently toying with the golden strands of her hair. I suddenly realized that the hair had to be a wig because she didn't have nearly that much hair when I met her last night; it had also been several shades darker. She was wearing a lot of makeup, but I guessed that too was part of the disguise. The sight of her made me inhale involuntarily. I immediately wondered what she did to stay in such spectacular shape.

"Hot yoga," she said.

I realized that her eyes were open and she was looking up at me.

"What?"

"You were wondering what I do to stay in shape." The voice was her own, not the one she had used in the elevator, and it startled me a little. "Everyone always does."

"I guess a real man would have been admiring your ass," I said, sitting on the lounge next to her, "but at my age, I can't do that without wondering what you have to do to keep it that way."

"Hot yoga. It's conducted in a one-hundred-degree-plus room. I do the advanced classes. Ninety minutes, five times a week. It's about my only concession to myself."

She still hadn't moved, but her eyes were locked on mine as I let them roam all over her body.

"And right about now," she continued, "part of you is saying, 'There is no way this chick can stay in that kind of shape with Yoga.'"

"Actually," I said, "I knew someone once who was very much into Yoga and was in similar shape."

"Knew?"

I nodded, looking away. "She died a little while ago."

There was an awkward pause and then Susan's voice shifted into its Southern accent.

"Well darlin', you arrived just in time to put some sunscreen on my back! Do you mind?"

I could hear someone coming up behind me and played

along. "No, I sure don't."

"Ricardo? Would you bring me a piña colada and bring this nice man a...""?

"Corona," I said. "Thanks."

The waiter retreated toward the beach bar.

"The sunscreen is in my bag."

"No problem," I said. I reached into the cloth beach bag next to her chair and retrieved a bottle of sunscreen. As I did, Susan lifted slightly and moved to one side of her chaise, revealing her breasts for a second or two.

"Yes, I'm topless," she said, watching my eyes again. "It's what they do at this hotel and it's part of the role I'm playing. Can you handle it?"

"I'll do my best," I said. I rose from my chair and sat on hers. The tube of sunscreen felt warm in my hands, so I squeezed it directly onto her back and began to rub it in. Her skin was soft but I could feel the muscles underneath ripple as I kneaded the lotion into her back.

"Ummm," she said involuntarily in her own voice. "That feels great. You have really strong hands."

I shrugged. "What do I call you, anyway?"

"Why my name is Sophia," she said, using the *voice* again, "Sophia Monachelli."

I chuckled. "Sophia?"

"Undercover identities require a lot of backstop work to be credible. You don't always get to choose the name you want. And this was the identity I was using when I met al Qudamah earlier this year."

I nodded as I continued to work. "It's a beautiful name. Sort of rolls off the tongue as you say it." I had my hands on either side of her tiny waist and was working the small of her back with my thumbs. I had always loved giving women back rubs. Something about non-threatening skin-to-skin contact I guess.

"Well hi there, Ricardo," 'Sophia' said. "Can you put those

nice drinks on the table there?"

"Certainly, Señora Monachelli," Ricardo replied. He wore a tropical, khaki-colored outfit with shorts and a short-sleeve shirt. It looked a little formal for the beach.

"Just put that on my tab with the usual tip," Sophia's voice instructed him. "Thank you, honey."

"De nada, Señora," Ricardo said as he left us and made his way over to another couple down the row.

"Mrs. Monachelli?" I asked when he was out of earshot.

She sighed. "Sophia Monachelli is the executive vice-president of an investment bank and the highly-neglected wife of a real-estate mogul in Reno, Nevada. We have two kids who are grown and through college; a girl, Kimberly who is a veterinarian and a boy, Fred, who is in law school. My 'husband,' John, is closing a real estate deal for a new casino complex and I just wanted to get away from the cold for a few days."

"Wow," I said, my thumbs reaching the waistband of the thong. "Impressive." I finished the massage by running my hands up the outside of her lats to her armpits. She shivered with pleasure.

"Now that was impressive," she said sleepily. "Every once in a while, this damn job does offer a fringe benefit or two."

"Anything else you need while I'm back here?" I asked, eyeing her legs and nearly bare butt.

"Later," she said.

"Your call," I said, placing the lotion back into her bag and reseating myself on my own chair. "I wouldn't want to see any part of you get sunburned."

"Took care of that before I left my room," she said lazily. "There's nothing worse than sunburned T and A."

I took my Corona from the table and deliberately inserted the lime all the way into the bottle, placed my thumb over the opening, and inverted the bottle to let the lime rise to the bottom. When the lime reached the glass there, I up righted the bottle and then slowly released the pressure, all the while keeping my eyes focused away from Susan who had pushed herself up onto her elbows and was sucking on the straw of her piña colada. Her breasts were clearly visible in my peripheral vision and her pink nipples were erect in the ocean breeze.

She was smiling at me as she drank. "This is making you uncomfortable, isn't it?" she asked. "Well don't look away on my account," she said. "I've never minded men looking at me and besides, I come from a family with seven kids and two bathrooms. When bath and shower time came, we cycled in and out of the bathroom wearing nothing or next to nothing. The whole nudity thing has never been an issue for me."

"I don't have a problem with it at all," I said, raising the golden beer and sucking down a long draught. "It's just not what I expected. You're you, but you're not you. It's like I don't know how to treat you."

"Well let's talk about that," she said, stirring her drink with her straw. "When anyone else is within earshot, I'm Sophia Monachelli, corporate big shot and trophy wife, looking for a good time while I'm away from my bastard husband. This will give you and me the opportunity to spend some time together and exchange information when you're down here in the hotel. When it's just us, we can talk freely, like we are now."

"Aren't you worried about distance mics or bugs or something like that?"

"We don't think Adam and company have that kind of infrastructure in place here yet. And even if they did, they have no reason to suspect me."

"The infrastructure might be more developed than you think. The doorman took my luggage when I walked through the door here. It was out of my sight for maybe five or ten minutes, but it was searched during that time."

Her eyes widened a little. "Thanks for that. We'll obviously have to turn the precautions up a notch." Then she paused and

I could almost hear the gears turning inside her head. "You threaten them," she said, thinking aloud. "That's interesting. I wonder why."

"I reached the conclusion that Adam wants to keep an eye on me. Typically, we crew-dogs don't stay at the same hotel that the passengers do. It's not comfortable. And this place is way out of my league anyway. So," I turned toward her, making a very valiant effort to look into her eyes instead of lower, "have you learned anything new since last night?"

She nodded, lowered her voice even further and leaned toward me a little. Okay, I did glance down at her breasts and saw something there that put her in an entirely different place in my mind. I was betting she'd nursed a few kids. Her breasts had that "lived in" look. It's hard to describe but I've always liked it. I prefer women who are more "down to earth" and women who are mothers are about as down to earth as it gets. I smiled unconsciously.

"After we found out that Spratt had this boat, we used our liaison with the Coast Guard. The Coast Guard Station in San Diego has a good working relationship with the Sea Police detachment of the Mexican Navy here. We discovered that Spratt's boat has been making trips out to sea on the dates that 'Adam' and Bill Spratt have been down here. It's highly probable Adam is using the boat as a mechanism to smuggle people and other things into Cabo from the sea which sort of fits with the scenario we're building."

"Makes sense," I said. "Maybe you could explain how you're keeping an eye on Adam and working on your sun tan at the same time."

She smiled and inclined her head toward the sea.

I looked over her shoulder and saw the long, sleek, white yacht cruising off-shore. I involuntarily took a breath. It was a thing of beauty with flowing lines and expansive decks.

"Impressive, isn't it? That would be *Bachelor's Toy*," she said. "I watched it leave its slip in the Cabo San Lucas harbor about fifteen minutes before you walked into the lobby of the hotel. Adam was aboard, along with Bill Spratt and a large party of male and female revelers. It's like a party cruise I guess."

"When did you get here?"

"Last night about midnight," she said. "Yesterday was a long day."

"I guess! So, what's next?"

"Exactly what we discussed last night. You're going to meet your vacation girlfriend, Sophia Monachelli, in the bar tonight for drinks and dinner. And then, we're going up to Adam's suite."

"And how do you expect to get us up there?"

"Evidently Bill throws some pretty wild parties in his suite whenever he's in town and the booze flows freely. I've also been told that almost anyone in the hotel is welcome, so you and I are going to try to get invited up there tonight and do a little wild partying so we can put on the necessary show to attract the required attention from you-know-who."

"I'm here to serve," I said after a long moment.

She swung onto her butt and sat on the edge of her chaise, her knees touching mine. Then she grabbed my hands with hers and placed my arms around her neck as she looked into my eyes. To a casual observer, this might have looked playful, but the expression I saw in her face was professional and serious.

"After you left last night, I questioned Amrine and Smith extensively about your last job. We discussed the whole scenario of using a cover-relationship between you and me as a mechanism to get closer to Adam and find out what's going on. They seemed to think you'd be able to rise to the occasion. So, I'll ask you the same question I asked you before. Do you think you can handle this? More specifically, do you think you can put aside your feelings for little Miss Pilot-Centerfold and handle this?"

I back at her and what I saw there was fascinating. It was like she was the same woman I met last night, but it was also like she wasn't. There seemed to be a different "light" on inside of her. I again felt a strange compulsion to get inside her head and find out what made her tick. But in the meantime, I nodded knowingly at her and delivered the standard punch line a man would provide when told he'd have to spend a lot of time close to a beautiful woman.

"It's a dirty job," I deadpanned, "but somebody's got to do it."

She grinned at me, took my face in her hands, and kissed me lightly on the lips. She was back in character again.

"Now let's get that nice Ricardo to get me another Piña Colada, darlin'," she said in the spoiled-bitch voice, "and in the meantime, I think I'm going to need some more sunscreen on the rest of me."

CHAPTER SEVEN

Contract Day Three
Thursday, 19 November
1900 Hours Local Time
Hotel Imperial del Cabo
Cabo San Lucas, Mexico

I stepped out of the shower a few hours later after some time in the sun and in the Pacific with "Sophia." I dressed with precision since I too had a certain role to play now. I was not just Colin Pearce, I was Colin Pearce trying to impress a woman he had just "met," so the clothes had to meet that expectation. I donned a pair of freshly pressed Brooks Brothers khaki-colored dress slacks and an olive-patterned Tommy Bahama shirt worn over the waistband of my pants. I added a pair of casual—but expensive—Johnston and Murphy boat shoes and a matching belt. Then I regarded myself in a mirror. The outfit looked presentable but not contrived. I combed my hair, ran a little gel through it, and was out the door, keycard in pocket and cane in hand.

The walk to the elevator and then from elevator to the hotel's main restaurant was much more pleasant with the cane to lean on. As I hobbled across the tiles through the enormous lobby, I wondered how much longer I was going to require the enhanced stability of the cane before my left leg would be able to reliably and comfortably support my weight. The doctor's prognosis had not been encouraging.

"You're lucky they were using subsonic bullets and not high velocity ammo, Mr. Pearce," he had said. "The high-velocity stuff would have torn your thigh to pieces, particularly if they had used hollow-point or expanding bullets. But they stuck with the tried and true full-metal-jacket military style rounds. Hence, the damage your muscles experienced is all from the hydrostatic shock of a foreign body lodging in your muscles and nothing more. The damage to your shoulder is even less since the round went through."

I remembered lying in my bed in the recovery area with my head swimming with drugs while the young doctor told me all of this and nodding my head in gratitude. I didn't feel so damn grateful when I woke up in pain about twelve hours later. The Vicodin had helped after that but I was afraid of getting addicted to it, so I didn't rely on it often, only when the pain became excruciating. Now it seemed that pain was becoming a companion in my life. It was something I lived with. Thank God for the performance enhancing drugs the CIA continued to provide. They were the only thing that gave me the energy to press on.

I entered the hotel's main bar and searched for a bar table with two seats. The bar's decorative motif echoed the lobby's with stucco walls, rich wooden furnishings, and high, beamed ceilings. After a little searching, I found an empty table for two between two others that were occupied and seated myself. The place was more crowded than I expected given the limited population at the beach today, and the conversation was lively and multilingual. As I slid in to the seat against the wall, I caught a glimpse of Adam and Bill at a big table in the back corner of the bar. They were surrounded by a mixed group of the young and attractive and Adam was quite animated as he 'held court' for the group. Bill's face was different. It looked like an empty imitation of the tabloid pictures for which he was famous. I felt sorry for him.

I suddenly sensed the crowd stirring and I turned my head to see the cause. "Sophia" was making an entrance. The golden-blonde hair was pulled away from her tanned face into some sort of contraption on top of her head from which it erupted like a fountain and cascaded down to her tanned shoulders. She wore a white, cotton sundress that was just sheer enough to see her skin through but opaque enough in the right places to make it chic and not obscene. The makeup was more lightly applied than it had been earlier, but it was offset by the glittering diamonds that adorned her ear lobes, neck, wrists and naval, the last clearly detectable beneath the thin cotton of her dress. Every head in the place, including Adam's, watched her as she sauntered up to my table.

"Hi cutie," she said in the *voice*. "Mind if I join you?"

I nodded. "Please do." I could tell that my stock in the bar had just risen several percentage points. Nothing will bring a man to another man's or woman's attention more quickly than a beautiful woman seeking his company. Sophia joined me on my side of the table where the seat was a sofa anchored to a half-wall, and she snuggled up close to me. She smelled fantastic with a light scent of shampoo in the background and a hint of perfume up front. I was almost tempted to close my eyes and just draw in the scent.

"Dolce and Gabbana?" I asked.

She smiled radiantly at me. "Very good," she said. "Light Blue as a matter of fact. And just how would you recognize that?"

"The same way that I recognize your dress is Diane Von Furstenberg. I hear a lot of conversations between the people I fly around and I pay attention."

She nodded. "I'm impressed."

I resisted the impulse to question her about the diamonds that adorned her. A cocktail waitress in a classy but skimpy black outfit sidled up to our table a few moments later.

"Señor and Señora, what may I get you?"

I inclined my head toward Susan/Sophia.

"Ketel One, up," she replied quickly. "Dry and a little extra dirty with blue cheese stuffed olives if you have them."

The waitress nodded as she wrote down the order. Then she looked up at me.

"Sapphire and tonic, please."

"Gracias," she said. "I'll be right back with those."

"Gin and tonic?" Susan/Sophia asked with a bit of incredulity in her voice, "Aren't you a single-malt Scotch guy?"

I looked at her. "Later in the evening," I said. "If I've earned it."

"I thought the classic gin and tonic was a T and T, a Tanqueray and tonic?"

"Tanqueray makes you taste a little like you've been attacked by a pine tree," I said, smiling. "Bombay Sapphire is crisp and distinct. It tastes the way a black and white movie feels."

She nodded in comprehension as I made a show of looking her up and down. She just smiled back at me, clearly loving the attention. "Well, you certainly made an entrance," I said at last.

"That was desired effect," she whispered. "I'm trying to impress our target. I didn't want him to miss it. With any luck, he'll come over here and talk to us at some point. But maybe we need to give him a little more ammunition." And with that, she snaked one of her lightly-scented arms around my neck, lifted her lips to mine, and kissed me. She was good. The kiss was the perfect length and intensity to communicate intimacy without being showy or overdone. When it was over, she leaned her head on my shoulder. "I guarantee you we just put Adam's brain into overdrive."

Adam isn't the only one. And then, out of nowhere, the memory of Sarah's lips on mine flashed into my mind. I mentally seized it and locked it down.

The waitress delivered our drinks a few moments later

and sure enough, Susan's plan had come through.

"Your drinks are courtesy of Mr. Spratt," the waitress told us excitedly. "He asked me to give you this!" She passed us a cocktail napkin with some handwriting on it.

I picked it up and read the distinctive script. *"Colin, you and your lovely lady friend are invited to my party in the penthouse tonight. Please join us after ten. Bill."* I inclined my head toward Susan. "Almost like you knew that was going to happen."

She squeezed my arm. "I've been doing this for a while."

"We'll have to talk about that later," I said quietly. I could feel her tense slightly at my side. If she hadn't been so close to me I wouldn't have even noticed.

"Let's get some dinner," she said.

We spent the next two hours over a meal of fresh seafood and wine. I listened to Sophia tell me all about her life back in Reno and her "shit of a husband." She was speaking just a little too loudly and by now, I knew that was intentional. "Sophia" wanted everyone to know who she was and why she was here. It also became increasingly evident that I was a temporary companion and I guess if I was proud by nature, I would have been embarrassed, but the truth was that I was enthralled just watching her weave the tale.

"I'm just so glad I found you, honey," she finished with a tone of voice that indicated she'd had more than a few too many. "I'd just be so bored."

We asked for the check a few moments later and were informed that our meal was paid for by the ever-generous Mr. Spratt.

"Damn," I said. "If I would have known that, I'd have had a shot of the Macallan thirty."

Sophia smiled at me with a gleam in her eyes. "Let's head up to the party, darlin'. I hear the penthouse has a private pool on the roof. I might be in the mood for a moonlight swim."

I helped her to her feet and we walked out of the restaurant with her leaning on me heavily, which reacquainted me with the pain in my left leg all over again. As the elevator doors closed to take us to the penthouse a few moments later, she quickly straightened herself up and spoke in her own voice. There was no trace of intoxication in her speech or her eyes. It was like she just snapped out of it.

"I know that hurt your leg a little," she said. "Sorry about that, but it was necessary to complete the scene. Now there is something we have to do before we get to the roof. You need to kiss me like you mean it."

I guess my jaw dropped open a little. She stepped forward and put her arms around me. "We've got to convince these people that we're two horny recent acquaintances who desperately need a room. The problem is that we'll be putting on an act, and an act requires a degree of practice. This is practice time. Now kiss me."

I leaned down, made a mental check to ensure that the memories of Sarah were still locked away, and did what I was told. When it comes to kissing a woman, the key is passionate intensity. I teased her a little at first, kissing her with my lips closed for a moment or two, then slowly opening her mouth with my tongue and entangling her tongue with my own. After that, my tongue wandered the inside of her mouth patiently and, periodically, I'd move my lips to gently suck on one of hers. At first, she felt stiff in my arms but as soon as her mouth opened, her body melted completely against mine and I could feel the heat radiating from her. I couldn't tell whether she was acting or genuinely yielding, and that thought bothered me a little.

As the bell for the penthouse floor chimed a few moments later, we parted and she looked up at me breathlessly.

"Okay," she said in a voice that started as her own and ended up as Sophia's, "that was very nice... darlin'." Avoiding my eyes, she took my hand and interlaced my fingers with her own. "Here we go," she whispered.

The elevator doors opened and a wall of noise hit us, the mixed sounds of conversation, music, and the general dull roar many people create in a confined space. I recoiled slightly and I felt Susan steady me.

"You don't like this, do you?"

"I've never been good with crowds. I'll tell you about trying out for the Thunderbirds sometime."

"Well, I'm supposed to be the spoiled, rich, entertaining bitch type, so I'll work the room, wowing at the décor, and playing little Miss Party Animal. Got it?"

"Got it," I said weakly. "Can I get a drink first?"

"That's part of the deal," she said.

We exited the elevator and found ourselves in the foyer area outside the Suite del Presidente, a penthouse which occupied the top two floors of the hotel. Two massive wooden doors, at least half-again as tall as I was, stood wide open and revealed the organized chaos of a large party in full swing. I wanted nothing more than to turn around and leave. I felt my palms beginning to sweat.

"Stay with me, Colin," Sophia whispered. "I can't do this alone."

"The things I do for my country," I muttered.

We stepped through the door and found ourselves face-to-face with two large, very serious-looking Mexican gentlemen in black summer suits with conspicuous bulges under their armpits.

"Señor Pearce, Señora Monachelli, you are welcome," the one on the right said as he nodded to us. "Please come in and enjoy the party."

I felt the hair on the back of my neck go up. The goon squad knew who we were. Great.

"Well, what can I say but gracias a bunch?" Sophia crooned in her slightly intoxicated voice. "Where is Mr. Spratt? I'd like to thank him personally."

"Around," the doorman replied, grandly motioning to the

apartment's vast interior. "He roams the penthouse during these fiestas."

"We'll just have to track him down," she said.

The doorman and his companion bowed slightly in response and Susan/Sophia and I made our way into the seething mass of people. I looked around and tried to get my bearings. It seemed that the penthouse surrounded the elevator shaft, and the central hall area we were in had full-length French doors on the front walls which faced the ocean and the back walls which faced the peninsula's interior. Nearly all the doors were open and I saw people congregated in groups outside the doors with drinks in their hands. The hall itself was two stories high and I could see a balcony above us that ran the entire length of the room against the back wall, but then turned and ran along the side walls before ending at the front wall. The upper level on the side walls featured sets of additional double doors.

"It seems that all the bedrooms are upstairs," I whispered to Susan/Sophia.

"Master suite at the far end probably," she answered. "While we put on our show we might want to wander into the study, if we can locate it. We might find something useful in there."

"If we run across Bill during this process, we might be able to get some useful information out of him."

She shook her head slightly while looking up at me with a radiantly beautiful smile on her face.

"Can't risk it," she said. "You can never predict how a parent will act when they know their child might be taken away." And while the smile remained, I saw her eyes get shiny. She quickly looked away.

"Good point," I said. "Didn't think about that."

We continued walking down the end of the great hall. At this end of the huge room, the floor was about a foot lower than the area where we had entered. All the furniture had been cleared away for dancing and a disc-jockey with a full sound system was ensconced in the far corner playing to the crowd of twenty- and thirty-somethings who were undulating their bodies to the beat. I noticed, with great relief, that there was also a bar down there.

"Do you dance, Mr. Pearce?"

"I can and I have," I replied, "but I'm not very good at it. Too self-conscious I guess." I didn't mention that I had no idea how well my leg would hold up with that kind of activity.

"Well, we may need to do a little of that," she said.

"Let me guess, to set the stage some more?"

She looked up at me and winked. "Partially," she said.

"Scotch first," I ordered. "If I'm going to dance with this damn leg, I'm going to need some alcohol to take the edge off the pain."

She squeezed my arm. "You're the boss, sweetie," she crooned.

"That'll be the day."

We stepped down into the throng of dancers and made our way to the rich, wooden bar at the back end of the open area. Sophia ordered herself another martini while I looked over the rather impressive single-malt collection. Then the waiter looked at me questioningly.

"I'd like a double shot of the Macallan twelve, neat," I told him, "a double shot of the Macallan thirty, and a bottle of Perrier Water. I'd like the two Scotches in glasses with large mouths." I made a large circle with the thumb and index fingers of both hands.

Susan/Sophia looked at me questioningly as the bartender quickly manufactured her martini and poured my Scotches. He was careful to place the two glasses of Scotch well apart.

"This one is the twelve and this one is the thirty," he said pointing first to the glass on my left and then to the one on my right. I nodded. I would have been able to tell by the color and the aroma anyway, but it was nice of him to make sure

I knew. I held the two glasses up, side-by-side. The color of the twelve-year-old was much thinner than the rich, caramel color of its thirty-year-old brother. I opened my mouth and swallowed the entire glass of the twelve in one gulp. Then I gulped several swallows of the Perrier, swishing it around on my tongue before I swallowed it. Finally, I raised the glass of thirty-year-old to my nose, inhaled a deep nostril full of the rich, malt aroma, and downed a small sip, allowing it to linger on my tongue for just a few seconds. There was only one way to describe the taste: elegant.

I inclined my head involuntarily. "Wow," I said to no one in particular, "it's good but it isn't that much better than the twenty-five."

I caught Susan looking at me with a bemused expression on her beautiful face. "Are you done?" she asked.

"For now," I said, eying her over the rim of my Scotch glass as I raised it again. It appeared that I was going to be unable to stall the festivities any longer.

"We need to dance," she said with a peculiar gleam in her eye. She took the Scotch glass out of my hand and placed it on the bar with her glass. Then she wrapped her arm around mine and led me over to the dancing masses. I had no idea what song was playing but the beat was regular, the guitar line was complex, and there were no black men shouting obscenities in the lyrics so I felt pretty good about it. We moved into the dancing bodies and she turned toward me. Despite the Scotch, I felt very self-conscious standing there, cane in hand.

She slid up to me and placed her hands on my hips while kissing my neck and then licking it slightly.

"Let me do everything," she whispered. She began moving her hips side to side with the rhythm and moving my hips to match hers. "Just move," she said softly, "move like this. That's all you need to do."

So that's what I did. For the next several songs, she moved

my hips to the beat while she moved with me. Sometimes she did it from a few inches away, other times she did it with her body right up against mine, and other times she'd turn around and press her firm ass into my crotch while she did it. The effect was slow, electric, and erotic. She appeared to be totally lost in the intensity of our movement together and I found I was losing myself to it as well. As she pressed her ass into me, I could feel myself stiffening. In response, she pushed herself into me harder and began to move up and down slightly, as well as side to side.

"That's not even fair," I whispered into her ear breathlessly. "A certain part of me doesn't understand that this is all an act."

She threw her head back at me and lifted her lips to mine briefly. Then she spun around and shoved her hips against me so that her crotch was now firmly rubbing my fully erect penis. She still had her hands on my hips and now she was moving my hips in circles. My pants were linen and the underwear I had on was very light cotton and it was rapidly becoming apparent that there was little or nothing under the thin cloth layer of her dress. I could feel the peculiar tingle in my lower body that indicated that an orgasm was imminent if we continued.

"Okay," I said into her ear even more breathlessly than before, "if we don't stop this, there's a darn good chance that I'm going to seriously embarrass myself here in front of everyone."

"Kiss me," she said as she lifted her lips to mine.

I did what I was asked and lost myself into her mouth and into her arms. As we continued to move against one another and explore each other's mouths, I could feel the tingling intensifying. It wasn't going to be long.

The kiss ended and she rested her head on my chest.

"Look at the other end of the hall, second floor balcony," she breathed.

It was Adam. He stood on the balcony railing, about seventy to eighty feet away. While a party-host's smile was pasted onto his face, his eyes were lifeless. And he was staring directly at me. My arousal was forgotten in an instant; and ironically, I found I was grateful for that.

"Well damn," Susan/Sophia whispered after a moment, "I was afraid that would happen if I pointed him out to you. He's been there for about the last fifteen minutes. I needed to make sure he saw us together like this."

"So now what?"

"Now the stage is set," she said as she turned around, wrapped my arms around her waist, and led me to the bar. "Now we can look around and let his jealousy build." I was immensely grateful for her presence in front of me for the next several minutes as the tent in my pants slowly deflated.

We spent the next ninety minutes or so roaming the penthouse and I followed her cues. Sometimes we'd make conversation with the groups of people we met, other times we'd lean against a wall or railing and make-out while people went by. She leaned on me, hugged me, held my hands, and generally crawled all over me, but she did so with a purpose in every single move. We made it in and out of every room in the place and while there was no time or opportunity for a detailed search under the conditions, the cursory search seemed fruitless. We didn't run into Adam or Bill in any of our travels, but in a place as large as this one, it was more than possible they were just in different areas than we were.

Finally, we descended back to the main level, strolled out the French doors facing the ocean, and walked down the railing toward the master bedroom side of the penthouse. We rounded a curve in the wall and found a private courtyard with a small plunge pool up against a decorative waterfall. The pool was empty but at the far end of the plunge pool was a Jacuzzi with several sets of bare shoulders and wet heads protruding above the water. Between the Jacuzzi and the pool was a spiral staircase, with waist-high stucco walls which formed a partial barrier between the two and led up to the seaside balcony outside the master bedroom suite. As I followed the stairway up with my eyes, I saw Adam standing at the railing above the Jacuzzi, having a heated conversation on a cell phone. I could overhear enough of the pieces of speech to know that he was speaking Arabic.

I nudged Susan and inclined my head toward Adam.

"Perfect," she whispered. "We need to give him one more really good show to reel him in."

"I hope I'm up for it," I whispered back. *Both literally and figuratively,* I thought.

She ignored me. "It'd be really nice if we could overhear what Adam is saying into that damn phone." She nodded toward the spiral stairway. "While I put on a little show for our friend up there, can you get close enough to record something with that BlackBerry of yours?"

"I'll do my best."

A few minutes later, I had discarded the cane and made it to the underside of the stairway which ended against the lower wall of the penthouse and away from the Jacuzzi. I had slipped all my clothes off except a pair of black boxer briefs and left them with my cane on one of the chairs next to the pool. As I reached the bottom step, I nodded at Susan. She had made her way to the far side of the plunge pool next to the waterfall, and in Adam's clear view, and began to make a show of testing the water with her bare foot. Adam's conversation diminished for a moment. I could sense that he was being distracted by Susan's presentation below him.

He might have been an Arab and a Muslim, but he was still a man and a man first. We were counting on that. As much as I was dying to see what he was seeing, the mission called and I crawled up the cement stairs on my elbows and knees, gritting my teeth every time my left leg encountered the pebble-covered cement. I worked my way up the staircase as quickly as I could, trying to stay against the outside as I ascended in the shadow of the staircase walls.

Above me, Adam was into rapid fire conversation again. His footsteps had stopped, though. He was against the railing upstairs looking down into the pool. I had the BlackBerry in my hand and it was in the video camera mode, which also allowed it to record sound. I held it at arm's length in front of me as I crawled to try to get it closer to where Adam was talking. Below me, I could hear conversation, laughs, and the Jacuzzi tub's pump and I only hoped that sound technicians at the CIA would be able to filter out the background noise from the important stuff.

The staircase had turned a hundred-and-eighty degrees now and I would have had nearly the same view as Adam if I stood. There were openings in the bottom of the wall every few steps, about twelve inches long by six inches high, presumably to allow for water drainage in the event of an infrequent rain storm. As I ascended, I couldn't help looking out of the openings. Susan appeared to lose patience about something and slowly lifted her white sundress over her head. She tossed it onto a nearby chair and regarded the water in the skimpiest white lingerie set imaginable. I shook my head to clear it and continued my ascent.

A few moments later, I reached the top of the stairs. About the same time, I heard a splash and I knew that Susan was in the pool. Adam remained motionless, although he continued to speak heatedly into his phone. I lay there against the wall and held the BlackBerry up as far as I could without risking discovery to allow it to capture his conversation. The plan was working perfectly. By now Susan was naked in the water and Adam was transfixed with the sight of a nude woman swimming in his pool. I was recording every word of his conversation.

I could hear the gentle lapping of Susan stroking back and forth across the small pool below me and while I couldn't see her, my mind created a highly-sensual image of her lithe, muscular body slipping through the water. My arousal from earlier in the evening was being reawakened.

"... Shukraan. Ma'assalama."

Damn!

In my momentary distraction, I almost missed the words. My Arabic wasn't great but I knew those two words. *Thank you. Goodbye.* Two words which nearly everyone used to end a phone conversation. I could hear Adam's shoes on the pavement next to me on the other side of the wall. I pushed myself down the staircase as quickly as I could and bit my tongue to keep from crying out due to the pain in my knee and from my skin being rubbed off in several places on the cement. I reached the bottom and could hear Adam's shoes descending the stairs above me. I prayed that the sight of Susan's naked body in the water would keep his attention diverted and allow me the time I needed. I half-hopped, half-limped over to the chair where my clothes were, practically ripped my underwear off, and slid the BlackBerry under them. Then I slipped into my side of the pool, which would have been just under Adam's field of view from his perch above.

As my shoulders hit the water, Susan smirked at me from the middle of the pool and called to me in Sophia's voice. "Was that enough of a show for you?"

"Yes ma'am, it was," I responded. "Now why don't you come on over here and let me show you my appreciation."

She slowly stroked over to me. The pool was about five feet deep where I was, so by bending my knees just a little, I could keep my shoulders underwater. Susan swam up to me and wrapped her legs around my waist as she put her arms around my neck. I ran my arms around her and we kissed each other. Behind me, I could sense Adam's footsteps on the pavement of the pool deck. The steps came toward us for a few paces and paused. He was watching.

"Here we go darlin'," Sophia whispered in my ear.

And then she made me completely forget he was there. I became focused on the incredibly sensual, naked woman who had her legs wrapped around me. She was kissing me intensely and I was responding in kind. The combination of warm air, warm water, and the excitement of the evening was surging through both of us. I was rock hard and her crotch was pressed against me so tightly, I could feel her bare lips on my skin. As the kissing continued, she began to grind her hips into my body and move her sex and up and down my shaft. The tingling I felt from earlier in the evening was back and raging through me. Then, just when I thought I couldn't endure anything more intense, she raised herself up and lowered herself on me in a quick, fluid motion and I was inside her. Almost immediately, she began to writhe on me. I could feel her tense and release her muscles around me and her hips began the sporadic movement of pre-orgasm.

"Come with me, Colin," she whispered just loud enough for Adam to hear as she dug her nails into my back and pushed her erect nipples into my chest. "Come with me."

Her last word turned into a loud moan and she ground her body into mine. At that point, I didn't care if she was acting and neither did my body. I pushed myself into her and felt the orgasm literally ripped from my body. Waves and waves of pleasure passed through me as her body squeezed my penis and pulled my seed into her.

We stood there holding each other in the water for several minutes as we came back to reality. Eventually, she lifted her eyes to the pool deck behind me and to the balcony above.

"He left," she said quietly. "We can go now."

I opened my mouth to speak and felt her finger on my lips.

"Don't talk," she whispered with a pleading look in her eyes.

We dressed in silence and then she wrapped her arms around me and put her head on my shoulder.

"Get me out of here," she said.

We remained intertwined as we walked to the elevator and stayed that way until the chime rang for my floor. For a second, I thought she was going to follow me to my room to complete the "act" but she quickly extricated herself from my arms and gently pushed me away from her and toward the elevator doors.

"E-mail the file to Smith and Amrine," she said. "They'll have someone standing by to interpret it."

I nodded.

As the doors began to close, she looked at me through the strands of damp blonde hair which cascaded down her face.

"You're a little dangerous," she said, as her lips formed a wry smile. "And that felt a little too good."

CHAPTER EIGHT

Contract Day Four
Friday, 20 November
1000 Hours Local Time
Hotel Imperial del Cabo
Cabo San Lucas, Mexico

I awoke the next morning after a fitful night. Sex was typically a guilt-free act for me but that wasn't how it felt this morning. This *show* Susan and I were putting on was pushing buttons inside of me that I didn't know I had. It wasn't supposed to be real, but somehow it *felt* real. And I knew that wasn't my imagination. I'd been with enough women to have seen the full gamut sexually, from pure physical fucking to passionate lovemaking, and I could tell when there was more to it than superficiality. Or acting. And now because there was a sense of reality about it, I felt curiously guilty.

But why?

Not because of Samantha. She had been dead nearly a month and while our feelings for one another had been intense, I had only known her for a few weeks.

It had to be because of Sarah, but that didn't make any sense either. Our time had been three years ago and now, emotions and issues notwithstanding, she was another man's wife and she was carrying another man's child.

So, what the hell? And why did I even care? Act or no act, the sex with Susan was positively mind-blowing. What did it matter if there might be more to it than fucking for our country?

Suddenly, there was this peculiar tapping inside my head. I opened my eyes and realized that I must have dozed off while running this shit through my mind. And now someone was knocking at the door of my suite and I heard the words "Room Service" uttered in a respectful tone. I threw my legs over the side of the bed and my left leg practically gave out underneath me as I stood up and put my weight on it. I fell against the wall, hopped over to the closet doors, threw a bathrobe over my naked body, grabbed my cane and stumbled out into the great room of my suite and to the front door.

"Who in the hell ordered breakfast?" I asked myself aloud as I hobbled across the ceramic tile. I opened the door to find a member of the hotel staff pushing a rollaway dining table heaped with breakfast items and two more hotel members behind the first with trays full of assorted drinks and accompaniments. And behind them all was the lovely Miss Sophia, dressed in a flowery wrap over some sort of bikini.

"Well, good morning, darlin'!" She stepped by the parade of hotel staff and up to me, slid her arms around my waist, and gave me a lingering kiss. "Here's your morning breakfast, as promised. I didn't know exactly what you liked so I had them bring a little of everything. Can they come in and set up?"

"Sure," I said, playing along as my head swam into the moment. "Please," I added, gesturing to the inside of my suite.

The crew moved in and began setting up the food and other goodies on the tiled kitchen bar while Sophia stayed glued to my side, clinging to me and kissing me intermittently while she spoke.

"Did you sleep well last night, sweetie? I sure hope I wore you out a little. I've got a nice little adventure in store for you today. Mr. Bill Spratt and his friend, the delightful Mr.

Archmere, have invited us out for an afternoon cruise on their yacht. Isn't that wonderful?"

I looked down at her questioningly.

"Oh, I know, darlin'. You don't like crowds and such, but Mr. Spratt promised there wouldn't be too many people on the yacht, just fifty or so—and after all, it is a private invitation. I mean how often do you get to go out on the water on a boat like that?"

The staff members had finished setting up the food and were bowing as they made their way out. Sophia put a fresh $50 dollar bill into each of their hands as they exited. She shut the door behind them, and I was about to say something when she spun around and slammed her body against mine.

"God, Colin. I need you to kiss me again like you kissed me last night." She lifted her lips to mine but as our eyes met I could see that there was something else on her mind. She rolled her eyes rapidly and I instantly got the gist. We were under some form of surveillance. Our lips met and once again we were immersed in that odd "created reality" that felt like it was bridge to something else. I ruthlessly locked any guilt or feelings or regret behind a door in my mind and mentally placed myself back on the stage.

"I think I need another dose of what you gave me last night," she said breathlessly, "and I think I need it right now."

We continued the kiss as we moved toward the bedroom. She untied my bathrobe as I clumsily attempted to unfasten her wrap. She kept her lips locked onto mine and impatiently tore the wrap from her body. Then she unclasped her bikini top as I pushed the bikini bottom over her hips and to the floor. Out bare bodies merged as we went through the bedroom door. I could see her kick it with her heel as we went through to ensure the door was open even wider than it had been.

She backed me up against the king-size bed still kissing me. I finally made it out of my robe and despite my earlier mental consternation, my penis was rising to its morning engagement.

Those performance-enhancing drugs had wonderful side effects. Susan/Sophia pushed me down onto the bed and then she straddled me. I looked up at her taut body, from her shaven-pubic area, to her flat stomach with its diamond navel ring, to her firm breasts. Then I raised my eyes to her face. She looked down at me with an expression of determination on her features. Then, she leaned forward until she was lying on my chest and her mouth was next to my ear.

"There's a wireless transmitter in your outer room," she whispered. "I detected it from the hallway. There is at least one microphone attached to it and probably a fiber optic camera. There's nothing in this room but the mic outside will be able to detect some sounds in here so we can't speak too loudly. We'll have to convince our listeners that we're fucking each other's brains out and then we can talk for a few minutes. Are you game?"

I nodded and she sat up and began to rub herself on me. Oddly, as her genitals contacted mine, I could tell that she was already wet.

It was over in just a few minutes and she ended up doing all the work. While the post-orgasm flush was still burning my face, she lowered her chest to mine, placed her mouth next to my ear, and whispered to me while she kissed my cheek and the side of my face.

"The tape you sent to Smith and Amrine last night yielded some interesting intel," she whispered.

"Mmmmm, that's nice," I mumbled, barely able to concentrate on her words.

"The gist of the conversation is that there will be one more trip to Cabo after this one and then they'll be ready for whatever they're planning. Adam was arguing with someone about what day the operation needs to happen. Apparently, this other someone is waiting for verification of something else but Adam has a 'perfect day' in mind."

Suddenly, I felt my guts clench and that must have tightened other areas of my body as well, because Susan/Sophia startled on top of me. She recovered quickly, of course.

"Ooooooh, Colin. That's nice. I'm game for another round if you are."

I turned my head to kiss her and made sure my mouth was obscured. "It's Thanksgiving," I whispered to her. "When I was cleaning up the jet after the last trip, I saw a piece of paper at the table where Adam and Felix Lopez were talking. I took a picture of it but I forgot to show it to Smith and Amrine. It was a list of every major football game played in the US on Thanksgiving Day."

She nodded gently as she moved her lips to my neck and began to nuzzle me there. "You need to send the boys an e-mail about that when we're done here and before we go to the boat."

I must have tensed a little.

"This boat thing is important," she said as she switched sides of my neck. "It will be my chance to get him alone. And we might stumble across something useful."

"So be it," I whispered back.

She sat up and stretched. "Well, nothing gives me an appetite like great sex," she sighed. She reached out for my hands, pulled me into a sitting position, and drew my arms around her. "C'mon, darlin'. Let's eat before it gets cold!" She kissed me again quickly and dismounted. Then she walked out into the eating area without stopping to pick up her clothes.

I slid off the bed and headed for my bathroom, BlackBerry in hand, and dashed off a quick e-mail to Smith and Amrine as I stood there and peed. I attached the picture I had taken and gave them my suspicions about the day and the target, but I couldn't help adding an additional note.

"You could have at least given me a little warning about this Susan/Sophia thing," I typed. "And by the way, what is up with this chick? It's like she's got a split personality or something."

I had set the device on the vanity in the bathroom and was running a brush though my disheveled hair when the BlackBerry vibrated. The boys had not wasted any time in replying. I clicked on the new e-mail.

"Copy all," the e-mail said. "Good catch on the date. Our analysts were leaning that direction anyway. You might cut Susan a little slack. She plays this game well and she's spent so much time away from home on covert ops that her ex-husband won a custody suit for their kids."

I felt my face flush again, only this time it was with embarrassment.

"Damn." I sighed angrily at my reflection in the mirror and felt a few pieces of the Susan/Sophia puzzle click into place. "Damn," I said again.

"Honey, are you coming outside to eat with me or are you going to make me eat all alone?"

I turned my head to see Susan/Sophia standing in the doorway to the bathroom, leaning against one side of the doorframe, eating yogurt out of small cup. She was still naked, of course, and from her tanned, toned body, to her sex-disheveled hair, to her bright and playful eyes, she looked absolutely ravishing. I felt myself stir again.

"On my way, ma'am," I said. "I had a little personal business to take care of. Let me get my robe and I'll join you."

She shook her head. "No robes allowed, honey. If I need to have my way with you again, I don't want anything in the way."

"Sounds good to me," I replied. I put the BlackBerry down, washed my hands thoroughly, and dried them. Then she offered me her hand and we walked into the main dining area. She had set everything out on the ceramic-tiled counters and bar like a small buffet line. Susan took a plate, handed me one, and then preceded me through our miniature smorgasbord. I took a little of each of the meats, one or two of the various types of eggs, and some fresh fruit.

As I helped myself to a mug of coffee that smelled distinctly like a Peet's brew that I liked, Susan sat down at the dining table.

"May I bring you something to drink?" I asked.

"No thanks," she replied, "I took care of that while some guy was making me wait all alone out here."

"Touché."

I carried my food and drink over to the table and after some minor consternation about where to sit, I chose the armless chair next to her. After a few bites of my food, I turned to her.

"Well done," I said. "This is excellent."

She nodded and laughed. "I order room service well, don't I?"

"Yes, you do." My left hand was in my lap and I could feel my fingers tingle. I felt the oddest urge to touch her in some sort of affectionate and comforting way but our "relationship," such as it was, provided no bridge for that sort of thing. "So, we're going on a boat ride this afternoon, are we?"

She turned to me and her eyes lit up. "Yes, it will be soooo exciting! Bill has this huge yacht called *Bachelor's Toy* or something. It's like two hundred feet long and can go really fast! We're going to go find a reef to do some snorkeling and then maybe do some fishing. Won't that be cool?"

I felt my stomach turn over. I never liked boats much and I hated being on one out of the sight of land. I suddenly found I had no appetite.

"I think I need to go get a shower," I said, pushing myself back from the table. "When are we supposed to leave?"

"In about an hour," she replied. "Hey, you've barely had anything to eat!"

"I'm fine," I said.

"No, you're not. Sit," she commanded. "I'm not ready to for you to get up yet, so it looks like I'm going to have to feed you." Before I could get up, she threw one of her legs over my chair and was straddling me, with her back against the table. She reached over to get her plate and fork and then leaned back to give me a brilliant smile before she proceeded to alternately put food in her mouth and in mine. From time to time, she'd put a piece of fruit in her mouth and offer it to me and I'd take it, chew it, and we'd finish with a long and juicy kiss. Also, she'd "accidentally" dripped some yogurt onto her nipples and would arch her back to offer me the opportunity to lick them off. I did so with relish.

As my lower body stirred yet again and the blood began to engorge me, I felt myself beginning to disassociate from what was happening. My old mechanisms, which had protected me so well in all the meaningless relationships in my life, were deploying and I welcomed them. This entire situation was getting too complicated for me to understand and it was time to retreat into the safe physical arena and close the door on the other shit.

We were sharing another deep kiss with our eyes closed when I felt her shift herself and then felt her lower herself onto my organ. The moment she was settled, she started to undulate her hips into me, slowly and smoothly at first, and then faster and more frantically. I was just along for the ride, again. All the meaningless and physically-oriented relationships in my life had taught me a few things and one of them was how to rapidly determine what a woman liked sexually. It was very apparent that Susan/Sophia liked running the show. The trouble was that I couldn't tell which one of her she was. Women who want sex to be impersonal don't typically cling to you while they're fucking you. They keep their distance. So, while I was sure that our frequent humping was for the benefit of mics or the cameras, I could also feel a woman clinging to me and kissing me while the lower part of her body did its thing. Ironically, in this context, the two didn't seem to go together.

Without knowing why I was doing it, I removed myself

from her and stood up. Then I led her into the bedroom, gently pushed her onto the bed, smoothly nudged her legs apart, and crawled up onto the bed, lowering myself upon her. I put one hand on the side of her face and used the other to gently brush the blonde hair out of her eyes. Then, I started to kiss her, slowly and unhurriedly, while I gently pushed myself into her as deeply as I could and lifted my hips up a little to ensure she was getting the maximum possible stimulation.

It doesn't get much more intimate than the classic missionary position; and the vibe I was getting from her was that despite the Sophia exterior, the inner Susan hungered for intimacy. I didn't know why I was pushing that button; perhaps I had to see which of the two women I was with.

My question was answered immediately. She completely yielded to me. Just like in the elevator last night. Her mouth couldn't get enough of mine, and her legs wrapped tightly around me. Her arms and hands couldn't decide if they wanted to hang onto my neck or grab my ass and pull me more deeply into her.

We moved together like that for several minutes and it was like being carried down a river on a gentle current that slowly grew more forceful. Soon our strokes became deeper and more purposeful and then I felt her fingernails dig into my back and her legs clamp around me.

"Colin, Colin, Colin," she whispered breathlessly in my ear. My body responded to her and we moved against one another quickly and deeply as our orgasms consumed us. We held each other for several moments afterward, catching our breath and enjoying the warmth of each other. Then my lips found hers and we kissed each other, slowly and tenderly. When the kiss was over, I lifted my head and looked down at her.

As she looked back at me, I saw a battle take place in her eyes, and before I could see who or what would triumph, she threw her arms around me and drew me to her while turning her head away from me.

"It wasn't supposed to be like this," she whispered in her own voice. "Goddamn it."

Then a few seconds later, Sophia was back and she slapped my ass playfully. The sound of the *voice* made my skin crawl a little. "Okay darlin', enough fuckin' for now. We've got a boat to catch. Get this hot little ass of yours into the shower."

I had no sooner entered the huge stone-walled rain-shower when Susan/Sophia joined me under the water. She had her own shower head and she stood under it and peered at me through the streams as she began to soap her own body.

We stared at each other silently for a few moments before she spoke. "You can't do that again," she whispered in Susan's voice. "I don't know what changed, but it went from professional to personal and it just can't or it will fuck up everything."

I just looked at her. I could have told her that I only acted on cues she was sending me but I knew that would make things worse. "I don't have any practice at this sort of thing," I said. "I'm doing the best that I can."

She came closer to me and I could feel the air around us starting to become electric with sexual tension.

"You need to understand something," she said. "You need to understand that I've met men like Adam Archmere before and I know how to get to them. That's what all of this is about. Remember our discussion back at the Marriott?"

It was suddenly like I was seeing all that she and I had done from a third-person perspective. Like we were on a stage. I heard the voice of an Australian pilot whom I flew with back in Saudi Arabia years ago. "You know the quickest way to make an Arab want something so bad he can't stand it, mate? Well, that's simple. You just show him it belongs to someone else and he can't have it."

"Adam had a thing for me when I was on that op earlier this year but he couldn't act on it. This whole thing between you and me has been designed to make him jealous and make a pass at me... at Sophia. And when that happens, I have to yield to him." She looked up at me. "Do you understand what that means? It means I have to be able to put you behind me and fuck him and pretend I'm enjoying it."

She moved in closer to me, wrapped her arms around me, and looked up at me with a look in her eyes that showed a mixture of remorse and purpose.

"There may be a time and a place for this," she said. "For an *us*. But it isn't now."

Then, abruptly, she kissed me and left the shower.

I remained under the water for a few more minutes and chided myself slightly for what I had done. I had never intended for there to be an *us*. I had merely intended to see if she thought there could be an *us* and apparently, she did. As I had suspected. So, notwithstanding her protestations, Susan did have a personal stake in what happened between us. And, I was willing to bet, she was just a little jealous of the loyalty I felt for Sarah.

The reason for the guilt was clear to me now. The conscience that I had spent my entire adulthood trying to ignore was making its desire known. It wanted me to choose.

But that choice had already been made.

Hell, it was made three years ago.

I smiled as the water cascaded down upon me. Adam/Abdullah was about to do me a favor. And he didn't even know it.

CHAPTER NINE

Contract Day Four
Friday, 20 November
1200 Hours Local Time
Onboard Bachelor's Toy
In the Waters Off Cabo San Lucas, Mexico

About thirty minutes later, Susan and I were aboard *Bachelor's Toy* and perched upon a pair of very comfortable chaise lounge chairs. As the huge yacht churned up the water behind us, we watched the tranquil harbor shrink into the distance. One of the ship's crew had deliberately placed us by ourselves on the large upper sun deck just behind the wheelhouse as all the other revelers partied in the small splash pool below and in the larger splash pool on the forward deck. We both maintained the requisite smiles on our faces as we nursed our drinks and waited for Adam to show himself.

It was just a question of time.

"Isn't this beautiful, sweetie?" Sophia asked me while "absentmindedly" stroking my leg with her non-drink-holding hand. Her fingers were precariously close to a certain area of my body and I was sure that was intentional. She *had* to touch me for some reason.

"It's lovely, Sophia. Simply breathtaking!"

"Well, here you two are!" Bill Spratt's voice sprung up

from behind us and startled me to the point that I almost dropped my beer. "Welcome aboard *Bachelor's Toy*." Bill walked around to the side of my chaise and sat down in a chair nearby. He was wearing white linen slacks and a flowered, button-down shirt. He looked every inch the party-boat host. Adam appeared next to Susan's chaise and seated himself on a chair near her. His outfit could have been coordinated with Bill's.

"Bill, Adam," I said politely, "thanks for inviting us aboard. This is quite a boat."

"Yacht," Adam said precisely. "It's a yacht."

I knew that. I had spent enough time around people to know the difference between the two. "Sorry," I said apologetically. "I don't know much about boats... er, yachts."

"Me neither," Bill Spratt said candidly. "I just woke up one day and decided I wanted one and went to Dubai and bought this one. Took delivery of it here. It's a prototype of a PJ something or other."

"Palmer Johnson PJ210," Adam corrected him. "I recommended it to him." Then Adam looked at me closely. "My family has several Palmer Johnson craft."

I kept my face absolutely impassive. *You couldn't have set that trap any more obviously, Adam. Do I really look stupid enough to react to that?* I shrugged non-committedly and kept my eyes on Bill. "Hey, to each their own toys. If you're happy with it, Bill, that's all that matters, right?"

He painted a half-hearted smile on his face and looked back at me. "Right," he said.

"Do you suppose I could get a tour of this beautiful yacht?" Sophia asked in as sweet a voice as she could muster.

"Well, I guess..." Bill began.

"I'd be delighted, madam," Adam interrupted him and stepped forward, extending his hand.

"Thank you, kind sir," Sophia replied, taking Adam's hand and rising to her feet. She turned and looked down at me.

"Are you coming, sweetie?"

It was almost comical. Both she and Adam were looking at me, standing side-by-side and both of their eyes were plainly indicating that my company would not be welcome. His communicated distain and hers communicated a resignation to duty and perhaps a hint of regret.

"No, you two go on ahead," I said cheerfully. "I think I'd like to remain here with Bill and find out how he keeps his libido going so well after all these years."

"Suit yourself," Sophia said with just a touch of disappointment in her voice.

And then she and Adam were off into the main wheelhouse behind us and Bill and I were alone. I took the embossed cocktail napkin my beer was sitting on and turned it over to the dry side and put it on my knee so that it was in Bill's field of vision and no one else's. Then I took out a pen and began to write.

"I HAVE FRIENDS WHO KNOW ABOUT ADAM AND WHO HE IS."

Bill looked at me with eyes like saucers. The expression in them went from despair to disbelief to hope in a fraction of a second.

I continued to write.

"THEY ARE LOOKING FOR YOUR DAUGHTER RIGHT NOW."

That got him. I saw tears welling up in his eyes.

"DO YOU KNOW WHAT ADAM IS PLANNING?"

He began to open his mouth and I shook my head once side-to-side, very quickly. He frowned for a moment and then his face brightened. He went into the wheelhouse and came back with a newspaper and made a point of showing an article to me. Then, he looked for words in the article and on the page that he could use and pointed to them one by one.

Don't.

Know.

Exactly.

Needs.

He pointed at the deck to indicate the yacht itself.

And.

Plane.

Hmmm, I thought. *I wonder what that means.* I jotted on the napkin.

HOW MANY OTHER PASSENGERS HAVE FLOWN UP TO BURBANK BEFORE I ARRIVED? DO YOU HAVE ANY IDEA WHO THEY ARE OR WHAT THEY DO?

He held two fingers up and then found the word "doctor" on the page and pointed to it. Then he found the word "Special."

I felt a cold chill run down my spine. *CHEMICAL-WEAPON?* I wrote on the napkin.

He shrugged and pointed to a few other words.

Last.

Package.

Kept.

Cold.

I looked at him intently and he pointed to the paper again.

Very.

Cold.

I felt something scratching at the back of my brain. *What would need to be kept so cold?* Then a wave of realization hit me. *That's why the suitcase was so heavy on the last trip. They had some of kind of cryogenic storage container inside of it.* I made a mental note to ask Smith and Amrine about this and put pen to napkin again.

HOW DID THE CARGO AND THESE GUYS GET TO CABO? I wrote.

He shook his head sadly and pointed to the deck of the yacht and put his hands together like the hull of the boat. Then he opened them.

I was stunned. The yacht had an undersea door on the bottom. The cargo and personnel were taken into the boat when it was parked somewhere, either in the harbor or when it was out to sea. Probably when it was out to sea, given the frequent party cruises. That meant that the cargo and personnel were probably brought in by submarine, which indicated that the forces behind this thing were well funded, indeed. I made a mental note to ask Smith and Amrine if the al Qudamah shipping fleet included a submarine.

Then Bill looked up at me with a frustrated expression on his face and pointed to some other words.

But.

Not.

Only,

2.

Men.

More.

Many.

More.

And.

Many.

He searched for a word on the page and seemed frustrated when he couldn't find it. He then raised his right hand to his chest and made a pistol with it. The message was clear. *Guns. Many guns.*

I felt my jaw opening in astonishment.

"Gentlemen? May I offer you some more drinks?" A uniformed steward appeared behind my chair and reached for my Corona bottle. "Take your trash, sir?" he said, indicating the napkin in my right hand.

I crunched the napkin up forcefully. "No, I'm all right for now." I looked at Bill. "Bill, I've been boring you with all this flying stuff. I'm sure you want to get back to your other guests."

"You haven't been boring me at all, Colin," he said standing up. "It's been a pleasure. But yes, I guess I should play the host." He patted me on the shoulder. "We'll talk again."

"I'd like that, sir." I said.

"Husam," he said to the steward, "can you see to the young ladies down on the lower sundeck? They seem to be in need of some more champagne."

There was a noticeable pause. "Yes, Mr. Spratt."

I guess it was the way the steward said it that made me look around at him. He had a glaring expression on his face that was not appropriate to the obsequious manner that should have been characteristic of someone in his position. One glance told me why that was. Dark, olive skin and wavy dark hair, along with the haughty carriage of one who thought he was better than those he served.

Husam was an Arab. I wondered if he came with the boat.

We stayed at sea for another four or five hours. The boat stopped at several places for swimming/snorkeling and even some fishing. I wondered at what point the hull opened and we gained more passengers or cargo. I also wondered how much of the conversation between Bill and I was observed by Husam, the watchful steward. I made a show of walking around the boat's railing and taking in the sights, the magnificent rocky coast of Baja California, and the nude or semi-nude female swimmers and sunbathers which adorned the light green waters or the highly polished teak decks. At one point, I made my way to a bathroom, tore the cocktail napkin into about one hundred pieces, and flushed them down into the holding tanks.

Susan/Sophia did not reappear until the ship was approaching the harbor in the early evening. She sat down silently on the chair next to me and did not meet my eyes. I looked over at her and wished I didn't possess the observational skills and dirty mind that I did. She had the slightly disheveled appearance of a woman who has just been fucked long and hard and hadn't spent quite enough time to conceal it. I should have kept my mouth shut, but I just couldn't.

"I hope it was worth it," I said into the warm Cabo air.

"Me too," she said softly.

#

We went to our separate rooms when we returned to the hotel without exchanging another word or even another touch. I assumed that my purpose in all of this had been served. I didn't know how to feel about that. While I had engaged in numerous meaningless relationships in my life, I had never used anyone. The rules were always made clear up-front and I ensured that the other party was okay with the scenario. This entire business had left an extremely bad taste in my mouth. Sure, the sex had been great, but it seemed empty now. I felt my mind wander back to another similar episode a few weeks ago on an island far, far away.

"God," I said to myself as I stripped to go to bed. "I am getting so tired of this shit."

I tapped out a quick e-mail to Smith and Amrine outlining what I had learned from Bill and turned the damn BlackBerry off. Then I called the front desk and told them that I was not to be disturbed for twelve hours. I hung up the phone and clicked off the lights and closed my eyes.

It took me awhile to get settled, but at last I fell into a deep and dreamless sleep.

CHAPTER TEN

Contract Day Five
Saturday, 21 November
0900 Hours Local Time
Hotel Imperial del Cabo
Cabo San Lucas, Mexico

The damn phone on my nightstand yanked me out of my first peaceful sleep in many nights.

"Yeah?" I answered, gruffly.

"Colin," Adam's voice said coolly, "have the jet ready for a 1200 departure please. We will have three passengers in addition to Bill and Felix."

"Yes sir," I answered in as civil and businesslike a tone as I could muster. My mind was spinning. Three additional passengers? They had only ever brought one at a time before. "Would you like me to order any catering for the flight back?"

"That won't be necessary," he replied. "But I have a little surprise for you when we return to Burbank. Also, I'd like for you to stay at the mansion until we return here in a few days if you wouldn't mind."

"That will be fine with me, sir. I'll see you at noon."

The line went dead.

Surprise? Now what the fuck did that mean?

I pushed the button for room service and ordered myself

a plate of Eggs Benedict, some orange juice, and a pot of coffee. Not typical fare for a Mexican hotel, but I imagined if any hotel south of the border could pull it off, this one could.

I showered quickly, dressed, and packed my things. The doorbell rang a few moments after I zipped my roller bag and pulled it into the entry corridor. I opened the door to find a waiter carrying a tray and Susan/Sophia right behind him carrying a newspaper and looking radiant as ever in a beige sundress. The sight of her caught me at a complete loss. It seemed we had one more scene to play for the cameras and I didn't have the script.

I motioned them into my room and the waiter set up two plates of Eggs Benedict, two orange juices, and two coffees on the dining table. Susan/Sophia stood well clear of me while the waiter did his work. I signed the check and he exited quietly, closing the door behind him.

"This is two days in a row," I said as I seated myself at the table. "I guess you're plugged into the room service crew," I sighed. "To what do I owe today's pleasure? I just assumed you'd rather be with the rich guy."

"I felt like I owed you an explanation, darlin'," she said in Sophia's voice, but looking at her, I saw Susan behind the make-up. She was trying to communicate something and I couldn't decipher it.

I raised my hand in resignation. "It's okay," I said, keeping my eyes on my food as I cut a bite of the luscious-looking eggs. I couldn't believe how creamy the hollandaise was. "Adam is obviously somebody and I'm not. You're obviously somebody and I'm not. It was fun while it lasted. You don't owe me anything."

She started to reply but didn't. I could tell she wanted me to look at her. Her body language cried out for attention. But the whole business was getting way too complicated for me and I focused on my food as I tasted the first bite. The English muffin was toasted delicately, the Canadian Bacon was tasty, and the egg was poached to perfection. And the hollandaise was fabulous. I would argue that a well-made hollandaise is one of the hallmarks of a good chef. Mixing it is a precise, delicate process, and making it creamy and fluffy, like this hollandaise was, showed real talent.

"So," she said at last, "what did you do on the boat yesterday while Adam was... showing me around."

"Bill and I talked for a while. Then I wandered around the deck and looked around. I got bored. Boats have never been my thing, really."

"Well, Adam showed me this most amazing area of the boat! Did you know they have a room below decks with a door that opens to the ocean?"

I feigned surprise for the cameras and the mics. "Really?" I said. "That's fascinating. What *else* did he show you?"

She blushed slightly and tried to shrug nonchalantly. It didn't work. "He just gave me a complete tour of the boat," she said, as she lifted a bite of eggs to her mouth. "I guess he helped Bill purchase it several weeks ago."

Silence ensued for several minutes as the two of us ate. I found myself entranced by the hollandaise. I could cut myself a nice bit of muffin, Canadian bacon and egg, and then literally pile the sauce on top of it. It was that creamy. Truly amazing stuff.

"I hear you're going back to California today," she said later.

"Adam called and told me that just about an hour ago. I'm leaving right after I finish this delicious breakfast."

"When will you be back?"

"I don't know, exactly."

"Well, hopefully I'll be here. Do you think we could have dinner or something if I am?"

I looked up at her. The deep, expressive brown eyes were twin kaleidoscopes of emotion. Sophia's voice had spoken, but it was Susan asking the question.

"I don't think that would be a good idea," I said coldly.

Her face fell. You would have thought I told her someone died.

"Adam is my boss and you're with him now," I continued. "And like most rich guys, he probably has this thing about his *property*. If I intrude on that, I could lose my job."

She and I both knew that wasn't true but it was a plausible script and she had no choice but to work with it.

"I see," she said. She slowly rose from her chair and collected her purse. She didn't even look at me but kept her eyes on the floor. It was most un-Sophia like. I felt a pang of sympathy for her but the script was the script and we had reached the end of it.

"Maybe I'll see you around?" she asked innocently as she walked to the door.

"Probably not," I said, as I cut myself another slice of the eggs benedict and heaped the wondrous hollandaise on it.

The door clicked shut a few moments later. I spent the next several minutes enjoying a guilt-free breakfast with a guilt-free view.

Two hours later, I was back on the G-IV. The jet had been fueled, the flight plan was filed, the APU was running, and all the navigation systems had been programmed. We were ready for engine start. I sat in the captain's seat in the cockpit and looked toward the FBO's front doors where I expected Adam and company to appear at just about any minute.

Suddenly, the glass doors on the ramp side of the FBO opened and Adam and Felix walked out along with a very well-dressed man who had a familiar face.

Where have I seen this guy before?

Behind them were two more men, both of who were dressed as well as the man who had to be their boss. They moved smoothly and agilely, and they each kept their eyes roaming all over the area around them.

"Bodyguards," I said to myself. "Definitely bodyguards." I stared through the cockpit glass at the man at Adam's side. He appeared to be in his mid-forties and he walked with a gait of supreme confidence. Like he owned the place. *Who the hell are you?* I asked myself as I stared at him.

Bill trailed behind the five men, his eyes focused sightlessly on the ground in front of him. I noticed that the obsequious member of the local constabulary was missing today. I left my seat and made my way down the air-stair as quickly and as smoothly as I could without the cane. I took up my position at the base of the stairs and awaited my passengers like a good Captain.

Adam was the first one to make it to me and his eyes flashed venom as he glanced my way and climbed the stairs. I grinned in spite of myself.

The folks monitoring my room told you Susan came to see me again, didn't they? And you're wondering what I have that you don't.

The two bodyguards stepped in front of their boss quickly and, faster than I could react, they adeptly frisked me. The one on my left turned to the boss, nodded, then practically leapt up the stairs. As the other moved back to assume a position behind his boss, I saw a black, metal object gleaming in a shoulder holster underneath his left arm.

The boss stepped up to the stairs and offered me his hand. He was a few inches shorter than I was but broader—built like an NFL defensive back. The way he moved indicated he was agile despite his size.

"Miguel Hidalgo," he said, watching my face closely.

Son of a bitch! It was everything I could do to control my facial muscles. *What in the hell are you doing here?*

"Welcome aboard, sir," I said, struggling to keep my voice inflectionless.

He smiled at me with a polite look on his face. He had distinctly aristocratic European features but his visage portrayed a life in the elements—a life of work. He was wearing a well-tailored white linen suit that could have been Versace or Armani.

Bill took up the rear and he winked at me as I shook his hand. Then he leaned in close and whispered to me. "I think he must be a new bodyguard for Adam. They're old friends. Adam hugged and kissed him on both cheeks when we greeted him on the boat."

I nodded. A cheek kiss from an Arab man, particularly a member of the royal family, would have been reserved for close friends or those he thought of as near-equals. Or superiors.

"Thanks," I whispered back. "Keep the faith." I didn't know what else to say.

As they all climbed the stairs into the cabin, I did my final walk around the aircraft to make sure once again that all the landing gear safety pins were pulled, there were no fluids leaking from the jet, the wheel chocks had been pulled, and the nose gear was configured correctly. The nose gear was pinned and fastened. We were good to go.

It also gave me some time to get my head together.

I climbed the stairs, and ensured all passengers were aboard. Then I hit the switch to raise the door. The standby hydraulic pump kicked in and the door began to rise.

"You didn't ask if I was ready for you to shut the door," Adam said from the right seat.

Oh boy, I thought. *Here we go.* "Sorry about that, Adam," I said, in just exactly the right 'contract pilot – I'm here to please you' tone of voice. "Is it okay for me to close the door?"

"Yes," Adam replied. "It is."

"Thank you, sir," I said as I locked the closing mechanism into place and verified that the red door warning light had extinguished on the warning lights panel.

I climbed into the left seat and strapped in. Then I donned

my headset. "How do you hear me, Adam?" I asked.

"Loud and clear," he replied.

"You're loud and clear, also." I presented the clipboard which had been stowed behind my seat. "We're cleared back to Van Nuys via the standard routing. Do you have any questions?"

He shook his head.

"Ready for engine start?"

He nodded.

I ran the pre-engine start flow and then punched the start button for the number two engine. The start valve and ignition lights came on and I watched the low-pressure fan spool into positive range and the high pressure fan spool up to about twenty percent. I brought the fuel cock lever up and added fuel to the engine. It started immediately.

"The book says fifteen percent," Adam intoned critically. "Why do you not raise the fuel cock at fifteen percent?"

"Cooler start," I said, ignoring him as the engine stabilized and I began a similar start process for the left engine. "By letting the HP turbine spin up to a higher RPM before adding fuel, I get more airflow through the engine and reduce the odds of a temperature spike during the start process."

"But the book says fifteen percent HP..."

"It says fifteen percent or greater," I corrected him.

The rest of the entire checklist after the start and takeoff was like that. He asked me questions or criticized my entire cockpit routine. It was quite a change from his near silence on the way down here.

After we took off and passed through 10,000 feet in the climb, he excused himself from the cockpit and I breathed a sigh of relief. As we climbed up to cruising altitude and traced the generic route back to Burbank, I enjoyed the solitude of the cockpit and the view of Southern California, which, interestingly enough, was not covered by fog or smog today.

As we passed through 10,000 feet on the descent, Adam

reentered the cockpit and took his position in the right seat.

"I'll be taking this landing," he said, as he donned his headset.

"No problem," I replied. "You have the airplane. We're level at 8,000 feet on a heading of 360 degrees at a speed of 250 knots. The autopilot is flying the airplane. We're with SOCAL approach and we've been told to expect the visual approach to runway 15 at Burbank. ATIS says the sky is clear, visibility seven miles, winds 170 at ten knots, and the altimeters are set to 29.88."

He nodded at me. "My airplane," he said, accepting control of the jet.

SOCAL vectored us to a ten-mile visual final for runway 15. I had the flight management system programmed to give Adam lateral and vertical guidance through the GPS for a visual approach. I asked Adam if he wanted me to call it up on his navigation display, but he refused. That would be arrogant mistake number one. Arrogant mistake number two came when he kicked the autopilot and autothrottles off shortly after we rolled out on final and began to hand-fly the airplane. I wasn't impressed. You show me a guy who insists on hand-flying a large business jet in the terminal area and I'll show you a guy with insecurity issues. The whole point of automation in the cockpit is to reduce the workload on the crew so that they can stay situationally aware of the world around them. The autopilot and autothrottle systems on the G-IV can practically land the airplane by themselves; and while most guys don't let it get anywhere near that close, by programming all the systems to do that, the pilots can stay "heads-up" in the cockpit, looking for errant aircraft or birds or just staying alert for stuff that isn't right. Typically, if I have an approach programmed and it's a clear day, I'll let the autopilot and autothrottles fly the aircraft down to about five hundred feet and then I'll kick them off and take over manually.

But all that was lost on Adam. He was going to show

me what a man he was by hand-flying the aircraft down to landing. After extending the two notches of flaps, he called for me to extend the landing gear, and the airplane slowed to nearly 150 knots before he added power to correct for the additional drag after the gear locked into place. Then he called for full flaps and the jet slowed to 130 knots before he added power—not a good move since our final approach airspeed was 135. We were level at about 2,500 feet—1700 feet above the runway and he didn't begin his descent to the runway until we were well inside five miles to the runway threshold. A standard glideslope or descent angle for landing is about three degrees. That means the aircraft descends three hundred feet vertically for every mile it travels laterally. So at five miles from the runway, the jet should be 1,500 feet above the ground to hit a three degree glide path.

Adam missed that.

So now we were inside of five miles and descending at about four to five degrees with a vertical velocity of about 1,500 feet per minute. The ground proximity warning system was not happy.

"SINK RATE," it warned. "PULL-UP."

At about a mile-and-a-half from the runway, Adam intercepted a normal glide path and added power to hold his airspeed. The problem was that he added too much power. We crossed the threshold of the runway on glide path, but at about thirty knots too fast. Adam pulled the power to idle and lifted the nose to flare for the landing. But, the G-IV was a nice, clean aircraft and it still wanted to fly. Rather than settle to the runway, it began to climb a little. Adam, pushed the nose down slightly and we floated down the runway about three thousand feet without touching down. Runway 15 was 6885 feet long and with 3500 feet left and over 150 knots, there wasn't much time left to be gentle.

"Push the nose over Adam, or go around," I said. "We're about to run out of pavement."

He did nothing. It was like he was frozen at the controls.

"My airplane," I said and slapped his hands off the throttles as I took the yoke with my left hand. I looked at the runway remaining and decided I needed to prove a point. I checked the power in idle, banked very slightly to the right, and applied a little left rudder. This was an aerodynamic maneuver called a "slip" and it dumped lift from the wings. Almost instantly, I felt the right main gear touch down followed by the left main gear a few seconds later. I pulled the reverse thrust levers up immediately and applied maximum brakes - we were still well over 100 knots. The 1,000-foot remaining marker flashed by. The nose came down and the anti-skid braking system and reverse thrust worked as advertised. The jet slowed to taxi speed about 500 feet prior to the end of the runway.

"Gulfstream november three six whisky mike sierra, where are you parking?" the tower asked as we rolled out.

I gave Adam about ten seconds to answer the call. He didn't move. I keyed the mic. "November three six whisky sierra, we need to go to customs first and then to Atlantic."

"Tower copies, turn left at the end and taxi to customs."

"Three six whisky mike sierra copies," I answered. I exhaled loudly with relief. "After landing checks, please Adam," I commanded.

He recovered from his reverie or trance or whatever it was and ran the checklist. By the way he slapped the switches and punched the buttons, his emotional state was evident. After we stopped on the Customs ramp, Adam disappeared into the cabin and Officer Bjellos made his way to our airplane once again.

Surprise, surprise.

He ascended the ladder, checked my passport and pilot's license matter-of-factly, and then vanished into the passenger cabin. After some time back there for the sake of appearances, he exited the passenger cabin, waved at me on the way out the door, and went down the stairs. I didn't notice if his pockets were thicker this time.

"Colin," Adam called from the passenger cabin, "can you taxi us back to Atlantic please?"

"Yes sir," I replied.

I raised the door, started the engines, and did as I was asked.

A few minutes later, after I shut down the engines in front of Atlantic, Adam emerged from the cabin with Bill behind him.

"I'm going to leave one of Miguel's men here to keep you company as you finish your checks of the airplane. Then the two of you can take the limo to the mansion."

I nodded resignedly. I was now, essentially, a prisoner. There weren't going to be any e-mails going out from my BlackBerry for a while. At least not while my "guard" was watching.

"Also, tomorrow, you and I will ride to Van Nuys for a little fun flying."

"Sounds good."

He smirked at me as he went down the stairs, like he was going to enjoy teaching me a lesson or something. I let him enjoy his moment of arrogance. If it had to do with airplanes, I was pretty sure I could kick his ass doing it. Especially after the performance I had just witnessed.

I did my normal interior clean-up routine while my guard sat there and didn't take his eyes off me. There wasn't too much to clean. Then I had an idea.

"I have to check the oil on the engines and perform a quick exterior inspection before we go."

Before he could say anything in reply, I went down the air-stair, found Manny the line guy, and asked for a ladder. I walked around the airplane, making sure the landing gear safety pins were in place and just generally checking the condition of the aircraft. When I returned to the bottom of the air-stair, Miguel's man was there with a rather impatient expression on his face.

"Here you go, Captain Pearce," Manny said, carrying an aluminum ladder over to me. "Just leave it under the wing when you're done and we'll pick it up. Do you have any trash or anything?"

"Nope," I said. "Nothing you can throw away anyway."

He nodded and headed toward another airplane that was taxiing into the ramp area.

I found Miguel's man staring at me with a "is this going to take all day?" expression on his face. I lugged the ladder around to left engine, placed it below the oil gauge access door on the left side of the cowling, and climbed the ladder. The engine had plenty of oil, but I fiddled inside the cowling for a good five minutes, while my guard watched me from the base of the air-stair, in plain sight from the road. I hoped like hell that someone was taking pictures. After a suitable interval, I switched to the right engine and took my time there as well. I felt the BlackBerry on my hip vibrate as I laid the ladder down on the tarmac underneath the wing and resisted the urge to take it off my hip and see why. I returned to the base of the air-stair, trying my best not to drag my left leg, which was really talking to me by this point.

"Do you have anything else you need in the cabin?" I asked my guard.

He shook his head slowly.

"I'm going to go up there and shut everything down and grab my bags. Be right back."

I hobbled up the air-stair, and kept my legs visible from the ground as I shut down the APU and turned off all the remaining systems. Then I turned to the closet to get my things. Out of view for just a few seconds, I checked the BlackBerry.

"GOT HIM" Was the title of the e-mail from Phil Collins. There was no text. I deleted the mail and made my way down the air-stair, bags in hand.

As I reached the bottom, Miguel's man gave me the once-over and motioned toward a limo which had just pulled out onto the ramp. I activated the switch to shut the G-IV's door and when the door was closed, I pushed the latch into place and locked the door.

The driver took my bags and placed them in the trunk as I slid into the limo's rear seat and Miguel's man slid in and took the seat across from me. We were heading out of the airport a few moments later and we turned west onto Sherman way, toward the 405 freeway. Once we reached the 405, I knew we would head south to Beverly Hills and Bel Air. Any other time, to be an invited guest at the Bachelor Magazine Mansion would have been the realization of a dream for your average American male. But at this moment, I was dreading it.

TOP SECRET/SPECIAL
COMPARTMENTALIZED INFORMATION
CLASSIFIED BY: US Central Intelligence Agency
DECLASSIFY ON: OADR

From: Special Projects Group [NCS]
Sent: Saturday, 21 November 2009, 1500 PST (21
November 2009, 2300Z)
To: Director, NCS
Cc: Special Projects Group [NCS]; damrine@cmail.cia.gov;
dsmith3@cmail.cia.gov

SUBJECT: Aircraft Movement Summary and Update –
Gulfstream G-IVSP N36WMS

(TS) Narrative:

1. (TS) N36WMS departed MMSD (Los Cabos International
Airport) at 1207 PST / 2007 Z and landed at KBUR (Burbank/
Bob Hope Airport) at 1410 PST / 2210 Z.

2. (TS) Those on board included Contractor 09-017 (Pearce,
Colin M), Abdullah bin Rashid al Qudamah, aka Adam
Archmere, Saif-al Din, aka Felix Lopez, William Spratt, Miguel
Hidalgo, and two of Hidalgo's bodyguards, Jose Rodriguez
and Alejandro Garza.

3. (TS) Intel provided by Pearce and OO Susan Turner has
revealed the following:

   a. (TS) Al Qudamah the elder and Hidalgo appear to have
   a working relationship and are jointly planning some sort
   of action against the United States;
   b. (TS) Initial indications are that the action will occur

on Thanksgiving Day;

c. (TS) Spratt's yacht, Bachelor's Toy, a Palmer Johnson PJ210, has been commandeered by al Qudamah and appears to be taking on personnel and cargo while at sea via a door assembly on the bottom of the hull. Numbers of personnel and types of equipment are currently unknown. *Note*: al Qudamah shipping does, in fact, possess a conventionally powered submarine which would enable this mechanism;

e. (TS) G-IVSP N36WMS has transported two persons of interest to the US from Mexico. Spratt has indicated at least one of these persons was a "special doctor." He mentioned that the last package brought into the United States needed to be kept extremely cold, which could suggest a possible cryogenic storage cell for biological weapons. He also indicated that "many men" and "many guns" had been brought about the yacht;

f. (TS) It is possible that the genesis of this operation dates back well over a year. Pearce believes that Sarah Morton Marciano's husband is not legitimate and lured her to marry him so that he could control the flight department to prepare for this operation. In a previous audio surveillance clip obtained prior to this trip, al Qudamah indicates that the planning for this operation did in fact extend back nearly two years so Pearce's suspicions may be correct.

(TS) CONCLUSIONS:

1. (TS) It is now apparent that the operation underway has been planned for some time. We believe an attack using a weapon of mass-destruction is planned to take place on or about Thanksgiving Day at a large outdoor venue. Possible targets may include football stadiums where games are scheduled in the Southwest US. The target with highest visibility is Candlestick Park where the San Francisco 49ers are scheduled to play the Green Bay Packers on Thanksgiving Day. Due to

the focus on the use of the Gulfstream G-IVSP N36WMS, it is apparent that some sort of aerial dispersal is planned, suggesting a chemical or biological agent.

2. (TS). We are in the process of building a detailed timeline of the chronology of this operation for your review but the basic outline is as follows:

a. (TS) May 2008: Damian Marciano begins dating Sarah Morton (unconfirmed link);
b. (TS) November 2008: Damian Marciano and Sarah Morton are married (unconfirmed link);
c. (TS) March 2009: Abdullah al Qudamah observed meeting with suspected associates of Miguel Hidalgo in Oman when weapons shipment hijacked (suspected link);
d. (TS) 28 September to 2 October 2009: Dubai Yacht Show (confirmed);
e. (TS) 2 October 2009: Spratt purchases Bachelor's Toy (confirmed), Damian Marciano and Shelly Spratt abducted (suspected);
f. (TS) 30 October 2009: Bachelor's Toy arrives at Cabo San Lucas and Gulfstream G-IVSP N36WMS arrives at Cabo San Lucas (Trip 1) (confirmed);
g. (TS) 2 November 2009: Gulfstream G-IVSP N36WMS returns to Burbank; those aboard include Sarah Marciano, al Qudamah (Archmere), Spratt and al Din (Lopez) according to CBP records (confirmed);
h. (TS) 4 to 9 November 2009: Gulfstream G-IVSP N36WMS makes second trip to Cabo San Lucas and back; those aboard include Sarah Marciano, al Qudamah (Archmere), Spratt and al Din (Lopez) according to CBP records (confirmed);
i. (TS) NOTE: According to information Pearce obtained from Spratt, the two additional personnel mentioned in paragraph D above were also transported during either

trip one or trip two. This could indicate that CBP records are unreliable. The CBP officer on duty for all arrivals of Gulfstream G-IVSP N36WMS was D. Bjellos. We have placed him under surveillance but he has not yet been apprehended (unconfirmed);

j. (TS) 12 November 2009: Gulfstream G-IVSP N36WMS makes another trip to Cabo San Lucas (confirmed);

k. (TS) 14 November 2009: Gulfstream G-IVSP N36WMS returns to Burbank with only al Qudamah (Archmere) and Sarah Marciano aboard (confirmed);

l. (TS) 16 November: Sarah Marciano makes contact with Pearce, Pearce hired as contract pilot (confirmed);

m. (TS) 17 November 2009: Pearce travels to Burbank (confirmed);

n. (TS) 18 November: Gulfstream G-IVSP N36WMS makes round trip from Burbank to Cabo San Lucas and back to Burbank. Those aboard on the return trip include Pearce, Sarah Marciano, al Qudamah (Archmere), Spratt and al Din (Lopez) according to CBP records; Pearce provided video footage to prove that a third, unnamed passenger also traveled who is not listed on the CBP passenger list (confirmed);

o. (TS) 19 November 2009: Gulfstream G-IVSP N36WMS travels to Cabo San Lucas; Pearce meets with OO Turner and Turner makes contact with al Qudamah (confirmed);

p. (TS) 21 November 2009: Gulfstream G-IVSP N36WMS returns to Burbank; see passenger list above.

(TS) ACTIONS:

1. (TS) Cross agency team still brainstorming additional possible targets, delivery mechanisms and counter action;

2. (TS) Surveillance assets now in place to monitor Bachelor Magazine mansion (off site) and at the Hotel Imperial del

Cabo (on site) to collect intelligence;

3. (TS) Place E-3 AWACS aircraft on alert to deploy to March AFB pending further confirmation of the threat;

4. (U) Will have slides ready for your meeting with DCI tomorrow AM.

(TS) RECOMMENDATIONS: Request E-3 AWACS aircraft be placed on alert immediately.

TOP SECRET / SPECIAL
COMPARTMENTALIZED INFORMATION
CLASSIFIED BY: US Central Intelligence Agency
DECLASSIFY ON: OADR

CHAPTER ELEVEN

Contract Day Five
Saturday, 21 November
1530 Hours Local Time
Bachelor Magazine Mansion
Los Angeles, California, United States

The limo pulled through the brick-pillared gate about forty-five minutes later, drove down a long asphalt driveway between two imposing rows of trees, and then entered an expansive parking area in front of the large mansion with the commanding brick frontage that had been featured on so many magazine covers. The brown masonry building towered above, with a roof that shifted from high gables on one side to the half-turret of a castle on the other, complete with niches in the top of the wall which could have allowed archers a clear shot of those at the front door. The thin, rectangular, metal-paned glass windows completed the facade and I had flashbacks to the 60's TV Show "Batman" and the scenes of the front of "Stately Wayne Manor" that were often presented before cutting to the interior shots.

It felt completely surreal.

I exited the limo with my jaws agape, looking at the house with a sense of wonderment. The driver retrieved my luggage from the trunk and stacked the computer bag on top of the suitcase before presenting it to me. I took the plastic handle and made my way toward the front entrance, double glass doors under a brick archway. The doors opened as I reached them and a professionally-dressed young woman stepped back and allowed me to enter. As she shut the door behind me, I noticed that the driver and Miguel's man had disappeared along with the car, obviously enroute to somewhere else on the grounds.

"Hmmm," I said aloud unconsciously.

"Good afternoon, Mr. Pearce," the young woman said brightly with a slight trace of a southern accent. "I'm Natalie. I'm playing receptionist today. Bill told us you'd be along. He asked me to look after you."

"Most considerate of him," I said nodding.

Natalie was brunette and had the flawless complexion of a twenty-something who had taken great care of her skin. She was dressed in a maroon business suit, complete with skirt and high heels.

"Your room is upstairs. I presume you'll want to freshen up before dinner?"

"Dinner?" I asked.

"Yes," she replied, leading me from the tiled foyer into a wooden beamed great room and toward a large staircase at the end of it. "Bill told me to have dinner prepared at seven for all his guests, including you and Sarah."

"How's Sarah doing?"

"Great," Natalie said, smiling genuinely. "We're all so excited! We can't wait to be aunts!"

"We?"

"Oh, sorry!" she said as we reached the base of the stairs. "I guess I just assume everyone knows who lives here. There are twenty of us who live here at the mansion. Former Monthly Mistresses all. Bill tells us there's always a place here for us if we want it. A lot of us like it here so much we just never leave."

I nodded, thinking more highly of Mr. Spratt by the moment.

I removed the computer bag from the roller bag handle and began to negotiate the stairs. My left leg was not happy. And now, of all things, my left shoulder was beginning to ache. Since I had come to California, I hadn't noticed pain from the shoulder wound much. But it seemed that my luck had run out.

Natalie must have noticed my hesitation. "Let me help you with those," she said and before I could protest, she took my roller bag and computer bag and effortlessly ascended the stairs in front of me.

I shook my head, disgusted with my helplessness, and followed her, not even bothering to regard her posterior in the process as I negotiated the stairs with my cane.

"Sorry about that," I said as I joined her at the top of the stairs, "I had an injury a few weeks ago and it's still bothering me. I guess as should feel guilty about a girl carrying my bags, but right now all I feel is grateful."

"No worries," she said smiling. "Body building is one of my hobbies. These were no bother at all. Let me show you to your room."

As she turned to lead me down the long, carpeted hallway, I inspected her calves for the first time. The mark of someone who is seriously into bodybuilding is the degree to which they train the smaller muscles. Natalie's calves could have been sculpted out of marble. They were distinctly feminine but highly defined - the product of several thousand sets on the calf machine.

Shit, I thought. *She can probably lift more than I can.*

"Here we are," she said, as she reached an alcove down on the left. "Bill put you up in one of the guest suites." As I arrived at her side, she already had the double doors of the entry opened. I slowly walked into the room.

"Wow," I said involuntarily, "I wonder what I did to deserve this."

"Bill and Sarah think really highly of you," Natalie said. "And if they like you, we like you."

"Good to know," I said.

"Do you need me to show you around the room?"

"Sure. If it's not too much trouble."

"No problem at all. This is the reception room. You have a full view of the back grounds from the windows and you can even see the pool from here. The fireplace is gas, so just flip a switch on the remote and you'll have instant fire. Obviously, that's a desk next to the window. There's an Internet hook-up there and instructions if you'd rather go wireless, along with a phone and a printer/copier/fax machine. The books on the shelves are part of Bill's private collection. Feel free to look through them and read them."

"The wood in this room is fantastic!" I said, examining the shelves, the crown molding, and the flooring.

"It was just redone last year," Natalie said. "Bill had the whole place renovated at Shelly's recommendation."

"Well, Shelly has good taste. "

"Yes, she does," Natalie said thoughtfully. "I sure hope she gets done with her business in Dubai soon. We miss her around here."

I nodded to myself again. My suspicions were confirmed. No one here had any clue at all about what was happening.

"I take it she runs things? I only know what I've read."

"It's more than that," Natalie replied, almost in a whisper. "Bill's lost without her. The whole father-daughter bond with them is so strong. He's definitely not himself when she's not around."

"You know that the papers sometimes carry it further than that."

She snorted.

"They don't know anything. Bill has girlfriends and Shelly has boyfriends. But the two of them are all the other has from a family perspective and since Bill gave the reins of the company to Shelly, Bachelor Magazine has done extremely well."

"Okay, so I have to ask the question that everyone else asks."

"How can we allow ourselves to be exploited?"

I nodded.

"No one comes through the front door of this place in chains," she said. "And no one is forced to pose for the magazine. Bill takes great care of us and is incredibly supportive when we want to go on and do other things. He's paying the tuition for several of the girls here to get graduate degrees, me included. He has a heart of gold and for many of us, he's the protective father figure we never had."

I nodded again. "What are you studying?"

"Medicine," she said. "I attend the Geffen School of Medicine at UCLA. Another former Monthly Mistress is the head Orthopedic Surgeon at the UCLA Medical Center."

"Wow," I said respectfully. "Do you have a specialty picked out?"

"OB GYN," she said. "It's the women-helping-women thing."

"Outstanding," I said.

"And I'm not the only one here," she continued. "Teresa is attending med school as well. We have several other girls getting advanced degrees."

I smiled and shook my head.

"What?"

I looked at her. "It just goes to show that stereotypes can be dangerous."

She nodded back at me. "Oh yeah," she said. "People see the looks and the bodies and they assume there is no ambition or brains to match."

"I flew with Julie Way a few years ago when I met Sarah. She was on the verge of getting her masters in physics."

"She's busy on her doctorate now and she's working in the Jet Propulsion Lab in Pasadena."

"Good for her," I said approvingly.

"I take it you're not threatened by strong women."

"Some of the strongest people I've ever met in my life were women," I answered.

Natalie reached out reflexively and touched my arm. "Sarah has good taste," she said.

"Thanks," I replied.

"Okay, so moving on with the tour, there is a wet bar over here that is pretty well stocked and through here is the bedroom." She led me through another double door and into a large bedroom complete with a king-sized bed, a chaise lounge, and yet another desk. "And the bathroom is through there. You'll find a full double shower, Jacuzzi tub, and the other normal things."

"Great. Thanks. What time is dinner again?"

"Seven o'clock. This place is huge so I'll ask Sarah if she can come by and lead you to the dining room."

"There's no need for that, I can go by her room."

Natalie shook her head and smiled back at me. "She's all the way over in the east wing, the girls' wing. You'd get lost going that way. Besides, I'm sure she'd want to take you down herself."

"Okay. That's fine then."

"She'll be by sometime before seven. See you at dinner!"

"Sure thing, Natalie. And thanks for the help."

She smiled at me again and marched out of the room, her long, muscled legs carrying her away. I heard the door click shut in the outer room and remembered that I hadn't asked Natalie for the dress code for dinner. I decided I'd wear dress slacks, shirt, and shoes and hope for the best.

I gazed at the clock on the nightstand and found myself yawning. 3:45 P.M. I had time for a nap before dinner. I removed my coat and shoes and lay down on the soft, down comforter. I was asleep in seconds.

"Hey, sleepyhead! You've got to wake up! It's dinner time!"

Sarah was calling me, which was didn't make sense because

she was standing right in front of me in a black bikini, holding a baby. And there were two guys standing behind her. One was Adam and the other was...her husband. Had to be. But I couldn't make out his face. It was obscured by a red and white checkered keffiyeh.

Why was Adam with him?

My eyes shot open and for just a second or two I forgot where I was. Sarah was standing over me and she was in a modest lavender maternity dress. As I came to, I had the most distinct sensation of something important escaping my consciousness, like a bird flying out a window.

"Damn!" I said unconsciously.

"What?"

"Uh, nothing," I stammered. "What time is it?"

"Almost seven."

"Wow. I must have really conked out."

"I guess. When did you get here?"

"Three-thirty-ish. Didn't Natalie tell you?"

She nodded. "I got the word you were here while I was getting my massage. I don't remember exactly when that was."

I sat up slowly. "Massage. Must be nice."

"Well, it was until Adam interrupted it." Then she put her hands on her hips. "So, who is this Sophia Monachelli?"

I shut my eyes and grimaced. *Now how in the hell? Adam! Goddamn it.* "A nice lady I met in Cabo. She took quite a liking to me until Adam decided he wanted her."

Her face took on a perplexed expression. This obviously wasn't the version she had heard. She began to open her mouth to speak and I jumped out of bed, grabbed my BlackBerry, and began to type while I created a show of looking through several menus.

"Let me show you a picture of her. I know it's in here somewhere. She was quite a dish. Here. Take a look."

She looked down at the words I typed.

"THIS ROOM IS PROBABLY BUGGED. TV & MIC."

She was good. I had to give her that. Her expression only changed slightly.

"Well," she said, in a voice that was trying to stay impersonal and not quite managing. "I'm glad you were able to have some fun down there without me."

"It started well. Until Adam showed us around Bill's yacht. He swept her away and I never saw her again. Oh well. Easy come, easy go."

"We need to get to dinner or we'll be late."

"Would you mind excusing me so I can change?"

"Why? What you're wearing is fine."

I still had my navy blue slacks and white shirt on.

"I feel a little wrinkled. Just give me a minute or two."

She nodded. "Okay."

I went into the outer room and retrieved my roller bag. Sarah followed me and took a seat on one of the overstuffed lounge chairs next to the fireplace. She had the oddest expression on her face.

I returned to the bedroom and changed shirts quickly, combed my hair, and splashed a little cologne on. I hoped that would be enough. As I hurried into the main room, I caught my right foot on the door frame and tripped. Instinctively, I transferred all my weight to my left leg to retain my balance and a spasm of pain shot through my leg like several-thousand volts of electric current.

"Holy fucking shit!" The words flew out of my mouth before I even knew I had said them. I threw myself against the back of the nearest sofa and took my weight off the leg. "Goddamn it!"

"What's wrong?" Instantly, Sarah was on her feet.

"My cane!" I said through clenched teeth. "I left it in the bedroom. Can you get it, please?"

She whisked by me, almost like a lavender blur; and before I knew it, the cane was in my left hand. "Are you okay to walk?" she asked.

"I have to be," I answered. "Let's go."

"Colin, dinner isn't that important. If you'd prefer to have us bring you something up here we can do that."

I shook my head vigorously.

"Well, all right."

She took my right arm and led me to the door, opening it to let me pass through first. After I did, she closed it behind me. I took a few more steps down the hall and then leaned against one of the walls.

"God," I whispered, "I so did not want them to see that!"

"Do you really think the room is bugged?" Sarah was beside me.

"It would make sense," I answered as I tried to get my breath under control. "My room in Cabo was bugged." I looked over at her. "Sophia Monachelli is the cover for Susan Turner who is a CIA agent sent to Cabo to get close to Adam. She had met Adam before using the same disguise in a previous operation and she knew he was into her. I was just the guy chosen to play the spurned lover so Adam could be quite the man and steal her away from me. It was all part of an act."

"Poor baby," she said with a sardonic smile on her face. "So how real was the acting?"

"Real enough to fool Adam," I said. "And it felt weirder than shit."

"So, I hear about you and this woman in Cabo and I get positively jealous. Now what's that about?"

I laughed and extended my arms to her. She came willingly and nestled against me.

"If you only knew," I whispered to her. "If it's any consolation, act or no act, the whole thing with Susan just felt wrong to me."

"Really?" She looked up at me. "And why was that pray tell?"

I looked down at her and kissed the top of her forehead.

"Because I came here for you."

She rested her head against my chest.

"You don't know how many times I almost called you," she said.

"Now you're just trying to make me feel better," I said. "I'm sure you were swimming in a sea of eligible suitors after I left three years ago. At least until numb-nuts came along."

She giggled and we began to walk down the hall again.

"Not so much," she said after a moment. "The time you and I had together left a mark on me. You were a hard act to follow."

I looked at her with an inquisitive look on my face.

"There was no bullshit with you," she said, answering my unspoken question. "You are who you are and you don't hide it. And you don't place expectations on anyone else. You have no idea how refreshing that is. And how rare."

I felt the wave of emotion again. I had heard nearly the same words from Samantha, the woman who had died in my arms, just a few weeks ago. Once again, I could sense the door that she had opened in my heart; the door that Sarah had walked through.

I owe you, Sammy.

"Did I say something wrong?"

I didn't realize I had stopped walking.

"No. Not at all."

"What?" I looked at her face and the hazel eyes sparkled at me in affectionate curiosity.

"I'll tell you someday," I said. "When all this is over."

"I'll hold you to it," she whispered, looking into my eyes.

"Of that I have no doubt." I offered her my right arm and we continued our walk to the stairs. "In the meantime, we have this whole *husband* thing to deal with."

She sighed loudly.

"Yes, we do," she said, as she looked down at her belly and gently rubbed it. "But once all this is over, I've got something to tell you about the *whole* pregnancy thing." She looked over at me, her arms went around me again and she hugged me tightly. Then she took my arm and we headed for the stairs.

Hmmmm, I found myself wondering yet again.

I hobbled down the stairs with her and she led me into the grand dining room. I wasn't prepared for what I saw. There, seated around the long wooden table, were more breathtakingly beautiful young women than I had ever seen in one place in my life. It's one thing to be in the presence of one or two beautiful women, but to suddenly find oneself in a sea of them is another experience entirely.

Bill smiled at me from the head of the table and I noticed Adam sitting immediately to his left. Miguel Hidalgo was nowhere to be seen.

Interesting.

"Welcome, Colin. Welcome. Sarah my dear, would you do the honors?"

"Certainly, Bill," Sarah said brightly. "This ladies, is Colin Pearce. He's flying our G-IV while I'm," she rubbed her belly, "a little too stout to fit in the cockpit."

"You look very familiar!" the nearest girl said. She was a darkly-tanned blonde with a mouthful of supremely-white teeth. "Have you flown with us before?"

"Yes, he has," Sarah said. "A few years ago. You may remember him."

"Hmm," the girl said. "I thought I had seen him somewhere else."

"Me too," another girl further down the table said.

"I get that a lot," I said quickly. But not quickly enough. At the end of the table, I saw Adam's chin incline slightly. Like an important connection had been made in his mind.

Oh Shit, I thought.

"Well, introduce us, Sarah!" another voice feminine voice said from the other side of the table.

Sarah did so and I rapidly learned the names of the women and just as promptly forgot them. They didn't care. As a novelty, I was rewarded with their full attention while we ate a fantastic dinner of blackened swordfish, fresh asparagus, and a delightful Sauvignon Blanc. The girls peppered me with questions. They were fascinated to hear that I flew fighters in the Air Force and even more fascinated to hear the story about how I was shot down in the first Gulf War. I didn't tell them the part about being captured and how I obtained my subsequent freedom. One of them, a gorgeous African-American named Shauna, was attending Cal Tech and majoring in Aeronautical Engineering. She began to ask questions about the aerodynamic principles of dogfighting, a subject I loved to discuss.

After some back and forth there, the conversation turned to corporate flying and the girls wanted to know all about who I had flown and where I had taken them. Without betraying any of the confidentiality agreements I had signed over the years, I gave them a peek into the world of celebrities and private jets. It wasn't really that fascinating, but they ate it up and the questions continued through dessert.

From time to time, I glanced toward the head of the table. Bill's eyes were always elsewhere, and the expression on his face was akin to a frown, like there was something going on that he didn't approve of. Adam's gaze also never met mine, but his expression conveyed something else. He looked supremely pleased with himself and struggled to keep the trace of a smirk off his face.

And then suddenly it hit me. I was being interrogated. The ladies had no idea they were playing that role, but their questions were just as effective nonetheless. I was no stranger to interrogation methodologies and the means to resist them, but this technique was brilliant. I was forced into telling the truth because it wouldn't make sense for me to lie and because the facts were easily verifiable.

Goddamn it.

For the questions the girls didn't ask, Adam had enough information to find out the rest of what he needed to know from other sources. As dinner was cleared and we migrated to the lounge area, Adam disappeared. I didn't know where he was going, but I knew what he'd be doing. By the end of the night, he'd know everything he needed to know about me.

Except, hopefully, my exploits of a few weeks ago.

I gave the girls my attention for the next few hours and even got to the point where I could remember their names. Sarah stayed at my side and I couldn't decide if she was there to help me with them or protect me from them. But my mind wasn't there anyway.

Instead, I was thinking about how thoroughly I'd been outmaneuvered and wondering what it might cost.

Chapter Twelve

Contract Day Six
Sunday, 22 November
1000 Hours Local Time
On the 405 Freeway
San Fernando, California, United States

About twelve hours later, I found myself back in the limo again, and this time it was just Adam and me. It was Sunday morning and the normally heavy traffic on the 405 freeway had abated. We were driving to Van Nuys Airport for Adam's "surprise." There was no conversation. Adam spent his time reading the *Los Angeles Times* or looking out the window; and since I didn't have a newspaper to read, I just watched the world go by. California may have nutty politics and taxes that are out of control, but it sure is a beautiful place when you can see it through the smog. I gazed at the treed hills in the foreground and the rocky peaks of the mountains beyond. Up beyond those mountains lay the high desert of California, the sight of the fight of my life a few weeks ago. It seemed like a million miles away and a lifetime in the past.

And then my thoughts turned to the previous night.

##

Sarah escorted me back to my room and instead of leaving me outside the door, she came inside, commanded me to sit on the sofa closest to the fireplace, turned on the gas log, and activated some soft, New Age music at a very low volume. I could hear the strains of Enya floating into the air. I smiled.

"What?" Sarah asked as she returned from the sidebar with a glass of single malt Scotch—Talisker, in fact—and placed it on the lamp table next to my arm.

"Every time I hear Enya, all I can think of is that she's the only woman I've ever thought about marrying because of her voice."

She laughed softly, and then exhaled like she was impatient. "Men," she teased. "You never know what they want."

I smiled back, but my eyes were on the fire. "That's because often we don't know," I said.

"Well, I know what I want," Sarah said decisively as she kicked her shoes off.

I looked up at her. "What's that?"

"I want somebody to snuggle up with for a few minutes. Are you okay with that?"

I rolled my eyes around the room to warn her about possible surveillance, but the way she had her jaw set, it was clear she didn't care. So, I smiled at her and she smiled back. She was just so beautiful. Her hazel eyes gleamed in the firelight and the blonde, silken hair gently reflected the illumination as well. The high cheek bones framed the corners of her mouth, and her lips looked moist and appealing. I let my eyes go lower and saw the swell of her swollen breasts and curve of her pregnant belly. I shook my head in wonder.

"What are you thinking?" she asked, as if she was afraid to hear the answer.

"I always thought that the whole 'glowing' thing about pregnant women was a myth," I said. "But you look even more lovely pregnant than I remembered you."

"Are you good for my ego!" she laughed.

"I'm serious," I said, looking up at her. "Bill should do a pictorial on you like this." I raised my right hand slowly and moved it toward her stomach. "Can I touch you?"

She responded by gently taking hold of my hand and placing it on her belly. I was totally unprepared for what I felt. Her belly was hard and soft at the same time. The skin was taut but elastic and it was like I could feel the life inside.

I looked up at her in awe. "That's unbelievable."

"You need to do it skin-to-skin," she said. Then she stepped back and began unbuttoning the back of her dress. "As you know, I never did like clothes," she said. "And it's not like you haven't seen me before. But," she looked me dead in the eyes. "No comments about the granny panties."

I laughed. "I promise."

The dress came over her head and she stood there in her underwear as if she was trying to make a decision. Then the decision was made and the bra and panties came off. She stepped forward again. "If you're going to see, you may as well see it all."

I'm not sure I have the words to describe how perfect she looked. I had never seen a nude pregnant woman in person before, and the sight of her in this state was almost more than I could take in. Her figure was a little more rounded than I remembered it but looked more appealing that way, not less. Her breasts were definitely larger than I recalled and they rested against her chest a little instead of jutting out like they used to, but that fit somehow. It just looked right. I followed the curve of her belly downward and my eyes were naturally drawn to her genitals, which I noticed were clean shaven, presumably to not clash with her new hair color. Overall, she looked like the very embodiment of femininity. It was an intensely sensual image, but not a sexual one.

"Wow," I said unconsciously, my throat dry.

"Well, I guess that's a good thing to hear," she said.

I looked up at her as I raised my hands to her belly. "You

look magnificent," I said. The skin under my hands was warm and smooth to the touch, and I swore I could feel the muscle in her uterus below my fingers.

And then I felt something bump into my hands from beneath her skin.

It should have startled me, but it didn't. Instead, I put both of my hands on the spot and immediately felt another bump.

"Oh my God, Sarah," I looked up at her in wonder, "he's kicking!"

She looked down at me with a tender smile on her beautiful features. Her eyes were shiny. "I don't know if it's a he or a she," she said with a slight crack in her voice.

"Oh," I said, still lost in the moment, "in that case, I hope it's a she. The world would be a doubly better place with two of you in it."

She literally threw herself into my arms. I fell back against the sofa and she turned her body so that her ass was in my lap. She wrapped her arms around me and buried her face at the base of my neck and clung to me like we were the last two people left in the world.

And she cried. At first, I could just feel the spasmodic bursts of her breath on my neck, but then her body began to shake and the breathing came in rapid fire bursts on my skin. And I could feel the wetness of her tears running down the side of my neck.

"What's the matter, Sarah?" I asked softly, even though I thought I knew the answer.

"There's just so much shit!" she sobbed. "I've messed everything up. Damian used me and I let him. Then after I did what he wanted me to do and got pregnant, he wouldn't look at me or touch me. I mean, I wasn't sure I even wanted him to, but it just crushed any self-esteem I had left. It was like he thought I was sub-human or something. Like he thought I was, I was... dirty!" She wailed the last word as she buried her head even further into the base of my neck.

I sat there and held her and felt the familiar fire rising inside of me. *He's definitely a Muslim. I am so tired of being right.* "Then with all due respect, he's obviously an idiot," I said in the most restrained voice I could muster. "But I think you already know that."

She laughed at that and the tears began to subside. I stroked her face with my hand and lowered my lips to hers. Her mouth rose to meet mine and our lips met and we kissed each other for a long time, not with passion but with something deeper. There was no frantic tongue probing or changes in the positions of our mouths. Instead, I poured everything I could into her to validate who and what I thought she was without stretching the bounds of propriety any further than they had already been. She drank it in slowly and gratefully, and when our lips parted, she placed her head back on my shoulder. I found myself marveling at how fulfilling a kiss could be. Especially in light of the last couple of days.

"Can you reach that blanket by my feet?" she asked. "I'm a little cold."

I reached out and retrieved the blanket. It was made of light, soft wool with an intricate design. I couldn't tell exactly what colors were woven into the fabric in the dim light. I spread the blanket over her, over us, actually. As I did that she inserted one of her hands in the gap between the cushion and the side of the sofa. Almost immediately, the sofa reclined into a nearly horizontal position.

"Do you mind if I sleep here for a while?" she asked. "I'm so tired of sleeping alone." Without waiting for an answer, she snuggled in to me and in moments, she was breathing evenly.

It's amazing how certain moments in life can just feel "right" regardless of the circumstances around them. I gazed down at her beautiful face and gently swept a few strands of hair off her cheek so I could see her more completely. She was nearly young enough to be my daughter, but not quite. But my feelings at that moment were more those of a father than a former lover. I wanted to protect her. I wanted her to be happy. I wanted her to be able to raise her son or daughter in a place where he or she could thrive.

"You were so worth the trip," I said to her angelic, sleeping face. Then I looked over at my cane, leaning against the end table where I had left it, and I thought about her husband. The rage was alive inside me. And I welcomed it.

"So, did you *sleep* well?" Adam's voice had just enough emphasis in it that we both knew what he was talking about.

"I did," I replied brightly, looking him right in the eye. "Like a baby. Amazing what a night of good rest in the right environment can do for your attitude."

The limo had turned off Sherman Way and north on Hayvenhurst Avenue. A few minutes later we reached a gate with a very business-like guard standing next to it. Adam lowered the window and held up a driver's license as we approached.

"Mr. Archmere to see Mr. Rose. I have an appointment."

The guard looked at his clipboard and nodded. "Do you know where the hangar is?" he asked.

"Three down on the right," Adam replied.

The guard nodded again. "The one with the Rose Aircraft sign on it. You can't miss it."

"Thank you," Adam said dismissively, raising his window.

Rose Aircraft. Probably the only place in the United States that renovated and sold ex-USAF T-38 and F-5 aircraft. They also provided jets to Hollywood productions and occasionally even to celebrities who felt "the need for speed." I suddenly knew what this was about.

The limo pulled up outside the main entrance on the street side of the hangar and we exited. An older man with grey hair and trim build in a subdued blue flight suit was waiting by the door to greet us.

"Mr. Archmere," the older gentleman said as Adam emerged from his side of the car, "I'm Chuck Rose, very nice to meet you."

Adam shook his hand and he must have flipped on an internal switch because he was suddenly Mr. Charming. "Hello, Mr. Rose, thank you so much for making your services available on a Sunday."

"Well, quite frankly, Mr. Archmere, the fee you offered was exceedingly generous. How could we not be available to you?"

Adam smiled in a way that was both gracious and condescending at the same time. I wondered if it was something he was taught in "Prince School." He turned and gestured toward me. "This is Colin Pearce. He's my contract pilot in the G-IV, but he's got over 2,000 hours in the A-10, another 2,000 hours in the F-16, and is a USAF Fighter Weapons School graduate in both jets." His eyes gleamed at me in triumph as he said the words. He had indeed done his homework.

Great.

Chuck Rose turned toward me and offered me a respectful nod. "Well, between Mr. Pearce's expertise in the F-16 and yours in the F-15 and F-5 while you were in the Royal Saudi Air Force, Mr. Archmere, this should be a fun hop for both of you this morning."

I produced the appropriate expression of surprise at Rose's announcement and inclined my head toward Adam.

Adam kept his smile in place but his eyes were alive with hunger. He had something to prove today. I kept my face neutral and mentally wrestled with the proper response. Should I let him thoroughly kick my ass up there? Should I put up a token resistance and then allow him to win? But the internal battle was over before it even began. I knew I'd fight him the way I always fought, balls to the wall and no holds barred.

Rose motioned us through the door of the building and we

soon found ourselves in a flight briefing room that inspired flashbacks to my USAF career and to the events of a few weeks ago. There was a white board, several framed posters of airspace diagrams and training rules, and a large LCD monitor with a Powerpoint presentation called up on it. The title slide had the logo for the Rose Aircraft Corporation on it and beneath it had been customized for us.

"Welcome Arrow and T.C.," it said.

"Colonel Archmere, or may I call you Arrow?" A tall, slim man with short, blond hair and a mustache extended his hand to Adam. "I'm Bill Henson; I go by 'Brace.'"

Adam shook his hand in a restrained fashion, like he was dealing with a lower form of life. "You may, Brace."

The blond man turned to me and regarded me thoughtfully. "And you must be T.C."

I could feel Adam's eyes on me as I accepted his hand.

"I am," I said flatly.

Brace nodded. Apparently, he knew the story behind the name. "This is your pilot." He motioned to his left where there was another tall guy with black, graying hair. "Bob Kesterman," he said, extending his hand to me. "You can call me Roo."

"Weren't we at Luke together?" I asked him as we shook hands.

He laughed. "I wondered where I had heard your name and handle before. Thanks for waking up the neurons. We were. I was the ops officer and commander of the 62nd while I was there."

"I was over in the 310th. I knew your ops officer when you were promoted to squadron commander. Broyhill, I think his name was. He flew with us for a while. Pretty sharp guy."

Kesterman nodded. "Best ops officer on the base. I signed the OPR that said that."

Introductions among fighter pilots were always about mutual acquaintances. It let you size the other guy up based on who he knows. Crude, but effective. I knew a lot about Kesterman because of what Broyhill had told me about him. "Outstanding commander," my friend had said. "And a superlative aviator." My opinion of him was already very high.

"So, you'll have to tell me where TC comes from," Adam said in his best imitation of a friendly voice. It didn't come out so well.

I'd like to show you, I thought. *And that time may come.* "Between putting me up at the best hotel in Cabo and the Bachelor Magazine mansion, you're well on your way to effectively bribing me," I answered, smiling.

Adam smiled back half-heartedly. His eyes were narrow slits.

"Shall we brief?" Brace asked.

"I'll leave you to it," Chuck Rose said. "See you at the ops desk for the step brief." He shut the door behind him. Adam sat down at the head of the rectangular table in the room. Roo and I sat on the adjoining side.

Brace nodded and began his pre-flight briefing. The graphics in his presentation were excellent, but mostly geared to an audience that didn't have the expertise Adam and I did. Brace quickly covered start, taxi, takeoff, the departure procedure that would take us to the airspace over Edwards Air Force Base, and then he covered the recovery, landing, and taxi back to the facility. In a fighter briefing, we call this "the motherhood."

Then Brace went into "the meat of the mission," BFM or basic fighter maneuvers, the USAF's term for one versus one aerial combat or "dogfighting." As he went through this portion of the briefing, the scenario was revealed. Instead of warming up with "offensive" or "defensive" engagements, where one jet starts behind the other and each jet has a clear positional advantage or disadvantage, we would fly one "high-aspect" or neutral engagement to a conclusion.

High-aspect BFM engagements replicate the geometry

encountered by opposing fighters as they merge with one another at the endgame of an intercept. Typically, the jets passed close to one another, heading in opposite directions, at the same altitude and at their best maneuvering speeds. This resulted in a condition of almost complete equality in their positional and energy states vis-à-vis one another. As the two jets pass each other, the "turning and burning" begins. Usually, each jet turns across the other's tail into two separate turning circles. This was known as "two-circle fight" geometry, as the flight paths of the two jets transcribe a large figure eight when looked at from above, what fighter pilots call a "God's eye view." Sometimes, one jet would turn across the other's tail, but the other jet would turn into the first jet's circle. This is the "one-circle fight" geometry because the two jets' flight paths transcribed opposite sides of the same circle. Regardless of the engagement's geometry, the winner would be the pilot who managed his kinetic energy (airspeed) and potential energy (altitude) better than his opponent, because over time he could turn his energy advantage into a positional advantage and wind up behind his opponent. From this position, he could employ ordnance and kill the adversary.

Of course, today's ordnance would be simulated, and would be limited to "guns only." The gun shot would be animated by a computer-generated video stream of bullets which would be captured by a camera shooting through the Head Up Display or HUD in each jet. HUDs were a commonplace fixture in modern fighters. They were plates of glass mounted in the cockpit, usually fixed to the top of the instrument panel glare shield. They were placed in front of the pilot's forward vision so he had to look though them to fly the aircraft. An on-board computer projects flight data on the glass which was focused at infinity so the pilot could see the data and the background behind the data without having to refocus his eyes. In addition to displaying altitude, airspeed, attitude information, and navigational data, they also could project a gun sight or pipper.

In the F-16, the HUD gave us all of that, as well as a bomb sight, missile engagement zones and a host of other things.

As Brace faced the screen and covered the "kill criteria" for the gunshot, distance between aircraft, amount of simulated bullets required, and pipper position, I could feel Adam's eyes on me. I didn't know whether he was trying to stare me down or see if he could discover my game plan by looking at my face. I nodded to him politely, and then looked back at Brace as he continued to speak.

And I fought like hell to keep a shit-eating grin off my face.

We walked out to our jets about an hour later, after sliding into borrowed flight suits and the necessary life-support gear. Rose had two aircraft waiting for us, both from the Northrop assembly line. I climbed into the front seat of the T-38, the sleek jet which had been the US Air Force's advanced trainer for nearly fifty years. The jet was small, fast, and had a tiny wing, which meant it wasn't terribly maneuverable. But it was a joy to fly and I was excited to be in it again. Roo had finished the external preflight and had come up the ladder after me to ensure I was strapped in correctly. I was surprised to see that the ejection set did not have the handles and triggers I remembered from pilot training, but instead, had the lanyard between the legs. I asked him about it.

"We replaced the standard ejection seats with ACES II seats," he said. "It was the only way that we could get our insurance underwriter to increase our liability limits to the level we needed to stay in business."

I nodded in comprehension. The ACES II was a capable ejection seat. There wasn't much you could get into in a jet airplane that the ACES II couldn't get you out of.

"Sucks that you get the T-38 and he gets the F-5," Roo said, as he tugged on my shoulder harness straps to make sure they were taut. But at least it's an F-5B and not an F-5F. We had one of those here a while back but we sold it recently."

I looked across the ramp to see Adam strapping into the

front seat of the two-seat F-5B. The T-38 was actually derived from the F-5, but the F-5 had a few things the T-38 didn't - like leading edge slats. The slats increased the area of the wing at low airspeed and made the jet considerably more maneuverable.

"Not surprising he'd have the better dogfighter since he's paying for this outing," I said, as Roo descended the ladder, returning to the ground to buckle his own harness straps.

"He has the slats, but you have a little more thrust to weight than he does. So, my advice to you," he said as he looked down and fastened his leg straps, "is not to get slow until you can kill him." He finished and looked back up at me. "Do you have a game plan?"

"This guy was a prince who flew in the Royal Saudi Air Force. In a culture where saving face is everything; how hard on him do you think they were? I'm just going to show him something he probably hasn't seen before and see what happens."

Roo lifted his eyebrows in surprise. Then he grinned at me and nodded. "I like it," he said.

He climbed into the jet's rear cockpit and strapped in. Then he talked me through the T-38's engine start checklist. The T-38 and F-5 both required air carts for engine start. The air carts were essentially small jet engines mounted in portable, wheeled, metallic boxes. A hose was connected between the cart and an air valve on the underside of the jet and then on cue, high-pressure air was pumped from the cart to turn the engine for start. It was a cumbersome but familiar process. My pilot training days were flashing back into my brain.

From twenty-eight years ago.

"Wow," I said involuntarily after the second engine had settled at idle.

"Let me guess," Roo laughed, "you were thinking you can't believe it's been that long since UPT."

I nodded, unconsciously. "I was."

"Everyone does," he said. I could see his face clearly in the rearview mirrors mounted on the T-38's canopy rail. "Time is a scary thing, isn't it?" he asked.

"Yes, it is."

After the post-start checklist, I tuned the jet's UHF radio to the frequency for Air Terminal Information Service and copied the recorded information on the current weather and active runway onto the pad on my kneeboard. A few minutes later, Brace checked us in on the Van Nuys ground control frequency. He was going to be leading the flight through all the radio changes since he knew the airspace and procedures here.

"Talon Flight, check," his voice came clearly over the UHF radio.

"Two," I replied. In a multi-ship formation, pilots always replied to radio calls with their position in the flight.

"Van Nuys Ground, Talons flight of two, taxi from the west ramp, information golf."

"Talon flight, Van Nuys Ground," the controller answered. "Taxi to runway one six right via alpha three and alpha."

"Talon flight to one six right via alpha three and alpha."

Adam and Brace's ground crewman removed the wheel chocks from the nose wheel of their jet and then motioned them forward with his hands. I watched the engine nozzles on their jet close slightly as Adam applied power to taxi, and then his jet began to move forward. I pushed the throttles forward to follow him. I marveled at how quickly the engines spooled up and spooled down in response to my movement of the throttles.

"Wow," I said, as I retarded the throttles to check my speed. "I thought the Viper's engine response was good."

"This is a straight jet, remember?" Roo said. "There's none of that fan lag we had in the Viper."

I nodded. Turbofan engines, even the high-thrust models we had in the F-16, still lagged in their throttle response just a little.

"So," Roo said into the intercom as we taxied, "speaking of the Viper and since it's just us girls, I heard a little something about a real dogfight over the high-desert a few weeks ago. You wouldn't know anything about that, would you?"

I looked at his reflection in the mirror on my canopy rail. "I know what I read in the papers," I said.

Roo's visor was up and his eyes were looking out of the side of the cockpit. "A friend of mine in the California Air Guard intercepted a lone Viper over the high-desert on its way into Edwards. The guy flying it told them who he was over the radio. He called himself T.C."

I paused just about a second too long before I answered. "Could be a coincidence," I said weakly.

He turned his head to look at me in the mirror. "Not likely. There's only one Viper pilot called T.C. I ever heard of. And I know a lot of guys in the Viper community."

"Roo," I said, "for the sake of conversation, let me ask you a theoretical question. If you had participated in an operation with a lot of government agencies which go by their initials, how eager would you be to talk about it?"

He looked at me thoughtfully and slowly nodded in comprehension. "Noted," he said.

"Glad we understand each other," I replied.

We taxied north on the parallel taxiway, stopped short of the approach end of runway 16R and waited for clearance from the tower to takeoff. When it came, Adam's gloved hand raised to his canopy. Brace, in the rear seat, Roo, and I raised our hands to our canopies in response. Then we all lowered our canopies in unison, locked them into place and taxied out on the runway, with our two jets side-by-side, each in the center of its half of the takeoff surface.

"Sure hope these engines are reliable," I said, as I clamped my oxygen mask onto my face. "Eight thousand feet is not a lot of runway for this jet."

"We've got a net barrier at the end of the runway if we have to abort, but I wouldn't worry about it. Our maintenance folks here are fantastic. You could eat off the inside of these engines."

Adam looked over at me and twirled his index finger vertically in the classic "run 'em up" signal. I advanced my power to 100% RPM and surveyed my engine instruments. All was normal.

"Engines are good," Roo said from the back seat. "You're cleared to release brakes."

"Roger," I replied.

Adam looked over at me again and I nodded. He nodded back and then looked forward. His jet immediately began to roll. Jet engines on fighter aircraft had nozzles that opened and closed with the movement of the throttle. When the power was advanced, the nozzles closed to restrict the exhaust, thus increasing the velocity and pressure of the exhaust gases, like the effect of restricting the flow of water out of a garden hose. This dramatically increased the amount of thrust an engine generated at MIL power, short for "military power" or 100% RPM without afterburner. Adam's nozzles were closed as he initiated his takeoff roll, but then a few seconds later, they flexed open and the twin blue flames of the J-85s' afterburners appeared.

I released the brakes with the power still MIL. The nozzle gauges indicated the normal range, about 0-20% open. Then, I pushed the throttles over the detent and all the way forward to MAX AB and received a nice kick in the back as the afterburners lit and nozzle gauges swung to 50-85% open. My mind and body went to a familiar, friendly place that I can't explain. There is something about rolling down the runway in a high-performance jet that can't be adequately described to someone who hasn't done it.

"God, there is nothing like that," I sighed into the intercom. The jet roared down the runway and the hydraulically-powered flight controls began to feel light in my hands. I saw 135 knots go by on the airspeed indicator and I applied back pressure to the control stick to deflect the control slab and lift the nose to five degrees pitch. At 155 knots, we lifted off and as soon as we were safely airborne, I raised the landing gear handle.

"Talon One Flight, contact departure, 298.85," said the tower controller.

"Talon roger," Brace's voice came over the radio. "Talons push button three."

I turned the channel knob on the radio control panel next to the throttle quadrant. The frequencies for our controlling agencies today were pre-loaded into channels in these radios. While I was back there, I found the applicable switch and raised the flaps as well.

"Talons check," Brace's voice said on the new frequency.

"Two," I answered.

"SOCAL, Talon flight of two, on the Newhall six departure, passing 3,000 for 5,000. Three-zero-zero knot departure."

"Talon flight, So-Cal approach," the controller responded. "Radar contact. Climb and maintain 10,000."

"Talon flight to 10,000."

"Sorry you have to deal with an old-fashioned radio control head," Roo said from the back seat. "The T-38Cs the USAF is flying now all have up-front controls like the Viper did. We're going to upgrade some of our jets to that standard, but just haven't yet. We're lucky we have HUDs and GPSs in these things."

"I'm just glad to be back in a real jet," I replied. "I've often said that flying business jets is like masturbating. It's fun and can be done with one hand, but it's not completely fulfilling and you don't brag about it."

It was time to concentrate on the formation join-up or rejoin, a maneuver that was usually straightforward. Having taken off ten seconds behind Adam/Brace, I had to close on the lead jet by using higher airspeed and cutting them off in the turn. Adam's jet was in a right turn to the north, and from the briefing, I knew he'd be holding 300 knots in the climb. I accelerated to 350, pulled the power out of AB and left it in MIL as I banked to the right, applied some back-stick pressure and "pulled" the nose of my jet to the inside of his turn. My airspeed advantage, combined with my flight path inside the arc of Adam's turn, created a geometry which closed the distance between us rapidly. A few moments later, when the distance between our aircraft was reduced to where I could just read the numbers on his tail, I smoothly pulled the power to idle and applied a little g to the inside of the turn to align our fuselages and to bleed off my extra airspeed. Then I moved into "fingertip" formation, with three feet of wingtip clearance.

Adam's visored face in the front cockpit regarded me momentarily, and then he turned his head to look out the front of his aircraft. In the back seat, Brace gave me a big thumbs-up. A second later, Adam's nose yawed left and right and I loosened my formation and moved out about 50 to 60 feet.

"The last time you did that was not in 2001 when you retired," Roo said quietly from the backseat.

"Maybe I've just got a good eye," I responded. "By the way, thanks for letting me fly the rejoin."

"It's me who should be thanking you," Roo said with a sigh. "It's great to finally fly with a fighter guy and a proficient one at that. Normally we do this with celebrities or wealthy types; and when they're not throwing up, they're trying to put the jet out of control and or kill me. It's funny. A lot of these guys actually own airplanes and can fly, but you put them in a machine like this and it's like a pig staring at a watch."

I laughed. "What made you leave the airlines and come do this? Last I heard you were flying for Southwest."

"That shit bored me to tears," he said. "I guess it works for some guys. Just didn't take for me. I actually went back into the Air Force for a while before I came out here."

"This gets into your blood," I said wistfully. "I've missed it flying corporate jets."

"I can imagine," Roo said, with just a touch of irony in his voice.

"Talon flight," the radio crackled in my ear, "contact Los Angeles Center on 351.9."

"Talon flight copies 351.9," Brace answered the controller. "Talons push button 4."

I clicked the radio button over again.

"Talons check," Brace said.

"Two," I replied.

"Los Angeles Center, Talon flight of two, passing 8,000 for 10,000, Newhall Six departure, Edwards transition."

"Talon Flight, Los Angeles Center, good morning. Climb and maintain flight level 230. Proceed direct Edwards."

"Talons to 230, direct Edwards."

We were passing through about ten-thousand feet now and the brown expanse of the high desert of California was coming into view. I saw Adam's jet make a course correction toward the tan outline of Muroc Dry Lake, which lay on the west shore of Edwards AFB.

"Nice of the Air Force to let you use their airspace on the weekends," I commented.

"They like our camera planes," Roo replied. "We have another T-38 equipped with gyro-stabilized cameras and a Lear 25 as well. We do them a few favors, they do us a few favors. Besides, if we ever have any issues, there isn't a better place in the world to land a sick or bent jet than Edwards."

We leveled off at flight level 230 a few moments later and continued the trek out to Edwards. The events of several weeks ago came back to me and careened about inside my head. The radio interrupted my recollection. Fortunately.

"Talon Flight, Los Angeles Center Contact Joshua Approach on 335.6."

"Talons," Brace said, "push button 5."

I tuned the radio accordingly.

"Talons Check," he called.

"Two," I replied.

"Joshua, Talon flight of two," Brace said over the radio, "looking for clearance into the Buckhorn MOA over the lake at 230."

"Talons, Joshua Approach," a female voice answered, "you're cleared into the Buckhorn MOA, 10,000 to 50,000. Monitor this frequency and call when you're ready for departure."

"Talons Wilco," Brace said.

We were flying toward the center of the large dry lake bed that adjoins Edwards Air Force Base. The beige sand of the dry lake contrasted sharply with the darker brown of the desert surrounding it and the black painted runway markings were clearly visible on the sand's surface. Adam's jet began to move up and down in a "porpoising" motion, the visual signal for me to deploy to tactical formation - 6,000 feet line abreast. I banked away from him, shoved the throttles into MIL and pulled into about 2-3 g's until my nose was pointed to the outside of the formation about 45 degrees. I let the separation between us build and then pulled the nose of the jet back so that I was paralleling Adam's course. We were about 6,000 feet apart.

"Talons, g awareness, in place 90 right, now," Brace called.

Time to get our bodies warmed-up for the g and make sure our anti-g suits were working. I pushed the throttles back into MIL and banked the jet to the right, setting the wings just about perpendicular to the horizon. Then, I smoothly applied back pressure to the control stick until my body told me we were at about 4 g's. The nose of the sleek jet tracked nicely across the brown, desert landscape off in the distance as the anti-g suit inflated, squeezing my legs and lower abdomen. I rolled out, left the power in MIL and let the jet accelerate to about 400 knots.

"Talons, g awareness, in place 90 left."

I banked to the left, got into my anti-g straining maneuver and pulled into about 6 g's. I smiled to myself as I felt the familiar T-38 aerodynamic buffet through the control stick. When a jet pulled g, the wings generated a lot of lift. A lot of lift meant a lot of induced drag and the T-38 didn't have the thrust available to overcome the drag at high g, so the jet decelerated as it remained under g and that deceleration caused the wing to generate airflow which buffeted the airframe, similar to turbulence. I could feel my checks drooping and the skin beneath my eyes bunching up with the g as the anti-g suit inflated again, squeezing my lower body with a vengeance. It was a great sensation. We ended up back in line abreast formation again, although considerably slower than we started.

All I could do was smile. I loved the feeling of g on my body in a high-performance jet. G-force, for the uninitiated, is generated by the centrifugal force of a turn. One g is equal to the force of gravity. If you've turned a corner too tightly in a car and slid across your seat, you've experienced more than one g. If you've been on a roller coaster that goes upside down, it's the force that holds you in your seat when you're inverted, which is at least two g's. In a high-performance fighter like the F-16, the pilot routinely withstands 6-9 g's as he commands the jet to turn in aerial maneuvering. The force makes him weigh six-to-nine times his normal body weight and makes everything he does in the cockpit six-to-nine times more difficult. It also makes his blood weigh six-to-nine times more and the blood will leave his brain unless he tenses his body or "strains" to keep it there. Blood leaving the brain would be bad, so the pilot "fights" to stay conscious as he fights his opponent in a dogfight. It's completely exhilarating. And while the T-38 couldn't sustain the g the Viper could, it would be enough for me today.

"God, I needed this," I said into my oxygen mask.

"I know what you mean," Roo answered quietly from the

back seat. "Everything else in my life can suck, but I can come out here, watch the world go by, and get a few g's on my ass and everything is better, somehow."

I nodded. "Well put," I said.

"Talon one is good," Brace's voice came over the radio, indicating the g-awareness turns had gone well in his aircraft, the inflation valves for the anti-g suits were working, and both he and Adam were physiologically okay with the g.

"Talon two same," Roo answered.

"Talons, as briefed, one high-aspect engagement until we have a winner and a loser. Talon one is ready."

"Talon two's ready," I said.

"Talons split," Brace commanded

It was time for Adam to take his medicine. We turned away from each other about 45 degrees to build some separation between us. I parked the throttles all the way forward in MAX AB, and pushed on the control stick slightly to help the jet accelerate. This "unloading" maneuver reduced the g on the airframe to nearly zero. Zero g, meant zero lift required. Zero lift, meant zero drag. Zero drag meant the aircraft accelerated rapidly. As I descended and gained airspeed, I watched the distance between my airplane and Adam's grow. The sleek, light blue aircraft was going to be hard to see against the intensely-blue desert sky, so I fastened my eyeballs onto his jet. Cardinal rule one of Basic Fighter Maneuvers: Lose Sight, Lose Fight. I was not going to be the one who lost sight today.

"Talons turn in," Brace commanded.

I had accelerated to 500 knots and since I didn't want to lose the airspeed I had gained, I had to be easy on the back pressure as I brought my nose to bear on Adam's aircraft. I banked left into the other aircraft—now, a barely discernible silhouette, and gently applied back pressure until I could feel a "tickle" on the control stick. The tickle was just on the good side of the airframe buffet. My nose began to track slowly but smoothly across the horizon, just a little faster than a turn in a business jet or an airliner. Ordinarily in a fight like this, I'd plan on pulling my power to idle after I finished my turn to reduce my heat signature and deny the forward aspect missile shot. But it was a guns only fight today and I was going to take advantage of that fact. The throttles stayed in MAX AB.

As I watched Adam's jet turn toward me, I could see his nose moving much more rapidly than mine.

I grinned under my oxygen mask. I had expected this.

"Talon one, visual." Adam's voice came over the airwaves for the first time today. He was indicating that he could see my aircraft and the hunger in his voice was unmistakable.

"Talon two, visual," I answered flatly.

"Talons, fight's on!" Brace commanded.

Adam's jet was pointed at me now, about three miles away. By unloading my aircraft, I had descended about a thousand feet below him. My nose was still about 45 degrees to the right of his and tracking left as I climbed up to meet him. From Adam's perspective, it would appear that I was allowing him both energy and positional advantage by giving him altitude above me and by allowing him to point his nose at me before I pointed my nose at him. It was a logical conclusion for him to make. And exactly what I wanted him to see.

"Oh, you are quite the asshole," Roo said with a knowing chuckle over the intercom.

"The bait's in the water," I responded. "Let's see if he takes it."

As if on cue, Adam rolled his jet to the left and I could see the top of his aircraft as his nose tracked toward me. He was trying to capitalize on what he saw and get behind me. And it was costing him a lot of energy.

"Hook, line, and sinker," Roo said as we watched Adam's jet move aft.

In an instant, I rolled into him and pulled into a maximum-rate turn. In a few seconds, my nose was pointed at Adam's jet. A few seconds later, we flashed by each other, about 500 feet apart, flying in opposite directions. I could almost see the look of surprise on his face through his visor as I went past him.

He hadn't seen anything yet.

I smoothly pulled back on the stick and sent my jet skyward like a rocket, climbing into the pure vertical at about 500-600 feet per second. As the T-38 shot into the blue desert sky, I threw my head back to peer over my left shoulder and see how Adam would react. The smart thing for him to do at this point was to be patient, stay in his plane of motion, accelerate, build energy, and wait for me to come down to him.

Predictably, he did exactly the opposite.

Almost instantly, I could see his nose track upward as he initiated his own climb. His nose moved rapidly, thanks in large measure to the F-5's maneuvering slats, and soon his jet was in a near vertical climb of its own. I was now about 12,000 feet above him and applying gentle back pressure to the control stick, bringing the nose of my jet back down the to the horizon. The T-38 was inverted now, with our canopy facing the ground and Adam's jet and our underside bathed by the desert sun. I kept a gentle 1-2 g's on the jet as I pulled, using the positive g to keep the nose moving and also to keep Roo and I in our seats. My airspeed had decreased to just over 200 knots, but I had translated my kinetic energy, airspeed, into potential energy, altitude. And the altitude gave me the most valuable of commodities in a dogfight - turning room.

"Just about any time now," I said into the intercom, as I watched Adam's jet through the top of my canopy, a blue triangular shape against the light-tan of the dry lakebed below.

"Yep, he won't be able to make it much further," Roo said, watching him as well. And then a few seconds later he added, "And down he goes."

The nose of Adam's jet had stopped tracking upward and his airplane was now falling off to the right. By pulling his nose into the vertical without the energy to do so, he had completely run his aircraft out of airspeed. And now it was doing what all heavier-than-air objects do when they aren't generating lift; it was falling back to earth.

My nose was through the horizon and nearly perpendicular to the ground as I continued to apply back pressure on the control stick and "pulled" it toward the F-5.

Adam's nose had fallen below the horizon and his jet had begun a steep descent. I wondered if Brace had to take control of the aircraft to perform a nose-high recovery and get some lift back onto the wings. The F-5 was about 6,000 feet away from me now, trying to regain maneuvering airspeed.

I continued to pull my nose to his jet. By this time, my flight path had transcribed a full 360 degrees in the vertical plane. A few seconds later, I rolled out about 3,000 above and behind him. Now that I was descending and under mild g, all the airspeed I had spent in the climb and ensuing vertical turn was coming back and I was accelerating once more.

"You know he's going to want to use those slats again," Roo said from the rear cockpit.

"Oh, I'm counting on it," I replied.

As if on cue, Adam's nearly vertical descent began to lessen as he recovered from his dive and pulled his own nose up toward the horizon. The airspeed display in my HUD said I had 350 knots. It would be enough. I applied the g and pulled into the heavy airframe buffet. My nose was now well inside of Adam's turn. I was gaining closure purely due to the geometry of our two turns. The three conditions for a successful air-to-air gunshot were coming together. I was in the plane of turn of Adam's jet, my nose was pointed in front of his so I had lead and now I was waiting to be in range. I was counting on Adam to solve that problem for me.

As soon as he saw my nose lining up for the shot, Adam pulled his own nose toward me, hard. He was trying to take the turning room away from me and make me fly outside his turn, but he didn't have the energy to do it. His nose tracked for a moment or two, and then rapidly stopped as it hit the accelerated stall. He had asked too much of the F-5's tiny wing with too little airspeed. By applying too much g, he stalled the aircraft and it stopped flying—again. I yanked my throttles to idle, deployed the speed brake and settled the gun sight or "pipper" onto Adam's canopy. Then, I pulled the trigger. In the HUD, a line of green video dots were generated that stitched a neat line right down the middle of Adam's jet.

"Tracking, tracking, tracking," I intoned into the microphone. "Kill one F-5 over Muroc dry lake bed, right hand turn, 14,000 feet."

"Talon copies kill," Brace's voice said smartly over the radio. "Talons terminate, Talon one terminate."

"Talon two, terminate," I answered him. I looked at my fuel gauge. All the use of AB had cost me a lot of gas, but it had been worth it. "Talon two's bingo," I said into the mic.

"Talon one copies bingo," Brace answered me, "Talons rejoin. Let's head back to base."

The flight back was uneventful; although I rediscovered that landing the T-38, a jet that flies final approach at 155 knots and had virtually nothing to stop it but brakes, was still a challenge. Since we had landed separately, Adam's jet had made it back to parking before we did. As Roo and I taxied in, I could see that Adam's cockpit was empty and he was nowhere to be seen. I shut my jet down, ran the After-Shutdown checklist and climbed out of the cockpit. As Roo and I unbuckled the leg straps for our parachutes, Brace walked over to us.

"Adam didn't want to stay for the debrief?" I asked.

Brace shook his head. "Apparently not," he said. "He said something about having an urgent business thing to get to."

"I see," I said. "Well, there goes my ride home."

"He said he'd send a car for you and I was supposed to tell you to wait here until the car came. He also told me not to let you out of my sight."

"Really?" I said. "I don't suppose you guys have got any

beer around here do you?"

"We do!" Brace said. "It's after 5:00 P.M. somewhere in the world."

I secured the leg straps on my parachute and three of us walked through the hangar and into the operations building.

"That was damn artistic," Roo said. "Damn artistic."

"I saw it coming as soon as he made the turn in," Brace said. "He only had about 400 knots and he was pulling so hard that he was bleeding airspeed all over the place. We must have pulled six g's on the turn in. Who pulls 6 g's on a turn in for a high-aspect BFM set up?"

"And then when he saw that your nose still wasn't on him, he thought the engagement was already won," Roo added.

"Well, a skilled pilot who didn't have anything to prove would not have been nearly so predictable," I said. "But a pilot brought up in an environment where saving face is as important as life itself, that's a different story."

"Indeed, it is," Brace said.

"So, what's really going on here?" Roo asked as we walked into the building and shed our life-support gear.

I looked at him and weighed what I was going to say. It was possible that Adam had paid these guys off and all their friendliness was an act, but I doubted it.

"I don't completely know," I admitted. "Sarah Marciano, Bachelor Magazine's chief pilot, is a good friend of mine. Adam took over the department several weeks ago and Sarah wasn't happy about it, but what could she do? I've been out here the last few days doing some contract work for their flight department. Along the way, it's become apparent that something else is going on and Adam's at the center of it. For reasons I won't bore you with, Adam suddenly felt the need to prove his superiority to me, which is what I suspect this was all about."

"Looks like that backfired on him," Brace said cheerfully as he motioned toward the bar area.

I nodded, suddenly wondering what my little display would cost. "Believe it or not, this business between Adam and I is about a woman we both met in Cabo."

We walked into their bar area and I went silent as my eyes took in the decor. Bars were my favorite places in the world and this one was decked out like a typical bar in a fighter squadron. Lots of photos of airplanes and pilots on the wall, camouflage netting draped from the ceiling, a pool table for "crud" games, and the obligatory rack of ceramic beer steins.

"Wow," I said involuntarily as I looked around me.

"Awesome, isn't it?" Brace asked, as he walked behind the bar counter.

"It's like the best parts of every squadron bar the two of us ever saw," Roo said, inclining his head toward Brace. "We designed it and Chuck gave carte blanche to have it built."

"Now, sir," Brace said from behind the bar, with a gleam in his eyes, "what's your poison?"

"Do you have any Stella back there?" I asked.

"Indeed," Brace answered, "on draft even."

"Excellent!"

Brace turned to the rack of ceramic steins, retrieved one that had the silhouette of an F-16 on it, and put it under one of the taps. He pulled the tap toward him and began the flow of the cool, amber nectar into the porcelain. I almost licked my lips.

I took a respite from the drama and intrigue around me and relished a beer with two fellow fighter pilots. We talked, we joked, and we laughed and flashed back to the squadron experiences we had all enjoyed so many years ago. We mourned the past and cursed the present and solved all the problems of the world in that short period of time.

And it was over all too soon.

CHAPTER THIRTEEN

Contract Day Six
Sunday, 22 November
1500 Hours Local Time
Van Nuys Airport (KVNY)
Van Nuys, California, United States

I made the limo wait an hour for me while I enjoyed my time with Roo and Brace. My BlackBerry buzzed with multiple text messages and e-mails while we drank together but I ignored them. Eventually though, duty called and I had to leave. We exchanged handshakes and contact information and when that was finished, the two of them looked at me solemnly.

"We know you're in some shit, TC," Brace had said.

"You need to let us know if there is *anything* we can do to help," Roo had added.

I promised that I would.

Now the limo was moving through the light Sunday traffic on the 405 Freeway, back to Bel Air and I was watching the diverse terrain of Southern California go by as I attempted to determine what would happen next.

I should have known better.

As Miguel's man eyed me from across the limo, his cell phone rang and he answered. A firestorm of Spanish went back and forth between him and whomever he was speaking with.

Then, I heard the driver's cell phone ring and he answered and a similar firestorm ensued only this time it was in Arabic.

This can't be good, I thought.

As the driver talked, I was struck by how stereotypical Miguel's man appeared. If you went to central casting and asked for a guy that looked like a "Mexican Gangster," this guy could show up. He was about 5'10" inches tall and appeared solid and athletic. He moved like a cat, smoothly and purposefully. His features had the look of mixed European and Mayan blood, with dark-olive skin, a wide, flat forehead, and a rectangular nose. The expression on those features was one of condescending professional interest. I had a mental image of an animal handler observing curious behavior in his charge.

As the driver finished his phone call, he said two words in English to my companion in the bank of the limo.

"Do it," he said.

Miguel's man was incredibly fast. I didn't have more than a second to gauge his reaction before he hit me and the world went black.

##

Sometime later, how much later I had no idea, I was dragged from the car. I could feel muscular arms around my torso and under my armpits as my feet slid roughly across sand and gravel. As I struggled back to consciousness, I found myself oddly grateful that I was wearing my Nunn-Bush shoes and not the Johnston and Murphy ones. Funny where your mind goes sometimes. A few moments later, I was thrown to the ground and my face found some wild grass and pine needles.

"Quien coño eres? Who the fuck are you, man?" my companion demanded. I almost laughed into the dirt. He sounded like Al Pacino in Scarface.

"Colin Pearce," I said groggily, as I tried to push myself up to a sitting position. "I'm a contract Gulfstream pilot."

"I know," the man said, in totally unaccented English. "We have to maintain appearances to some degree."

Incredulous, I started to get to my feet and the guy held his hand up and made a pushing gesture, indicating I should stay sitting down. He looked back through the bushes, the way we had come, ostensibly to make sure we had not been followed. I looked up at him. His face had changed somehow, like he had taken a mask off.

Finally, he appeared to be satisfied and walked over to me, extending his right hand. "Joe Sanchez, DEA," he said, as he helped me to my feet.

I guess my jaw dropped a little.

"Surprised? I've been deep cover inside of Miguel Hidalgo's organization for about three years." He gestured to the side of my head. "Sorry for the smack earlier," he said with a small grimace. "I was instructed by my handler to make contact with you and I had to figure out a way to get you out of the limo and away from our driver. Archmere was really pissed about something when he called Miguel to send me to get you. Then the driver and I both got these instructions to take you somewhere and teach you some humility. So, the theory is I'm out here roughing you up on the boss' instructions. It all came together at the last minute."

I smiled at him while I rubbed the side of my head where he had hit me. "I guess I did embarrass him a little."

"No shit, man! He was out of control when he called Miguel! I could hear the conversation from across the room." Joe paused and looked at me with a bemused expression on his face. "No, Miguel Hidalgo isn't his real name. No one knows what his real name is. Do you know anything about Mexican history?"

I nodded, still rubbing the side of my head. "What the hell did you do to me? You put me right out!"

"Just a light tap on your temple. I was in the SEALs before I joined the DEA," Joe replied. "I can do that about ten different ways."

I nodded. "I have a little experience with you guys," I said. "I should have known. So, can you tell me what's going on?"

"We need to talk quickly or the driver is going to get suspicious," he said. "I guess the DEA was thinking this was all about drugs, the implication of Hidalgo's name notwithstanding. But now I'm hearing that there may be a hell of a lot more to it than that. That makes this an information exchange for both of us. What can you tell me?"

"Here's what I know. Several weeks ago, Bill flew his G-IV to Dubai with Shelly, his daughter, to attend a very exclusive VIP boat show. Sarah and her husband, Damian, acted as crew. Damian is the one who got Bill invited to the show. My personal feeling is that Damian is a plant but the CIA hasn't been able to verify that yet. Anyway, Spratt and company were in Dubai for several days. On the last day, Damian and Shelly were snatched, presumably by someone working for Adam because he took responsibility, and Adam commandeered the jet and they flew it back to the US. It's become apparent that Bill bought that big-ass boat while he was there. Whether he was coerced or enticed to do so is open to interpretation. Evidently, the boat has doors on the bottom of it that open for small submarines or divers or whatever. It appears that the boat makes trips out to sea, picks people up. Apparently two of these people have been transported to the US via the G-IV on one the trips Adam is directing back and forth between the US and Cabo. Bill told me that one of the men they had picked up was a doctor of some sort and he thought they might be working on a WMD. He said whatever they brought aboard must be kept very cold. The CIA thinks it might be a bio-weapon. Spratt also told me that they had picked up *many* people and *many* guns."

Joe was nodding. "Miguel is paying the Naval Sea Police

off to look the other way while Adam makes these pickups at sea. But they're definitely picking up more people and cargo than are going back on the G-IV. There's a whole bunk room in the center of that boat that can sleep 50-100 people or so. I also know that when the boat arrived, it was carrying a huge shipment of weapons from some place in the Middle East, AKs, RPGs, heavy machine guns and shoulder-fired surface to air missiles. They're all on the boat."

"Enough for a platoon-sized unit," I said, thinking out loud. "I wonder what they're up to."

"Well, based on what you've told me and what we've already learned, there's got to be a whole lot more to it than drugs," Joe said. "Miguel has huge influence in the country in general and in Baja California in particular. He doesn't need additional manpower or weapons to increase the size of his empire in country."

"Well, our guys seem to think that Adam and company are working on a terrorist strike. I found a schedule of football games for Thanksgiving Day in the airplane."

"Miguel did say something about coming up here to check on his investment," Joe said, shaking his head. "But I'd be surprised if he was involved in something like that. That's not his style. He has this code of honor that he lives by. No non-combatants are ever engaged. He's meticulously surgical and if one of his men violates the code, they're done. Period. It's one of the reasons why he's so widely respected. He doesn't kill women, unless they are combatants, never kills children, and actually has been known to pass money to orphanages and charities."

"Sounds like he's running for office," I said under my breath. "And he wouldn't be the first person to change his tune as if he was getting more ambitious." I paused for a moment to collect my thoughts. "So, what now?"

"I've been given instructions to support you no matter what. And let me tell you something, that must come from pretty high up because we've been building a case against Hidalgo for a long time and my boss is really hot to get him."

"I won't call on you unless there is no other option," I promised. "So, is there a catch phrase?"

Joe nodded.

"Just use the word 'Magillicutty' in a sentence," he said. "And I'll take it from there."

"Something tells me it won't get that hairy while Miguel is around," I said. "But thanks. I'll remember."

"I guess we're done then," Joe said, eyeing me apologetically. "But I guess I do need to rough you up a little."

"We do have to maintain appearances," I said remorsefully. "I wonder how Adam is going to rationalize beating up the help."

"I guess you'll find out." He looked at my face like he was looking over a menu. "Can you limp a little more and hold your side like I punched you there?"

I nodded.

"Okay, we're going to need a little blood and a good-looking bruise to sell this. I'm going to hit your nose lightly and then smack you under one of your eyes. Neither blow will hurt much, but they'll look like I really fucked you up."

There are times in life when you just have to face the music.

"I'm such an idiot," I murmured.

"What'd you say?" Joe asked.

"Let's do this, Joe," I said. "We're not going to find out anything else standing here."

He was helping me up again a few moments later and pushing me back to the limo a few minutes after that. I was bent over at the waist, clutching my imaginary stomach wound with my hands and limping as if my left leg was killing me, which it was. As I went through the door of the limo and into the back, I caught a glimpse of the driver's face in the side view mirror. He was grinning broadly.

Damn Arabs.

Joe was fully back into character as we made our way out of the woods where we were parked and back onto the 405 Freeway. He even snarled at me once or twice as we rode the fifteen minutes back to Bel Air. Then, he unceremoniously deposited me at the grand wooden front door of the mansion. I opened the door slowly and breathed a sigh of relief when I found the grand foyer area unoccupied. As quickly as I could, I hobbled up the stairs and down the vacant hallway to my room.

Where the hell is everyone?

I went through the front door of the room and plodded across the rich carpet to the bedroom, stripping my shirt and t-shirt off en route. I tossed the clothes onto the bed, now remade by the housekeeping staff, and threw my socks, pants, and underwear next to them. Then I padded into the bathroom and inspected myself in the mirror.

"Jesus Christ," I said involuntarily.

Joe had done well. The entire left side of my face, from just under my eye to my nose was grossly discolored, angry-red and blue. Blood was crusted on my upper lip and chin and my nostrils looked flattened and distorted. Yet, despite the apparent damage, there was very little pain. The area under my left eye was a little tender, as was my nose, but it didn't feel nearly as bad as it looked.

"Un-fucking-believable," I said to my reflection.

I looked at the shower and Jacuzzi tub and settled on the tub, turning on the water spigots and emptying the complimentary miniature bottle of bubble bath into the rapidly rising water. The tub was large and triangularly shaped so that it fit neatly into the corner of the bathroom. It looked like it was made from a solid piece of light brown marble, and judging by the level of tasteful extravagance I seen elsewhere here, I didn't doubt that it was.

I adjusted the mixture of the spigots to ensure the water temperature was just this side of scalding, and then eased into the foamy suds and seated myself comfortably in the recliner-shaped portion of the tub, built into the wall to my left. I put a towel into the corner of the tub, laid my head on it and luxuriated in the soft, slippery suds as the water climbed up my body. When it reached my chest, I turned the spigots off with my feet, and then turned the jets on. Instantly, my body was pelted by millions of tiny bubbles under pressure and I felt my muscles respond to the gentle kneading. Odds were I'd be sore from the g today, since I wasn't used to it. A half hour or so in the tub would go a long way toward relaxing my fatigued muscles.

As I lay there, with the regular hum of the tub's pump providing an oddly soothing audible rhythm, and the tub's jets providing a tactile one to match, I closed my eyes and recounted the dogfight, smiling as I remembered the frantic motion of Adam's helmeted head in the cockpit as my gun sight pipper settled upon it. I could see his visored face turning toward me in realization and expected to see some indication of panic or resignation. But that's not what I sensed at all. Somehow, I had the distinct feeling that underneath the oxygen mask and visor, the handsome Arab face was smiling at me. Like I had played right into his hands.

"Jesus Christ, Colin, what did they do to you?" A feminine voice roused me from my reverie and I lifted my head and opened my eyes to find Sarah standing over me with an anxious look on her beautiful features. She was wearing a flowery sundress, and her shoulders were bare. Impulsively, she leaned over the side of the tub, extending her hands toward me to help me up.

"How long have you been in here?" she asked.

I shook my head unknowingly and reached for her. Then, as I rose, we both became aware of the fact that I was naked and even more of the aware that a certain part of my body had awakened in the warm water.

"Here," she said hastily, handing me a towel.

I took it from her dumbly, and began to wipe the suds and water from my body.

"I guess this makes us even," I muttered, trying to fill the awkward silence and remembering the view of her naked body last night. No doubt in my mind that I had enjoyed the better deal there.

"You've been working out," she said, looking at my body and taking great pains to keep her eyes above my waist.

"Part of my last job," I responded. "I wish I could tell you I had the discipline to do it myself. Is there a bathrobe around here anywhere?"

She walked into the bedroom and then returned with a white terrycloth robe a few minutes later. By then, I had managed to exit the tub, turn the jets off, and dry myself. I threw the drenched towel on the floor. I've never been terribly modest where the whole nudity thing was concerned.

"Colin," she said, as her eyes took in my battered body, "oh my God! You look like you've been through hell!" She handed the robe to me as her eyes continued to take in my wounds. I guess I did look pretty bad. Her eyes bounced between my pummeled face, the small pockmark on my left shoulder, and the three angry-red indentations on the front of my left thigh. She shook her head back and forth in disbelief as I donned the robe and tied it in front of me. "I've never seen gunshot wounds before," she said at last, her voice barely audible.

"By this point," I answered, "they probably look worse than they feel, although my damn leg is still pretty tender."

"So, what's with your face?" she asked.

"Let's continue this is the main room," I answered her and pointing to the air around me. I wanted any mics and cameras to hear our conversation.

She knelt next to me on the sofa a few moments later and began to tend to my face with a moist washcloth. She wiped the blood off my nose and chin, and then dabbed around the area on my cheek. I did my best to be a big boy and not wince.

"You were going to explain to me how this happened?" she inquired.

"I guess Adam felt he had something to prove and it totally backfired on him," I began. I followed with a version of the events in the air which emphasized Adam's recklessness and ineptitude. Sarah caught on quickly and asked several questions which allowed me to go into detail about Adam's specific errors and she laughed at all the proper moments. If I had given her a script, she couldn't have performed any better. "I guess I bruised his masculinity a little," I concluded. "So, he had a goon work me over. It was one of the guys who works for the passenger we flew up here yesterday. Miguel something?"

Sarah's face went white. "Not Miguel Hidalgo!"

I brightened for the camera but felt myself go dead on the inside. "Yeah," I said, in a tone that I hoped communicated nonchalance, "so what?"

"He's the most dangerous drug lord in Mexico! And he's personally threatened the President of Mexico and half the Department of Justice in the U.S.! He's an animal!"

I put my best devil-may-care look on my face and tried to grab Sarah's gaze with my own. "Oh, he's just another passenger as far as we're concerned, Sarah. You know me. As long as I'm getting my daily rate, I don't care who we're carrying back there. But, if getting beaten up is part of the job description, I may have to increase my fee."

"I'm the one who writes those checks," Sarah said. "At least for now. I'd say you've earned yourself a nice bonus."

"Well, then," I smiled at her, "that makes things a little better."

She leaned back a little and surveyed my face. "I got the blood off," she said. "But I'm not sure there's much else I can do. You're not really cut anywhere."

I nodded, thinking of Joe's words. He obviously knew what he was doing. *Where the hell do you get skills like that?* I wondered.

"Did you sleep okay last night?" she asked. She had an odd expression on her face. "I didn't keep you awake or anything? You seem awful tired."

"I slept great," I said, "but the exertion from this morning along with getting beaten up has worn me out a little. The whole getting old thing sucks."

I suddenly became aware of our physical proximity. She was kneeling on the sofa next to me and her pregnant belly was pressed against me. I could feel the sensual warmth of her even through my robe. She had put the washcloth down and now had one hand on my shoulder and the other on my knee. It was like the atmosphere was charging up between us.

Almost unconsciously, she took her hand off my shoulder and ran her fingers though my hair. "You don't look old," she said, as if she was talking to herself.

I looked back at her. "What's that line from Indiana Jones in the first *Raiders* movie? 'It's not the years honey, it's the mileage.'"

She smiled as her eyes explored my face and her hands continued to work their way through my hair. "I really missed you," she said softly. "I guess I didn't realize how much until last night."

"I missed you too," I said because the moment seemed to require it. The fact that it was the truth didn't hurt.

"Would you have really come back if I had asked?" she whispered.

"Hmmm," I said, stroking my chin, "let me think. Remain in my townhouse in Wilmington, flying for random people who are largely pudgy and ugly, or come to Southern California and fly with the most beautiful woman who has ever given me the time of day?" I eyed her. "You can see how I would have been torn."

She grinned and smacked me playfully. "You always were able to make me giggle," she said. "I do remember that."

I looked back at her. She regarded me with an air of longing. I didn't know what to make of it.

"So, when's dinner?" I asked.

"We don't usually do a formal dinner on Sundays," she answered. "I was going to ask you what you wanted and run down to the kitchen and get it for you."

"Oh my God, Sarah," I exclaimed, "I'm not going to have a pregnant woman fetching me food! Next thing you know I'll be wearing wife-beater t-shirts and moving to a trailer park."

"Please, Colin," she rolled her eyes at me, obviously making reference to the possible cameras and mics, "I've been asked to keep you in your room here tonight. Adam wants to depart for Cabo early tomorrow morning and he wants you to be rested for the flight."

I straightened. "That's fine," I said. "I can still help you out in the kitchen. Let me get some clothes on."

She lowered her right hand to my knee and squeezed it hard while she opened her eyes in a pleading expression. I got the message. Adam didn't want anyone to see me.

"On second thought," I said, "leaning backward against the sofa, "I am still feeling a little out of it. What's for dinner?"

"What do you want?" she asked brightly.

I guess my eyes went soft as I looked back at her and she squeezed my leg again, this time more tenderly.

"Just about anything is on the menu," she continued.

"Really?" I asked.

"Oh, yes," she replied softly.

"You know honestly, I'm not that hungry. If you could find some cheese and crackers and a nice bottle of red wine, that'd be plenty." I thought for a second. "But wait a minute, I forgot you can't drink. That's not fair."

"I can have a small glass," she said, "and cheese sounds great. But instead of the crackers, I'm betting I can find a baguette or some bread downstairs. I'll be right back." She squeezed my leg again and rose to leave. "Don't go anywhere," she teased.

"Wouldn't think of it," I replied, leaning back against the leather of the sofa. "It's pretty comfortable right here."

She hit the remote control for the fireplace and activated the room's music system. Immediately, soft tones of some sort of Celtic music became audible.

"Oh," I said appreciatively, "that's nice." I pulled the release to allow my side of the couch to recline. "I love this music," I continued as I leaned back. "You know my last name is Irish. I hope to God it's for real and not some legally-changed thing somewhere along the family line."

"I did know that," she said softly as she reached the door to room, "I looked it up after you and I were together." She paused as if she was going to say something else and then abruptly seemed to change her mind. "Back in a bit," she said and went through the door.

I closed my eyes and listened to the music for a few moments as I relaxed on the sofa, enjoying a rare moment of real peace. The soothing strains of Clannad reached out for me and beckoned me to drift off into sleep. As tempting as it was, I sat up abruptly and decided to inspect the books on the shelf. They were all richly leather bound and included a host of different subjects from literature to history to biography. The range was impressive and I was reminded of the volumes in my own library. I felt an unexpected pang of homesickness for my townhouse in Delaware.

And then I found the camera.

I had bent over to remove one of the books in a multi-volume biography of Thomas Jefferson from a shelf just above waist high, when I saw the black flexible tube of the fiber-optic device on the underside of the shelf. The tube went through the facing on the shelf and its black color was almost undetectable in the pattern on the wood. It was positioned to afford a view of the entire room and especially the sofa. I was betting Adam and company had gotten an eyeful last night.

I couldn't help myself. In as nonchalant a manner as I could muster, I replaced the volume clumsily on the shelf and banged the camera tube several times in the process. It popped out of its niche in the facing and drooped down. I removed another volume and looked through it in a leisurely fashion for a few minutes. Then I stuffed it back into the shelf, doubling the camera tube over onto itself and pushing it against the rear wall of the bookshelf.

Feeling ridiculously proud of myself, I returned to the sofa and reclined back onto a resting position with a satisfied smile on my face.

About seven songs later, Sarah reentered the room, pushing a rolling table with several trays on it, as well as bottles of wine and water. She was wearing a reddish-brown silk robe and sandal style slippers.

"I hope you don't mind if I changed," she said. "Maternity clothes are designed to be more stylish than comfortable. It seems I spend nearly all my time in my robe these days."

My mind recalled the sensual image of her nude body from last night and broadcasted it into my mind's eye. I felt a stir beneath my own robe and mentally paused to chastise myself. "Nothing wrong with that," I said. "You're in your robe and I'm in my robe and we'll just hang around in our robes."

She cocked her head at me and I realized what I had said.

"Is this making you nervous?" she asked, with just a trace of a smile on her face.

"A little," I confessed. "But I'll be okay." I motioned toward the tray in an effort to change the subject. What do you have there?"

"Come over and see!" she replied brightly.

I rose from the sofa and walked to the table. There was a mouth-watering array of cheeses, artistically arranged on a rectangular platter, along with a tray of both red and white grapes. A basket of sliced baguette bread lay next to them. An open bottle of Greg Norman Estates Reserve Shiraz and two wine glasses completed the ensemble.

"Letting that breathe," I said, inclining my head toward the wine.

"Someone I knew once told me it was a good idea," she said, winking at me. "If you carry the cheese and fruit, I'll get the wine and bread."

I grabbed the two trays and took them over to the dark cherry wood coffee table that rested between the sofa and the fireplace. Sarah put the bread and wine down, and then returned to the roller table to get the glasses and a few plates. A few minutes later, the wine was poured and we were both well into the different cheeses on the tray, interspersed with some grapes every few bites. We exchanged a few comments about the excellent tastes of the cheese, fruit, and wine but we did more eating than talking. At times, I would find myself just looking at her while she ate and while she spoke, watching the way the glow of the artificial firelight was reflected in her perfect skin, or the way her eyes crinkled slightly when she smiled or laughed.

"What?" she said, startling me from my trance. I realized she had caught me staring at her.

"Sorry," I said sheepishly, sighing. "When we were together before, I couldn't believe how lucky I was. And now here we are and I can't believe my luck again."

She smiled radiantly at me in the flickering light and I saw some wonderful things in her eyes, some of which I could fulfill and most of which I couldn't. At least, not now.

"Of course," I said despondently, "circumstances this time are a little different."

The spell of the moment was broken and she looked away and sipped her wine. I saw her shoulders slump just a little and realized that I had taken the wind out of her sails. I didn't know exactly what she had in mind just then, but I knew her well enough to know that if we crossed a certain line, she'd end up regretting it. Even if she and her husband weren't getting along.

We finished eating and carried our dishes over to the roller table.

"Do you have any idea what time Adam's going to want me at the airport or when he wants to depart tomorrow?"

She nodded as she stacked our plates.

"He wants you at the airport at 11:00 a.m. and he wants to be airborne at 12:00."

I nodded. "I get to sleep in a little, then."

"Yes, you do," she said quietly.

She rolled the table out of my room a few moments later. I sat down on the sofa, thinking she'd return shortly, and was just mildly surprised when she didn't after several minutes. I nodded to myself.

"Well done, Colin," I said to the air around me. "You managed to hurt the feelings of one of the few people in the world who actually gives a shit about you. Well done."

I glanced up at the music unit and saw the LED clock on the front of it. It was nearly 10:00.

"Where the hell did all the time go?" I asked myself.

I went into the bathroom, peed, and then brushed my teeth. Then I doffed the robe and got into bed.

"Wow," I said involuntarily as I crawled into the bed. The sheets were softer than anything I had ever slept on and I wondered what sort of cotton they were made of. I lay on my back, hands behind my head, staring at the ceiling and thought of Sarah and Susan and Adam and Miguel Hidalgo and Joe and Smith and Amrine.

"Pearce, you have a supreme talent for getting yourself into some shit," I said to the ceiling.

Eventually, I fell asleep.

I dreamt I was lying on an island beach somewhere and

the sun was beating down upon me. There was sudden gust of wind which chilled me for a moment; but after that, the warmth returned even more than before.

And then I smelled her hair.

I opened my eyes to find Sarah in bed with me. She was curled up on her side next to me, her right arm over my chest and her head snuggled neatly onto my shoulder. Her bare stomach and breasts were pressed against my flesh and the heat she was generating was more than enough for both of us.

She must have sensed I was awake because I heard her words float up to me in the darkness.

"Don't send me away," she said softly. "You're going to think I'm crazy or something, but I feel very safe with you. I need that right now." She buried her face into my chest. "I used to look down on women who talked about that sort of thing and now I'm one of them. I don't know if it's the hormones from the pregnancy or all the shit that's going on, but I just need to feel safe right now. I know we can't do anything else, but can I just borrow you for this?"

I felt a surge of protective affection run through me, followed by something even deeper. I gently stroked her soft hair with my hand and I felt the tension leave her body, evaporating into the darkness. My throat tightened and I felt my eyes water.

"As long as you want," I said, when I could trust my voice.

She kissed my chest softly and snuggled up to me a little more closely. Almost immediately, her body completely relaxed and her breathing became deep and even.

I stared into the darkness for a long time with a satisfied smile on my face. After a long while, the warmth of her body and the comfort of her presence lured me to sleep again.

And I dreamt of beautiful things.

CHAPTER FOURTEEN

Contract Day Seven
Monday, 23 November
1045 Hours Local Time
On Interstate 405
San Fernando, California, United States

I sat in the back of the limo—alone—and watched the terrain go by on my way back to the Burbank airport. Once again, I was reminded of the cyclical and repetitive nature of the life of a business jet pilot. Land the jet, put it to bed, take some form of transport to a hotel or lodging facility, stay there for a day or two, then back in the transport, back to the jet, and back in the air. The locales and faces might change, but nothing else did. It was the same script, over and over again.

But I had slept better these last two nights than I had in a long while. There was something about Sarah curled up next to me that took the tension out of my body and angst out of my mind. When we awoke earlier this morning, we had just laid there in each other's arms for a long time, enjoying the closeness. While the proximity of our nude bodies to one another was sensual, there had been a line there which we both intuitively understood.

"You were very good for me," she said, as she rose from the bed to leave. "I never told you that when we were together.

But you were good for me."

"I'm glad you thought so," I said seriously, rolling over on my side to watch her don her robe. "It was my honor and my privilege."

She retrieved her robe from the floor and faced me while she slid her arms into it. The expression on her face was one of both gratitude and regret. "I don't know when I'll see you again," she said.

I rose from the bed to embrace her one last time. "Be careful," I whispered as I held her. "Adam doesn't like the fact we're spending this sort of time together and for the life of me, I don't understand why."

She nodded into my shoulder, gently brushed my lips with hers, and left the room.

##

Now, back in the limo, I could feel a myriad of emotions coursing through me and pain was intertwined with them all. I found myself wondering if relationships were like a transactional analysis, the payoff was not being alone but the payment was the pain you'd suffer as a result.

"Well, that depresses the shit out of me," I said into the limo's interior.

I arrived at the airport, conducted all the normal preflight activity, and had the jet ready when Adam and Bill showed up at noon, accompanied by Miguel Hidalgo and his two guards, one of which was Joe. Felix/Saif was not with them and no one even looked twice at my bruises. Bill walked like a zombie back into the cabin and didn't acknowledge my presence. The three Mexican men followed him aft without a word. Adam closed the main door and took his place in the right seat. Other than the challenges and responses required to accomplish the checklist, he said nothing to me. No greeting, no apology, no acknowledgment. After we passed through flight level 180 on the climb out, I found myself alone in the cockpit again and enjoying the view of the Pacific coast from 45,000 feet.

It's funny how certain circumstances can possess and transport your mind. Being alone in the cockpit did that to me. Even though these days it happened only when the other crewmember went aft for one reason or another, the solitude still took me away. To another place. A place that felt familiar and safe. I liked seeing the change in the color of the atmosphere from this altitude. The light-blue hue of the troposphere was darkening into the blue-black of the stratosphere. Up here, alone, was just about the only venue in which I allowed myself to contemplate the existence of God. And then, as they always did, the words of John Gillespie Magee, Jr.'s "High Flight" came to my mind, unbidden.

Oh! I have slipped the surly bonds of Earth
And danced the skies on laughter-silvered wings;
Sunward I've climbed, and joined the tumbling mirth
Of sun-split clouds,—and done a hundred things
You have not dreamed of—wheeled and soared and
swung
High in the sunlit silence. Hov'ring there,
I've chased the shouting wind along, and flung
My eager craft through footless halls of air...
Up, up the long, delirious burning blue
I've topped the wind-swept heights with easy grace
Where never lark, or ever eagle flew—
And, while with silent, lifting mind I've trod
The high untrespassed sanctity of space,
Put out my hand, and touched the face of God.

As always, a lump formed in the back of my throat when the words ran their course. Try as I might, I could never understand the reason for that. I felt a moment of exhilaration. A moment of hope and of joy; the joy of flight, which was just about the only joy in my life these days.

"God, no matter what other shit happens, I've been lucky to do this," I said into the cockpit intercom. "So lucky."

I sat back into the sheepskin-covered pilot's seat, listened to the muted roar of the air going by the cockpit windows at Mach .85, and enjoyed my temporary place in the heavens. Things were going to heat up soon. I could feel it. But for now, I was in my element and all was well.

Adam returned to the cockpit as we descended through 10,000 feet back into Cabo Approach's control area. He dutifully ran all the checklists required and we landed uneventfully and taxied to the ramp. Once again, as usual, he and Bill and the gang were out and gone immediately after engine shutdown. This time, however, I was left to my own devices with no supervision.

I put the airplane to bed and locked it up. Then I retrieved my bags and my cane and went into the terminal. I was utterly unsurprised to find Juan in the waiting area holding a sign that said "COLON PERCE" in neat, block letters.

"Hello, Juan," I said, as I walked up. I pointed to the sign. "You forgot the 'A.'" I didn't tell him that he had also made my first name equal in nomenclature to an asshole. I figured I deserved that.

Juan looked down at the sign and his brown skin turned a dark shade of red.

"*Ay coño!*" he spat.

"It's no big deal," I said.

"I am so sorry, *Señor* Pee-arch," he said, "so sorry. Forgive me, *por favor.*"

"No problem," I said, now feeling like an ass for even mentioning it. "Are we going to the same hotel?"

He nodded rapidly. "*Si, si, Señor* Pee-arch. *Señor* Adam, he tell me to bring you *rapido*. I get your bags."

Into the van we went and to the hotel we drove.

From: Special Projects Group [NCS]
Sent: Monday, 23 November 2009, 1430 PST (23 November 2009, 2230Z)
To: Director, NCS
Cc: Special Projects Group [NCS]; damrine@cmail.cia.gov; dsmith3@cmail.cia.gov

SUBJECT: Aircraft Movement Summary and Update – Gulfstream G-IVSP N36WMS

(TS) Narrative:

1. (TS) N36WMS departed KBUR (Burbank/Bob Hope Airport) at 1202 PST / 2002 Z and landed at MMSD (Los Cabos International Airport) at 1359 PST / 2159 Z. Those on board included Contractor 09-017 (Pearce, Colin M), Abdullah bin Rashid al Qudamah, aka Adam Archmere, William Spratt, Miguel Hidalgo, and two of Hidalgo's bodyguards, Jose Rodriguez and Alejandro Garza. Saif-al Din, aka Felix Lopez, was not aboard.

2. (TS) DEA agent Joseph Sanchez, aka Jose Rodriguez, who has been involved in a deep cover intelligence-gathering and sting operations as a lieutenant for Miguel Hidalgo, has been introduced to Pearce to facilitate cooperative intelligence. Sanchez has confirmed that Bachelor's Toy has taken on many personnel who are confined to a crew living area below decks on the vessel. Sanchez has also confirmed Hidalgo's receipt of the shipment of hijacked weapons from Oman including:

small arms, crew-served weapons, man-portable surface-to-air missiles, and personal explosive devices. These weapons are reportedly aboard Bachelor's Toy with the personnel who have also been uploaded. Sanchez does not believe that Hidalgo would participate in an operation where bystanders would be killed or injured. Analysis of Hidalgo's past operations indicates that he has, in fact, avoided collateral damage at all costs.

(TS) CONCLUSIONS:

1. (TS) The existence of an armed force of possible combatants changes the range of options for al Qudamah and Hidalgo. We still believe a biological or chemical attack is planned to take place on Thanksgiving but we are now considering additional options which include the use of a platoon-sized ground force. As of this moment, there are no ground venues or events during the Thanksgiving timeframe schedule of which we are aware against which a platoon-sized force would present a reasonable threat;

2. (TS) We believe the possession of the hijacked weapons aboard Bachelor's Toy constitutes confirmation of a formal partnership between al Qudamah and Hidalgo and that this confirmed partnership warrants an increase in the inter-agency threat level.

(TS) ACTIONS:

1. (TS) Increase interagency threat level from ELEVATED to HIGH;

2. (TS) Continue intelligence collection and analysis by cross-agency team;

3. (TS) Request deployment of an E-3 AWACS aircraft to March AFB. We believe 24-hour airborne radar coverage of the Southern California area is warranted to detect off-airway movement of Gulfstream G-IVSP N36WMS;

4. (TS) Request placement of USAF-trained Air Traffic Control liaison officers at SOCAL (Southern California) Approach Control, located in San Diego with terminal control responsibility for all airports in Southern California. Also request placement of liaison officers in the Los Angeles Air Route Traffic Control Center. Both locations will monitor inbound traffic for hostile indications.

(TS) RECOMMENDATIONS:

1. (TS) Approve increase of interagency threat level from ELEVATED to HIGH;

2. (TS) Approve deployment of an E-3 AWACS aircraft to March AFB; and

3. (TS) Approve placement of USAF-trained Air Traffic Control liaison officers at SOCAL (Southern California) Approach Control and the Los Angeles Air Route Traffic Control Center.

CHAPTER FIFTEEN

Contract Day Seven
Monday, 23 November
1515 Hours Local Time
Hotel Imperial del Cabo
Cabo San Lucas, Mexico

When I checked in at the front desk, I did something I don't normally do. I made a fuss. After ranting about the uncleanliness of my room during my last visit, I insisted on a room that had been freshly cleaned. There were two different, but equally beautiful girls behind the desk this time; and after attempting to reason with me, they spent several minutes on their computers and even got their manager involved. And lo and behold, they found me a room that had just come open.

I had no sooner made it up there and shut the door behind me when my BlackBerry rang.

"Colin Pearce," I said, as I answered.

"Nice display, Pearce," said Amrine's voice in my ear. "Effective, but do you think you could have attracted any more attention?" I could almost see the smirk on his surfer-like face. "And those poor girls at the desk, you gave them so much shit. We're getting a little spoiled, aren't we?"

"Just trying to pick a room that Adam hadn't wired," I said tiredly. "I figured if I picked one that had just been cleaned he wouldn't have been able to get a crew in first. He can't have every room in this place bugged."

"Good call," Amrine said, with a respectful tone in his voice. "You're learning. In the future, we need to give you some noise-generating devices to travel with. Makes this sort of thing much simpler and easier on the service staff."

"I'm glad you called," I said, as I walked to the large windows and looked out at the ocean. "I was wondering, have you done any background work on Damian Marciano, Sarah's husband?"

"Damn," Amrine said. "No, we haven't gotten to it yet and bad on us. We've been trying to brainstorm what al Qudamah and Hidalgo are up to and it's taken a lot of our time. But I'll get someone on that ASAP." He paused and I could hear the sound of pen on paper. He was obviously writing himself a note of some sort. "You realize the whole thing with Damian might just be a coincidence, don't you?" he asked a moment later.

"How typical are coincidences in this line of work, John?"

"Believe it or not, more common than you might think. When you spend your entire career worrying about shit that might happen, you start to see conspiracies and motives behind everything. But in this case, I personally think you might be on to something. It fits and given the al Qudamah boys' cash limitations, basing a whole scenario on using someone else's jet is actually pretty brilliant, as is hiding inside the flight operation for a men's magazine. It is quite literally the last place anyone would look to find Islamic militants."

"So, on a different subject, obviously I met with Joe Sanchez yesterday and we exchanged what intel we had. Do you have any other info about Miguel Hidalgo's role in all of this? It shocked the shit out me when he got on the airplane two days ago."

"Cash and influence as far as we know," Amrine said, thoughtfully. "The al Qudamah brothers have long been cut off from funds sufficient to do any major damage and both of them like the ladies and the luxuries in life a little too much to sacrifice dollars from their personal trust funds to pay for anything big. We're thinking the al Qudamah boys diverted a shipment of arms his way in exchange for some big bucks so they could do their own thing."

"WMDs can be pretty expensive," I said, thinking aloud.

"Agreed," Amrine answered. "The chem or bio-weapon and business jet scenario fits, but the thing that's baffling us is the whole boatload of guys and guns thing. It appears Spratt bought the boat because the al Qudamahs made him do it. But a boat isn't the best platform to dispense a chemical or biological weapon and you sure don't need a lot of guys with guns to do it either. It appears the boat is a concession to Hidalgo. But for what purpose? We're scratching our heads like crazy trying to figure it out. Hell, we're still trying to figure out exactly what the hell al Qudamah plans for the G-IV at this point."

"Joe did say that Hidalgo was in California 'checking on his investment' yesterday, so I guess that's something," I said resignedly. "But I guess at this point there are still a lot more questions than answers."

"Exactly," Amrine replied, "which sort of fits in with the main reason I called you. We want to get you up in the penthouse tonight so you can place some surveillance gear. We need to get some more information."

I was puzzled.

"Isn't Susan still down here? I'd think she and good old Adam/Abdullah were both having the whole reunion scene up there right now."

There was a pause.

"She seems to have... um... disappeared," Amrine said after a moment, sounding distinctly embarrassed.

"What?"

"We can't find her and we can't contact her. She checked

out of her room in the hotel and she doesn't answer her phone or other devices. We heard an unconfirmed report that she moved up to the penthouse yesterday, but nothing other than that. Which is another reason why we have to get some eyes and ears inside the penthouse."

"Don't you have specialized teams for this sort of thing?"

"Yes, we do," he sighed. "But we're having difficulty getting assets because we can't seem to convince anyone that there is a real threat here, even with Miguel Hidalgo involved. We can't get a team in here to do a full black bag job on the penthouse. We have all the video and audio feeds covered but whoever is minding their store is good. We got a short audio clip through a computer that was online a few days ago, but other than that, nothing. We need to get devices in there and you're going to have to help us do it."

I exhaled in resignation. "What do you need me to do?"

"Get invited to another party upstairs. They'll have one tonight. They do it every night Bill and Adam are in town. We think they use the noise and confusion to conduct meetings in the background."

"And just how am I supposed to get invited?" I asked.

"Bill has a standing dinner reservation," Amrine replied. "He'll be in the bar and restaurant tonight along with some of his beautiful people. We'll supply you with a date, so to speak. She'll have the devices with her. Spratt likes you. Use that charm of yours and get invited to the party. Then get up to the penthouse, get the devices in place, and look around. Getting intel is paramount, but it'd be nice to know what's up with Susan." His tone became more somber. "At worst case, we have to make sure that they're not using Susan as a source of intel or we're all screwed."

"You know if they catch me," I said, "any cover I have remaining will pretty much be toast."

There was a pause.

"That's a chance we'll have to take. I have this overwhelming

237

feeling that we are way behind the power curve in figuring out what's going on here. We have to risk cranking things up a notch."

"So be it," I said. "Especially if Thanksgiving is D-Day. That's only three days from now."

"I know," Amrine said quietly.

"Hey John, one more thing."

"Yes?"

"Do you have a surveillance team on the mansion?"

"We have someone watching the mansion, in addition to other duties."

"Can you have him or them make Sarah part of the crosscheck? She didn't ask for any of this and I'd hate to see her hurt if it goes bad."

"You and the ladies, Pearce," Amrine chuckled, "you and the ladies."

"John, please, I'm serious," I said.

There was another pause and I had a feeling he was remembering the events of a few weeks ago. "Sure, Colin, sure. I'll make it happen as soon as we hang up."

"Thanks," I said gratefully. "I appreciate it."

The line went dead and I put the BlackBerry into its holster. Then I went outside on the stucco-walled balcony and stared at the gently lapping waves until the sun set into the bright blue Pacific.

A few hours later, I was limping across the ceramic tile toward the bar area, cane in hand, and again reflecting on the cyclical nature of my life. Looking over at the reception desk, I could see the same two girls I had harassed earlier glaring at me, the fire in their eyes contradicting the "customer service smiles" on their elegant faces. I smiled and walked over to them, thanked them profusely for all they had done, and raved about how clean my room was. Then, with a small flourish, I gave each of them a crisp one-hundred-dollar bill. Their eyes lit up and suddenly, I was their best customer. I considered it a good investment. You never knew when you'd need friends at the front desk.

It was a Monday night here in Cabo, but the hotel bar was doing a booming business. A crowd was already forming around the large corner booth where Bill and Adam held court. I eyed the group as I made my way to an empty seat at the bar, and wondered how in the hell I was going to break into the group and get invited upstairs.

"What may I get for you, señor?" asked the well-groomed barman.

"Shiraz," said a female voice from behind me, "Jacob's Creek Reserve, 2007."

"Si señorita," he answered and turned to get the drink.

I turned to find myself looking nearly eye-to-eye with a beautiful woman of color. She was smiling at me with an expression of anticipation on her face. She was lighter skinned with long, luxurious black hair tied behind her head and hanging a long way down her back.

And she looked very familiar.

"I don't know if it will rival the shirazes we poured by the glass the other evening, but perhaps it will be close," she said.

I wanted to smack myself on the side of the head. It was the girl who had played cocktail waitress at the Burbank Marriott. But tonight, instead of a uniform, she wore a cocktail dress which was exquisite, even to my untrained eye. It was aqua in color, with small, red sequins, gathered just under her perfectly-proportioned breasts and clung to her body below. The colors offset the coffee hue of her skin beautifully.

"You get around," I said at last.

"I travel a lot for my job," she said, flashing me a brilliant smile.

"Your Shiraz, señor," the bartender said.

I turned to take the drink and to sign the offered room charge check. As I turned back, the girl was looking at me. "Well, taste it," she said.

I swirled the wine in the large glass and then lowered my nose to smell it. A rich, fruity, and spicy bouquet greeted my nostrils. I eagerly put the glass to my lips and drank. The taste of ripe plums with a little pepper rolled across my tongue, balanced by soft grape and oak tannins. The finish was smooth and lingering.

"Wow," I said eloquently.

She laughed. "Not too shabby?"

"Between you and a couple of guys I know, I'm going to have to give up the cheap stuff."

She smiled at me brightly and took my arm. "So Mr. Pearce," she said teasingly, "care to show a girl a good time tonight?"

"Let me guess," I replied, "you're already 'in' with Bill's local entourage and have a standing to the party tonight."

"Close enough," she said.

I shook my head and smiled. "You guys don't leave much to chance, do you?"

"This kind of work has enough chance built into it."

"That's too bad," I said. "I was so looking forward to turning the old Pearce charm on for some unsuspecting young lady tonight." I couldn't finish the sentence with a straight face. "If there was any," I added.

The girl reached out and grabbed my free hand with hers. "Just because I'm a sure thing doesn't mean you shouldn't try," she said. "Besides, you do have this sort of bad-boy thing going on. It's kind of sexy."

I laughed. "Be careful," I paused, wanting to use her name and realizing I didn't know it. "You obviously know who I am. Who are you... I mean, what do I call you?"

She smiled and tilted her head toward me a little. "You can call me Sharona. Sharona... Brown."

"I like it. Maybe one day someone will write a song about that name of yours."

"Maybe they will," she said.

She took my arm and led me toward Bill and Adam's table. "Sharona" was a dish. She was built like a model, tall and lithe, and she moved with a restrained elegance. I felt privileged to even be in the same room with her. I could feel the eyes of several of the other men and women on me as we walked the short distance. For those who had seen my display with Susan only a few nights previously, I'm sure they were wondering how someone who looked like me wound up with women who looked like Susan and Sharona. If someone had asked, I don't know what I would have told them. *I'd rather be lucky than good,* came to mind.

A few minutes later, Bill Spratt showed up, surrounded by the usual bevy of beautiful women. He slid into the booth, regarded the crowd, and noticed Sharona and I sitting there. He gave us a broad smile and eagerly motioned us to join him. My status with the crowd, already high because of my companion, now soared even higher. We slid into the booth and then as my ass hit the seat, a realization hit my brain.

Adam wasn't here. And that could only mean one thing.

I casually slid my arm around Sharona's shoulder and pulled her to me. I kissed the corner of her mouth and then placed my lips next to her ear.

"Excuse yourself, go to the ladies' room, and tell the boys that Susan is definitely in the Penthouse."

She was a professional. She didn't even tense as I spoke. Instead, she kissed my cheek and ran her tongue lightly and sensually across it.

"How do you know?" she whispered.

"Adam's not here," I whispered back. "That means he's with her."

##

Three hours later, after six courses of food, several bottles of wine, and a round of after-dinner drinks, we all rode the elevators up to the penthouse. Throughout the meal, Sharona had become progressively more friendly, and now as we rose to the top of the building, she had her firm body practically wrapped around mine.

"I hope there's a room up there we can use for a little while," she said breathlessly, just loud enough for everyone in the elevator to hear. "I'm going to need to have you *very* soon."

"Oh really," I said, playing along, "well at the rate things are going on my side, we won't need the room for very long."

The folks in the elevator laughed at that. I was just so funny.

The doors open and into penthouse we went. The roar of music and conversation was like a slap in the face.

"Let's dance," Sharona whispered in my ear as we passed through the entryway.

"Looks like I picked the wrong week for leg recuperation," I sighed. "I'll do my best, but I'm warning you, I'm not very good."

"You don't have to be," she said. "I am." She squeezed my arm comfortingly. "And don't worry, it won't be for long. I just need to get an overview of the layout here and this is a non-obvious way to do it."

We made our way through the throng of people and down to the dance floor. I found myself unconsciously biting my tongue as I anticipated the pain in my leg that would inevitably come with the activity to follow. The evening's alcohol intake had dulled it somewhat, but it was still there, lurking below the anesthesia of the booze. And I knew it would be back with a vengeance.

The music was a mixture of Latin and Salsa tonight, and Sharona picked up the beat immediately. She masterfully led me through some complex moves while making it look like I was the one in command. Eventually, the tempo slowed for some body-to-body stuff. Playing her role, she rubbed herself against me and kissed me and did all the things required of her. This time, however, I could keep my emotional distance and play along. It was actually kind of fun, in an odd sort of way.

"So, you've been up here before," she said into my ear after a particularly spectacular kiss. "Where do you think they have her?"

"I'd be really surprised if she wasn't in the master suite," I said. "That's where Adam stays and odds are he's up there banging her right now."

Sharona moved her head back and looked at me with a surprised look on her face.

"Really?" she asked.

I nodded. "I think she's been here all along."

"Wow," she said. "But she's been out of contact."

"Could be a number of reasons for that," I replied, letting my voice trail off. The question I was asking myself was whether her stay had been voluntary or involuntary. Neither option was a particularly good one.

"Okay," Sharona said as she raised her lips to mine again. "So now we have to go upstairs and try to find a place to be alone and hopefully find Susan in the process."

"How far do you want to take this?" I asked between kisses.

"Depends on the audience," she said, looking around. "The more eyes there are, the hotter it will have to be." She pressed her lower body firmly against mine. "And we may have to get a certain part of your body involved," she said. "My understanding is you've done this kind of thing before."

You mean have sex for show? I wanted to say, but didn't. Instead, I nodded. I did have a question for her though.

"The theory is you have these *devices* to plant," I said. "But you've got this skimpy little dress on and a purse that barely has room for a cell phone. Where are the devices?"

She put her mouth next to my ear.

"Sequins are a wonderful thing," she whispered. "And now, if there are no further questions," she continued playfully, "let's get to it."

She took me by the hand and we slowly ascended the staircase at the end of the large room and went up to the second floor. People were milling about up here as well, in and out of the assorted rooms and on the terraces. We worked our way into each room and as we repeatedly stopped to kiss and grope one another, Sharona would surreptitiously peel sequins from her dress, and place them in places that were just out of sight but would be able to pick up to casual conversation easily, like behind pictures and under the arms of chairs. In one of the nicer bedrooms, Sharona needed to place a device behind a headboard, which required a lengthy kissing session on the mattress in full view of those who strolled in and out of the open doors.

"Jesus, Colin," Sharona laughed after we rose from the bed.

"What?" I asked.

"Did you take Viagra or something tonight?"

"Performance enhancing drugs," I said. "Provided by one of your doctors to help me heal more quickly. They have certain... side effects."

"No kidding!" she said. "That's amazing! And this isn't my first time to the rodeo."

"What can I say," I replied. "What I don't have in talent or ability I make up for with technology."

We continued to work our way across the floor toward the master suite and stopped about two rooms down as our little act continued. I had Sharona against the wall and was kissing her deeply as I cupped her firm ass in my hands. Her own hands were busy holding my hips against her and she had one of her legs wrapped around mine.

"Check it out," I whispered, inclining my head toward our objective.

The entrance to the suite was obvious. There were two grand columns on either side of the ornate wooden doors and two dark-complexioned men on either side. They looked as hard as the stone they were standing next to.

"Damn," she said, "don't think we're going to be able to get past those two without attracting some attention."

The main entrance door and columns were bracketed by a pair of large, curved windows cut into the curved walls on either side of the door. There seemed to be no way in other than the front.

And then I saw the side door.

The curved wall nearest to us ended in an alcove, and there, barely visible to us and just out of sight of the guards, was a single door.

"Well, well, well," I said. "Darling, we may have found our room."

We walked into the alcove with just the right amount of urgency to attract the guards' attention, but not their interest.

As soon as we were out of their view, Sharona was all business. She pushed me against the door, and very quickly and adeptly, unclasped my belt and undid my fly. "Drop your pants," she said.

"What?" I asked in astonishment. Sharona knelt in front of me, opened her purse and pulled out what looked like a small I-Pod music player. Then she reached behind her neck and unclasped her necklace, which looked like a very chic silver tube, about a quarter of an inch in diameter.

She looked up at me impatiently.

"I want to get some video surveillance into the master suite, which means we need to get through this door. And I need to see if there is anyone on the inside, which means I need to get on my knees and if someone comes by..."

I nodded.

"Jesus," I breathed. "The things I do for my country."

I pushed my pants and underwear down obediently as she snapped one end of the tubing into the I-Pod. Then, ignoring my erect penis, which was literally directly in front of her face, she threaded the free end of the tube between my legs and under the bottom edge of the door.

Then we heard the click of footsteps on the ceramic tile hallway.

She hid the I-Pod in the pile of my trousers, immediately grabbed my penis with both hands and wrapped her mouth around it. She began moving her head up and down rhythmically.

I inhaled involuntarily with pleasure and closed my eyes just in time to hear the footsteps stop behind us.

"Wow," a female voice said, "that's so hot. Let's go find another place so I can do that to you."

The footsteps scurried off, but Sharona kept at it, her head moving back and forth.

"Damn," I whispered, "you don't have to keep this up, they're gone." I didn't mention that the odds of my coming in her mouth were increasing by the second.

"Guard will come now," she said, with her mouth still around me.

He's not the only one, I thought.

Sure enough, as she continued to do her thing, another set of heavier, more deliberate footsteps, made their way down the walkway toward us. I could feel the first drops of pre-ejaculate begin to seep out of me.

"Not yet," she whispered. "Hold it back. I need you to stay like this for a while longer."

"I'm doing my best," I hissed though clenched teeth. "Goddamn, you're good at this."

The footsteps got closer. And Sharona lifted her head to look at me as she continued to stroke my penis. "Wow, baby," she said loudly enough for the approaching guard to hear. "This is getting me so wet. We're going to need to find a place

246

or I'm going to have to fuck you right here." She went back to work with her hands and mouth. And I tried to think about aircraft operations limits, Federal Aviation Regulations, and just about anything else that would distract me from the fact that a beautiful woman was giving me some of the best oral sex I'd ever had.

The footsteps stopped nearby and paused there for a few seconds. We heard a grunt of acknowledgment and then the footsteps moved away. Sharona kept at it for another minute or so and then lifted her mouth from me. She had aroused me so much I could still feel myself tingling.

"Fuck!" I said.

But she wasn't paying any attention. She had retrieved the I-Pod and was looking down at it. On the screen was some sort of infrared display. I leaned over to see more clearly. In a superb display of multi-tasking, she put her lubricated hand on my shaft and used it to force me back against the door in my position as she gazed downward at the screen.

"You need to stay where you are," she said.

"Okay," I said weakly. "What is that thing?"

"It's an infrared, fiber-optic camera, I'm checking to see who or what is in this room."

"And?"

"We're in luck. It appears to be a small den or reading room. If we can get in, I can put a bug in the common wall to the master suite and we might be able to get some eyes and ears in there."

"How are you going to get in?" I asked, as she continued to stroke me while she regarded the display.

"Pick the lock, obviously," she said. She looked up at me. "I'm going to need both hands to do a few things, but you need to keep yourself suitably...ready in the event we have to continue the act. Understand?"

I nodded dumbly.

"Then do it," she said, taking her hand from my penis to

go back into her purse.

I did as I was ordered, feeling more odd and awkward than I had in my entire life.

Sharona retrieved a small leather case that looked like a manicure set. She removed two tools and set to work on the door lock. I heard the click of the latch a few moments later.

"Come on, Colin," Sharona chided me. "I can't do everything around here."

I looked down and found that my penis had lost a fair amount of its enthusiasm. She applied her hands and mouth to me for a minute or two and I was tumescent once again.

"Now keep it that way!" she ordered.

She checked the screen for a moment, to make sure no one was in the room I presumed, then slid the door handle down and pushed the door open.

There were two sofas facing one another across a glass-covered coffee table. A long bookshelf covered one side of the room and it had an opening for a fireplace in the center at floor level.

There was a set of double doors into the master suite next door, but they were as solid as entry doors. Perhaps this was a waiting area for suite guests.

"Sit there," she pointed to the sofa closest to the door. "I want your pants and shorts around your ankles. Do it!"

Like a cat, she swept around the room placing sequins under the end tables and at strategic places on the bookshelf. Then she zipped over to the double doors on the far wall.

In the meantime, pants in one hand and cane in the other, I had awkwardly made my way to the sofa along the near wall, sat my bare ass on the luxurious cloth, and pushed my pants and underwear to my ankles as I was told. Fortunately, maintaining the required physical state was made easier by the appealing visual of Sharona bent over, sliding the fiber optic tube under the double doors. Her dress had hiked up somewhat and a generous portion of her splendid, muscular ass was visible, her light-brown skin reflecting the dim light coming through the entry door. I may have been mistaken, but I didn't see a trace of a thong or undergarments of any kind.

"Sit in the middle of the couch, stay hard, and listen for footsteps," she hissed.

"Yes, ma'am!"

After peering at the fiber optic display and adjusting the viewing angle several times, she appeared to see what she wanted. Then she leapt up onto the sofa across from me, moved a large picture that was in the center of the wall aside, placed her fingertip against the wall and gently tapped.

"This should work," she whispered.

She pulled what looked like a fat lipstick from her purse, along with another tube that looked like mascara. A drill bit came out of the mascara and plugged into the lipstick. Then came the soft, high-pitched whine of a drill.

"Hopefully that won't attract too much attention," she said. "And hopefully the interior wall construction in this hotel is as cheap as it is in most places."

About fifteen seconds later, the drill came out and I could just barely see a stream of dim light coming in from the fresh hole in the wall. The mascara and lipstick went back into the purse and an eyebrow pencil came out. She took the end cap off and then gently inserted the pencil into the hole until it went all the way through. Then she turned it slightly and a red pinpoint of light appeared on the end of it.

She took out the I-Pod, fiddled with a switch or something on the inside, and then smiled over at me.

"We're in business!" she said.

And then we heard the footsteps in the hall.

Faster than I would have believed possible, she replaced the picture and flew across the room to the sofa where I was seated, hiking her dress up as she did so. I had a glimpse of a runway-shaped thatch of dark pubic hair and then she was upon me, straddling me on the sofa, her genitals up

249

against mine. She had one arm locked around my neck and was leaning back, in a perfect impression of a woman on the pre-orgasm plateau.

"Um baby, oh baby, that feels so good," she cooed at me. "You're going to make me come right here."

The footsteps became more audible and there was a brief conversation in Arabic outside the door. Then, out of my peripheral vision, which was surprisingly engaged at this point, I saw two men step through the door we had entered.

"Excuse me," a polite voice with an Arabic accent interrupted. "You must leave this room."

Sharona and I did a perfect impersonation of two lovers embarrassed in the middle of a public tryst. We rearranged our clothes hurriedly and left the room with polite apologies to the guard who had interrupted us.

He didn't even ask our names.

A few moments later, we were out on the lower floor balcony of the penthouse, overlooking the ocean in a secluded spot, and Sharona was fishing the I-Pod back out of her purse.

"Great work, Colin!" she said. "You're a natural at this!"

"Well I've certainly been getting a lot of practice recently," I said, as I finished buttoning and rearranging. "I have to ask a question," I said haltingly. "What do you do if you actually have an orgasm while you're putting on an act like this?"

"Enjoy it!" she said, as she fiddled with the I-Pod. "It's one of the few perks of the job. If that guard had taken a few seconds longer to get into the room, I would have been there. I was getting pretty hot." She looked down at the I-Pod's screen. "Okay, here we go. The smaller pick-ups we installed," she motioned to the sequins on her dress, "are like little wireless mics and they push to a central collection point we installed on a balcony on the floor below this one. They operate in the same radio range as cell phones and they're voice activated, so they're very hard to detect. But this video feed is different. It operates on a different frequency because we need HD quality to get the detail required. We can't get too far away from the transmitter I installed in that room because it doesn't have a lot of range; and if we install a signal booster, any normal electronic sweeping equipment will pick it up. Hell, if they have the right gear they might have picked it up already."

She turned to lean back against me.

"Put your arms around me, please. I'm cold."

I complied and wrapped my arms around her as she tuned the I-Pod to display the bug unit she had just installed.

The picture was tiny and infrared. The scene was of a bedroom area, with a four-poster, king-sized bed against the wall on the far side. Sure enough, a man and a woman were on the bed. She was on her hands and knees and he was on his knees behind her. Even with the limited detail in the small screen, it was easy to see she wasn't happy about it.

Sharona pulled a headset out of her purse to get the audio. She plugged it in and offered me one of the ear pieces.

"This was part of the deal, remember?" Adam's voice came clearly through the headset. The audio was amazingly crisp.

"I thought what I told you *was* the deal," Susan said meekly.

"No," Adam replied. There was no mistaking the arrogance in his voice. "What you told me was for the money. This is for getting you and your kids out of the country."

"But I thought..."

"I didn't pay you to think, I paid you for information from your friends in the Secret Service. But that money doesn't get you out of the country." He stroked her upper body and then smacked her ass, hard. "This is what gets you and your brats out of the country. This." He spat the last word into the palm of his right hand and used the spittle to lubricate his penis.

I shook my head in disgust.

He grabbed her hips firmly with one hand. Then he positioned his penis between the cheeks of her ass. He paused for a diabolical moment. Then he roughly shoved his hips forward and pulled her onto him.

"Jesus," she gasped.

"I've had several American bitches who liked it in the ass. You'll get used to it."

I watched the screen with the same conflicted emotions you feel watching a car wreck. Part of you wants to look away and another part of you simply can't. I felt an odd mixture of sympathy and frustration for Susan because of her predicament. The familiar hunger was rising inside me along with a slow eruption of raw anger. A confident and beautiful woman whom I had come to respect was being degraded. But another part of me was playing the conversation repeatedly in my mind. *What information was she giving him?*

"I thought I recognized you when you came into this place," said an angry male voice with a heavy Arabic accent. "What are you doing here?"

Sharona tore the ear pieces from our ears and the I-Pod disappeared into her purse in a flash. We turned and found a man in the generic business suit worn by the guards standing in front of us. He was swarthy, olive-complexioned and looked disturbingly familiar. He also had an automatic pistol of some sort in his right hand.

"Oh, I'm sorry, sir," Sharona said meekly, "are we not supposed to be here? I thought Bill said we could go anywhere out here." She made a show of snuggling back up against me. "We just had to get away from all those people in there. It's just so crowded."

The man wasn't fooled by her act. He knew who she was. He knew who I was. His eyes narrowed as he looked at our faces. He was the same guy Sharona had arranged to have thrown out of the bar at the Burbank Marriott. Even if he had half a brain, he would have been able to put the pieces together.

He motioned with the muzzle of the pistol toward the nearest door back into the penthouse. "They thought I was crazy. That I was seeing things. But I will show them. We will go see the boss now," he said, stepping forward.

He's balls deep in a woman's ass, I thought. *Good luck with that.*

"Oh my," Sharona said, leaning forward a little and raising her left hand to her mouth, "I'm not feeling well." Then she fell forward, toward the man.

He hesitated for half-a-second. And it cost him his life.

Sharona used the momentum from her fall to step into him. With her left hand, she grabbed the wrist with the gun and rotated his arm in a direction that was physically impossible. The sound of the bone snapping was just barely audible over the music and conversation coming from inside. Even as the weapon fell to the tile, Sharona was stepping even closer to the man and had her right hand swinging in an arc behind him. The man's eyes had been widening as they had registered the pain of having his right arm broken, but now they registered surprise for just a moment. Then, they became empty.

To the casual observer, it might have looked like she embraced him.

"Little help here, Colin," she whispered as his body went limp in her arms.

I moved forward and helped her with the now inert guard.

"Hey buddy, are you okay?" Sharona asked just loudly enough for those within earshot to hear. "Maybe you need to sit down for a while."

We half-walked, half-dragged him across a few feet of tile to a table and chairs and sat him down into the nearest chair. As she took her hand away from the back of the man's head, I saw her withdraw a long stiletto from the area where his skull met his spinal cord.

"Holy shit," I whispered involuntarily. "Remind me never to piss you off."

Sharona ignored me as she positioned him at the table to make it look like had had put his head down on his hands and fallen asleep. She also arranged the hair at the base of his skull to conceal the wound. Then she looked around quickly. The partiers on this area of the balcony were sparse and it appeared the scuffle had gone unnoticed.

"Let's casually make our way out of here," Sharona said. "We need to get to a place where we can talk with Bart and Bruiser. I don't know what this means, but we need to get it to someone who does."

"Bart and Bruiser?" I asked.

She laughed. "They never told you their handles? Their code names? Bruiser is Smith. You don't want to get on his bad side. He has more ways to kill you than you've even heard of. And Amrine is Bart." She smiled at me in the dull light. "Like Bart Simpson? Blonde hair, smart-ass attitude?"

I grinned at that. "What's your handle?"

"Angel," she said. "Not the good kind."

"That sounds a little ominous."

She took my arm and we began to walk off the patio area and back inside the main area to depart.

We didn't make it to the elevator. We didn't even make it into the inner hall. As we approached the large French doors to enter the hall, we found ourselves face-to-face with three large guards. Each of them was dark complexioned, at least my height and about one and half times as wide as I was. Behind them was one of the Mexican "head guards" that manned the main entrance and had admitted Susan and me my first night here. I remembered that he had been quite pleasant when I had met him before. Tonight, he still had a pleasant expression on his mouth but his eyes were all business.

I felt Sharona tense at my side, like she was coiling.

I don't know what I expected them to do. Especially, in a place crowded with witnesses. Maybe I expected a speech, a la the James Bond movies. Or maybe I expected them to "escort" us somewhere gently. All I know is that I did not expect what happened next.

Suddenly, the forehead of each of the three guards sprouted

a red spot, about the size of a pencil eraser. They appeared in startlingly quick succession, one, two, three. The looks on their faces were identical, a combination of shock and surprise.

And then each of their heads vibrated suddenly and they collapsed to the floor. Sharona immediately took my hand and we turned and ran back out onto the patio. She quickly pulled me to the left, around the corner and into the area where the plunge pool was. We then flattened ourselves against the wall that hid us from the walkway down which we had just come. She appeared to be counting to herself.

"We need a distraction. In a second, I'm going to tell you to go jump in that pool and when you do, you need to make as much noise as you can."

"Okay," I said, unclipping the BlackBerry from my belt and taking the wallet from my pants and laying them both on the ground along with my cane in a rare moment of mental presence.

"Now!" she hissed.

I limped/ran to edge of the pool and jumped as high as I could. Then I put my legs straight out in front of me and perpendicular to my body, while covering my face. The "king-sitter" dive was perfect and I heard the giant slap sound my legs made when hitting the water and knew the splash to follow would be most impressive. When I came up for air, Sharona was peering over the side of the stucco wall on the walkway and to the ground several stories below. I exited the pool and limped to her side.

"There goes another damn good stiletto," she said, as I approached.

I looked over the side and saw the crumpled body of the lead guard impaled on the spikes of a wrought iron fence several stories below.

"What now?" I asked.

"Well, we're not getting out the front way, that's for sure," Sharona said.

"Why do you think they were coming after us?" I asked. "They couldn't have found the guy you put down so quickly."

She was shaking her head.

"They couldn't have found the bug," she said. "Unless they had an alarm set up for listening devices."

"How did you...?"

She raised her hand and showed me a small automatic pistol. "Point one seven caliber with exploding shells. Small, easy to hide, but devastating. I used the bullets that just explode internally. If I had used the ones with the larger charge, it would have gotten pretty messy in there."

"I'll say. I'm not trying to tell you how to do your job but wasn't that a little extreme? They'll be onto the fact that you guys know now."

"They already know," she said. "Weren't you listening to the I-pod earlier? Barbie sold out on us. I don't think they expected you at the party tonight but somebody made you and in the process, they made me. We were being collected for questioning. For you it was just a question of time. I was a bonus."

She glanced around.

"Part of my mission is to get you out of here. And if we can't go down, maybe we should go back up." She pointed to the stairway which went up from the pool to the exterior balcony of the master suite. "The last place they'll look for us is right next to the boss' quarters."

I shrugged. "You're in charge."

She nodded. "Let's go."

After I retrieved my BlackBerry, wallet, and cane, Sharona led me past the hot tub at the base of the stairs and up the concrete steps. We hunched over to avoid detection and quickly made it to the upper balcony, outside the master suite. The balcony was about ten feet wide, and for the moment, uninhabited. We low-walked over to a corner, next to the wall of the suite, and knelt there while we plotted our next move.

My eyes found something interesting. I nudged Sharona and pointed.

There was a door, a single, steel door on the wall next to us and near where that wall met the lower wall of the balcony. It was the sort of door typically found on exit staircases.

"You don't think?" I asked.

"Only one way to find out."

We low-walked over to the door and tried the latch. It was unlocked and the door opened into a dimly lit stairwell; and judging by the pattern of landings and metal rails below, it was evident the stairway went down quite a distance.

Sharona shook her head. "Odd place for a fire exit stairway."

"Not really," I said. "We're at the far southern edge of the building. There's one of these staircases on each end of the hotel, I bet."

"Never look a gift horse in the mouth, I guess," she replied. "It's not like we have a lot of other options. I'm going first to check things out. Stay right behind me."

She went through the door, crouched down, with her small automatic at the ready. I paused to give her just a second.

And then my brain detected a sound that was out of place in the now-quiet night. It was the sound of a leather-soled shoe scraping the concrete patio, in a dead sprint, heading toward us.

"Go," I whispered to Sharona and pushed her into the stairwell. I turned, slammed the door shut after her, and threw my weight back against it as I watched my assailants approach. They were the two guards from outside Adam's door. They were big, agitated, and heading right for me. I didn't have much time or much to work with. I just knew I needed to give Sharona time to get away.

I grabbed one of the light-weight aluminum chairs next to me and tossed it toward the first guy's feet. It landed in front of him and skidded closer to him. He tried to jump it, and had it not been moving when he did, he might have made it. But his rear foot got caught on one of the legs of the chair and down he went.

One down, one to go.

There was a trash can next to the door, a plastic forty or fifty-gallon version encased in a decorative container that was plastered in stucco to match the wall. As the second guard approached me in full-defensive-lineman tackle mode, I grabbed the trash can, lifted it, and swung it around to put it between us. His head smashed into it and he went down.

Two down and time for me to go. I had no illusions about my being able to handle these guys in a fair fight.

I dodged the second guy as he crumpled and evaded the first guy as he tried to regain his footing and lunged toward me. I gritted my teeth and ran to the edge of the upper balcony, did a little mental math, and then jumped onto the edge of the balcony wall and sprang down. I hoped like hell I'd land in the plunge pool below, knowing I probably wouldn't be able to walk if I didn't.

I splashed down a microsecond later, cane in hand, and was out of the pool nearly as quickly as I had landed. I limped down the balcony walkway, next to the edge, with no other plan but to make a run for it and try to get to the stairs at the other end of the building.

I entered the more open area of the downstairs balcony and was relieved to see a door that looked like an exit at the far end, set into the stucco wall with a lighted sign over it. Since there were actually people on this section of the balcony, I made my way toward the door as nonchalantly as possible. Even though I was soaking wet, I barely attracted a second glance from the partiers on the balcony and I was at the door very quickly. Looking around, I depressed the handle, opened the door, and slipped around it and into the stairwell as hurriedly as I could.

The stairwell was well lit and I hobbled my way down the cement stairs to my floor as quickly as I could, with my leg complaining the entire way. At any moment, I expected to hear the stairwell door I had just entered slam open followed by footsteps coming after me.

But it didn't happen and I made it to my floor without incident.

Feeling ever-so-cautious, I opened the door to the hallway and checked to ensure there were no other people in the hallway. Once I verified I was alone, I slipped through the stairwell door and closed it quietly behind me. Then I tiptoed to my room, which was only a few doors down. I reached into my right pocket and panicked for a moment when I thought I had misplaced my keycard. But as I dug further down, I found it was still where I had left it.

"Damn deep pockets," I muttered to myself.

I slipped the keycard into the slot and turned the handle to slowly open the door, wondering why I was being so cautious. I opened the door to my suite and walked in, noting it was quite dark and wondering why I hadn't turned any lights on when I left.

I placed my keycard, my now-soaked wallet, and my BlackBerry on the entry table, and then reached up to turn on the lights. And I saw that I was not alone.

CHAPTER SIXTEEN

Contract Day Seven
Monday, 23 November
2200 Hours Local Time
Hotel Imperial del Cabo
Cabo San Lucas, Mexico

Miguel Hidalgo sat at the head of my table, his back to the floor-to-ceiling French doors, smoking a cigar and nursing a glass of what I assumed was single-malt Scotch. He looked at me curiously but respectfully. Oddly enough, I wasn't terribly surprised to see him there. Perhaps I should have been, but I wasn't.

His same two bodyguards, Joe and the other guy, stood between the two of us, but off to the side, perhaps to interdict any attempt on Miguel's life that I might make. I was slightly surprised to see both Adam/Abdullah and Susan seated at the table as well. For two people who had been naked and fucking mere moments ago, they looked remarkably put together and composed.

"Come in, amigo," Miguel said. He gestured to the room around him. "You will forgive our use of your room, of course. Our accommodations above have become somewhat inhospitable." He pointed at the chair at the opposite end of the table from him with his cigar. "Have a seat. We must talk."

"What if I'm not in a terribly talkative mood?"

Miguel smiled and tilted his head toward Adam/Abdullah without taking his eyes off me.

"Then I send a text message and my good friend Saif, whom you know as Felix, and he walks up to Sarah's room back at the mansion and cuts her throat," Adam said. "But Saif enjoys his work. He may not cut her throat right away, he might play with her awhile..."

Miguel lifted his hand in a silencing gesture and Adam immediately stopped speaking.

So much for not harming non-combatants. Then I corrected myself. *If he thinks Sarah's involved, that makes her a combatant. Damn.*

I hobbled toward the table and immediately, Miguel's guards stripped me of the cane and frisked me quickly but thoroughly. When they were finished, I was offered the chair at the opposite end of the table and I sat down.

"We already know who you're not working with," Miguel said, as he raised the glass of liquor to his mouth and took a sip. "The DEA."

"What makes you so sure?" I asked.

He laughed and pointed at me with his cigar. "First of all, you should be glad, because if you were DEA, your head would be on its way to Virginia in a box. I have a reputation to maintain."

I smiled crookedly.

"But you should be more careful, my friend. Between our background check on you and the display this evening, we know you're working with the CIA. What is important to us is how much they know."

I looked back at him and tried to keep my face expressionless. But deep inside, I was trying to draw upon the instruction I had ages ago during resistance training at the Air Force Academy. Particularly, the stuff they taught us on resisting interrogation. The trick was not to play silent, I remembered. The trick was to mislead. But do so in a way that the interrogator would believe.

"So, if you'd like to stay intact and alive and would like Miss Marciano to remain the same, you'll tell me just that. How much do they know?"

How the hell should I play this? I was sure Miguel had administered many interrogations and would be expert at detecting a lie.

And there was another variable in the equation that had ominous consequences.

How much had Susan told them?

I pointed at Adam. "Apart from the fact that they know your buddy over there is a Saudi prince with a name I'm not even going to try to pronounce, they don't know shit," I said.

I saw Adam's eyes light up with fury but Miguel's face was unmoved.

"Look," I said, "I'm here because Sarah and I have some history. She asked me to help her and I came. Now I get out here and discover that there's a lot of other shit going on. I don't particularly care what the outcome of said shit is as long as I get paid and no one I care about gets hurt."

Hidalgo raised his eyebrows at me, obviously expecting more.

"The point is," I continued, "I've got no reason to lie to you. They don't know shit. They suspect a lot, but they don't have leads on anything or proof of anything."

"You're leaving out an important piece of the puzzle, Mr. Pearce," Miguel said patiently but ominously. "How do you and the CIA have such a cozy relationship?"

A part of my training replayed in my brain. "Often," the instructor said, "the interrogator will ask you questions he already knows the answers to. He's testing you. Trying to see if you're lying to him. If you can afford to, in these situations, tell the truth."

I nodded. "You already know the answer to that," I said.

"I did some contract work for them about a month ago. They feel like they have a claim on me now."

"A claim?"

"Mr. Hidalgo, the CIA keeps tabs on me and they know who Adam is. When they put together the pieces of me working for him, they wanted more information. There are entities in the world you don't say no to. The CIA is one. I imagine you are another."

Miguel smiled at that comparison. Never resist stroking the ego of someone in power when it will benefit you, I always say.

"One more thing," I said, hoping to improve my case by telling some more of the truth. Or at least a piece of it. "They were very concerned about her." I nodded toward Susan. "The whole thing tonight was about finding her."

Miguel tried to keep his face impassive, but a quick glance and accompanying scowl in Adam's direction confirmed that he had already suspected that. I found myself wondering if the combination of Adam's ego and libido had been a liability to 'the operation,' whatever it was.

"Are you going to believe him?" It was Susan's voice this time. "Are you actually going to buy this bullshit? He's working for *them*. The agents in charge are friends of his!" Her voice had just a trace of desperation in it.

I looked right into Miguel's eyes calmly.

"And you and your female friend saw or heard nothing?" he asked me.

"She didn't see anything useful and I was just along to provide cover," I sighed and looked over at Susan. "I seem to have been doing a lot of that recently."

"Too bad you suck at it," she hissed at me.

There were all sorts of sharp comebacks that rushed into my brain, but I kept my mouth shut.

Miguel looked carefully at my face and seemed to make up his mind. He motioned to the guards.

"Time to leave," he said.

"Leave for where?" The surprise in Adam's voice was obvious.

"For my hacienda, further north on the peninsula. We will take your plane."

"But why..."

Miguel shot a quick glance at him that cut him off in mid-sentence. "We obviously cannot stay *here* any longer," he snapped. "If we are not under surveillance now, we will be. There will be a CIA team on site very quickly and we need to move before the locals are mobilized. Even with my influence, multiple deaths at this hotel will not go without investigation."

"What about Spratt?" Adam asked, appropriately subdued.

"We'll put him on the boat for appearances and we'll leave the boat here until we're ready to stage." Miguel returned his gaze to me. "You may still yet be useful, Mr. Pearce. My understanding is that you're a rather gifted pilot."

"I have my days," I said.

"I hope you have your nights, because you're going to fly that G-IV into my private airstrip tonight."

"I've had a little bit to drink," I answered. "Does that matter to you?"

"'Does it matter to you?' is the question. If something bad happens, you'll be the first one to the scene of the crash."

I smiled. Miguel had a sense of humor.

"You're just going to need to be on your game," he said, still looking at me. "We're going there without a flight plan and without radar control. The strip is lighted and paved, but it is four-thousand feet long by sixty feet wide. I built it for smaller aircraft, like Beechcraft King Airs."

"Do you have some exact longitude and latitude coordinates for the end of each runway?" I asked.

"Yes," he answered with a knowing smile on his face.

"No problem." I shouldn't have asked the next question, but I couldn't help myself. "Adam's qualified in the G-IV. Why don't you want him to fly?'

I could feel Adam's eyes burning to me like twin laser beams but I kept my eyes on Miguel. He glanced over at Adam and then back to me.

"Because I'd like to get there alive," he said.

CHAPTER SEVENTEEN

Contract Day Seven
Monday, 23 November
2330 Hours Local Time
Los Cabos International Airport (MMSD)
San Jose Del Cabo, Mexico

One hour and fifteen minutes later, we were airborne, climbing out of the Cabo airport and headed up north to Miguel's hacienda and airstrip. I was at the controls, Adam was sitting next to me in the right seat, and Miguel was on the jump seat between us. I didn't know if Miguel was there to keep Adam in line or to provide vectors to his airstrip, but I was grateful for his presence, in an odd sort of way. The rest of the entourage, including Susan, Joe, Miguel's henchmen, and a few other miscellaneous men and women were sitting in back along with our hurriedly-loaded baggage.

"Stay on your present heading, head out to the coast, and turn right when you're clear of Los Cabos," Miguel said once the gear and flaps were retracted.

It was a typical, clear, desert night and since we had taken off to the south, the white lights of the highway to the coast were readily visible underneath us. Beyond that, the line of the southern coast was clearly outlined, just a few miles away.

"Altitude?" I asked, as I pushed forward on the yoke to

slow our climb. The autothrottles retarded to maintain our speed at 250 knots.

"Between five and ten thousand," he answered. "It will make for a long flight, but at that altitude and 250 knots, we won't attract attention. They might even think we're on a sightseeing tour."

I leveled the G-IV at 8,000 feet and engaged the autopilot. For the first time since we left the hotel, I had a few moments to think as I settled into my element once again. Next to me, I could see Miguel's cold features reflected in the glow of the display units as he calmly regarded the night sky. I don't know what stereotype I had formed in my mind where drug lords were concerned, but Miguel Hidalgo was not what I expected. He was thoughtful, literate, and intelligent. Nothing at all like *Scarface's* Tony Montana. And I was sure that made him more dangerous.

I knew the only reason I was still alive was because I was useful. I also knew that the moment I ceased being useful, my time was up. I just had to try to stay useful until the cavalry arrived. If it ever did.

My CIA BlackBerry was in Miguel's possession and I was sure he had turned it off, assuming it was even still operative after having taken a swim when I jumped off the balcony earlier. So much for the Feds tracking my position. I just hoped one of the radar controllers at the Cabo approach control would remember where we flew or that another radar agency would track us.

Almost like he was reading my mind, Miguel pointed down at the multifunction radio control units.

"Is this where you control the radar transponder?" he asked.

I nodded. The transponder was the device that illuminated our aircraft on radar for controlling agencies. Without it, we were just a "*skin paint*" and much harder to detect.

"Turn it off," he said.

Miguel's hacienda was on the west coast of the Baja Peninsula, about five-hundred miles north of Cabo San Lucas, near a small town called Santa Maria, about two-hundred miles south of Tijuana. During the flight northward, Miguel showed me a topographical map of the area. There was a natural harbor there which was roughly in the shape of the letter "U," with the open area of the U oriented north, northwest. The airstrip was on the land between the arms of the U. All 4,000 feet of it.

Using the coordinates Miguel had given me, I programmed the location of the southern end of the runway into the G-IV's flight navigation system. Then, using the magnetic heading of the runway, about 330, I constructed a virtual final approach course and glide path to the runway. Assuming Miguel's coordinates were accurate, the jet would basically fly itself down to just above the runway. And that's when the work would start. I'd have to get about thirty tons of jet traveling at 140 knots stopped in less than four-thousand feet. I hoped all the coffee I'd been drinking since we left the hotel would have the desired effect.

Just over two hours after takeoff we reached a point about fifty miles south of Miguel's airport and I commanded the jet to begin a slow descent to fifteen-hundred feet above ground level (AGL). We were flying over the water just off the west coast of the Baja peninsula. The partial moon was bright and the sky was clear, making the distinctive shoreline easy to see. I had programmed a point five miles from the end of the runway into the jet's navigation system and extended the centerline of my virtual final approach course from the runway to that point and into infinity. Now, as the jet descended, I commanded it to intercept my virtual final at about the seven-mile point.

"Why are you descending so early?" Adam asked, impatiently. "If we stayed high, we could intercept your glide path and follow it down."

"Because I want to get the airplane down, completely configured and stabilized before we get on the glide path," I answered as I monitored the jet's descent. "I never pass up the chance to get ahead of the airplane." I looked over at Miguel. "Radio frequency for the lights?" I asked.

He nodded. "You'll need to do it on two radios at the same time. Use 124.7 on one radio and 133.2 on the other. When the time comes, click three times on the first frequency, wait one second, and click four times on the second. Don't do it until you're about a mile out on final because the lights only stay on for sixty seconds."

Adam tuned the two aircraft radios to the VHF frequencies Miguel provided. Pilot-controlled airfield lighting at uncontrolled airports was a common thing. The pilot tuned a frequency in his radio, then keyed the mic switch to get the lights to come on. By using two radio frequencies, Miguel had ensured his airfield lights would never be accidentally activated by someone who didn't know the code.

As the G-IV descended through about 2,500 feet above the water, the radar altimeters ranged in and began to display. We adjusted our barometric altimeters to match the radar altimeters since the elevation of Miguel's airfield was essentially zero and the jet leveled off at 1,500 shortly thereafter. I allowed it to slow down, and then we deployed the flaps and landing gear. The jet intercepted the programmed final approach course and turned itself onto final. I adjusted my chair and then placed my hands on the yoke and throttles. I could feel my heartbeat increase in my chest. This was for all the marbles. I had to get this right or we'd be swimming.

"I guess I should have asked this earlier," I said to Miguel. "Any runway markings?"

"None," Miguel said. "But the runway lights will give you sufficient guidance."

I shook my head in admiration. *Smart*, I thought. *Very smart.*

During the day, there'd be nothing to define the piece of pavement as a runway. In fact, I was betting the color of it was deliberately camouflaged. But at night, for those who knew where to find it, there'd be an easily identifiable runway.

The G-IV's throttles retarded automatically and the jet began its descent down the glideslope. I did a little quick math in my head. At our approach speed of 140 knots, we were a little over two minutes from touchdown.

"We'll click the mics at about five-hundred feet, Adam," I said. "And we'll get the landing lights after they come on."

His head begrudgingly nodded in my peripheral vision.

"Just a word of warning," I said. "This isn't going to be a greaser. I'm going to touchdown firmly and get right into max braking. It's probably going to be overkill for four-thousand feet but I'm not taking any chances."

I peered through the windscreen and into the darkness below. With the light of the partial moon, I saw the coastline line clearly, but I barely made out the shape of the lagoon area where the airstrip was located. In between was a large, brightly-lit house which I presumed was the hacienda itself. But there were no other significant references and for all intents, we were descending into a black hole.

"ONE THOUSAND!" the audio warning from the ground proximity warning system enunciated in my headset. We were a thousand feet above the ground and just over three miles from touchdown. I re-checked the placement of my hands on the control yoke and throttles and began to get in sync with the movements of both. I'd be kicking the auto-pilot and auto-throttles off at the five-hundred-foot point.

"FIVE HUNDRED!" the audio warning announced a few moments later. Immediately, Adam began clicking the mics to get the runway lights to come on—and they did. Then he reached up to turn on the aircraft landing lights and all hell broke loose.

As the landing lights illuminated the ground below us,

the area to the left side of the airfield erupted in small-arms muzzle flashes. And then I saw a larger flash from the left, followed by a corkscrew smoke trail. Heading right at us. Someone had just shot a shoulder-fired surface-to-air missile and we were the target.

"Son of a bitch!" I spat into the microphone. "Adam, flaps 20, gear up!" I kicked the autopilot and autothrottles off and turned directly toward the flash at about 2 g's, as much g as I could muster without overstressing the airframe. At the same time, I shoved the power as far forward as I could and not tear the engines apart. A small, fiery spot flew by the aircraft so closely that I could discern the body of the missile as it passed us. A split-second later the reflection of a bright-yellow glow was visible on the water below. The missile had detonated behind the aircraft. I looked at the engine gauges and saw no evidence that they had been affected. We had been lucky. So far.

Shit, I said to myself. *That was a proximity fuse. That means they're not shooting the older stuff.*

Adam was frozen in the seat next to me. His brain may have been processing what was happening, but he wasn't reacting. I reached over and raised the gear handle, then moved the flap lever to the 20 degree position.

"Miguel," I grunted as I rolled the G-IV out and descended slightly, "I'm not sure your people completely control the territory around your airfield."

"Microphone for 133.2!" he ordered.

I checked the radio displays to find which radio was tuned to that frequency and tossed him the applicable mic.

Miguel keyed the mic and uttered a stream of rapid-fire Spanish. A few seconds passed, and someone replied over the cockpit speaker, also in Spanish, with the sound of small arms fire in the background.

"My people are engaging them," he said.

"I hope we last until they do," I replied. Not trusting Adam to respond, I raised the flaps to zero as the G-IV continued to accelerate.

"You are going toward them," Adam said at last, with a touch of panic in his voice. "Why are you going toward them? Are you trying to kill us?"

"The missile they're shooting is probably a plume-tracker," I said. "If you remember your RSAF days, that's a missile that goes after hot exhaust, not hot metal. It also has a minimum range of about a half mile or so, which means they might shoot it at us, but it won't guide if we're inside that distance. I'm trying to build up some maneuvering speed while we're inside their min range."

A stream of Spanish came over the radio. Miguel replied with a few words. "My people are closing on their position, but they haven't been eliminated yet."

"Who the hell are they?" I asked.

"Competitors," he spat. "I was hoping they didn't know about this place."

I nodded. We passed over the airfield as the jet accelerated to 300 knots at about five-hundred feet above the ground. I waited a few moments, and then banked up to the left to turn out to sea. As the nose came around, I looked back to the left, in the general area where the first missile launch had come from. And I saw the reflection of our landing lights on the water below.

"Holy shit," I spat. "Our lights are still on!"

As I reached up to the overhead panel to turn them off, there was another flash and another cork-screw smoke trail reached out for us, like the crooked finger of the grim reaper. I pulled both throttles to idle, rolled the aircraft up to about 60 degrees of bank, and then pulled the nose around rapidly, hoping to reduce our exhaust plume and make the missile overshoot our flight path before it detonated.

We almost made it.

The spot of fire started to rapidly drift aft as I watched it;

then suddenly, the missile's guidance computer must have realized it couldn't get it to its programmed trajectory, and it made an abrupt turn forward and detonated with a bright flash just behind us. The shockwave from the explosion rattled the airplane. That wasn't good. The warheads on these missiles were small and if it was close enough to produce a shockwave it was probably close enough to produce some damage.

I glanced down at the engine display and noticed that the number two high and low pressure turbines were beginning to fluctuate. And then the internal engine temperature began to rise rapidly. The right engine was failing.

"Adam," I said as calmly as I could, "shut down number two please."

I retarded the right engine throttle to idle as I applied left rudder to counteract the now asymmetric thrust and waited for him to reach down and shut down the right high-pressure fuel cock. He did so, a second later, and the engine began to slowly spool down.

"Any words on how your boys are doing down there, Miguel?" I asked. "We're actually going to have to land now."

Miguel spat another stream of Spanish into the microphone and was rewarded with some frantic words amid a very intense fire-fight. I continued my turn to keep the missile's firing position off my left wing, but I wasn't sure how much good it would do. I had to apply additional power on the left engine to keep us flying, and that was increasing the size of our exhaust plume. I allowed our altitude to creep upward in the event I had to do some rapid maneuvering to avoid the next missile.

Then, as my eyes roamed over the engine instrument display, I saw something else I didn't like. The oil pressure for the number one engine was decreasing. Steadily.

"Well, it looks like we're royally fucked," I said, to no one in particular.

"What?" Miguel asked, microphone in hand.

"We're losing oil on number one. I pointed at the oil

pressure display. If it keeps dropping at that rate, the left engine will eventually seize. We're only going to be flying for about another five minutes or so."

Miguel keyed the mic again and spat a stream of Spanish into it. After a pause, his man on the ground replied, but this time the return conversation was more composed and the small arms fire was more sporadic. Miguel nodded in satisfaction.

"Muy bien," he said. "My people control the field again. The intruders have been neutralized."

"Let's get this bitch on the ground before it falls out of the sky," I said. "Adam, with the right engine shut down, we won't have the flight hydraulic system. All we're really going to lose is the yaw damper and the right thrust reverser. Everything else should work; we're just going to have to be a little deliberate about extending the gear and the flaps."

I rolled the aircraft out on a heading of about 150 degrees and leveled off at 1,500 feet. " Can you reconfigure the FMS and get me an inbound course for the runway again?"

Once the jet overflies a certain point, the flight management system sequences guidance past that point so I needed Adam to recall it from memory and build me a new course. Adam fumbled with the FMS control unit for a moment or two, but then I saw the steering guidance reappear on my attitude indicator, horizontal situation indicator, and navigational display.

"Well done," I said dryly. "Flaps one."

Adam deployed the flaps to 10 degrees as I began a turn to the left to re-intercept the final approach course. We were about five miles south of the field and I didn't want to waste a moment getting us on the ground. I glanced down at the oil pressure display for the number one engine. It was only about 10 PSI above the minimum. We didn't have much time.

"Flaps two," I commanded, as I rolled us out on final approach again.

Adam deployed the flaps to 20 degrees as I intercepted the glide path guidance and began our descent to the runway.

"Gear down," I said.

Adam lowered the landing gear handle and when we had three green lights indicating the gear was down and locked, he checked the landing gear weight on wheels switch, and then armed the ground spoilers.

"ONE THOUSAND!" announced the ground proximity warning system. While I was grateful we had survived an attempt to blow us out of the sky, there was still some serious flying to do. I still had to stop a now wounded sixty-thousand-pound-plus airplane on 4,000 feet of runway and the pressure was on because if I screwed up, the odds were good that we wouldn't be flying or walking away.

"Flaps three, Adam," I said. "Before landing checklist."

"But we're single engine," he replied. "The checklist says…"

"I know," I said impatiently, "flap setting is optional. But landing is basically assured because we probably won't be able to go around, and I need the slowest possible speed on final so I can stop on that miniscule piece of concrete down there."

Adam opened his mouth for a moment, apparently thought better of it, and dutifully deployed the flaps to 39 degrees. Then he finished the checklist and re-activated all the exterior lights.

"Before landing checklist complete."

"Let's get the runway lights on a little earlier this time. I need to see what I'm up against here."

Adam and Miguel keyed their mics in the right sequence to get the runway lights to come on. Two miles in front of me, two parallel rows of white runway lights illuminated, and I swallowed hard when I saw them.

Goddamn. That's a tiny fucking runway. It looked even smaller than it did the last time.

"FIVE HUNDRED!" announced the GPWS.

I began to slowly ease the power back on the number one engine to reduce our approach speed. Every extra knot meant more stopping distance required - distance we didn't have.

"APPROACHING MINIMUMS!" said the GPWS. Adam had set the decision height for the approach at two-hundred feet above ground level.

"I'm going to duck under just a little," I announced. "If I fly this glide path to touchdown I'll waste runway. Click the lights again so I don't have to land in the dark."

I pushed forward on the yoke just a little to get under the three-degree glide path Adam had programmed into the flight management system. I had to be careful though. As I noted from our previous approach, there were serious visual illusion possibilities here. Runway lights with no surrounding features could create the infamous black-hole approach illusion which made the pilot want to get too low, too early, and impact short of the runway. We obviously didn't want that.

"MINIMUMS!" the GPWS announced.

We were two-hundred feet above the ground. I began to slowly move the left throttle back to idle. Typically, I don't do that until I cross the runway threshold, but there was nothing typical about tonight's landing. Approach speeds are calculated at a 1.3 times the stall speed for the landing configuration, so I had a small speed margin to play with and the G-IV was a very clean airplane, aerodynamically speaking.

"You're below V ref!" Adam called out, obviously concerned that I was allowing the jet slow below approach speed.

"Noted," I said tightly. "It's intentional. You're going to need to hang on, by the way. This is going to be a firm touchdown. I'm going to try to dissipate some energy with the landing."

The two rows of lights seemed to be reaching up for us out of the blackness below. I looked to the end of the runway quickly, and then back to the approach end to ensure my eyes were correctly focused.

"You're V ref minus ten!" The pitch of Adam's voice was a little higher. He was scared.

I allowed myself a smile. *How the fuck did this guy ever*

fly fighters?

"Noted," I said. We were still well over 100 knots. Any moment now the GPWS would begin its final descent countdown.

"FIFTY!" it said.

I checked the left throttle in idle.

"FORTY!"

I checked our glide path and descent rate. About 2.5 degrees and six-hundred feet per minute. Just where I wanted us.

"THIRTY!"

I checked the wind readout in the flight display. About five knots on the nose. *I'd rather be lucky than good.*

TWENTY!"

The lights at the end of the runway went under us. On a normal approach, I'd cross the end of the runway at fifty feet. For this landing, I was on profile.

"Get ready on the speed brakes, Adam." I didn't want to rely on automatic ground spoiler deployment.

"TEN!"

Normally, this was where I'd lift the nose to round-out for touchdown and give my passengers a nice soft landing. But not tonight. The G-IV, like most swept wing aircraft, flew final approach in a nose-up configuration due to the required angle of attack to maintain the lower airspeed. I maintained my pitch attitude.

The main gear hit the runway solidly, but not brutally; and I allowed the nose to come down immediately instead of holding it up for a few seconds as I would have for a normal landing. I was already applying full brake pressure as the nose gear came to rest. I began to deploy the left thrust reverser as I simultaneously applied right rudder to counter the asymmetrical drag.

"One-hundred knots," Adam said, as he pulled the speed brake handle rearward. Fortunately, his action there was redundant. The ground spoilers had deployed.

"Your yoke," I replied, dropping my left hand from the

yoke to the steering tiller on the left side panel.

The runway lights seemed to be going by very rapidly, and unlike most airports, Miguel's private strip didn't have runway remaining markers so I had no idea how much pavement I had left. I could feel the anti-skid system cycling the brakes as we decelerated.

"Reverser deployed," Adam said. "Eighty knots."

I nodded. I had seen the blue REV DEPLOY light on the panel to my right. My mind flashed back a few weeks when I was trying to stop an F-16 with a flamed-out engine and dead brakes on the runway at Edwards AFB. But then, I had an arresting hook on the aircraft and the runway had an arresting cable. No such luck tonight.

The runway lights continued to go by, but the pace seemed to have slowed somewhat. There still seemed to be several more rows in front of us.

"Sixty knots," Adam called.

Normally, I'd stow the thrust reverser at about this speed but tonight I wanted all it could give me.

Then, the pace of the passing lights began to slow markedly and the anti-skid began to cycle less frequently. I began to think we might actually survive this.

And then I saw the truck.

It appeared in the landing lights in front of us a few hundred feet away and with only sixty feet of runway width to play with, there was no way we'd be able to go around it. It was lying on its side and there was smoke rising from the engine. Apparently, it had been engaged in the gun battle that preceded our landing. It was three tons of American pickup and I had time to wonder what make it was.

"Holy fucking shit," I spat.

There was only one thing to do. I reached down and pulled the emergency brake to its full extension and instantly fed 3,000 pounds of unmetered hydraulic pressure directly to the braking system. Adam, Miguel, and I were violently flung forward in our harnesses and I heard a dull thud in the back of the aircraft. Someone had been thrown onto the floor.

The jet skidded forward but slowed down rapidly and after an agonizing few seconds, came to rest mere few feet from the vehicle in front of us. The truck was now clearly illuminated by the bright landing lights of the aircraft. I could see several bullet holes in the windscreen and dark spatters all over the interior of the cab.

"F-150," was all I could say.

I exhaled forcibly and suddenly realized I had been holding my breath.

"Miguel," I said, "get on the radio please and tell your guys to stay away from the main wheels. Those brakes have got to be extremely hot. They don't want to be anywhere near them if we blow a tire."

It took a moment for my words to register, and then he raised the mic to his lips and began to speak deliberately and slowly. After he had received an acknowledgment, he turned to me as if waiting for further instructions.

"Do you have a hangar or building to put this jet inside of?"

He nodded. "It's built to look like a barn. It's on the western side of the field. Once this truck is cleared away, you can taxi there."

"We can't actually." I was looking down at the left engine instruments and the oil pressure for the number one engine had just gone below the minimum level for idle power. I started the APU as quickly as I could to keep power on the airplane, and then shut down the left engine. "There's a tow bar in the aft compartment. Do you have any tow vehicles here? "

He nodded again.

"Let's let the brakes cool down for about thirty minutes or so, and then we get towed in."

He shook his head.

"We need to be out of sight as soon as possible. I'll have

my men move that truck and then they can get the tow bar and hook us up."

"It's too dangerous," I warned him. "If those tires blow, it could kill someone."

"If they don't get us inside quickly, I'll kill them," he said flatly.

I began to unstrap.

"If that's the case," I said. "I better get down there and tell them how to do it. Can I ask you to get up so I can get through the door?"

He didn't move for a moment.

"You saved my life tonight," he said solemnly. "Not once but twice."

"Well, as you so eloquently put it earlier, I would have been the first one to the scene of the crash if I hadn't."

He shook his head.

"It doesn't matter. The deuda de honor, the debt of honor, stands. I owe you. Ask whatever you want. Your freedom, money, whatever it is in my power to give you, is yours."

Admittedly, my mind wasn't in the most rational place at that moment and several images flew through it. First, I saw Adam screaming in agony and then I saw myself in a Caribbean villa looking out over the ocean being waited on by an assortment of beautiful, scantily-clad women. But both visions vanished nearly as soon as they were created. If one of the most powerful drug lords in the world was going to make a promise, there was only one thing that mattered enough to me to ask for.

"I've never cared much about what happens to me," I said. "Life happens the way it happens. But there is one thing you can do for me."

He nodded, and I could see his eyes fill with realization. He knew what I was going to ask before I asked it.

"Sarah Marciano and her unborn child are now out of this," I said. "They are non-combatants. No matter what happens. They need to be untouchable. I don't give a shit what you do to me but Sarah and her child live. I want them out of Adam's reach."

"Done," Miguel said, without missing a beat. "Miss Marciano will be designated a non-combatant."

And as I looked into his eyes, I realized he totally meant it. *I'll be damned.*

"But Miguel," Adam protested, "without the woman we won't have any leverage."

Miguel shushed him with a gesture that was both dismissive and contemptuous.

"Te doy mi palabra. I give you my word," he intoned, "my word of honor." He paused a moment and looked me over with a degree of respect in his eyes that hadn't been there previously. I might not have been an equal or a friend, but somehow, I wasn't quite an adversary any more. "So, what are we to do with you, then?" he asked, after a long moment.

I could see Adam's eyes blazing with hatred in my peripheral vision, but I ignored them and kept my eyes focused on Miguel.

"I'm thinking you need to get this jet fixed and then somehow get it back into the United States undetected."

He nodded slowly.

"I know how we can do that."

From: Special Projects Group [NCS]
Sent: Tuesday, 24 November 2009, 0200 PST (24 November 2009, 1000Z)
To: Director, NCS
Cc: Special Projects Group [NCS]; damrine@cmail.cia.gov; dsmith3@cmail.cia.gov

SUBJECT: INCIDENT REPORT – Intel Collection Mission and Gulfstream G-IVSP N36WMS Disappearance

(TS) Narrative:

1. (TS) Last evening at approximately 2130 hours local time, Contractor 09-017 (Pearce, Colin M.) and Operations Officer 53-3445 (Code name: Brown, Sharona) attempted an intelligence gathering operation at the penthouse apartment of the Hotel Imperial del Cabo to gain additional information on the intentions of Abdullah bin Rashid al Qudamah, aka Adam Archmere, and Miguel Hidalgo as well as to ascertain the whereabouts of Operations Officer Susan Turner. After successfully planting several audio devices and one audio/visual feed, the two were apprehended by security personnel working for al Qudamah and Hidalgo. An altercation followed which left five hostile personnel dead on the scene. While Brown evaded capture, Pearce was taken prisoner. His current whereabouts are unknown. The GPS tracker on his phone has not responded to multiple attempts to track him. While al Qudamah, Hidalgo and company apparently fled the scene shortly after the altercation, the video surveillance device

provided some intelligence which may indicate that Turner may be providing information to al Qudamah. The content of this information is discussed below. Turner was located during the operation, but she was not recovered and may no longer be reliable.

2. (TS) Also last evening, at approximately 2340 hours, Gulfstream G-IVSP N36WMS disappeared from radar coverage about ten miles south of Los Cabos International Airport (MMSD). Since our requests for AWACs coverage were denied, non-cooperative radar tracking was not available. HUMINT surveillance assets were not in place to monitor the departure and we currently have no information as to passengers and crew on the aircraft.

3. (TS) Bachelor's Toy remains at anchor in the Cabo San Lucas harbor. No movement of the yacht has been attempted.

(TS) CONCLUSIONS:

1. (TS) The intelligence gained from the surveillance device appears to indicate that Turner has provided information to al Qudamah in exchange for money or to possibly take custody of her children and flee the country. (You will note that Turner was placed on administrative leave 18 months ago while a custody battle for her children was underway. See Turner's personnel folder for further details.) The intelligence gleaned appears to indicate some connection to the US Secret Service which may have implications for Presidential or Vice-Presidential security. The video clip from the surveillance device is attached to this e-mail (Caution: objectionable material).

2. (TS) While we suspect using the G-IV to escape was merely opportune, we still believe Archmere intends to use the aircraft

as an aerial delivery vehicle for either a chemical or biological weapon.

(TS) ACTIONS:

1. (TS) A sterilization team has been dispatched to the Hotel Imperial del Cabo to deal with the aftermath of the operation there, as well to collect any latent intelligence.

2. (TS) We will use Embassy resources to liaise with the terminal approach control at Los Cabos International Airport and attempt to see if we can derive track information for Gulfstream G-IVSP N36WMS.

3. (TS) We reiterate our request to deploy E-3 AWACS aircraft in an orbit between Los Angeles and San Diego to look deeper into Mexico and monitor the border for uncontrolled aircraft crossings.

4. (TS) We need to read the Secret Service into this operation and also investigate any connections/acquaintances that Turner may have had in the Secret Service. We will need cross-agency interaction at the DCI level to gain access to the information and personnel necessary to complete this task.

(TS) RECOMMENDATIONS:

1. (TS) Gain permission from DCI to read the Secret Service in on this operation to assess potential presidential security implications, as well as to pursue information on Susan Turner's connections.

2. (TS) Suggest briefing to National Security Advisor and National Security Council on this operation as soon as possible. This will necessitate a formal name for the operation in

progress. Using the next sequence letters in the secure op list, we propose naming the operation "Baja Sunrise."

TOP SECRET / SPECIAL
COMPARTMENTALIZED INFORMATION
CLASSIFIED BY: US Central Intelligence Agency
DECLASSIFY ON: OADR

CHAPTER EIGHTEEN

Contract Day Eight
Tuesday, 24 November
0600 Hours Local Time
Miguel's Hidalgo's Hacienda
Near Lazaro Cardenas, Mexico

"Wake up, man"

I blinked my eyes open to find Jose/Joe standing over my bed with a bemused expression on his face. I could tell there was a lot he wanted to say but nothing that he could, given the circumstances. He had a look on his face that was a cross between respect and disbelief. It was an odd combination.

"The boss say he want you downstairs."

I nodded and pushed myself up on my elbows.

"Wow," I said sleepily. "I never even undressed last night." I looked over at the clock radio on the ornate cherry nightstand. "It's six o'clock already? I feel like I just went to sleep."

"The boss, he say you have a lot to do today. He want you to get started early."

"He's right," I said, swinging my legs over the side of the bed "We do have a lot to do."

Joe gave me a quick set of directions to Miguel's study and then left to pursue his other duties. I sat on the edge of the extremely comfortable bed and spent a few moments recounting the events of the previous several hours.

#

We had managed to get the jet towed into Miguel's hangar/ barn structure last night without blowing a tire in the process. Then, once it was inside, I had him turn every light in the place on and provide me with a ladder. Armed with a flashlight to provide additional point illumination and fighting the pain in my leg, I inspected the elevator, horizontal stabilizer, rudder, and vertical stabilizer. I was relieved to find no indications of damage. The engines, of course, were a different story. The damage on the right engine was easy to find. There were several holes on the underside of the aft third of the engine cowling. Some as small as a pencil lead and others as large as my finger. They were spread over an area about a square yard. I was grateful to not find any large horizontal gashes.

"Simple frag warhead," I said to myself. "Doesn't look like a titanium rod warhead."

The damage on the left engine was significantly more difficult to locate. After about twenty minutes of searching, I found myself wondering if the decrease in oil pressure had been due to some sort of coincidental mechanical failure and not the surface-to-air missile fire. But then, as I trained my flashlight along the hinge of the cowling that was on the underside of the engine on the fuselage side, I saw a hole that was about as big around as a pencil eraser. After placing the ladder where I had better access, I examined the hole more closely and detected the usual ragged edges of metal made by a perforation. I also stuck my pen into the hole and removed it to find oil around the nub.

"Unusual frag pattern," I said to myself aloud. Explosive fragmentation patterns weren't always consistent or uniform, so this could have been caused by the same warhead that caused the damage on the other engine. But it was also possible it was generated by the first missile, the one that I had thought missed us.

I limped down the ladder to find Miguel and Adam waiting for me.

"Well, Pearce?" Adam asked.

I paused for a moment to consider my options. With the jet broken and Sarah under Miguel's protection, it seemed all my mission objectives were complete. It was possible I could stall the repairs and maybe even stop what they were planning for Thanksgiving Day, but there was a high probability that would get me killed. Besides, I knew I wasn't seeing the entire picture and if I didn't stay useful, I wasn't going to see it. Sometimes the devil you know is better than the devil you don't.

"We're going to need to change the right engine," I said, resignedly. "I think we may have just taken some damage to an oil line on the left engine, but I'd order a second engine just to make sure. You'll need diagnostic equipment, a hydraulic mule, and whatever they use to raise the engines into place."

I deliberately focused my gaze on Miguel and not Adam. "When do we need to fly?"

Miguel paused for a moment while he considered his answer.

"It's going to affect how many maintenance technicians we need," I said.

Miguel nodded, satisfied. "Thursday morning."

Great. I thought. *It's Thanksgiving Day, after all.* "Okay," I said. "I'm not an expert, obviously, but I know some people who are. I'm guessing it will take two full teams. I have some ideas about who to call."

"We will, of course, monitor those calls," Adam said.

"I expected that and have no issues with it. Not that it would matter if I did." I looked at Miguel. "How long does it take to drive up here from Cabo?"

"Depending on traffic, about twelve to fifteen hours."

I thought for a moment. "What's the heaviest aircraft

you've ever had land on your runway?"

He looked at me and cocked his head, like he was trying to see inside my mind. "A C-130," he said, at last.

"Okay," I said. "That'll work. When it's 9:00 a.m. on the east coast tomorrow, I need to start making calls." I looked at Miguel intently. "Is this place going to stay safe now?" I asked. "Having an enemy fire team sneak inside your perimeter again will really fuck things up."

His face flushed slightly and I prepared myself for an angry outburst. But when he spoke I realized he was more embarrassed than angry.

"We underestimated the threat in this area," he said. "We won't do that again. There are some in this country who object to my goals."

Your goals? What the hell did that mean?

"The crew who fired at us was given orders to shoot down any aircraft attempting to land here. Apparently, they wanted to create the impression that this area was not under my control. Measures are being taken to ensure that impression has been corrected."

"Do those measures include more security forces?" I asked.

Miguel nodded heavily. "By the morning, no one will be able to sneeze within five miles of this place without me knowing about it."

So here it was a few hours later just after 6 a.m. Pacific Time, which meant it was just after 9 a.m. Eastern Time. I looked down at my wrinkled clothes and took a quick sniff under my left armpit.

"Whew," I said to the empty room. "Somebody needs a shower."

And before I could bemoan the lack of clothes to change into, I saw my roller bag neatly arranged on a suitcase stand against the wall next to the door with my cane strapped to it. I walked over to it and opened it up to discover that while my clothes, shoes, and toiletries were present, they had been thoroughly searched.

"Par for the course," I said to the empty room.

I selected a pair of khaki slacks and a polo shirt and limped across the tiled floor to the bathroom. It was only then that I took a moment to examine the room around me.

Either Miguel or his decorator had good taste. The room was done in a comfortable, luxurious, and southwestern motif with a large sleeping area on one side near the door and an open conversation area on the other side under a large window. Dark brown mission-style furniture abounded and the fabric colors on the sofas and chairs featured a series of earth-toned browns and alternate shades of hunter green and maroon. I liked it.

I peered out the window and took in the scenery below through the paned glass. My room looked out the rear of the house. I could see a large lawn with a classic Roman pool next to the house. Beyond lay the blue expanse of the Pacific Ocean.

"Wow," I said unconsciously, "what a view."

I made my way into the equally opulent bathroom and accomplished my morning routine as quickly as I could. Fifteen minutes later I was half-walking, half-limping down the tiled semi-circular staircase in the two-story foyer and found myself again silently commending Miguel's taste. Overall, his hacienda was luxurious, but understated. There were rough-hewn beams, stucco walls, wrought iron railings and ceramic floors. All the colors melded together very naturally and accented the rich wooden furniture and earth-toned colors of the fabrics on the chairs and sofas. The artwork was southwestern, but it was placed sparingly so as not to draw the viewer's eye away from the richness of the house itself. The house wasn't at all what I would have expected from a drug kingpin. It was very casual and refined.

I reached the bottom of the stairs and made a U-turn to parallel the staircase as I headed toward Miguel's study. There was a spectacular gathering room to my left that ran the entire width of the house, open to the foyer in the front of the house, and ending in a two-story floor-to-ceiling window at the back. The room featured several conversation/seating areas arranged around an ornate bar and a huge fireplace. Over the fireplace, a large painting dominated the wall. It displayed a man on horseback wearing a 19th century European military uniform and looking thoughtfully off into the distance. I could barely make out the name plate from across the room as I walked by; but when I read it, it gave me pause.

General Antonio Lopez de Santa Anna, 1794-1876.

I stopped and stared to make sure I read what I thought I had read.

I'll be damned.

You don't make it far in the military without knowledge of military history and I knew a fair amount about Santa Anna. He was the leading figure in Mexican politics for most of the 1800s and fought for Mexican independence from Spain, served as president of the new nation several times, and led the attempt to crush the Texas rebellion in the in 1830s with what the history books called "a take no prisoners" attitude. He was probably best known for his "victory" at the Alamo in 1836 where his four-thousand-man force suffered six-hundred casualties in a thirteen-day siege at the hands of less than two-hundred Texas patriots. After the defenders were killed and that battle won, Santa Anna ordered their bodies burned. He followed this victory with another one at Coleto Creek three weeks later where he ordered the massacre of three-hundred prisoners of war. Of course, Texas won its independence shortly thereafter; but in spite of this defeat and a subsequent defeat in the Mexican-American War, Santa Anna remained the most powerful man in Mexico until 1853 when he sold millions of acres of what is now New Mexico and Arizona to the United States. Disgraced by liberal opposition against his actions, Santa Anna left public life and never regained the spotlight. The history books all said the same things about him when they summarized the choices he made in his life: "Santa Anna repeatedly put his own interests above those of his country."

It was noteworthy that his portrait occupied a central place in Miguel's home. I made a mental note not to question him about it. Santa Anna was a controversial figure. I was sure that Miguel had some very strong opinions about him.

Just then, I heard Joe's words in my ears. "No, Miguel Hidalgo isn't his real name."

I looked at the painting again.

Hmmmm, I thought. The historical Miguel Hidalgo had been a selfless priest and a leader of the Mexican War of Independence. I wondered what he would have thought about someone who was a Santa Anna fan using his name.

Miguel's study was next to the gathering room through a pair of ornate wooden double doors. It was a long, rectangular room lined with books and 17th century military relics. Miguel sat at a large wooden desk in front of a windowed wall with a pair of French doors off to one side. The view behind him was something you'd see in *Architectural Digest*—the Roman pool immediately outside the house and then the large, immaculately-manicured green lawn and the Pacific Ocean extending into the horizon beyond.

In front of Miguel's desk was a rectangular table with a conference phone set in the middle of it. Next to the phone lay a legal pad and several pens. My computer had been set up on the table and my computer bag sat on the floor next to the table. Miguel lifted his eyes to me as I entered the room and motioned to the table.

"Since we've confiscated your BlackBerry, I thought you might need your computer for contact information."

He gestured to a side board where a small, continental

breakfast buffet had been set up along with an urn of strong-smelling coffee. "Help yourself to some breakfast and then get to work," he said.

I nodded, leaned my cane against his desk, walked over to the side board, and lifted a plate from the stack, noting that it was real bone china. A glance at the inverted coffee cups on the saucers next to the coffee urn confirmed it, Royal Doulton was stamped on the bottom.

Miguel had some class, no doubt. He was a paradox. Obviously well-educated and well-spoken, but he had the hands of a laborer.

Prison? Hard labor?

I glanced over at Miguel as he worked at his desk. He was wearing a linen shirt with long sleeves. I wondered if the long sleeves were meant to hide the requisite prison tattoos. On the other hand, I might just be imagining the whole scenario. I found it only slightly curious that there was no guard stationed in the room to keep an eye on me. Miguel was a big guy and he looked to be in decent shape. He also undoubtedly had more hand-to-hand fighting experience than I did. I was also sure there was a gun somewhere very close by.

But still, there was an element of trust here. It was most curious.

I sat down with a plate loaded with cold cuts, cheeses, a croissant, and a cup of steaming coffee, appropriately diluted with cream and some sugar.

"Is Adam going to join us?" I asked.

Miguel looked up at the ceiling with a clearly exasperated look on his face.

"I suppose," he answered. "When he's *done*."

I couldn't help smiling.

As I ate, I made a task list on one of the legal pads. When I was finished, I rose and offered it to him.

"Just so we're on the same page. This is what I think needs to be done."

He read the list and nodded.

"Before we go any further with this, I need for you and I to have an understanding about something." I looked him directly in the eyes.

He leaned back in his chair, crossed his arms, and regarded me silently.

"I'm about to make arrangements to bring twenty-to-thirty people here to work on this aircraft; and you're obviously going to offer them a ton of money to do this work, right?

He nodded once more.

"They won't know who you are or what any of 'this' is about. Hell, I don't even know what 'this' is about. But I need your assurance that they'll make it out of here and live to spend all the money you're going to pay them."

"How much do you know about me, Mr. Pearce?"

"Not much," I admitted.

"I'm a drug dealer," he said, with a smirk on his features. "The largest in Mexico, perhaps one of the largest in all of Latin America, and if you believe the press, one of the most ruthless. This has gained me a certain reputation."

I gulped and nodded. *Alrighty then.*

"A reputation that is very useful, even if it is based more on myth than fact. The truth is, Mr. Pearce, I am a businessman but I am also a military man and I abide by a code of honor, like my ancestors before me. The workers you bring in will be considered non-combatants. As long as they maintain that status, they won't be harmed."

I nodded. "Fair enough. Now here's a question. I can find the people and I can find the equipment, but I don't know how to get them here. I was thinking we could fly them into Cabo and then truck everything and everyone up here; but that will obviously take too much time. So, we're going to have to bring everything and everyone here on a cargo plane. I'm assuming you don't want to highlight your location, so how do we get all that stuff here without attracting a lot of attention?"

Miguel looked up at the ceiling for a moment and rubbed his weather-worn chin.

"Make arrangements to get them to Cabo," he said. "I'll take care of getting them here."

"Not Tijuana? That's obviously closer."

He shook his head. "Too visible."

I nodded. "Roger that."

I sat down at the table and turned on my computer. After Bill Gates took the usual ten minutes to get everything up and running, I opened up Microsoft Outlook and found the phone number I was looking for. As I reached for the conference phone in the center of the table, Adam walked into the room. He looked tired, but his complexion had a slightly flushed look that tended to come from a particular activity that often takes place early in the morning, largely because a certain part of mens' bodies tends to rise before the rest of us does.

"Good morning, Miguel," Adam said brightly.

"Buenos dias, Adam," Miguel replied begrudgingly.

"Is Mr. Pearce about to make himself useful for a change?" Adam helped himself to some food and coffee and took a seat across the table from me.

"I'm about to get on the phone here, Adam," I said. "Apparently I need to make these calls so you guys can hear them, but I'd prefer that the people I'm calling not know they're being overheard. They might not be quite as forthright as I need them to be."

Adam shrugged his shoulders and began eating as if he couldn't have cared less. There was something about his manner that I found irritating. In his eyes, I had become a necessary annoyance. Like a servant that was needed, but not pleasing to have around.

I keyed a number into the conference phone's keypad. Out of the corner of my eye, I could see Miguel watching a computer screen with a number readout at the top and map in the center. He was tracing my call. I saved him the trouble.

"The guy's name is Ken Martin and he lives in Palm Beach, Florida. His business card says he's a maintenance consultant. But his specialty is putting together unconventional repair packages. I've known him for about five years. And no, he doesn't know that I've done work for some folks in Washington. If he did, he probably wouldn't take my call."

The phone rang five times before the gruff voice I remembered answered it.

"Who the fuck is this?" the voice said sleepily.

"Well, hi Ken," I answered. "Did you tie one on last night, or is that the way you greet everyone who calls you these days?"

There was a moment's pause.

"Pearce?" Ken asked incredulously. "Colin Pearce? No shit? How the hell are you?"

"I'm okay, Ken," I answered. "But I've got a G-IV that isn't. And I need to get it fixed in big hurry without too many questions about how it got broken."

"What's broken and how quickly does it need to be fixed?"

"Do you remember that business we worked together about two years ago?"

Another pause. I knew he'd remember. I looked directly at Adam as I waited for Ken to answer.

"You mean in Saudi Arabia?"

Adam almost choked on his croissant. I smiled at him.

"That would be the one. It's the same sort of damage. We're going to need at least one engine change and possibly two. And we need to fly in the morning on Thursday."

"Holy shit, Pearce!" I could hear him scribbling something down and counting under his breath. "Jesus, that's going to be tight. Where's the jet?"

I looked at Miguel. He nodded.

"In Mexico. I'm going to need to fly the team and the parts into Cabo San Lucas."

More scribbling and counting. "That's not as bad as it

could be. At least you're not in Asia. It's still going to be tight though. So, what's my cut to put all this together for you?"

I looked at Miguel and he looked back at me, inclining his chin in my direction. He was giving me the reins.

"I'm thinking your cost plus about twenty-five grand," I said.

"You're on drugs!" Ken came back immediately. "Two engines, stands, crews to work around the clock for like thirty-six hours and I probably have to arrange a freighter to get it all down to Cabo too. Cost plus two-hundred grand. And that's a bargain."

I couldn't help smiling. Ken was a man after my own heart. I sighed loudly. "Cost plus one-hundred grand, Ken. And I'm really pushing it here."

A pause with some scribbling again. I could hear some more counting and then more scribbling. I wondered how many pens he went through in a day.

"One twenty-five, Pearce. And that's the 'friend who saved my ass' rate. It's as good as it gets. Hell, I'll even come along to supervise."

The mute button on the conference phone came on without my having touched it and I realized that Miguel had a remote control for it on his desk.

"Did you get it?" Miguel asked Adam.

Adam nodded. "It should arrive by truck today. They can load it in Cabo."

Miguel looked at me. "Tell him one fifty," he said. "And tell him to bring a painting crew."

From: Special Projects Group [NCS]
Sent: Tuesday, 24 November 2009, 1600 PST (25 November 2009, 0000Z)
To: Director, NCS
Cc: Special Projects Group [NCS]; damrine@cmail.cia.gov; dsmith3@cmail.cia.gov

SUBJECT: UPDATE – Operation Baja Sunrise

(TS) Narrative:

1. (TS) After an extensive review of the digital archives of the radar control agencies with coverage of the Cabo San Lucas area and Baja California, an approximate track of the Gulfstream G-IVSP N36WMS has been derived. The aircraft departed Los Cabos International Airport (MMSD) at 2330 PST (24 November 2009, 0730Z) with no flight plan filed. The weather was VFR (Ceiling 250 BKN, Visibility 10SM). The aircraft flew approximately 10 miles south of the airport and leveled off at altitude below 10,000 feet. It then made a turn to a westerly heading at 2340 PST and maintained that track until it was approximately five miles off shore, then it turned to the north at 2353 PST and maintained that heading for approximately 200 miles. The aircraft disappeared from radar coverage at approximately 0042 PST. No airports on the Baja peninsula or in Southern California reported landings of an aircraft of this size and the Aerostat radar balloons which monitor the US/Mexico border showed no indications of a border incursion. Satellite passes over the Baja peninsula have

not revealed an aircraft of N36WMS size on the ground at an uncontrolled airport. No wreckage has been detected.

2. (TS) Miguel Hidalgo reportedly maintains a summer home on the coast of Baja California in the vicinity of Santa Maria, a village just south of Lazaro Cardenas. Satellite reconnaissance of the area has shown an estate on the ocean in this area although official records indicate the property is owned by a holding company based in the Cayman Islands. Photographic analysis has revealed a length of pavement which could be a runway although the size (4000' long by 60' wide) is more suitable to lighter aircraft than to aircraft the size of a G-IV. There is a large building adjacent to the runway which could house a G-IV-sized aircraft. Infrared analysis of the building reveals no abnormal indications. We suspect the building may have infrared shielding installed.

3. (TS) As you are aware, the Secret Service had refused to share confirmed information about presidential or vice-presidential movements over the next several days without confirmed intelligence that a direct threat exists to POTUS or VPOTUS, although a Secret Service advance team is on the ground in San Francisco and is scouting positions in and around Candlestick park. The Philadelphia Eagles will play the San Francisco Forty-Niners at 1300 PST Thursday, 26 November (Thanksgiving Day) and VPOTUS is a known fan of the Eagles. Despite reports that POTUS will be spending Thanksgiving Day at Camp David, Secret Service advance personnel have been spotted at Orange County/John Wayne airport in California.

4. (TS) Bachelor's Toy remains at anchor in Cabo San Lucas Harbor. William Spratt has been seen aboard. He does not appear to be under guard but he has not left the vessel.

(TS) CONCLUSIONS: Based on analysis of available intelligence, we believe:

1. (TS) Abdullah bin Rashid al Qudamah, aka Adam Archmere and Miguel Hidalgo are working in concert to conduct a hostile act against the United States using airborne dispersal of a chemical or biological weapon;

2. (TS) The intended target of the hostile act is VPOTUS while he attends the football game at Candlestick Park on Thursday, 26 November;

3. (TS) Gulfstream G-IVSP N36WMS will be used as the dispersal platform for the weapon and is currently at an undisclosed location being fitted for the weapon;

4. (TS) Operation Officer Susan Turner's role was to provide confirmation to Archmere and Hidalgo about VPOTUS schedule; and

5. (TS) At this time, Bachelor's Toy and its associated personnel and equipment does not seem to be part of the plan.

(TS) ACTIONS:

1. (TS) We will monitor FAA Temporary Flight Restrictions (TFRs) closely. The presence of a short-notice TFR with restrictions that match VIP criteria usually indicates POTUS or VPOTUS movements;

2. (TS) Continue to request deployment of an E-3 AWACS to monitor border crossings and southern approaches to San Francisco;

3. (TS) We recommend NORAD be notified of the possible

threat so that air defense fighters can maintain as high an alert status as possible;

4. (TS) We will continue to monitor Bachelor's Toy for movement and activity;

5. (TS) We are deploying a human surveillance team to monitor Miguel Hidalgo's supposed summer home. We have been unable to get the NRO to re-task a satellite to support this surveillance on a continual basis; and

6. (TS) We will update slides for your presentation to the National Security Advisor. We understand the briefing was postponed due to pre-Thanksgiving ceremonial commitments.

(TS) RECOMMENDATIONS:

1. (TS) Continue to petition Secret Service for access to Susan Turner's contacts and potential intelligence related to those contacts;

2. (TS) Continue to request E-3 AWACS support; and

3. (TS) Continue to push for briefing to National Security Advisor and National Security Council on this operation. We believe this intelligence indicates a credible threat to VPOTUS.

TOP SECRET / SPECIAL
COMPARTMENTALIZED INFORMATION
CLASSIFIED BY: US Central Intelligence Agency
DECLASSIFY ON: OADR

CHAPTER NINETEEN

Contract Day Eight
Tuesday, 24 November
2000 Hours Local Time
Miguel's Hidalgo's Hacienda
Near Lazaro Cardenas, Mexico

Almost as if it had been conjured out of the darkness, the C-130 seemed to appear on Miguel's unlighted runway before us. Adam, Miguel, Joe and I were standing outside of the barn/hangar building looking toward the runway when I heard the light screech of the tires contacting the pavement and then the unmistakable high-pitched drone of turboprop engines going into reverse thrust. Only then did I see the blunt-nosed cargo plane decelerating in front of me. The crew had flown in using night vision goggles. Miguel wasn't taking any chances. I wondered how the passengers felt about landing in the dark.

Wasting no time at all, the aircraft exited the runway and taxied quickly over to where we were standing. The ramp area in front of the barn/hangar was fairly large and the plane had plenty of room in which to maneuver. It slowed to a walking pace about fifty feet in front of us and then began a very tight hundred-and-eighty-degree turn. I could see the cargo ramp already lowering as the turn continued and I could also see the insignia of the Mexican Air Force on the fuselage and tail.

While Ken and I had arranged to get the personnel and equipment to Cabo, Miguel had apparently arranged for a Mexican Air Force C-130 to bring everything and everyone from there to here.

How does a drug lord command that kind of loyalty inside the Mexican Air Force?

Miguel's earlier words replayed themselves in my mind "… but I am also a military man and I abide by a code of honor, like my ancestors before me."

There was a bigger picture. And I wasn't seeing it.

The aircraft finished its turn and stopped, leaving the engines running. The cargo ramp lowered to the pavement and almost immediately, a red Lektro tug, a vehicle typically used for towing airplanes, slowly backed down the ramp, pulling a plastic-wrapped Rolls-Royce Tay 611-8 jet engine on a wheeled cart. The Tay was nearly eight-feet long, just over three-and-a-half feet in diameter and weighed over 3,300 pounds; so the tug driver took his time. Once the tug and engine were completely on the pavement, they headed directly for us. I didn't recognize the man driving the tug, but I recognized his passenger. Ken Martin was good to his word. He was here to supervise. The tug stopped directly in front of us and Ken hopped out, his stocky frame clad in the standard working clothes for maintenance technicians: dark blue, heavy-cotton pants, and a light blue shirt. The usual baseball-style cap was on his head, one of an entire wardrobe he possessed. This one said *Gulfstream,* of course. He walked up to me and pumped my hand vigorously.

"Damn good to see you again, Pearce," he said with a tobacco-stained grin.

"You as well, Ken," I said, smiling back at him. "Thanks for making this happen."

"With enough money, anything is possible." He motioned to the aircraft behind him and the men who were making their way down the ramp, wheeling large tool chests behind them. "Believe it or not, finding the people was the difficult part of this project. The engines and support equipment was easy. Thank Christ the General Dynamics folks in Dallas had some spares."

I looked at him intently. "You've worked with these guys before?"

He nodded. "They're actually a crew that specializes in no-notice heavy work deployments like this. They just got finished doing an engine change on a G-550 in Cairo. It got trashed during the recent round of protests there. I intercepted them when they got back into Miami this morning and rerouted them to Dallas where I met them. Of course, the charter operator for the cargo plane they were traveling on was very happy to get the extra dinero for the diversion to Dallas, and then onto Cabo. And the boys were very happy about the amount of money you were willing to pay. So, what do you say? Let's make them earn it."

He looked briefly at the building behind us where the doors were opening and the G-IV was becoming visible. "I take it we'll be doing the work in there?" he asked.

I nodded.

He looked briefly at Adam, Miguel, and Joe.

"Gentlemen, I'm not going to introduce myself to you because you already know who I am and I don't need to know who you are. I know what needs to be done and we're going to bust our asses to make it happen. If you're unhappy with anything you see or anything my guys are doing, please tell Mr. Pearce about it and he'll tell me and I'll either explain it or fix it. Now if you have no objections, I'll get these guys started."

There was silence.

"Pearce," he nodded in acknowledgment.

Then he turned and began directing traffic. The tug made its way into the building with the first engine while the mechanics filed off the C-130 and into the barn/hangar with the huge, wheeled tool carts. Professional aircraft mechanics were very particular about their tools; and if they'd been in the business for a while, it wasn't uncommon for them to own a toolkit worth twenty to thirty-thousand dollars. These guys typically didn't go to Sears and buy Craftsman tools off the shelf. Everything was professional grade, and it seemed that Snap-On was the preferred vendor. Each guy had his own cart and each cart seemed to reflect its owner. Some were pristine and shiny; others were adorned with different stickers that were replicas of military unit patches or logos for aircraft products. There were about twenty mechanics all together and it was easy to see that they were veterans in the business and that they'd worked together before. There wasn't a lot of talk or chatter; instead there was a focus on what needed to be done.

As they entered the barn/hangar, Ken began instructing them on where to set up. Meanwhile, the red tug had uncoupled from the first engine and was threading its way through the people and back up the ramp on to the C-130. A few moments later it reappeared with the second engine and towed it into the barn/hangar. It made a few more trips back into the C-130 to get the remaining heavy support equipment while the mechanics filed in and found areas for their tool kits. As soon as the tug came off the ramp for the final time, towing a trailer with several large drums on it, the ramp was retracted and the C-130 began adding power to taxi for takeoff. It roared into the air a few minutes later.

I found myself shaking my head in wonder at the precision with which the entire offload had been conducted. The airplane might have been on the ground for a total of twenty minutes. As I turned to go back into the hangar, Adam's voice hissed at me.

"We'll be watching you, Pearce. We'll be watching everything you do and say. Jose will be at your side the whole time."

I turned to face all three of them. "We have no secrets, guys. You want this jet to fly by Thursday morning and I want to fly it for you, if for no other reason than to get the hell out of here. I don't have any idea what you're planning to do with it, and frankly, I don't give a rat's ass. As I told you the other night, the only reason I even came here was to help Sarah. I didn't want to get tangled up in any of this other shit and now that Miguel has guaranteed Sarah's safety, as soon as I set foot on US soil again, I'm done with this mess. Until this jet is fixed, though, I'm obviously not going anywhere. So, I'm going to get to it."

And I left them standing there and limped away, again hoping I wasn't laying it on too thick. As I entered the hangar, the doors closed behind me and we were sealed into our working space. In response to my request, a food buffet had been set up on one side of the hangar complete with cold cuts, bread, condiments, chips, drinks, and cookies. I helped myself to a Diet Coke and made my way into the crowd of mechanics. They were all huddled around Ken under the aft end of the G-IV. In the mere few minutes since they had arrived, they already had both engine cowlings open and were evaluating the damage.

"You were right about the number two engine, Pearce," Ken said, as he climbed down from a ladder. "We're definitely going to have to change it. The high and low-pressure turbine sections are both blown to shit. But we got lucky with the number one engine. You were right about that as well. It's just a busted oil line. We can repair that pretty quickly. Looks like we'll only need to change one engine. That leaves more folks to do some painting. What did you have in mind?"

I used my cane and pointed to the paint drums on the trailer that had arrived with them.

"We didn't even know that was paint," Ken snorted. "The drums aren't marked. The whole jet?" His voice was incredulous.

I nodded. "It doesn't have to be perfect, like you'd get from a paint barn. It just needs to be covered."

"Well, it's obviously not going to be fucking perfect if we can't pull all the surfaces off and do it right. But it will look pretty good when it's done. What color is that shit?"

I smirked at him. "It's like a dull, military gray-blue."

"It won't be terribly pretty," he said.

"No, it won't be," I said. "But it will be effective."

He raised his eyebrows at me. "So, what is that shit?"

"I'm betting that it's probably RAP," I said. "Radar absorbent paint."

At midnight, I excused myself to get a few hours of sleep. By that time, the number one engine oil line had been replaced and the process to disconnect the number two engine was approximately fifty percent completed. While one part of Ken's crew worked on the engine repairs, the other mechanics began masking and wrapping the aircraft for painting, which seemed to be slow tedious work. Ken had divided his men into shifts; and I had an office area off of the hangar floor converted to a bunk room so that he could rotate rest periods for his men as they worked through the night. Aircraft maintenance was extremely detail-oriented work and tired mechanics, like tired pilots, could make mistakes that might end in disaster.

Joe accompanied me back to the main house and left me on my own. As I climbed the stairs to my bedroom, I found my left leg wasn't screaming at me quite as much as it had in the past. Perhaps all the exercise was making it stronger. I could hear Adam and Miguel's voices coming from the direction of Miguel's study as I ascended, as well as a faint aroma of cigar smoke. There was the sound of a woman's voice, too. Susan was with them.

As I reached the top of the stairs, I had the choice to go right, in the direction of my room, or left, which took me to the other wing of the house and a position which was more directly over Miguel's study. I looked around, saw no one, and headed left, doing my best to stay low and against the wall away from the railing so I wouldn't be visible from the foyer or gathering room below.

With the open design of the foyer and rooms, I suspected I could hear the conversation more clearly from above; and as I approached, I wasn't disappointed. It was apparent that the doors to the study were open and that Miguel and Adam weren't concerned about being overheard. I lay down on the ceramic tile and inched forward so that my face was very close to the wrought iron railing of the walkway.

"So, it's confirmed then?" I heard Miguel ask solemnly.

"Yes," Susan answered. "He'll definitely be there. My contact in the Secret Service is on his protection detail."

"How do you get him to tell you these things?"

"He's in love with me," she said simply, "and he likes to impress me with how important he is."

"Very good," Miguel replied with a note of irony in his voice.

There was a pause and I could barely make out the sound of liquid being poured. I found myself suddenly craving a shot of single-malt whiskey.

"Well, gentlemen," Susan said. "I'm off to the kitchen for a snack and then off to bed. It's been a long day."

"Good night, Miss Turner," Miguel said.

No doubt the room she shared with Adam was up here. I was going to have to move soon. Susan's heels clicked across the ceramic tile and I heard the kitchen door close a few moments later. As soon as the door closed, Adam spoke in a very soft voice that was barely audible.

"She's been useful," he said flatly.

"You know what must be done, of course," Miguel said.

"I do," Adam replied, with some ice in his voice. "Saif will be waiting for us with the device. He'll take care of her and Pearce both. The device will be installed and we'll launch for

San Francisco."

I was back in my room a few moments after that.

Forewarned is forearmed.

I went to my roller bag and located the plastic bag of single malt miniatures I traveled with. I opened a small bottle of Oban and poured the contents into one of the glasses I found on the dresser. Then I sat down in the conversation area of my room and looked out the window at the dark sea outside. I raised the glass to my nose, closed my eyes, and breathed in the rich and fruity sweetness along with a note of sea salt and peaty smokiness. I could feel my heart rate and breathing slowing.

It's not every day you hear your death sentence pronounced. I was no stranger to having my life threatened, but hearing it spoken out loud was a new twist. I put the glass to my lips and took a healthy sip of the rich whiskey, letting it linger on my tongue and enjoying its fruitiness and malty dryness before it seeped down my throat with a long sweet finish and a touch of oak.

So be it, I thought.

"Hitting the Scotch again, Pearce?" Susan's voice wafted across the expanse of my room. I hadn't even heard her come through the door.

"Don't you have *duties* elsewhere?" I asked, without looking at her.

"Are *you* judging me?" she asked sarcastically.

I shook my head. "I'd never judge anyone," I said. "I've made so many fucked-up decisions in my own life that I've lost count."

"Then what?"

"While I never judge anyone," I said, looking down at the amber liquid in my glass, "I do try to understand them. And I don't understand you." I looked over at her. "At first, I think you're this dedicated CIA agent. Then I see that you're a brilliant covert operative, then you use me for sex to get

Adam to notice you, but then there seems to be something else between us that I can't define. Then I find out that apparently you and Adam are working together. So, I find that I don't have a clue what you're about or what you're after."

She paused for a second as if considering her answer. "I'm just like you," she said at last. "I'm in it for the money."

"Fair enough," I said, shrugging. "If that's what you need to tell yourself to make it easier."

She wanted to turn her back and walk out then, but she couldn't and we both knew it. She needed me to understand, which was the whole reason she was in my room in the first place.

"What in the hell do you mean by that?" she asked, as her voice rose.

"You better keep your voice down, Susan. Adam might hear you in here and think you're doing me again. He wasn't pleased the last time you did that."

I was watching her face and the range of emotions that swept across it was impressive. Fear, hate, self-loathing, anger, determination, and despair were all there. I couldn't help myself. I had to push the buttons some more. And for the life of me, I didn't know why.

"I know you had to fuck me to play the game," I said. "But what about *it can't get personal?'* What the hell was up with that?"

The emotional storm raged over her face again. "Why do you give a shit about that when you've got your little playmate at the mansion?"

There it was - the jealousy that I had wondered about. But why? Susan and I had just met each other. Why did she even care that I felt something for Sarah and didn't for her? And then as I looked at her standing there, and saw the plea behind all the other expressions on her face and heard the echo of the timbre of her words, it hit me. It was the damsel-in-distress syndrome. Susan wanted something or someone to save her from her own life. I had seen it so often in the lives of women who had made choices they'd regretted. Hell, on occasion, I'd allowed myself to be used as a tool of sexual salvation by women who had needed to escape from those choices. But I had never made promises as part of the process.

But I had made promises to Sarah and Susan was jealous of that.

You can't save everyone, Pearce. And you've made your choice.

"Sarah is very sweet," I said, without thinking. "But she's also married and carrying another man's child. I care about her very much, and a part of me would like to believe we could be together. But that's not real life."

Sarah's too good for you anyway. The thought came without warning and I closed my eyes in acknowledgment.

"Why are you really doing this, Susan?" I blurted out after a long moment. "It's not just for the money. You can't shit a shitter."

"For my kids," she said angrily. "I've given my entire adult life to the government and when it finally came time for the government to stand up for me, they let my shithead husband take my kids away."

I sort of knew what that felt like. The government had turned its back on me after many years of faithful service as well. But while I had walked away from it, I had also never directly turned against it either. Of course, that had probably been more about circumstances than any morality on my part.

I nodded. "I guess I can understand that. How old are they?"

Her face took on a very tender look and any tension in it vanished. "My little boy is seven and my baby girl is four."

I didn't want to say what had to be said next. God knew that someone with my history of ambivalence had no business saying it. But it had to come out. She had to hear it. "When they are of age," I said quietly, looking away, "how are you going to teach them to stand for anything when you will have betrayed your country to raise them?"

There was nothing she could say in reply. The door slammed a few moments later and I was left alone with my glass of Oban and the dark Pacific sky.

TOP SECRET/SPECIAL
COMPARTMENTALIZED INFORMATION
CLASSIFIED BY: US Central Intelligence Agency
DECLASSIFY ON: OADR

From: Special Projects Group [NCS]
Sent: Wednesday, 25 November 2009, 1145 PST (25
November 2009, 1945Z)
To: Director, NCS
Cc: Special Projects Group [NCS]; damrine@cmail.cia.gov;
dsmith3@cmail.cia.gov

SUBJECT: UPDATE – Operation Baja Sunrise

(TS) Narrative:

1. (TS) Gulfstream G-IVSP N36WMS has still not been located.

2. (TS) Contractor 09-017 (Pearce, Colin M.) and Operations
Officer Susan Turner are still missing in action.

3. (TS) A ground surveillance team arrived at Miguel Hidalgo's
reported summer home on the coast of Baja California in the
vicinity of Lazaro Cardenas at 0800 PST. Due to the terrain
and the extent of Hidalgo's property, they have been unable
to find a position where they can set up visual and infrared
surveillance and attain line of sight to the main house or the
outbuildings.

4. (TS) Per our expectation, an FAA Temporary Flight
Restriction (TFR) has been established for tomorrow for
San Francisco International Airport (KSFO) and Candlestick
Park from 1200 PST to 1800 PST. Although still not confirmed
by the Secret Service, VPOTUS is apparently attending the

Eagles/Forty-Niners game tomorrow.

5. (TS) A TFR has also been imposed over John Wayne/ Orange County Airport (KSNA) and Santa Catalina Island for the same time period as the TFR over Candlestick Park and San Francisco International Airport tomorrow. The FAA refuses to provide the source for the TFR request.

6. (TS) The Secret Service continues to refuse requests for information concerning POTUS and VPOTUS travel tomorrow, as well as requests concerning Susan Turner's contacts.

7. (TS) Bachelor's Toy departed Cabo San Lucas Harbor before sunrise this morning. No float plan was filed. The yacht was last seen on a westerly heading. William Spratt was escorted off the yacht prior to its departure along with an unidentified female matching the description of his daughter, Shelly. (Note: If the unidentified female is his daughter, we have no information about when or how she came aboard the vessel. Multiple people were seen boarding the vessel last night and it is possible she may have been one of them. We are searching the immigration records at Los Cabos International Airport for aliases that may have been used to bring her into the country.) They were escorted back to the Hotel Imperial del Cabo and remain under guard in one of the rooms there. We have them under surveillance and are prepared to retrieve them if required.

8. (TS) Per Pearce's request, we have conducted a background check into Damian Marciano, Sarah Morton Marciano's husband. The social security number and date of birth matching Damian Marciano's name correspond to a child who died at age 7 in Downingtown, PA, 30 years ago. The man posing as Sarah Marciano's husband is using an assumed identity and we are now using facial recognition software on his driver's

license picture to determine his real identity.

9. (TS) We understand that the National Security Advisor still refuses to receive the briefing on this threat.

(TS) CONCLUSIONS:

1. (TS) We stand by our previous conclusion concerning action against VPOTUS while he attends the football game at Candlestick Park on Thursday, 26 November;

2. (TS) The short-notice TFR over Southern California and the Secret Service's reticence to provide answers are troubling; we suspect that POTUS may be traveling to Southern California on a sensitive matter without the usual protection or preparation;

3. (TS) Originally, we suspected Turner's role was to provide confirmation to al Qudamah and Hidalgo about VPOTUS schedule. We now suspect that VPOTUS' schedule was known and that Turner's role was to provide word about the secret movements of POTUS; and

4. (TS) A ship of the size and speed of Bachelor's Toy, with a suspected armed force aboard, presents a significant threat if indeed POTUS will be in Southern California without the usual defenses in place, especially if POTUS is on Santa Catalina Island.

(TS) ACTIONS:

1. (TS) Request Coast Guard forces be placed on alert for watercraft approaching Santa Catalina Island;

2. (TS) Request deployment of A-10 Aircraft from Davis-Monthan AFB, AZ to maintain alert status at March AFB, CA

or North Island, NAS, CA;

3. (TS) Request deployment of E-3 AWACS to monitor southern approaches to San Francisco;

4. (TS) Maintain NORAD air defense fighters on high alert; and

5. (TS) We will continue to update slides for a potential presentation to the NSA.

(U) RECOMMENDATIONS:

1. (TS) Petition DHS to place Coast Guard forces on alert for watercraft approaching Santa Catalina Island;

2. (TS) Petition JCS to deploy A-10 Aircraft from Davis-Monthan AFB, AZ to maintain alert status at March AFB, CA or North Island, NAS, CA;

3. (TS) Reiterate need for deployment of E-3 AWACS to NORAD to monitor southern approaches to San Francisco;

4. (TS) Maintain NORAD air defense fighters on high alert;

5. (TS) Continue to push for briefing to National Security Advisor and National Security Council on this operation. We believe this intelligence indicates a credible threat to VPOTUS and possibly to POTUS.

Chapter Twenty

Contract Day Nine
Wednesday, 25 November
1600 Hours Local Time
Miguel's Hidalgo's Hacienda
Near Lazaro Cardenas, Mexico

Ken's maintenance crew had been on site for twenty hours now and the results were impressive. The damaged right engine had been removed, the replacement engine was on the pylon, and most of the connections were in place. The dull, blue-gray radar absorbent paint now covered the fuselage back to the mid-point of the wings, the entire left wing and engine cowling, and a good portion of the vertical stabilizer.

"How much longer?" I asked Ken when he joined me at the food table after inspecting some of the engine work.

"About another two hours for the engine and another three hours after that to finish the paint. We'll have to run and trim the engine after that, of course. I'd also like to run the number one engine for a bit, just to make sure that leak is fixed. Let's say six hours total." He looked at me and lowered his voice. "I'd love to ask you what this is about. It's not every day that we use radar absorbent paint."

I didn't answer him. Of course, Joe was standing nearby but I wouldn't have answered anyway. I was determined to keep my word to Miguel if it meant keeping Ken and his guys safe.

"So, it's like that, is it?"

I shrugged.

"Well, that's what I expected. I should learn to stop thinking out loud. Maybe someday we can have a beer and talk about this," he said.

"I'd like that," I replied. *If I live that long.* "If I tell our host to arrange for your transportation to arrive in about six-and-a-half hours, you'll be ready?"

"Make it seven," Ken said. "You know how maintenance is. Something always goes wrong at the last minute."

I nodded and looked down at my watch. "I'll be back in a few hours. I've got somewhere I've got to be."

He nodded and went back to join his men. I limped back to the main house with Joe at my side and we made our way to Miguel's study. The doors were closed as we approached and I could hear a heated conversation taking place inside. The other guard was standing outside the doors and held a hand up to motion us to stop. He and Joe exchanged a few words in Spanish.

"We wait over in that room," Joe motioned toward the gathering room.

"That's fine," I said, and walked across the tile and into the richly-furnished room. Out of curiosity, I walked up to the ornate fireplace and looked up at the huge picture of General Antonio Lopez de Santa Anna. It was an amazing portrait. The general looked lifelike and charismatic.

"He's Miguel's ancestor," Joe whispered in his normal voice as he stood next to me. "I told you Miguel Hidalgo wasn't his real name. I overheard him on the phone yesterday. His real name is Antonio Lopez de Santa Anna, the fourth."

I stood perfectly still as I digested what Joe had told me. *Holy Shit! Why would an ancestor of Santa Anna be playing drug dealer?* The answer came to me immediately. Drug lords were the most powerful people in Mexico.

"Pearce?" Adam's voice called from the direction of Miguel's study. "Get in here. It's time to plan."

I walked into the study and found Miguel pacing back and forth in front of his window while he puffed on a cigar. He was obviously very agitated about something.

"I gave them the chance," he said to himself. "I gave them the chance."

"The maintenance folks will be done in a little less than seven hours," I announced.

Miguel snapped out of his inner dialogue and nodded.

On the table where I had sat earlier, Adam had a 1:500,000 scale map of northern Mexico laid out, as well as some sectional aeronautical charts for the southwestern US which were the same scale. I could see several highlighted areas on the sectional charts. There was also a ruler, a map plotter, and a selection of pens and highlighters.

"You need to plan a route to get us from here to the Burbank airport," Adam said. "And we need to avoid detection by the border surveillance radar balloons. So that means we need to go in at low altitude."

"Not necessarily," I countered. "We could do something much easier."

"And that would be?"

"Do you have any high-altitude IFR charts for this part of Mexico?"

He nodded and looked at me warily. "What are you suggesting?"

"We climb out of here up to an altitude in the mid-30s and orbit over one of the standard air routes into the United States. With our radar transponder off, of course."

"And?"

"We wait for an aircraft flying northbound along that route, intercept it, fall into trail behind, and follow it in."

Adam's jaw dropped open and Miguel stopped his pacing.

They both looked at me like I was crazy.

I looked at Miguel. "Without trying to pry into your business, may I ask if you send aircraft into the United States at low altitude on a regular basis?"

He nodded.

"What fraction successfully enters the US without detection?" I asked.

He paused for a moment. "Just over half," he said.

"The customs folks expect low-altitude entry because that's what everyone does. If my boys at the CIA are looking for us, they'll have an AWACS posted somewhere to watch for low-altitude approaches. They'll never expect us to come in high. And if we follow another aircraft closely, we might as well be invisible."

"We won't be invisible," Adam insisted. "They'll see our skin paint on radar!"

"You didn't pay enough attention in radar class, Adam. If we stay close to another aircraft, we'll be inside the resolution cell of the air traffic radar. It won't be able to detect us."

He looked at me blankly. Over his shoulder, I could see Miguel's eyes keen with interest.

"Okay back to Radar 101. The resolution cell of a radar is defined by the pulse width or duration and the vertical and horizontal beam widths of the radar. It's like," I searched for the right words for a moment, "it's like this. The shape of a radar beam is sort of like a cone with the point of the cone at the radar and the open area of the cone out in the airspace. The vertical height of the cone is the vertical beam width and the horizontal width of the cone is the horizontal beam width. The closer you get to the radar, the smaller the cone is. The further you get from the radar, the larger the cone is. Are you with me so far?"

Adam nodded.

"Okay. Now the radar doesn't transmit continually. It transmits and listens and transmits and listens. The amount of time it transmits is pulse width. So, if we go back to our cone analogy, a resolution cell is a three-dimensional space defined by the lateral dimensions of the cone and a depth which is defined by the pulse width, like slices of the cone. At any one time, we have this series of slices traveling through the air. When a target is detected in that space, the radar sees a hit. If there are two targets in that space, the radar still sees only one hit. Hell, if there are ten targets in that space, the radar still only sees one hit because that's all it can resolve."

"But radars are different," Adam said. "Some radars have better accuracy than others."

I nodded. *You're a good straight man, Adam.* "Target-tracking radars need greater accuracy; so to continue with our analogy, the cones would be smaller at the open end and pulse widths would be shorter so that the radar can pinpoint the position of whatever it finds very precisely – the slices would be thinner, so to speak. Some airport surveillance radars, like those that monitor approaches, are very precise. But long-range air traffic control radars don't need a lot of precision so the 'cones' they use are quite large and the pulse widths are quite long, relatively speaking, so the slices are much, much thicker. That three-dimensional slice is huge. We could have a party in there and the ATC agencies would never know it. Like I said, we'll be invisible."

"But what about the contrails?" Adam asked. Contrails were the white plumes of vapor generated by jet aircraft at altitude. "Other aircraft will see us."

"Well, it would certainly be better if we did this at night, but we can manage it during the day with a piece of information Miguel's friends at the Mexican Air Force can provide us and some smart flying," I answered.

"What information will you need?" Miguel asked.

"The level above which contrails will form," I said. "In the USAF we called it the 'Con Level.' Any military weather forecaster will predict it. We stay below that level until we intercept our aircraft, then fly formation with them until we cross the border. If we're lucky, we can follow one all the way up to LAX or part of the way to SFO before we separate and go land."

They both looked at me and I looked back at them. I could almost hear the cogs in their brains turning.

"There's another advantage as well," I said. "The USAF maintains fighters on air defense alert. They wouldn't hesitate to scramble them against an unidentified low-altitude target, but they'll think twice about scrambling against an airliner, especially when the ground control agencies are in contact with that airliner, and the airliner is following their instructions. All we'll be presenting is a primary skin paint target to the radar in one of the busiest air traffic control zones in the world. Even if they suspect anything at all, our target will vanish the moment we get close to another aircraft with its transponder on."

To my surprise, I saw Adam nodding. Then Miguel was nodding too. I had them convinced, and I had also provided them a perfect mechanism to penetrate US airspace and attack targets on US soil. Now all I had to do was live long enough to stop them.

Eventually, after deciding on the route, running navigation and fuel calculations, and a quick dinner, I made it back out to the hangar. Joe wasn't even bothering to escort me anymore. I guess I had been officially deemed harmless. I couldn't decide how I felt about that.

Ken's maintenance crew had finished connecting the replacement engine and was in the process of buttoning up the cowling when I arrived. The paint crew was standing by to paint the cowling. The rest of the aircraft was finished.

"That used to be a pretty kick-ass paint job," Ken said, as

I walked in. "Now it just looks boring."

I nodded. "That's the plan I guess." I tried to look around me without looking like I was looking around me. "Ken, I need you to do something for me." I fixed my gaze on the airplane. "If I give you a phone number, can you call it when you get to a place where phone calls are possible?"

"Sure," he said. "What do you want me to tell them?"

I recited Dave Smith's cell phone number to him. He didn't write it down but he didn't need to. He was a maintenance guy. Numbers lived in his brain. "Just tell them what you did here and who you did it for."

I could feel the suspicion rising off him. "Exactly what the fuck are you involved in here, Pearce?"

"Nothing that will affect you or your business, Ken, I promise you that. But it is something that could have some very grave consequences further north."

"What does that mean?"

"Honestly? I have no idea yet. I'm just going to have to ride along and stop it."

"Is there anything else you'd like me to tell them?"

"Yes. Describe the appearance of this aircraft and tell them we'll be landing at Burbank about twelve o'clock noon tomorrow. And tell them to have an ops team there."

Two hours later, the painting was done. Ken and his crew connected the tug to the G-IV's nose wheel and towed the jet outside so that they could run the newly-installed engine and ensure the throttle mechanism and engine control computer were talking to each other and to the avionics on the aircraft. They also ran the number one engine and, as expected, the oil line repair had fixed the leak issue on that engine. When the runs were completed, we fueled the aircraft using an apparatus that pumped fuel from an underground holding tank that lay under the ramp area. I was somehow unsurprised that Miguel had his own fuel facility. He seemed to be a man who thought of everything.

Once the aircraft was fueled, Ken's men backed it into the hangar and performed a thorough preflight inspection. They also performed all the necessary maintenance documentation to indicate what work had been completed and what parts had been used. Aircraft records were legal documents; and for business jets, the completeness of those records had a direct impact on the value of the aircraft. In addition to technical procedures compiled with, part numbers and serial numbers of the parts installed, the records often contained the very tags from the parts themselves. Ken and his crew were professionals, so I didn't try to talk them out of this particular function, but I couldn't help view their diligence on the paperwork as wasted effort in this case. I was convinced that the jet would be a smoldering collection of wreckage within twenty-four hours. I just hoped I wasn't part of it when that time came.

Finally, at about 2300 hours local time, Ken and his crew packed all their tools and equipment and readied the damaged engine for return to Gulfstream where it would be repaired and restocked. I was sure that it would be inspected by some men from the government as well. They had no sooner finished their packaging process when the Mexican Air Force C-130 re-materialized out of the darkness once again and collected them. Ken and his crew were gone before I even had time to shake his hand a final time.

Miguel walked up to my side as I watched the C-130 lift off into the darkness. "You chose well with them, Pearce," he said softly. "And I will honor my word. They will not be harmed. But..."

I felt my heart leap into my throat.

"They will be detained by customs in Cabo San Lucas for about twelve hours or so. Just to make sure that their arrival in the United States doesn't generate any suspicion."

I forced a smile onto my face and nodded at him. "Fair enough, Miguel."

"In the meantime," he continued, "you need to get some rest. Your flying skills will be severely tested once again tomorrow."

I hadn't really thought about it, but he was right about that. Although I had recently become reacquainted with the geometry required to run a successful intercept, that had taken place in an F-16 where I had thrust, maneuverability and most importantly, an air-to-air radar. Tomorrow, I was going to have to do it all visually in an aircraft that was not designed for it. I had my usual ridiculous confidence that I could make it work, but I knew I needed to sit down and run some calculations first.

"Any chance I can have some time with my computer and an internet connection to run some numbers? You're welcome to have Joe or someone look over my shoulder while I do it, of course."

Miguel nodded. "You can do them in my office and I'll watch. Besides, there's something I'd like to discuss with you over a glass of very good Scotch."

I looked at him. "I'd never turn down a glass of very good Scotch, sir."

About forty-five minutes later, I had all the numbers I needed; and after giving Miguel a course in intercept geometry, I stowed my computer, put my calculations aside, and he and I repaired to the gathering room. True to his word, Miguel poured us a couple of tumblers of the Balvenie Port-Wood 21-year-old, one of my favorites. Miguel even had a pitcher of spring water handy and he added a dash of the water to each tumbler, a tasting trick used to release the bouquet of the spirit.

We took seats in front of the fireplace and, coincidentally, in front of the picture of General Santa Anna. Adam was nowhere to be seen and hadn't been around all evening. I was sure he and Susan were busy fucking each other's brains out, her thinking she was buying her freedom and him using her one last time before he had her killed tomorrow.

It felt very odd to sit there with that knowledge.

I raised the tumbler to my nose and inhaled the soft bouquet, a little woody with a touch of pepper spice and a lingering aroma of ripe grapes.

"Cheers," I said reflexively, and I put the glass to my lips. The palate was fruity and just a little bitter, but somehow remarkably creamy. And the finish was reminiscent of hazelnut. "Wow," I said. "It's been a long time since I've had the port-wood twenty-one. I've missed it."

"It's my favorite," Miguel said quietly. "Which is why I own the distillery." He looked over at me. "I fly over there about twice a year."

"Scotland is beautiful," I said. "Unfortunately, except for a few hours on the ground at RAF Lossiemouth many years ago, I haven't had the opportunity to spend any time on the ground there."

"Which brings me to our discussion," Miguel replied. "How much do you make working for the CIA?"

I could have tried to talk around the subject or divert the discussion. But Miguel was smart and I was tired. Besides, I had the feeling that if I played it straight I might actually learn something useful.

"Ironically," I said, "the CIA has never paid me directly. They paid me through a holding company for my last and only job with them and the money was pretty good although I had to risk my life for it." I thought for a moment or two. "I guess they paid me about twice as much as I'd make on a daily contract gig."

"You seem to be a fairly gifted pilot, Colin. It's also apparent that you possess some leadership talent and can manage aircraft maintenance and logistics. How would you like to run my flight operation? I'd pay you well. About a million dollars per year, taxes paid, to start."

I looked down at my whiskey. A million dollars per year? My bank account was already pretty fat, but it wasn't that fat. I could be set for life in just a few years. I weighed the options and tried to tap into the moral ambivalence with which I had lived most of my life. But unfortunately, now, when it would have done me some financial good, that ambivalence seemed to be profoundly absent.

Well, shit.

"With no disrespect intended, Miguel, a lot of money doesn't do me much good if I'm behind bars."

"Life does indeed have its risks, Colin. But in this case, they may be unfounded. I wasn't talking about smuggling. I use subcontractors for that anyway. It's the only way I can maintain sufficient distance from them. No, you would build me an operation that would transport my cadre and would also allow me to implement a plan I've been working toward for several years."

I thought for a moment or two. "I don't want to get into your business, sir. But would this plan involve anything illegal?"

"Nothing that is illegal in the United States."

That doesn't help much.

"I see," I said, even though I obviously didn't.

He sat forward in his chair and turned toward me. The expression on his face was calm, but earnest. "If your country had lost its honor and it was in your power to restore it, would you not take steps to make that happen?"

I considered his words. "Well," I said slowly, "the US has lost a lot of its honor. Unfortunately, no one person can restore it. We need to do that as a nation. So, I guess I can't really relate to your question."

"Suppose for a moment that it was in your power," Miguel's face became animated. "Suppose you could clear away those whose interests were only for themselves and replace them with those who would serve the country alone and return it to greatness. Suppose you could clear away the corruption and inefficiency and turn your country into an economic powerhouse where all people would benefit and no one would live in poverty. Would you not see it as your moral duty to make that come to pass?"

Miguel rose and stood next to the fireplace in front of me. As I looked up at him, standing under the portrait of Santa Anna, the family resemblance, even with all the years between the generations, was unmistakable.

"I am Antonio Lopez de Santa Anna, the fourth," he said. "And it is my goal to overthrow the current government of my country and return honor both to my country and to my family. You seem to be something of an adventurer, Colin. I invite you to join me on my quest and become part of the new history of this great nation. You will not only fly my cadre and me, you will also build the new Mexican Air Force and lead it into battle against those who would oppose us."

He looked down at me keenly.

"And there are those who would oppose us, those who wish things to stay as they are, like those who attempted to shoot us down as we landed here night before last. But we will overcome them. What say you, my friend? Do you wish to make history or merely read it?"

To say I was taken aback would have been the understatement of the year. There was no reasonable reply I could utter in response.

"But Miguel, or er, Antonio," I blurted without thinking, "I don't even speak Spanish."

"That's not a problem," he said, without flinching. "Nobody is perfect."

TOP SECRET/SPECIAL
COMPARTMENTALIZED INFORMATION
CLASSIFIED BY: US Central Intelligence Agency
DECLASSIFY ON: OADR

From: Special Projects Group [NCS]
Sent: Thursday, 26 November 2009, 0145 PST (26
November 2009, 0945Z)
To: Director, NCS
Cc: Special Projects Group [NCS]; damrine@cmail.cia.gov;
dsmith3@cmail.cia.gov

SUBJECT: UPDATE – Operation Baja Sunrise

(TS) Narrative:

1. (TS) At 2100 PST, our ground surveillance team monitoring
Miguel Hidalgo's reported summer home saw a Gulfstream
G-IV towed outside of one of the large outbuildings on the
property. No registration numbers were visible on the aircraft
and the paint scheme did not match that of N36WMS. The
aircraft started and ran engines for some time. Then the
engines were shut down, the aircraft was refueled, and the
aircraft was replaced in the hangar/outbuilding.

2. (TS) At 2310 PST, a Mexican Air Force C-130, with no
exterior lights illuminated, made a landing on the property
on the pavement previously identified as a possible airstrip.
It stopped outside the outbuilding and men and equipment
were loaded onto the aircraft. Contractor 09-017 (Pearce,
Colin M.) was seen monitoring the departure.

3. (TS) At 0100 PST, a Mexican Air Force C-130 landed at Los
Cabos International Airport (MMSD) where it was detained

by customs personnel. The personnel aboard filed routine notifications with the US Embassy and with US Customs and Border Patrol.

4. (TS) At 0130, Operations Officer Smith received a call from a Ken Martin who, acting on instructions from Pearce, described maintenance work he and his crew had performed on Gulfstream IVSP N36WMS at Miguel Hidalgo's reported summer home. This maintenance work included replacement of an engine which had sustained fragmentation damage from surface-to-air missile fire. He also said the aircraft had been painted in radar absorbent paint and was scheduled to arrive at Burbank/Bob Hope Airport (KBUR) tomorrow at approximately 1200 PST. Martin said Pearce had requested an Operations Team on site when the aircraft arrived at Burbank. Martin further indicated no non-standard devices or equipment had been affixed to the aircraft. Lastly, Martin said that Pearce had indicated that he (Pearce) had no knowledge at all about intentions or targets with the aircraft.

5. (TS) Operations Officer Susan Turner remains missing in action.

6. (TS) Initial facial recognition analysis has tentatively identified the man claiming to be Damian Marciano as Mohammed bin Rashid al Qudamah, Abdullah bin Rashid al Qudamah's younger brother. Mohammed was/is a radical Wahhabi Imam who supported Al-Qaeda and violent action against western countries. He disappeared approximately 18-24 months ago, approximately the same time he was introduced to Sarah Morton Marciano.

7. (TS) A full presidential advance team is now in place at John Wayne Airport in Santa Ana, California, although the Secret Service refuses to comment on POTUS movements.

8. (TS) Per your request, the USAF has tasked an E-3 AWACS from Tinker AFB, OK. The aircraft will arrive on station no later than 0800 PST (1600Z) today.

(TS) CONCLUSIONS:

1. (TS) The repairs and schedule for Gulfstream G-IVSP N36WMS are further corroboration of action against VPOTUS while he attends the football game at Candlestick Park on Thursday, 26 November. We believe that the aerial dispensing device will be fitted to the aircraft upon its arrival at Burbank airport and then the aircraft will be flown to the target area. We will not attempt to intercept the aircraft on its way into the US, instead we will have an operations team at the airport to greet the aircraft. We understand additional assets have been approved.

2. (TS) The timeline for the introduction of Mohammed bin Rashid al Qudamah as Damian Marciano to Sarah Morton approximately 18 months ago indicates that the timeline for the current operation extends back to well before Bachelor's Toy was purchased at the Dubai Yacht show in late September. Apparently, the purchase of the yacht was the trigger for the current phase of operations and the exchange of Mohammed for his brother to supervise the final phase of the operation was part of the timeline. We suspect the yacht was used to transport the diverted weapons shipment from the Middle East to Hidalgo in Mexico. The exact nature of the relationship between Miguel Hidalgo and the al Qudamahs remains unknown although laundered funds from drug transactions held in banks in North America are much easier to use for financial transactions than funds originating overseas. Additionally, Hidalgo's influence in Baja California would make the use of Cabo San Lucas as a staging point much easier.

3. (TS) Bachelor's Toy has been at sea for over 18 hours now.

In another 12-14 hours, it could easily be in range of Southern California. We believe the vessel and the armed force aboard her represent a significant threat. While we understand that the DHS refused to place the Coast Guard on alert due to orders from the Office of the President, we must revisit that request or task US Navy assets stationed in San Diego.

(TS) ACTIONS:

1. (TS) Operations team tasked for reception of Gulfstream G-IV N36WMS tomorrow;

2. (TS) Maintain current E-3 AWACS orbit to monitor border crossings and southern approaches to San Francisco;

3. (TS) Task Coast Guard forces to deploy and monitor watercraft approaching Santa Catalina Island;

4. (TS) Request deployment of A-10 Aircraft from Davis-Monthan AFB, AZ to maintain alert status at March AFB, CA or North Island, NAS, CA; and

5. (TS) Maintain NORAD air defense fighters on Alert 5.

(TS) RECOMMENDATIONS:

1. (TS) See action items 3 and 4 above.

2. (TS) Inform the Director of the Secret Service of the nature of this threat and ask him to reconsider POTUS and VPOTUS travel tomorrow.

CHAPTER TWENTY-ONE

Contract Day Ten
Thursday, 26 November
0900 Hours Local Time
Miguel's Hidalgo's Hacienda
Near Lazaro Cardenas, Mexico

It was yet another clear and sunny day in Baja California as the hangar doors opened in front of us and the G-IV was towed out onto the ramp and under the bright, azure sky. Adam was still in the back of the airplane with Susan, so I was left to start the APU and run the pre-start checks by myself.

I didn't mind. I had a lot to think about.

First, there was Miguel's offer from last night. When I told him I needed some time to consider it, he didn't seem surprised or disappointed by my answer. Instead, he offered me a piece of advice that I found intriguing if not a little disturbing.

"Keep your cane close at hand, amigo," he had said, with a sly smile. "And be first. If you are, then we can talk again." He had then shaken my hand warmly and we had each gone off to our own rooms to get our ration of sleep for the night.

This morning, he was nowhere to be seen.

The other thing I had on my mind was the fate that awaited me when we reached Burbank. I was reasonably certain the

CIA would have men in place but I wasn't counting on it. And then when I had met Adam for breakfast and we had briefed the flight, he had seemed remarkably composed and professional for a man who planned to have me killed in a mere few hours. That seemed a bit spooky. But maybe I should have expected that.

Before we were towed out, our bags were brought down to the hangar and we loaded them in the passenger seating area instead of the baggage compartment on Adam's instructions. That confirmed where they intended to install the device. The G-IV had a baggage door that could be opened in flight without damaging the aircraft, assuming the aircraft was not pressurized. A device designed to disperse its payload in aerosol fashion would work very handily there.

Once the bags were stowed, Adam shut the door to the vestibule so he and Susan could be alone in the back. Where they remained.

When the aircraft was stopped outside the hangar, I lowered the door, ensured the nose wheel steering pin was properly installed, and removed the landing gear safety pins. Then I returned to the aircraft and raised the door. The door to the vestibule remained closed. I wondered if Adam was having one last interlude with Susan before he had her killed. It fit the profile.

I finished the pre-start checks and got the flight management system and performance computers online. Then, I programed them with the route I intended to use and the holding pattern from which I intended to watch for the intercept. The route I had selected was UJ9, a high-altitude airway which ran directly over the Gulf of California and joined the arrival routes into both San Diego and Los Angeles. The plan was to orbit six miles to the west of the route and watch for aircraft headed northbound, and then execute a well-timed turn to end up about one-to-two miles in trail of the target aircraft and close to a position where we were directly under and behind it. Hopefully we could then just follow it as far north as it would take us. There were two possible flaws with the plan. First, there was a possibility someone might see us. That was remote but plausible. The second was that I had never flown a purely visual intercept before and the odds were at least fifty-fifty that I wouldn't get it right the first time. Which was why we had brought along a little extra gas.

Still, no Adam in the cockpit.

I started the engines and ran the post starting-engines checklist before he finally joined me. His hair was slightly disheveled and his cheeks were flushed. It was all I could do not to smack him.

"Checks are done," I said. "With the current temperature and our gross weight, we have just enough runway so that we don't have to lie to the FMS for it to give us speeds. I'll be doing a static takeoff. If we have any problems, we'll take the jet into the air and deal with them there because numbers or no numbers, I'm not even going to try to abort a takeoff in a sixty-thousand-pound aircraft on four-thousand feet of runway with no emergency vehicles. Do you have any questions?"

He shook his head impatiently at me as he donned his headset.

I released the parking brake and applied power and the G-IV began to move forward. Since there was no air terminal information service to give us the wind direction and velocity or altimeter setting, I eyeballed the few trees that were around the property and determined that the wind was out of the south. We set the altimeters to just above sea level in elevation. The taxi route to the north end of Miguel's runway took us about forty-five seconds, and I paused at the entrance to the runway for a moment to make sure all the pre-takeoff items were complete.

"FATS," I said over the intercom.

"Flaps," Adam said.

"Twenty selected, twenty indicating," I replied, looking

down at the flap indicator.

"Airbrakes."

"Stowed." I also checked the annunciator panel. It was clear.

"Trims."

I looked down at the G-IV's trim indicators. The aileron and rudder trip were zero and the elevator trim was set in the takeoff range.

"Speeds."

I looked in my flight display and could see that all the speeds we needed for takeoff we appropriately labeled and displayed. V_1, V_R, V_2, V_{FS} and V_{SE} were all there. "Posted left," I said.

"Posted right," Adam said.

"Are you ready?" I asked.

Adam nodded impatiently. He was clearly anxious.

I taxied out on to the runway.

"Aren't you going to move a throttle up so I can arm the ground spoilers?"

"Nope," I replied. "The only way we'd need ground spoilers is in the event we're planning on aborting the takeoff and like I told you, I have no plans to do that on this runway."

He shrugged in response.

The runway was only sixty-feet wide, so it didn't allow for a lot of maneuvering, but I put the left main gear as close to the approach end as I could before I turned the aircraft to point down the runway. Then, after making sure the nose wheel was precisely aligned with the center of the runway, I stood on the wheel brakes and slowly applied power. The exhaust pressure ratio reached 1.17 and I armed the autothrottles. They moved swiftly and deliberately to the max power position. The G-IV started to vibrate.

"Power is set," Adam said, as the EPR gauges reached the takeoff index.

"Here we go," I replied.

Static takeoffs weren't uncommon in business aviation, particularly if passengers wanted to go into smaller airfields and escape the hustle and bustle of larger airports. Usually though, the pilot flying will release the brakes gradually for passenger comfort. That was the last thing on my mind today, and I instantly released brake pressure and put my heels on the floor so that just my toes were on the rudder pedals. Immediately, the powerful business jet leapt forward, propelled by over twenty-six-thousand pounds of thrust from the big Tay engines.

I glanced down at the right engine gauge. All indications were normal and matched with the left gauge. My eyes found the left oil pressure display and it read normal as well. Ken and his folks had done well.

Meanwhile Adam, as the pilot monitoring, was staring out of the windscreen with a look of apprehension on his face as the end of the small runway rushed toward us. In theory, it was his job to read airspeeds off to me so that I'd know when to perform my tasks. Apparently, though, he was otherwise engaged.

The airspeed tape accelerated past 80 knots.

"My yoke," I announced, taking my left hand off the steering tiller and putting it on the yoke. I also removed my right hand from the throttles and put it on the yoke as well, something I typically didn't do until after V_1 but I wasn't aborting today.

V_1 went by and the airspeed tape accelerated to V_R. Adam was literally pushing himself back into his seat as if to prepare for some sort of impact at the end of the runway. I smiled to myself and pulled the yoke aft a little more quickly than I normally did. The G-IV's nose smoothly rotated to the takeoff attitude; and for a scant second or two, the jet remained in that position, nose up and main gear still on the runway as the lift required for takeoff continued to build. I could feel Adam's tension building from across the cockpit. Then the wings gained the lift required and the heavy business jet rose from the small runway and climbed into the blue Baja sky.

I looked down at the altimeter and vertical velocity indicator. Both indicated a positive rate of climb - something Adam should have noticed and called out, but he was clearly recovering from a self-perceived brush with death.

"Gear up, Adam," I commanded.

He started as if I had disturbed him from some sort of dream state and raised the gear handle without even looking down to verify we were indeed climbing.

Guess I'm going to be playing single pilot today, I thought to myself.

"Flaps up," I said, as we climbed through four-hundred feet above the ground. I banked the G-IV to the right and we turned out over the Pacific Ocean while I waited for him to comply with my command. His hand found the flap handle about ten seconds after it should have and the flaps began their retraction. Ordinarily I would have asked a co-pilot to set the avionics up for the climb, but since it was apparent that Adam was still not completely with me, I set my heading marker to 270 degrees and commanded a target speed of three hundred knots for the climb. Then I rolled out on the heading and allowed the jet to accelerate as we climbed slowly away from the rugged Mexican terrain below us.

We needed to reach the high twenties or low thirties to find an airplane we could follow; but to traverse the altitudes without radar control and avoid hitting another aircraft, I needed to find airspace that would be relatively free of traffic in which to make our ascent. My plan was to fly about fifty miles out over the ocean, just west of the major high-altitude north-south airway off the coast of Baja California, and then climb into the high-altitude structure. At 300 knots, about ten minutes on a westerly heading would do it.

As the jet reached 300 knots, I retarded the power and allowed the jet to slowly creep upward as we continued out over the water. We hit the ten-minute point at about 10,000 feet and I began a slow turn to the south as I commanded maximum continuous thrust for the climb and raised the nose to maintain the airspeed. The G-IV began to climb rapidly and soon we were climbing through 18,000 feet.

"2992 set," I commanded, as I reached down to change my altimeter setting to 29.92 inches of mercury, the standard setting for the high-altitude flight levels. Adam seemed to be mentally present with me now and he ran the climb transition checklist and ensured the remaining altimeters were set correctly.

"Did Miguel get you the con level, Adam?" I asked him.

He nodded. "Flight level 340 over Baja today."

"Perfect," I replied. "We'll level at thirty-two five." Ordinarily, aircraft operating under instrument flight rules or radar control fly at odd altitudes if they were on a heading of 360 to 179 and at even altitudes if they were on a heading of 180 to 359 degrees. I wanted to offset those altitudes by five-hundred feet to avoid running into other airplanes I might not see and I also wanted to be further below the con level than five-hundred feet for the simple reason that weathermen were often wrong. Contrails would be a big deal for us today. At high altitude, without proper training and/or technology, other aircraft are hard to see if they're not generating contrails. I intended to take full advantage of that fact.

We reached FL325 a few minutes later and I turned us to the east. With the aircraft now on autopilot, I called up the airway we were going to troll—UL9—in the flight management computer and displayed it on our navigation screens. The white line of video now ran perpendicular to our flight path about one-hundred miles in front of our nose. According to my calculations, at our speed and altitude, the turn diameter for the G-IV would be roughly six miles and a 180-degree turn would take about seventy-five seconds. That meant I needed to be six miles offset from the airway traveling the opposite direction, and begin my turn when the target aircraft was about ten miles away, assuming we were traveling at the same speed.

"Wow," I said out loud, as I programmed the offset turn into the guidance computer, "I'd kill to have an air-to-air radar and a fire control computer to make this more precise." I finished programming the turn and entered a random series of digits in the transponder.

"Why are you setting up the transponder?" Adam asked. "Won't that alert the other jets to our presence?"

"Once we see another jet conning out there, I'm going to turn it on for a few seconds and use the TCAS like a poor man's air-to-air radar."

He nodded at me slowly, but I could tell by the expression on his face that he didn't agree with my thought process. TCAS stood for terminal collision avoidance system. It was a computerized system built into the transponders of modern-day aircraft. When two aircraft had their transponders on, the TCAS boxes in the aircraft talked to each other and each aircraft would get a display of the other aircraft's approximate range and azimuth, as well as the difference in their altitudes. If the two aircraft were on a collision course, the TCAS boxes would work together to command guidance to avoid the collision. This latter feature would require me to ensure the transponder/TCAS was off during the end game of the intercept. The flight path I planned to fly would make the TCAS box in the target aircraft think we were going to hit it.

A few moments later, I began the turn to parallel UL9 six miles to the west.

"Okay, heads up," I said. "It's show time."

I had set up twenty-mile legs for our orbit pattern and we did two full orbits and spent about fifteen minutes without seeing an aircraft on the airway. I even cheated and turned the transponder on for a few seconds to see if the TCAS detected any other aircraft. I was rewarded with a blank screen for my attempts. I was beginning to think that I had chosen the route poorly as we rolled out southbound for the third time when a distant set of contrails caught my attention.

"Houston, we have a target," I said.

At high altitude, with the horizon well below, it was difficult to determine if another aircraft was above you or below you when they were far away. In this case, though, we were lucky because the aircraft was conning and we weren't. But we still didn't know how high above us he was.

"Okay, here goes with the transponder," I said.

I activated the box and waited for the TCAS to range in.

"Shit," I said when I saw his altitude.

"He's 8,500 feet above us," Adam said. "We'll never get up to him in time."

"It'll definitely be a challenge," I agreed as I turned the transponder off. "You want to wait for the next guy?"

Adam looked at his watch and did some mental math. We had launched early to allow extra time for our ingress plan, but I didn't know where we were on the timeline. He did.

"No," he shook his head. "Let's try this one."

"Roger that," I said. "Here goes."

I increased our speed to get us as close to the airframe limit as I could. Maintaining level flight in a turn requires more lift, and I expected to bleed off airspeed in the turn at this altitude. If we got too slow in the turn, we'd end up in a tail chase behind the target with opening velocity. I turned the transponder on again to check the target's flight path and distance from us. Once the TCAS ranged in again, I could tell by the movement of the blue diamond representing his aircraft that he was definitely on UL9. He was now at about twenty miles in range. I called up the elapsed time counter on the G-IV's avionics display. Then I turned the transponder off again and started the clock. Assuming we were both traveling about Mach .8, our closing velocity was approximately sixteen miles per minute. When my clock reached thirty seconds,

I kicked the autopilot off and began my turn, immediately losing sight of the target aircraft as we banked up and the target was obscured from view under the belly of the G-IV. I reset and restarted the clock.

"Isn't this too early?" Adam asked. "I thought you wanted to start the turn at ten miles range."

"That was before I knew I had to make up an eighty-five-hundred-foot difference in altitude," I replied, keeping my eyes on the flight display in front of me. "The last thing we need to do is wind up in a tail chase with an altitude delta. We'd never catch him before he reached the border. As it is, if this guy turns out to be a 75, 76, or 77, we could still be screwed." Most airliners cruised at .8 Mach or below but the 757, 767, and 777 could go faster—and often did.

I kept my eyes glued to the pilot's flight display, maintaining just the right amount of back pressure on the yoke to sustain level flight and keeping the roll indicator exactly at 45 degrees of bank. This was a steep turn, a maneuver we routinely performed on simulator check rides, but it was usually performed at 10,000 to 15,000 feet where the air was a lot more dense and not at all like the thin atmosphere in the thirties. Pitch control was more sensitive up here and thrust available, in relation to the lift and drag required, was much less. Typically, we flew these turns at 250 knots indicated airspeed in check rides also, but up here indicated airspeed didn't mean nearly as much to me as Mach number did and I needed to ensure our Mach number didn't go below .8.

The clock ticked past 37 seconds—we were halfway through the turn.

"Shouldn't we roll out and check our position?" Adam asked, just a little frantically. "How do we know if this is working?"

"We have to fly the parameters, Adam. This guy isn't a maneuvering target. If we fly the numbers, it will work."

"But I can't see him!" Adam exclaimed, as he tried to look

over the side of his windscreen while we maintained the bank angle.

"He's 8,500 feet above us and we're in 45 degrees of bank," I said. "Do a little trigonometry. We won't see him until we're 8,500 feet apart or just over a mile. And that won't happen until after we roll out."

The clock reached 75 seconds and I rolled out, headed northbound on the airway. The sky seemed to be completely empty in front of us. I could feel Adam radiating impatience next to me and for a moment, I felt an overwhelming urge to ask him how eager he would be to race to his own execution but I didn't.

Instead, I turned the transponder back on and let it range in for a moment. There was only one other aircraft visible on the TCAS display. Our target. Just behind us and 8,500 feet above.

It was perfect.

I turned off the transponder and began a gentle climb, checking the power in max and maintaining .8 Mach.

"Okay," I said. "Up we go."

The target was at flight level 410, 41,000 feet on an altimeter setting of 29.92 inches of mercury. I engaged the autopilot and set a 900-foot-per-minute rate of climb for the G-IV. We maintained .8 Mach and by the time we reached FL 380, the target had still not appeared in front of us. Apparently, it was maintaining .8 Mach as well. Even though we were slightly in front of the target, I had no worries about its crew seeing us, largely because visibility over the nose in an airliner is terrible. But also because I knew from many of my friends in the industry that while in cruise, most airline pilots don't spend a lot of time looking outside. Instead, they read newspapers, magazines, or used laptop computers.

There was one thing to be concerned about, however, and that was the target's radar altimeter. Once we got within 2,500 feet below the jet, it was possible its radar altimeter would detect us. While it would give the crew a false terrain warning, it would still startle the crew out of their normal high-altitude routine, and I didn't want that.

"Alrighty, then," I said, as I leveled off and rotated the speed command back to .79 Mach. "Let's see how we did."

About two minutes later, the target aircraft, a Boeing 737, became visible directly above us, as it slowly began to move ahead. I clicked off the autopilot and autothrottles and resumed our climb. I could feel Adam tensing beside me. Our air combat flight the other day notwithstanding, it was obvious he hadn't flown formation for a while. I, on the other hand, had some recent experience.

Our position was going to be a challenge though. We had to stay out of sight of the crew and passengers of the aircraft, which meant we had to stay directly behind the 737. We also had to try to ensure our contrails blended with the contrails of the other aircraft, so we had to stay nearly directly under it, but not so far under it that we activated its radar altimeter. The G-IV had relatively heavy control forces and to fly good formation position, I couldn't trim off all the control forces because I needed to maintain some "feel" on my hands.

This was going to be tricky and tiring.

I leveled us off about a hundred feet below the 737 with our nose just under the airliner's vertical stabilizer. We were close enough to hear the roar of the airliner's CFM 56 Engines and clearly see the winglets on the end of each wing. It was a 737-700 or newer. Probably. I could feel the wake turbulence generated by the 737's wings on the G-IV's elevators so I knew I was at the right height. Now all I needed to do was stay here until we crossed the border. And hope no one looked too closely at us.

"Adam, as you probably remember, when you fly close formation as a wingman, it's hard sometimes to pick up on turns or changes in altitude. As soon as you see either of those things, please let me know."

I saw him nod out of my peripheral vision.

Flying formation required total concentration on the leader's aircraft because that aircraft is the wingman's sole source of reference. And once a pilot was proficient at flying formation, his responses became reflexive, automatically changing pitch, roll, yaw, and power to maintain position without thinking about it.

The other thing about flying formation was that it was hard work. The G-IV's cockpit was cold, largely because the air on the other side of the windscreen was at about -57 degrees Celsius, but I could feel trickles of sweat running down the sides of my body and feel the hair under my headset getting damp. I flexed my toes to keep the blood flowing and as I kept control pressure applied with one finger on my left hand, I allowed my other fingers to flutter for a moment or two to keep them relaxed. I found my mind drawn to one of my longest flights in the F-16. I had led a flight of four jets from Korea to Alaska for a Cope Thunder exercise and spent roughly ten hours in the air on the wing of a KC-10 tanker. To maintain sufficient power and maneuverability for air refueling operations, we hadn't cruised any higher than the mid-twenties and the weather for that deployment had been miserable. We had flown close formation on the tanker for hours at a time, the monotony broken only when we were refueling, which required more concentration than flying formation did.

"We just crossed the border," Adam said, after what seemed like an eternity but was probably only about fifteen minutes. "Now it looks like we're headed north toward Thermal and Palm Springs. How much longer do we need to do this?"

"Let's stay with him until he reaches Palm Springs," I said. "It will be easier if we make the approach to Burbank from the north, from around Palmdale. If he drops us off at Palm Springs, we can skirt the mountains to the north and squawk VFR once we get down closer to the airport."

"You're not worried about ATC radars picking us up once we're no longer behind this airliner?"

I shook my head.

"ATC radars aren't optimized to return skin paints without transponder enhancement. And once this guy makes his turn, I plan to drop like a rock. "

"Okay," Adam said flatly. "And by the way, we're not going to Burbank. We're going to Van Nuys."

My head was still swimming over the destination change several minutes later when the 737 began its descent and turned left, obviously entering one of the arrival corridors for the LA basin. Reflexively, I retarded the power to idle, opened the speed brakes, and let the jet descend at 300 knots. The descent rate increased to about 4,000 feet per minute and then held steady. We came through 18,000 feet just east of Big Bear Lake and I began a slow turn to the west as I continued the descent. This was the same terrain I had fought the air battle of my life over just a few weeks ago, but apart from registering it in some far corner of my mind, I didn't think about it.

Instead, I thought about how I was going to fight the ground battle awaiting me in about fifteen minutes or so. The CIA was going to be at Burbank and we were going to be at Van Nuys. The two airports were only about five nautical miles apart. A 15-minute car ride in good traffic.

They may as well have been on different continents.

And Felix Lopez/Saif-al Din, the sword of the faith, would be waiting. He had his weapon and I had mine. I just hoped mine would be enough. I silently thanked Miguel for the warning about my cane. I intended to keep it very close indeed.

As we passed through 10,000 feet, I slowed us to 250 knots

and dialed in the radio frequency for the weather information service for Southern California Logistics Airport—which used to be George Air Force Base—to get a local altimeter setting.

"30.14," I said, when I heard it over the radio and I adjusted the two altimeters on my side of the cockpit accordingly. "You want to run some checklists over there, Adam?"

It was obvious that I had caught him daydreaming or distracted about something. He quickly ran the descent and approach checklists.

I then dialed in the automatic terminal information service for Van Nuys Airport which was just barely audible due to our altitude in relation to the mountains that separated us from the airport.

"Looks like they're landing on 16 Right," I said. "We'll plan the ILS." I looked over at Adam. "So, is it up to me to bullshit our way into the airport as well?"

He looked back at me with what could only be described as a gleam in his eye and nodded.

"Great," I said sarcastically.

I leveled us off at 9,500 feet, set the transponder to the VFR code of 1200 and turned the unit on. Then, I had a sudden flash of inspiration. If I could get SOCAL Approach to issue us an IFR clearance into Van Nuys, it was possible the Feds would pick that up, assuming they were monitoring the approaches to Burbank. The same Sector Controller for SOCAL had responsibility for both airports. I nonchalantly found a frequency for SOCAL approach and dialed it in.

"SOCAL approach, Gulfstream November 36 Whisky Mike Sierra."

There was a pregnant pause as the controller on this frequency checked his flight data and his screen. Typically, Gulfstreams flew on IFR flight plans and were handed off by other radar control agencies. We were pop-up traffic.

"Gulfstream November 36 Whisky Mike Sierra, SOCAL Approach," a male voice finally answered, "are you sure you're on the right frequency sir? I have no record of you."

"We're VFR just about twenty miles east, southeast of Palmdale on a ferry flight and we'd like to pick up an IFR clearance to Van Nuys."

There was another pause as he spoke to one of the other controllers around him.

"Gulfstream November 36 Whisky Mike Sierra, squawk 3423 and ident."

"Gulfstream November 36 Whisky Mike Sierra copies 3423 and a flash." I dialed in the digits, and then hit the ident button which highlighted our transponder return on his radar.

"Gulfstream November 36 Whisky Mike Sierra, SOCAL approach, radar contact. What kind of Gulfstream are you?"

"Gulfstream November 36 Whisky Mike Sierra, we're a Gulf Lima Fox four slant quebec with three souls aboard, sir."

There was a pause while he entered the data he needed into the computer and then waited for our clearance.

"Gulfstream November 36 Whisky Mike Sierra is cleared to the Van Nuys Airport via radar vectors. Squawk 3423. Maintain 9,000."

I repeated it back to him and we were on our way. I just hoped to God somebody who mattered was paying attention.

About ten minutes and several frequency changes later, we were on final approach to runway 16R at Van Nuys, the busiest general aviation airport in the United States. It was a struggle to keep my mind on all the flying details when I knew what awaited us. I kept trying to think of additional ways to call for help or alert the CIA, but with Adam sitting right next to me and listening to every detail, it just wasn't possible. As we approached the field, I searched for signs of official vehicles or flashing lights, but the airport looked dismayingly normal. It wasn't even particularly busy today.

As soon as the wheels touched down and we slowed to taxi speed, Adam had his cell phone out and made a call. After a few quick words in Arabic, he hung up.

"We're going to the Rose Aircraft hangar," he said. "You remember where that is, yes?"

I nodded and swallowed hard.

Goddamn it. The folks at Rose aircraft had apparently committed the unpardonable sin of allowing me to embarrass Adam/Adbullah so now they had to pay with the use of their facility. And quite possibly their lives.

I announced our intentions to the ground controller and he gave us taxi clearance to get there. Then he wished us a happy Thanksgiving. I returned his wishes and wondered if it would be my last.

Rose Aircraft's hangar was on the western side of the airport and at the end of a row of hangars off the main taxiway. It was very well-concealed from prying eyes, especially on a day when the level of activity at the airport was low. As I taxied the G-IV toward the hangar, an Arab-looking man walked out onto the taxiway to direct us into the hangar. He obviously wasn't one of Rose Aircraft's technicians—not a good sign.

Typically, you don't taxi a jet into a hangar with engines running. Instead, you completely shut the airplane down, and then it's towed in. That wasn't the plan today. The man was motioning with his hands rapidly for us to turn and taxi completely into the hangar. I hesitated for just a moment— and that's when I felt the barrel of a pistol against my neck. It was almost amusing, the sensation of the deadly, cold metal against my skin had absolutely no effect on me. It wasn't that I was particularly calm at that moment. It was just that I had expected it for so long that it was almost a relief of sorts.

"Calm yourself there, Tex," I said, as I turned the aircraft into the hangar. "If you pull that trigger the bullet will go right through me and you won't be flying this jet anywhere."

"You act very calm for a man whose life belongs to another," he said.

I glanced over at him.

"I've been threatened by people who are a lot scarier than

you, Abdullah."

His eyes flashed at the mention of his real name.

"So, I have a question for you," I continued recklessly. "What in the fuck do you hope to accomplish today? And why do you guys have such a hard-on for the US anyway? Is it because you can't reconcile the Muslim thing with all the shit you enjoy about the western lifestyle—or is it because if it wasn't for the good old US-of-A, you'd all still be herding fucking camels around? Or would that be fucking herding camels? I have difficulty remembering."

I could feel his hand shaking with rage.

"Do not push me, Pearce. We don't need you or any of your *special* skills any longer."

As I taxied the G-IV into the hangar, I could see Rose's T-38 and F-5 had been pushed up against one another to make space for our airplane. Apart from a man in a technician's uniform who was bound and gagged on the floor and the Arab who was marshaling us, there was no one around. It seemed that today was a perfect day for foul play. After our tail cleared the hangar door, I was given the signal to stop and shutdown engines. I did so with a degree of resignation and prepared to run the APU shutdown and securing checklist.

"You will leave the APU running and complete the aircraft turnaround checklist," Adam said, as he unstrapped. "We will offload our cargo and then take off again." He handed me a clipboard with a new flight plan on it. "And you will load this into the FMS."

I just looked at him, measuring the distance between us, and wondering when the fuck the cavalry was going to arrive.

If it arrived.

"So, who is going to fly this thing?" I asked. "You?"

He smiled at me triumphantly and motioned with his head toward the front of the airplane. I looked in the direction he indicated with a sinking feeling in my chest. There were several men dressed in coveralls entering the hangar from a door that opened to the street. Three of them were pulling a cart which carried a rectangular object with some sort of metallic canister attached to it. I instantly knew what it was, but I didn't dwell on it.

Instead, I looked beyond the cart and saw two more people, one of which was a shorter man wearing a worn, brown suit. The few wisps of hair on his bald, freckled scalp were standing up in the breeze. It was Felix Lopez, aka Saif-al Din.

But he wasn't alone. There was another person alongside him, obviously coming along reluctantly and moving with some difficulty. As this person's head rose to look at the aircraft, I saw wide, hazel eyes and a wild mop of blonde hair.

"No Pearce, I am not flying this aircraft to its glorious target," Adam/Abdullah said gleefully. "Your precious little whore is."

It took me a moment to process this. "But what about Miguel?" I said at last.

"By the time he finds out, we will be long gone," Adam said with a maniacal grin on his face. "Of course, he'll also find out that he's missing the man he assigned to guard your little whore as well. But by then, it won't matter."

I shook my head in amazement. "How fucking stupid are you?" I asked him. "This guy is so powerful that he has the Mexican Air Force in his pocket. Do you honestly think there is anywhere you can go where he won't find you?"

"Allah will protect me. We are doing his will," Adam said with a tone that was both self-righteous and indignant.

I snorted. "I sure as hell hope your life insurance is paid up. Allah seems to use up a lot of fanatical idiots like you with this jihad bullshit."

That remark pushed the right buttons. Adam drew his left hand back rapidly, presumably to pistol-whip me, but he never got the chance. Fighter-pilot reflexes have some universal applicability. Without even thinking, I reacted, using the opening to hit him with most viscous right hook I could muster in the tight quarters of the cockpit. The feeling of my knuckles impacting his jaw was most gratifying, but the "thud" of his head hitting the circuit breaker panel behind his seat was even better. Before he could react, I smacked him again and this time, I felt the cartilage in his nose break as my fist made the impact. I stripped the pistol from his hand, gripped it, and shoved the barrel as roughly as I could into his now-shattered jaw.

"Tell that monkey of yours to let Sarah go," I hissed at him. "Or I'll blow your fucking brains out. Right here. Right now."

But my macho interlude was short lived.

Even as I finished speaking, I heard the sound of two gun shots in the hangar. Against my will, I turned my head to look out the cockpit window to see Saif grinning up at me and holding the barrel of his pistol to Sarah's stomach. I was grateful to see that she wasn't bleeding. Apparently the two shots were meant only to get my attention. But Saif's intent was unmistakable. If I proceeded, he'd kill Sarah's unborn child—and then kill her.

Then I heard the incomprehensible sound of Adam's laughter. I turned back to him to find him laughing at me through the blood and the mess of his shattered jaw and broken nose.

"You are so predictable, Pearce," he said between cackles. "Just like all Americans. You focus on the little things and lose sight of the big ones. If you were willing to let her die, this might have been over and you might have won. But because you won't, we will win and she'll die anyway."

As he spoke, the air-stair door was lowered and I knew it would be a matter of moments before another pistol barrel dug itself into the back of my head. Whatever opportunity I might have had was gone.

"Son of a bitch," I said.

I tossed the pistol into the vestibule behind me.

An arm flashed into the cockpit and handed Adam a cloth

of some sort. He used it to wipe the blood from his face while he watched me for several moments. Then, without a word, he inclined his head toward the avionics panels, his meaning clear; I was to do as I had been commanded. I was to program the jet for the next flight—the flight in which Sarah would lose her life.

He had me and he knew it. And there wasn't a damn thing I could do about it. I did as I was told.

From: John R. Amrine, GM-14, OOIC, via Secure BlackBerry
Sent: Thursday, 26 November 2009, 1220 PST (26 November 2009, 2020Z)
To: Director, NCS
Cc: Special Projects Group [NCS]
SUBJECT: URGENT ALERT MESSAGE – Operation Baja Sunrise

At 0915 PST, Gulfstream G-IVSP N36WMS departed Miguel Hidalgo's reported summer home in Baja California. The aircraft was last seen headed west out over the ocean and was subsequently not detected on radar by either Mexican or United States control agencies.

At 1155 PST, Gulfstream G-IVSP N36WMS contacted Southern California, Approach Control (SOCAL) from a position approximately 50 miles northeast of the Van Nuys Airport (KVNY) requesting an IFR clearance to the airport. The voice on the radio has been positively identified as that of Contractor 09-017 (Pearce, Colin M.). The aircraft landed at KVNY at 1210 PST. Due to delays in notification, we were notified only moments ago and are now enroute to the Van Nuys Airport with the Operations Team. We will provide further updates as they become available.

CHAPTER TWENTY-TWO

Contract Day Ten
Thursday, 26 November
1225 Hours Local Time
Van Nuys Airport (KVNY)
Van Nuys, California, United States

I completed the Turnaround Checklist and finished reprogramming the avionics, a chore which took only a few minutes. Adam stood behind me in the vestibule, licking his wounds and trying to simultaneously keep an eye on me while supervising his crew as they took the baggage off the airplane and loaded the device on it. Susan had left the airplane and was standing off to the side, next to her luggage and all by herself. The expression on her face was one of discomfort and impatience. It was apparent that she wanted to get out of here very badly. A few feet away stood Sarah, dressed in a flowered maternity top and blue pants, her hands bound in front of her by a plastic tie. She looked forlorn and afraid. Saif-al Din stood beside her, with his long-barreled automatic pistol in his right hand and a serene expression on his face. His jacket was unbuttoned and I could see the handle of a long knife sticking out of his trousers.

I glanced behind me for a moment and saw that Adam had his back turned to me again. I incremented the flight plan display of the flight management computer to the next screen and scribbled the longitude and latitude coordinates down as quickly as I could on a scrap of paper. I had managed to get about the first five or six points of the route copied when Adam was supervising the crew and not paying attention to me. But there were several more points I didn't get and didn't think I'd get the chance.

"Are you finished, Pearce?" Adam asked impatiently.

"I guess," I said, shoving the paper into my pocket.

He motioned at me with the gun as he stepped back into the vestibule toward the passenger cabin.

"Out."

I took note of the way he handled the weapon. Guys who shoot people for real, like Special Ops types, always keep the weapon at the ready position, at about a 45-degree angle to the ground or pointed in at their target. If they give instructions, they do so with a free hand. This told me that Adam had not been formally trained and may not have ever used his weapon for anything other than show. I wondered if I would have an opportunity to exploit that knowledge.

I contorted myself appropriately to exit the cockpit and made a show of grimacing as I put my weight on my left leg in the vestibule. I reached for my cane—which I had stowed in the coat closet somewhat frantically—and put some weight on it as I turned to begin my trek down the stairs. I could see a confident smile on Adam's face out of my peripheral vision.

I adopted my awkward three-legged gait down the stairs; and when I reached the bottom and walked far enough to the side to clear the wing, I was proud of the little show I had managed to put on.

And that's when Saif-al Din raised his pistol and shot me.

It was so unexpected and he was so nonchalant about it that I had no time to prepare or react. His hand came up with the gun and then I felt two impacts in my tender left leg even as I heard the echo of the two shots. The leg immediately decided it was incapable of supporting any weight at all and I fell to the hangar's cement floor. Surprisingly, there was very little pain.

His eyes betrayed no emotion about what he had done. I didn't know if he was immobilizing me as a precaution or taking vengeance because I had slugged his boss.

"Colin!" Sarah screamed. "Oh my God! Colin!"

"I'm all right, Sarah," I muttered through clenched teeth. "They're not getting a virgin here."

Sarah swung her bound arms at Saif-al Din in a wild attempt to hit him. Saif merely moved his upper body out of the way and backhanded her to the ground in a manner that was both casual and contemptuous.

"Saif," Adam yelled from the doorway of the G-IV. "Enough!"

Adam rapidly descended the air-stair and then raised the door after he had reached the ground. He gave some commands to his crew in Arabic and they began the process of removing the wheel chocks from the airplane so the jet could be pushed outside of the hangar. I noticed they had an electric tug connected to the nose wheel and I found myself wondering when they had done that. Probably while I was absorbed in the cockpit.

Adam walked over to where Sarah lay sprawled on the ground and roughly yanked her to her feet. Then he pulled her across the hangar floor so they were both standing over me.

"Behold your hero," he spat at her. "In all his glory."

She looked up at him with venom in her eyes. "You're a piece of shit," she spat back at him. "I don't care what you want me to do. I'll never help you. Never."

"What about for the sake of your husband?" Adam asked with a peculiar edge to his voice.

I couldn't help myself, I laughed. Even with two fresh bullet wounds in my leg and the imminent deaths of both Sarah and I looming, I couldn't contain myself. "Is that the best you can do?" I asked Adam. "Really? For the sake of her husband? Everyone knows he was a plant, Adam. Sarah knows. I know. The CIA knows. He's a fucking Saudi just like you are. For all I know, the two of you might even be related. What the hell does it take to be a prince in Saudi anyway? Do you just have to know somebody? Aren't there like four or five thousand of you?"

I hadn't intended to get a rise out of him. I was probably in shock from the bullet wounds and just mouthing off. But as he registered my words, I saw something in his eyes that told me I had struck a nerve.

"He *is* related to you!" I said. "Holy shit! He is related to you!"

And that's when Sarah looked over at Adam's face and saw something that seemed to strike her for the first time.

"Oh my God," she whispered, the shock on her face evident. "Oh my God."

Adam pushed her away. "For someone who knows so much, Pearce, you haven't been able to do much with it." He gestured to the jet behind him. "In mere minutes the glory of Allah will be revealed as this symbol of American decadence will be used to spray a particularly virulent form of *Yersinia pestis* all over the city of San Francisco. And there's not a thing you or your government can do about it."

"Hey, Adam," I shot back, "you know I work for that government and you know that they've been watching this jet." I nodded in the direction of the G-IV. "Don't you think they'd be monitoring ATC frequencies for it?"

Adam looked like he had been slapped in the face.

"We must go immediately!" he yelled. "Saif, take Pearce away and hold him as we discussed." Adam turned to Sarah while pointing at me. "You will do what I say or Pearce will die."

I knew he was lying. He intended to kill me anyway. But I had to buy time for the cavalry to arrive. "Do what he says, Sarah. I'll be okay."

Sarah was brave. She was so very brave. She accepted her fate and didn't protest. She walked over to me quickly, dropped to her knees, placed her hands on my cheeks, and kissed me. "I love you, Colin Pearce," she said, her eyes glistening. "Don't forget that."

I couldn't help smiling through the pain that was now making itself known in my leg and another, greater pain that was tearing into my heart. "You always were too good for me, Sarah," I replied. "Be brave. Help is coming."

She nodded again and Adam pulled her up and across the hangar floor and outside where the G-IV was now waiting.

"Adam!" Susan Turner had apparently grown impatient at being ignored. "What about our plans? What about me?"

Adam nodded to Saif dismissively and as Susan's jaw came open in suspicion, Saif turned to her and flashed a disarming smile. He raised his left hand in a gesture that looked helpful— and it was then that I noticed that the gun was no longer in his right hand. A long silver knife was there instead.

In a movement that was terribly and horribly fluid, Saif took Susan's hand and spun her around so that she was facing me. Then his hand swept up her body and went over her mouth in a manner that that was gentle and even tender. But then his right armed moved rapidly upward and I saw the silver tip of his knife emerge from the front of Susan's body, just below her right breast. Dull, dark-red-colored blood began to seep from the tear in her flesh and it stained the front of her stylish, white satin dress. The look on her beautiful face was one of utter disbelief.

Behind me, I could hear the G-IV's engines starting. They'd be moving in a moment. I didn't have much time. My cane was near. It had, in fact, never left my hand. Saif and Susan were only about five feet away from me. I looked up at the two of them and even as Susan's eyes registered recognition as to what was happening to her, they also registered understanding as I began to move.

Saif was in his own world. For him, stone killer that he may have been, it seemed the actual act of taking a human life so personally had sensual implications for him. As he held Susan to him and held the knife in her body, his eyes were only about half open, his lips were parted and his cheeks were flushed.

I launched myself across the five feet of concrete, gritting my teeth against the now fiery pain in my left leg. At the same time, I turned the barely visible catch on the upper part of my cane with my thumb and shook the cane away from me with a rapid snap.

The blade emerged and it was a thing of beauty. I had ordered it from a specialty sword maker after realizing that a cane would be my constant companion for several weeks or months. While stiletto swords were the typical style found in sword-canes, mine was different. The cane itself was not round; it was oblong in cross-section and allowed a flat blade to be concealed therein. I had always liked the look and feel of the *katana*, the primary weapon of the Japanese Samurai, and the blade was modeled after it. It was about two feet long, very flat, very thin, and razor sharp.

As the G-IV's engines spooled up to taxi, the sound of the bottom part of my cane clattering to the floor was almost lost in the jet noise. But not quite.

Saif's eyes recovered from their quasi-orgasmic reverie and he saw me coming at him. He tried to pull the knife from Susan's back but in a heroic effort, she pushed herself back against him, pinning his hand between their bodies and making his knife irretrievable. Impatiently, he pushed her away to his right side and reached underneath his coat for his pistol.

But I had reached him by then.

He should have been wearing boots. Boots might have saved him. But instead he was wearing dress shoes—and as he leaned and turned, his pants hiked up slightly, making the line of his Achilles tendons on both legs very visible beneath his brown, nylon socks. And as I slid by him on the floor, I whipped the blade in a savage horizontal cut about three inches parallel to the floor and severed both of his Achilles tendons.

The effect was instantaneous. He went right to his knees on the concrete floor and the crack of his knees hitting the concrete was distinctly audible. But he wasn't out of the fight yet. The gun emerged in his right hand. But I was behind him and to his left, so he tossed the gun from his right hand to his left hand in attempt to train it on me. He was already pulling the trigger as the weapon came around and in a peculiar moment of temporal distortion, I could see the action cycling and the shell cases being ejected, even as the sound of the gun became audible as the G-IV taxied away.

I grasped the handle of the small sword with both hands, raised it, and made a vicious vertical cut at his arm before he had a chance to understand what was happening. The sharp ribbon of hardened steel hit him at mid forearm and never even slowed down. There was a splash of blood and three more shots from the pistol as it and the severed hand separated from Saif's body and spun end-over-end. Then he completely collapsed in front of me and his body came backwards. As his head hit the hangar floor, I saw a single bullet hole on the left side of his forehead. I looked over to where his arm and his gun had come to rest and I saw that it was on the ground, upside down, pointing at him, the finger still tight against the trigger.

Saif-al Din's own hand had killed him.

"Colin?" It was Susan Turner's voice, barely above that of a whisper.

"Holy Shit! Susan!"

I had nearly forgotten about her. I crawled around al Din's body and made my way to her. She lay on her side in a pool of dark, red blood.

In the background, I could hear sirens and tires screeching.

"Susan, hang on. They're almost here. Stay with me. You'll make it. Help is on the way."

She smiled up at me. "You're such a liar," she whispered. Then her eyes took on a pleading look. "Colin, please hold me, I don't want to die alone. I know I've been a shit, but please hold me."

Probably violating every rule of first responder medical protocol, I lifted her upper body and wrapped my arms around her, carefully avoiding the tip of al Din's knife which still protruded from her body.

"That's better," she said with a smile on her face. "Much better." Then her expression became urgent. "You need... to understand. There's... more... to it," she said, gasping.

My face must have displayed a look of confusion. I could see frustration on her features even as the light inside of her was fading.

"Boat," she said. "Need... to... worry... about... boat."

"Susan, what do you mean? Bill's boat? What about it?"

"Presidents," she whispered. "Both presidents." Then her eyes began to cloud over and tears began to flow. The reality of her death was upon her.

I looked down upon her helplessly, knowing she was leaving two kids behind and that I was helpless to prevent her departure.

"Colin," she whispered again, her voice barely audible. "Can... you... tell... my kids... I died well?"

In the background I could hear the sounds of Tay engines whining at high RPM as the G-IV took to the sky.

Shit!

I nodded down at her frantically, even as I heard the sounds of cars screeching to a halt outside the building and commands being barked. There were even a few bursts of automatic weapons fire and some men shouting.

I ignored them.

"Yes, I will," I promised. I briefly considered trying to

ask her more questions, but it was clear that she was almost gone and her mind wouldn't register my words. Somehow, though, she commanded the strength to bring a hand up to touch my face.

"It... could... have... been... good... you and me," she said.

Then, her hand fell and her head turned to the side—and her eyes went sightless.

"Jesus Christ," I muttered to myself.

And that's when I heard the footsteps running up.

"Damn, Pearce!" said a voice I recognized. "Is there a place you go where people don't get cut up?"

I looked up to find both Amrine and Smith looking down at me, both clad in black tactical gear and both with Glock semi-automatic pistols in their hands. As their eyes registered recognition of the body I was holding, their jaws dropped open in unison.

"Al Din killed her," I said. "On Archmere's orders." I couldn't keep all the names straight. "But she said something before she died that I can't make sense of. She said we needed to worry about the boat and then something about the president," I thought for a moment and then corrected myself. "No," I said. "She said *both* presidents. I'm assuming she's talking about Spratt's boat, but I don't have a clue about the presidents thing."

Both faces filled with tension.

"That's not good," Smith said. "That is so not good."

"What?" I asked.

"We think the president is going to be at Santa Catalina Island today. The Secret Service won't say anything about it, but we think he'll be there. That'd be an easy target for a boat with lots of men and lots of guns."

"Why would the President be at Santa Catalina?" I asked.

"That's the ten-thousand-dollar question," Smith said. "And we can't get anybody to fucking answer it. You'd think he was signing a secret treaty or something."

"Can't you station the Coast Guard or the Navy around the Island to guard it?"

Smith shook his head in disgust. Both have been specifically instructed by the National Security Council *not* to draw attention to the island for reasons they alone are aware of."

Treaty. Why did that word resonate? My brain went back to the discussion I had with guy who installed my carpet back in Delaware.

"*Hell of thing about that treaty, huh?" he had said, as he handed me the clipboard.*

"*What treaty?" I had replied absentmindedly as I searched the document for a signature block.*

"*That US-Mexican thing," he said, clearly impressed. "I mean, if the US and Mexico are going to combine forces to close the border and deal with those damn drug cartels, that might really do it!"*

Then the narrative from the news story I had heard while I was waiting for my luggage after I first arrived rapidly ran through my head.

"*Hidalgo, whose influence inside Mexico rivals that of the president's, has vowed he will stop the treaty by all means necessary. White House sources have revealed that a secret meeting between the two presidents for the formal signing ceremony has been under consideration since the negotiations began."*

Finally, I remembered my conversation with Miguel Hidalgo back at his hacienda.

"*I am Antonio Lopez de Santa Anna, the fourth," he said. "And it is my goal to overthrow the current government of my country and return honor both to my country and to my family.*

"No," I said out loud. "No way. No fucking way."

"What?" Smith demanded.

I gently lay Susan's body aside and struggled to my feet. My left leg was screaming at me but I ignored it for the moment.

There was so much here to think about.

"I think I know what this may be about. I'm going to tell you some shit," I said, "but in the meantime, we've got a plane to stop."

"You saw them load something on the G-IV?" Amrine asked.

I nodded. "A metallic device. They installed it in the baggage compartment. Adam said it was going to spray something he called a particularly virulent form of," I paused for a moment to recall the words, *"Yersinia pestis."* I congratulated myself for remembering the words exactly. But the horrified look on the faces of the two agents quickly whisked that feeling away.

"Yersinia pestis? Are you sure?" Amrine asked. *"Yersinia pestis?"*

I nodded.

"Jesus," Smith said. "That's gruesome stuff." He looked at Amrine. "We need to get the CDC on the line right now."

Amrine nodded back at him.

"So what the fuck is it?" I asked.

Smith looked at me. "Bubonic plaque," he said. "The Black Death from the Middle Ages. Typically, it can't be spread person-to-person, but our friends the Russians developed some weaponized strains during the Cold War which can be aerially dispersed and are incredibly contagious and lethal."

"Damn," Armine said. "Damn. Damn. Damn. The jet took off just as we were pulling up. We couldn't get word to the tower in time to stop them. Who's aboard?"

"Adam and Sarah," I said resignedly. "And I copied the first few points on their route. They're heading north at low altitude. To San Francisco."

"The VP is attending a football game there," Smith said, looking at his watch. "And they kick off in about ten minutes."

"We can scramble fighters," Amrine said. "And persuade them to land or blow them out of the sky. If the jet explodes, the agent would be neutralized."

My heart sunk at those words. A part of me knew that was an option but saying it made it real. I swallowed hard. I knew what had to be done. And I hated myself for it.

"Goddamn it," I said angrily. "Your fighters won't find them. They don't know the route and they don't know the jet. I do. Besides, the jet is coated with radar absorbent paint and probably flying a speed that will make it blend in with slower traffic. I can find them and I'll lead the fighters to them."

"Flying what?" Amrine asked.

I pointed to the T-38 and the F-5 parked against the wall of the hangar.

"One of those."

I looked around and saw the Rose Aircraft technician who had been bound and gagged milling about and rubbing his wrists. He was also probably cursing himself for choosing to work on Thanksgiving Day. I recognized him from the day Adam and I had done our flying here.

"Robert?" I asked. "How quick can we get one of these things ready to fly?"

He stared at me in disbelief for a second and then looked me up and down. "I'm not really authorized to release an aircraft to someone..."

"Robert!" I snapped at him and pointed to Smith and Amrine. "These two guys work for the CIA and this is a matter of national security. They can give you any authorization you need."

He looked at Amrine, and then at Smith and took in their garb and their attitude as if seeing them for the first time. Then he nodded slowly.

"I can have a jet ready for you by the time you go into life support and get suited up," he said. "Which one do you want to fly?"

"The one that has the most gas," I said.

"So, what about this shit you need to tell us?" Amrine asked me impatiently.

"If you promise you won't get aroused or embarrassed by watching me strip, I'll tell you while I'm getting dressed to fly," I said. "And by the way, do you have a medic on your team? I'm going to need a little bandaging and some really good drugs."

From: John R. Amrine, GM-14, OOIC, via Secure BlackBerry
Sent: Thursday, 26 November 2009, 1305 PST (26
November 2009, 2105Z)
To: Director, NCS
Cc: Special Projects Group [NCS]
SUBJECT: URGENT ALERT MESSAGE – Operation
Baja Sunrise

We arrived at the Rose Aircraft hangar at Van Nuys Airport
(KVNY) at approximately 1250 hours local time. Upon
arrival, our operations team engaged hostiles presumably
under the employ of Abdullah bin Rashid al Qudamah,
aka Adam Archmere. Three hostiles were killed and the
remainder surrendered. After brief but intense interrogation,
no information was gleaned on the action underway. Upon
arrival we also found Saif-al Din, aka Felix Lopez dead at the
hands of Contractor 09-017 (Pearce, Colin M.) after some sort
of altercation. Also killed in the altercation was Operations
Officer Susan Turner. Pearce indicated that Turner provided
some possibly valuable intelligence regarding the operation
underway. Turner told Pearce that "we needed to worry
about the boat," presumably Spratt's boat, Bachelor's Toy.
She also said something about "both presidents." Pearce said
that Miguel Hidalgo revealed himself to be Antonio Lopez de
Santa Anna, IV, the descendant of the Mexican General of
the same name. Hidalgo informed Pearce that he intends to
overthrow the current Mexican government to "restore honor
to his country." *(QUESTION: Is it possible Hidalgo used
his status as a drug dealer to acquire power and funds for*

political action?) Based on the information from Pearce and Turner, we believe Hidalgo funded the intended operation and that he intends action against the President of the United States to initiate turmoil in US/Mexico relations to facilitate a coup. (Pearce also revealed that Hidalgo is well connected in the Mexican Air Force and that, in fact, the Mexican Air Force flew the repair crew into Hidalgo's summer home—a fact our ground surveillance team verified.)

Pearce also confirmed that G-IVSP N36WMS has been loaded with an aerosol device that will disperse *Yersinia pestis* and that the target for the aircraft/device is San Francisco.

IMMEDIATE ACTIONS REQUIRED:

1. We must have further information concerning Presidential presence and activity on Santa Catalina Island ASAP. If POTUS is there, he may be in extreme danger.

2. We must be allowed to task Coast Guard and /or US Naval assets in the vicinity of the Island.

SIGNIFICANT ACTIONS TAKEN:

1. Pearce has launched out of Van Nuys Airport in a T-38 Talon, N5494D, in an attempt to find Gulfstream G-IVSP N36WMS and guide Air Defense Fighters to it;

2. We have scrambled a flight of two F-16s from March AFB to assist Pearce in either forcing the G-IV to land or eliminating it; The CDC has been informed and Bio-Hazard and HAZMAT recovery teams have been alerted and are moving to support this operation; and

3. The A-10s which were deployed to NAS North Island based

on your request have placed on Alert 5 status.

We will provide further updates as they become available.

****

Message ends.

TOP SECRET / SPECIAL
COMPARTMENTALIZED INFORMATION
CLASSIFIED BY: US Central Intelligence Agency
DECLASSIFY ON: OADR

CHAPTER TWENTY-THREE

Contract Day 10
Thursday, 26 November
1320 Hours Local Time
At 500 Feet AGL and 420 KCAS
Near Paso Robles, California, United States

"Dragnet, Talon N5494Delta. Any luck?"

There was a pause over the radio as the airborne weapons director on the E-3 AWACs regarded his radar display yet again.

"Talon N5494Delta, Dragnet, negative contact."

Shit, I thought. *I should have caught them by now.*

I had been airborne for about twenty minutes and with a complete disregard for the rules of low altitude flight outside of protected airspace, I had kept the T-38's power up and averaged about 420 knots, 7 nautical miles per minute, as I flew along the first five points of the route, across the Los Padres National Forest and up the mountain range that ran just east of Lompoc and Vandenberg Air Force Base. From there I had flown to a point just east of San Luis Obispo, then to another near Santa Margarita, and finally I had arrived at the last point I had, which was a road intersection just west of Paso Robles. I presumed from there that the route would fly along the mountainous terrain just east of the California coastline and probably terminate at Candlestick Park. I had backtracked once to investigate an aircraft that AWACS had directed me to, but it turned out to be a Beechcraft King Air just enjoying the sights. Given that the entire distance between Van Nuys and San Francisco airport was only about three-hundred nautical miles or so if I followed the logical extension of the first five points on the route, I had covered over half the distance to San Francisco and had not found them.

Apparently, I was missing something. Again.

Of course, the fact that I didn't have an air-to-air radar wasn't helping matters. The F-5 had one but it was inoperative and the T-38 had more gas, so I wasn't regretting my choice of aircraft, but I was getting frustrated. And AWACS, with all its technology, had been useless. AWACS was designed to operate in a warzone and to detect and target enemy forces moving in specific directions and off designated friendly routes. It was never meant to find one airplane out of many in a civilian environment; to find the proverbial needle in a haystack.

To make matters worse, as I tried to concentrate on finding the G-IV, I had these other thoughts tumbling around in the back of my head. *The treaty.* Santa Catalina Island. Miguel Hidalgo, nee Antonio Lopez de Santa Anna. What did it all mean?

The words I had left Smith and Amrine with were simple and blunt. "You need to find out exactly what the fuck the President is doing on Santa Catalina Island," I had said. "That's the key to this whole thing. If he's signing that damn treaty there, then it won't just be him but it will be the President of Mexico as well. That's both Presidents and that will make it a fucking lucrative target for Miguel."

And the suspicion I had when I had taken off moments ago was growing inside me.

I was going there next.

Fortunately, for the first time in weeks, my left leg wasn't complaining. Even though there were two fresh, small-caliber bullet wounds there. I had been bandaged quickly and methodically and told I'd need to get serious care within a few hours. Then I had been injected with enough local anesthetic to make the pain go away followed by a healthy injection of cortisone. Physically, I almost felt like my old self again.

I looked down at the T-38's fuel gauges. I had taken off with full fuel, a little less than 4,000 pounds, and now was down to about 2,500 pounds thanks largely to flying around at low altitude and high throttle setting for the past twenty minutes. Less than an hour of flight time remaining.

Jesus. Why is there never enough time?

"Bear check," said a new voice on my radio frequency.

"Two," replied his wingman.

"Dragnet, Bear Zero One, flight of two F-16s, on station, two AIM-9Ms, two AIM-120s each, forty minutes of playtime."

"Bear, Dragnet copies. I'm working with Talon N5494Delta, also on this frequency."

"Bear copies."

The F-16s were here to back me up and I had nothing to give them. But their arrival and the fact that they carried the quite-capable APG-66 radar gave me an idea.

"Dragnet, Talon N5494Delta, can you get Bear's radar on me?"

"Dragnet, affirmative. Bear One, look bullseye 145 for 150, low." The AWACS controller was giving Bear flight the usual directions for air-to-air target detection, a radial and distance off a known ground point, or bullseye. Today, the bullseye was San Francisco International Airport.

"Bear One, looking."

"Bear," I asked. "Can you interrogate IFF?" Most F-16s didn't have the capability to read transponders; but if these jets came off the production line equipped for air defense, they might be able to do that.

"Bear One, negative."

That figures. If they could paint IFF with their radar, it would make the task of finding me much easier. I hoped these guys were up-to-speed with their radar mechanics.

"Bear One, radar contact, bullseye 145 for 142, 2000, tail."

I looked at my barometric altimeter and smiled. It read 2100 feet. These guys were on their game.

"Bear One, Talon 5494Delta, I'm going to make a 90 right and then a 90 left back on course. Now."

I rolled the T-38 up on the right wing, applied some back pressure to the stick, and pulled the nose to the right. Then I reversed the turn and pulled the nose to left and back on course.

"Talon, Bear One. We got ya."

Shit hot.

"Okay Bear, now I need you to look between me and the bullseye and see if you can detect any other traffic flying at approximately 250-300 knots at low altitude along that route."

There was silence on the radio but having been a Viper Flight Leader for several years, I knew what was happening. Bear One and Two were talking over their intra-flight VHF radio. The wait was excruciating.

"Bear One, negative," came the verdict at last. "We're both clean. All traffic along your route is either not at low altitude, not in that speed envelope, or both."

Well shit. Where the fuck did they get to?

"It's possible we're just not painting them, Talon." The flight leader's voice sounded almost apologetic.

Yes, that is possible, I thought. *Goddamn it.* Ordinarily a jet as dirty as a G-IV with huge engine nacelles and antennas sticking out should be easy to paint with a radar like the APG-66, but I had no idea what effect the radar absorbent paint might be having.

Then a thought came to mind—a thought that should have occurred to me much earlier. Adam didn't strike me as the suicide bomber type, and yet he was with Sarah in the

G-IV when they took off. The jet was destined to dispense a biological weapon and would probably be destroyed. Adam struck me as many things, but he wasn't martyr material.

He didn't plan to stay on the jet!

Which meant he planned to bail out somewhere along the route. And where could he do that so he could guarantee he'd be picked up quickly and with no interference? A bailout over land would be too risky. The terrain was rugged along most of the route; and where it wasn't, the population density was high.

It would have to be over water.

But where?

In theory, he could have planned a route that took him out to the west over the water, but I had reviewed the plot of the route on the navigational displays after I had programmed the avionics, but I didn't remember seeing and places where the route made a severe bend to the west.

Then a word popped into my mind. A word I had programed into the flight management computer: ISIFU.

It was a five-letter identifier for a navigational fix on a low-altitude airway. I fumbled with the low altitude IFR chart I had stashed on the console next to me in the cockpit.

"Jesus, Pearce!" I cursed at myself in the intercom when I saw where the fix was. "You are such a fucking idiot!"

"Dragnet and Bear, both of you look bullseye 170 to 150 at about 75 miles or so. There's a navigational fix there called ISIFU, india, sierra, india, foxtrot, uniform. If you don't see anything there yet, keep watching."

I pushed the throttles to the firewall and allowed the sleek little jet to accelerate to 480 knots. I knew where to find them.

Monterey Bay. ISIFU was a fix over Monterrey Bay. A perfect place to bailout over water and where a boat could easily get to you, pick you up, and then disappear into the crowd of boats that frequented the bay and the numerous marinas there. It was brilliant.

I didn't know how far the F-16s were behind me, but I knew we didn't have much time, regardless.

"Dragnet, radar contact a single target, bullseye 160 at 80, 4,000. Contact is slowing to 200 knots. That's ten nautical miles south, southwest of ISIFU."

Bingo.

Of course Adam wouldn't want to hurt himself with too much windblast as he dove out the baggage door on the G-IV. But then how would the airplane get to its target? Sarah wouldn't voluntarily fly it there.

The answer was obvious. Adam would obviously have the flight management system programmed to advance the autothrottles to a higher speed after he left the aircraft and he would also have the jet programmed to take the aircraft exactly where he wanted it to go at whatever speed and altitude he desired. Since the flight management system would tell him the exact time it predicted the jet's arrival over the target, he could set the timer on the device appropriately.

I knew Adam well enough to know he would take no chances about Sarah interfering with his plans. She was dead, unconscious, or incapacitated in some way. Regardless, the jet would have to be blown out of the sky to prevent it from reaching its target. In fact, if I knew Adam well enough—and by this point I thought I did—he'd have intentionally left her alive. Perhaps tied to a chair in the cabin. He'd want her to be alive when the end came. He'd want her to see it.

"Dragnet, Talon," I called, fighting to keep my voice under control, "snap me to that target."

"Talon, Dragnet, snap 350 for fifteen now, 4000, you're already gaining on him rapidly."

"Talon copies. Bear, Talon, I'm going to positively ID the target and you guys will be cleared in hot."

"Bear Copies, Talon."

At twice nearly 300 knots above the G-IV's airspeed, I was closing the gap between our two airplanes by a factor of five miles a minute. I applied a little back pressure on the T-38's control stick and allowed the jet to climb slightly. I still wanted to stay below the G-IV's altitude so that it would be easier to see, but I wanted to be able to focus more on looking for the aircraft and less on not hitting the ground.

"Talon, Dragnet, look 355 for 5 now. 4,000."

I peered through the T-38's heads-up display and even looked around and above it. Just ahead, the rugged California landscape opened up into the blue elliptical shape of Monterey Bay. We'd be over the water in seconds. I could see Santa Cruz on the far side and did a little mental math to determine how much time Adam would have over the water to make his jump. Then I returned my eyes to the sky in front of me.

Almost immediately the familiar silhouette of a G-IV zoomed into focus out of nowhere, at my left eleven-o'clock position and slightly high. Just as my eyes fully registered the jet and noted the dull grey paint job, I yanked the throttles to idle, and deployed the speed brakes to slow down as rapidly as I could. And as I did so, I saw the man-shaped silhouette separate from the aircraft, down and away to my left.

Goddamn it.

I keyed the mic. "Dragnet, Talon. Mark my position and relay it to the authorities. I just saw someone depart the target aircraft via parachute over the bay."

"Dragnet copies."

"Talon, Bear," the F-16 flight leader asked, "do you have eyes on the target?"

I didn't answer.

I had slowed and was making a 360-degree turn to the left, trying to keep the G-IV in the center of my circle. I closed the speed brakes and reapplied power to maintain about 300 knots as I continued the turn. It was our G-IV, all right. The paint job was a dead giveaway, as was the open baggage door, inside of which the metallic device was just visible. Part of me knew that I should break off the turn and try to locate

Adam's parachute, but another part of me wanted to stay where I was and scan each aircraft window and the cockpit for a sign of Sarah.

And that's the part that prevailed. I wasn't going anywhere.

One of the risks of spending a lifetime hiding from feelings is the fact that they can catch up with you at the most unexpected and inconvenient times. I felt like an anvil had been dropped on my heart. Even as I raised the shaded visor on my helmet and peered through the Plexiglas of the T-38's canopy, desperately looking for the wild mop of blonde hair that I become accustomed to, I could feel the moisture pooling in my eyes. I searched every window, hoping beyond hope to catch a glimpse of her and knowing full well I wouldn't.

"Talon, Bear, we're five south at ten thousand. We're contact you and contact the target, say intentions."

The northern edge of the bay was coming up and I could see San Francisco looming to the north. It was time to act and stop this thing.

"Bear, Talon," I said resignedly into my microphone. "I'm separating to the south at 5,000. You're cleared hot."

"Bear copies. Bear flight, green 'em up."

Green 'em up. Master arm switches to the "hot" position. It was time for them to employ ordnance. And a fireball in the sky which contained Sarah was the last thing I wanted to see. I rolled out of my turn headed south and cast one final glance at the G-IV as it continued northward.

"Goodbye, Sarah," I whispered. "Goodbye, sweet Sarah."

"Talon, Dragnet. Climb to Angels 30 and proceed southbound at maximum speed."

"Dragnet, Talon copies."

I pushed the throttles to military power, full power without afterburner, and lifted the nose to climb. I glanced down at the fuel gauges. Just under 1,800 pounds of fuel. Not a lot. Impatiently, I wiped my eyes with my gloved hands.

"Talon, Dragnet, push frequency 235.9."

"Talon," I answered, and dialed the new UHF radio frequency in on the control head. "Dragnet, Talon is up 235.9."

"Talon, this is Delta Sierra," said Dave Smith's voice over the radio. "We know what Catalina is about. As we suspected, POTUS and the President of Mexico are there in a secret meeting to sign the new mutual cooperation border treaty. It's happening right now."

And the pieces finally came together. That would be a slap in the face to someone like Antonio Lopez de Santa Anna. He would never want the treaty to occur. And what better way to stop it than by having an armed force storm the treaty signing site and kill or capture both presidents? A platoon-sized unit with the right weapons could easily overwhelm a Secret Service detail, particularly when the Secret Service had tried to keep the visit low key and minimize personnel. It was perfect.

"Roger that," I replied. "Where's the boat?" I asked.

"Satellite feed indicates it is twenty miles due west of Santa Catalina Island."

"Can you get the Coast Guard out there?"

"Negative," Smith said. I could hear the frustration in his voice. "Secret Service refuses to acknowledge viability of the threat."

How could anyone be that fucking stupid? I asked myself.

"How quickly can you get there?" Smith asked me.

I pushed the power up until the airspeed approached the Mach. About ten miles per minute. Maybe even a little more.

"Thirty minutes," I said. Assuming the gas held out. "Dragnet, you need to clear a corridor in front of me."

"In progress, Talon," came the quick reply.

"Delta Sierra, do you guys have any other assets you can call upon, maybe something with some air-to-ground ordnance loaded?"

"Roger that. We have a flight of A-10s on ground alert at North Island Naval Air Station in San Diego, but we don't have approval to launch them in support of this mission."

I thought for a moment.

"Can you get approval to reposition them to another base?"

There was a pregnant pause.

"Yes," Smith said.

I reviewed the geography of Southern California in my mind, especially the stretch between San Diego and Los Angeles.

"I think they need to be moved to the Marine Corps field at Camp Pendleton," I said. "Right away."

Camp Pendleton was about thirty miles east, southeast of Catalina Island. At A-10 speeds, that was about five minutes away. I hoped it would be close enough.

"They're starting engines now," Smith replied, after a few moments. "They'll be airborne in five."

I nodded.

"Tell them that they need to do some pattern work at Pendleton," I said. "Tell them not to land."

CHAPTER TWENTY-FOUR

Contract Day Ten
Thursday, 26 November
1345 Hours Local Time
Descending through 20,000 feet at Mach 1.03
Near Los Angeles, California, United States

The green and gray shapes of the Channel Islands appeared just to the right of the sleek nose as I pushed forward on the T-38's stick to increase my descent rate. I could see Oxnard to the left and my eyes followed the indentation of the coast where it headed down to Santa Monica, LAX, and Redondo Beach, as well. It was yet another clear day in the LA basin and the deep blue of the water contrasted beautifully with the sandy beaches and green hills.

"Talon, Delta Sierra, A-10s are airborne. Heading to Pendleton."

"Talon copies," I said reflexively. I found I was having difficulty concentrating.

Directly off my nose, about sixty miles away, lay Santa Catalina Island. Less than six minutes away at my current speed.

Santa Catalina was about twenty-two miles long and was, coincidently enough, twenty-two miles south, southwest of Los Angeles. It was oriented approximately northwest-southeast and was eight miles across at its widest point. A popular tourist getaway for people in Los Angeles, its development was largely funded by chewing gum magnate William Wrigley.

How did I know all this? Sarah had taken me there on a spare afternoon when she and I had worked together, those few years ago. We had hiked and eaten and found a bar from which to watch the people go by for several hours. And talked about everything and nothing. I found myself smiling as I recalled the memory.

Sometimes you never know how much something means to you until it's taken away.

I couldn't remember where those words came from but they were ricocheting inside my head like a pinball on steroids. All I could think about was Sarah. How her voice sounded when she laughed and what she felt like to hold.

"I love you, Colin Pearce," she had said. *"Don't forget that."*

And I had just handed her and her unborn child off to be killed.

What kind of fucking monster are you, Pearce?

Guilt was an emotion I had done my best to avoid throughout my adult life. God knew I had endured enough of it during my childhood with an alcoholic mother to take care of and younger brothers to raise. But it was back and flowing through my veins now. And it was working like acid, eating away at me from the inside.

I glanced down at the T-38's fuel gauges. Five hundred pounds per side. One thousand pounds total. The fuel had held out better than I had any right to expect. But there wouldn't be enough left to get me to a runway after I found the boat and got the A-10 pilots' eyes on it. I was going to be jumping out of this jet at some point when the engines flamed out. Of course, that depended on whether I cared enough to even pull the ejection handle when the time came.

And at this exact moment, I wasn't sure I did.

"Talon, Delta Sierra, we've lost contact on the boat. We're going to need you to assume a search pattern starting west of the island and working your way toward it."

"Wouldn't it be better to start from the island and work west?" I asked.

"Affirmative," Dave Smith replied, "but the Secret Service doesn't know you're coming and they might actually shoot at you."

Lucky me.

"Roger that. Do we have any idea where exactly POTUS is?"

"Somewhat. Avalon, the town on the southeast side of the island. That's the best we can do right now."

Avalon was the larger of the two populated areas and the one with the most amenities available. And if the boat was going to go after him there, it would have to make its approach from the southwestern side of the island where it could remain somewhat unobserved until it rounded the southern side.

But then a thought occurred to me. Why the focus on a boat, and a fast boat at that, if the action was going to take place ashore? Wouldn't there be issues with a large boat storming into a harbor, even a small harbor, and off-loading gunmen to make an attack? Wouldn't there be better ways to stage that kind of assault? Miguel was a very deliberate and careful guy who, by all reports, avoided collateral damage at all costs. He'd have all the available intelligence. He'd take no unnecessary chances. He'd select an engagement zone where civilian casualties could be avoided.

"Delta Sierra, Talon, I don't think this meeting is taking place ashore. I think it's on a boat. Can you get any additional intel on that?"

The altimeter clicked through 15,000 feet and I pulled the throttles back to save a little gas. Malibu went by on the left side and I could see right down the runways at LAX as I descended. I banked about 15 degrees to the right and allowed the nose of the jet to track west of Catalina. I also began straining my eyes to look for *Bachelor's Toy*. I was thankful that it was a two-hundred-foot yacht. There couldn't be that many of them out here. But then again, this was Southern California.

"Talon, Delta Sierra, we have a surveillance team on the ground now in Avalon and they confirm that POTUS and the Mexican president are aboard a yacht, parked in the harbor at Avalon. It's the biggest one there. Our Secret Service liaison has also relayed that if you can confirm that *Bachelor's Toy* is a threat, they will upgrade their security status."

"That's mighty fuckin' big of them," I muttered into my oxygen mask. "Roger that," I replied over the radio.

Through 10,000 feet now and the small rock that was Santa Barbara Island went under the nose. I made a mental note to begin the level off at 5,000 feet. I was hoping that from that altitude, I'd be able to see the detail I needed and yet still cover a large enough area to make the search go quickly. As I drew nearer to the water and looked ahead and down at the seas to the west of Catalina, suddenly it seemed as if there were boats everywhere. Apparently, between the sunny skies and calm seas, it was a great day for boating.

Maybe this wasn't going to be as easy as I had hoped.

I broke the descent rate as I went through 5,000 feet and zeroed the vertical velocity indicator at about 4,000 feet. I didn't even need to use the symbology in the heads-up display to do it. Instead, I just superimposed the end of the pitot tube which protruded from the T-38's nose a few inches below horizon. I retarded the throttles to maintain about 280 knots of airspeed and reflexively clicked in some nose-up trim to ensure I wouldn't sink as the lift generated by the jet's little wings lessened with the reduction of airspeed. I glanced down at the fuel gauges again. About 700 pounds total left onboard. I didn't remember what the minimum or emergency fuel numbers were for the T-38, but I was sure I was getting close to them. I needed to find that damn boat soon.

The problem with conducting visual reconnaissance in a high-performance aircraft is that visibility over the nose is very limited, especially as altitude increases. To adequately examine an object on the ground, you must first acquire it several miles away, and then turn the aircraft slightly to offset the object so you can see it as you go by. At lower altitudes, the visibility over the nose improves, but then you have to worry about other things, like hitting the surface or even running into the object itself.

I looked to the east and could see the outline of Santa Catalina clearly, and its highest point, Mount Orizaba, plainly visible against the horizon. I estimated that I was twenty miles due west, approximately in the same position where *Bachelor's Toy* had been spotted by satellite approximately twenty-five minutes ago. I banked to the left and gently pulled the T-38's nose to a course just to the right of Catalina's southernmost point. I was hoping it was a rough approximation of the boat's path.

I had lowered my shaded visor to give my eyes some respite from the glaring sunlight on the flight down the coast from Monterey, and now I raised the visor again so that I would have the minimum possible layers between my eyes and my quarry. It was time to begin the search in earnest.

My eyes hopped from craft-to-craft on the dark blue sea below me. Since I wasn't really a boat person and didn't really recognize the different classes and sizes of sea-going vessels, I couldn't discard any one of them without at least a cursory glance. Also, with no surface detail to provide background scale, I had no frame of reference. I tried to look at each boat, but between the number of them out there and my speed, there just wasn't time to take them all in. I realized that I was going to have to make wide 360 degree turns that slowly translated south to be able to examine each boat. I banked up to the right to offset the probable trail a little further to the west and then prepared to begin my slow circle to the east when I suddenly saw something off my nose that drew my attention.

It was a boat. A big boat. And it was churning up a huge, white wake behind it.

I could have smacked myself.

Of course it would be going fast and generating a wake. Size or no size, to get to where it was going in time, it would need to be moving quickly.

"Jesus, Pearce," I muttered to myself impatiently. I keyed the mic. "Dragnet and Delta Sierra, Talon, I've got a possible contact just to the left of my nose for a few miles. It appears to be approaching the southernmost point of the island."

"We copy you, Talon, can you get closer and confirm?"

"Roger that," I said. "Be advised, when I do they're going to know we're on to them."

"Copy, Talon," Smith's voice answered. "That's a risk we'll have to take."

Easy for you to say, Dave, I thought. *You're not in a place where they can shoot at you.*

As I closed in on the yacht, more detail came into view. I could see the indentation of the splash pool just behind the main salon and the steps that went down the starboard side to the lower aft deck. There were several people on deck and a few in the flying bridge. They all seemed to be wearing some sort of white uniform. I could see three radar domes on top of the single, dark mast. It all looked very familiar. I thought I could make out the deck just behind the wheelhouse where Susan Taylor and I had lounged just a few days ago.

It was hard to believe that she was dead.

And by now, Sarah was also dead.

I mentally willed away the wave of grief that beckoned for me and retarded the T-38's throttles, allowing the jet to descend even further. I wanted to get close enough to read the name on the back of the boat and close enough for them to see me. They were going to get a good look as I went by at about a hundred feet and 200 knots.

Of course, I should have been smarter than that knowing that there were guys with automatic weapons and possibly surface-to-air missiles on that boat. I should have been thinking about how vulnerable a jet like the T-38 would be in an airspeed regime where it was on the edge of its aerodynamic envelope. A regime where the level of induced drag was so high that the thrust required to maintain level flight would generate a huge heat signature. A regime where any sort of maneuvering to avoid automatic weapons fire would immediately create controllability issues in a jet with a tiny wing and no leading-edge devices.

But I didn't think about that. I'm not sure I was thinking at all. The world-famous Pearce compartmentalization and concentration mechanisms seemed to have taken the day off. I just knew I needed to get a good look at them and I wanted to make damn sure they got a good look at me.

The yacht was now just about a mile in front of me and to my left. The radar altimeter that Rose Aircraft had installed in the jet was indicating about a hundred-and-thirty feet above the water. As the airspeed went below 220 knots, I lowered the flaps, and then added some power to maintain the airspeed. The nose of the aircraft came up slightly due to the increased angle of attack at the lower speed, and I trimmed the control forces off the stick and fixed attention on the boat ahead.

The yacht was about half-a-mile in front of me now and I could distinctly see several men in uniforms that looked like those that a ship's crew would wear. I tore my eyes from them and regarded the stern of the yacht where the name was painted.

It read, *Viva Mexico*. Doubt crept into my mind. Had they changed the name? Was this even the same boat?

But then as I neared the ship, some of them crew stepped out onto the rear deck to monitor my approach—and suddenly

I could discern sand-colored load-bearing equipment strapped to their bodies. The pouches which contained spare magazines came into focus, as did muzzles of assault rifles which protruded along the sides of their bodies from the weapons carried across their backs. Suddenly, one of the men on the flying bridge leaned over to shout something to the crewmembers on the foredeck and he pointed at me as he was talking.

That's not good.

It was like a light switch had been thrown in my mind and one clear, lucid thought instantly made its way through the emotional haze. It sounded like the opening statement of a scenario back at USAF Fighter Weapons School.

You are a non-maneuvering target within the real-time envelope of automatic weapons.

Jesus Christ!

The temptation was to slam the throttles right into full afterburner. But I wasn't in an F-16 with a sophisticated digital engine control computer to schedule engine acceleration. Rapid throttle movements in the T-38 could cause compressors stalls or even flameouts. I smoothly pushed the throttles forward as I came abeam the yacht and slapped the flap handle up. I checked the engine gauges to verify that the engine RPM was increasing and then, as I looked back to the left, I saw muzzle flashes in my peripheral vision.

They're shooting at you, asshole.

Even as my eyes detected the flashes, I could feel and hear multiple thumps on the nose and fuselage of the jet. A hole appeared in the left side of the canopy next to my head along with a matching one on the right side as the oxygen mask on my face was blown into several pieces.

There were many more thumps behind me but now I had the throttles in full afterburner and was pushing forward on the stick. With low airspeed and a tiny wing, any application of back pressure to climb would have caused the sleek jet to stall, so I pushed the nose down to reduce the lift requirement slightly as the aircraft accelerated and to generate a three-dimensional problem for the guys shooting at me. Thank God the engines were still working.

"You fucking idiot!" I screamed at myself. "What in the hell were you thinking?"

Line-of-sight rate. I had to generate line-of-sight rate. And I had to get out of the real-time envelope of the guns.

Shooting airplanes with guns is exactly like shooting birds. You can't aim at them; you have to aim in front of them by a distance equal to the time of flight of the projectile to that location. You must lead them. The higher the lateral rate of target motion from the shooter's perspective, the higher the line-of-sight rate, the more lead required. Unless, of course, the bird is stupid enough to fly so close to you that it's within real-time envelope of the gun, close enough that the time of flight of the projectile is nearly negligible. So close that you can simply point and shoot.

Right where I was—in the real-time envelope of the guns the guys on the boat were using, probably some kind of assault rifle shooting a projectile with a nominal 3,000 feet-per-second muzzle velocity. And until I was out of that envelope and even out of range, I was going to have to move my aircraft so I didn't get hit again.

The waves of the Pacific Ocean reached out for me as I descended to them, and I leveled off close enough to get sea spray on the canopy. The jet was accelerating rapidly now, going through 300 knots, but I was still an easy target to hit, even as I headed away from the shooters. I rolled up on the left wing and pulled the stick into my lap for all I was worth, turning the jet across the bow of the yacht, in an attempt to generate a high line-of-sight rate and throw off the aim of the guys with the guns. To my left and only a few feet away, the dark blue curtain of ocean became a wall which meant instant death and destruction if the vector of my turn was even slightly too extreme. To the right, the light blue of the cloudless sky beckoned, but with the climb came additional vulnerability and the chance to get my airplane peppered with more bullets. I stared out the front of the T-38's windscreen and dragged the pitot tube across the horizon, mentally willing the bullets not to hit me and hoping like hell that I didn't hit the water.

The T-38 doesn't turn very rapidly. Maybe ten degrees per second if conditions are optimum, a function of its small wing and limited thrust. I needed to turn approximately 90 degrees and then accelerate away to the north. It was an agonizing few seconds as the nose seemed to crawl across the horizon. And then I could see the island dead ahead of me and I rolled out and let the jet accelerate toward it. I didn't feel or hear any more thumps or bumps. I wanted at least a two miles of separation before I climbed, so I checked that the airspeed was still at least 300 knots and increasing. I glanced down at the engine instruments and was relieved to see nothing out of the ordinary. Then I raised the nose of the aircraft and looked back over my left shoulder as I started a turn back to the west.

The yacht was now rounding the southernmost tip of the island and turning to the northeast to parallel the coast. The harbor at Avalon was only a few miles away. Time was running out.

I continued my turn through south as I passed about two miles behind the yacht. I leveled off at 5,000 feet and pulled the throttles out of afterburner.

"They're definitely hostile," I exclaimed, when I caught my breath. And then, as I keyed the mic to speak, I realized that my oxygen mask and its embedded microphone were gone and I had missed getting my face shot off by mere inches. *I'd rather be lucky than good*, occurred to me about the same time I realized that I couldn't transmit any details about the yacht or its intentions.

"Well, shit," I muttered. Then I thought of something. My transponder was still on and operating—or at least as far as I could tell it was. I rotated the thumbwheels for the Mode 3 code to 7700, the universal code for airborne emergencies—a code that would highlight my radar return on any display that was monitoring my position. I also located the emergency locator transmitter switch and turned it on. The ELT was a separate transmitter and was mandatory on every civilian aircraft in the United States. Now every radio tuned to the UHF of VHF emergency frequencies would also know there was an aircraft in distress. Rescue centers could also triangulate on that signal. Hopefully some of this would get me some attention and maybe even get those A-10s headed my way.

As I continued the turn, I rolled out on a parallel course with the yacht as it continued up the coast to Avalon, now visible about two miles ahead. I could now see a row of large yachts parked in the mouth of the harbor and one which dwarfed all the others set well off by itself, further out to sea. *Viva Mexico*—formerly *Bachelor's Toy*—was heading right for it.

The cavalry wasn't going to get here in time. It was up to me. Once again.

Here I was in an airplane with no weapons and just about out of fuel. What was there to do?

Unbidden, the equation for kinetic energy popped into my head. $KE=MV^2$. Kinetic energy equals mass times velocity squared. And there was only one thing at my immediate disposal that could generate kinetic energy—the airplane around me.

And I'd have to guide it to impact.

And that was as it should be, I thought to myself. The only person who ever gave a shit about me was dead. Maybe it was time for me to join her. Maybe we could be together in whatever place we ended up. Maybe we could even be happy. I glanced down at the fuel gauges. I had only a few hundred pounds of gas remaining. It would be enough to turn this jet into a weapon.

And that's when the guys on the boat must have gotten

the same idea, because that's when they fired the SAMs at me.

There was a flash low and to my left, and then the white trail reached out for my jet, followed by another flash and another trail a few seconds later.

Tactical instincts are deeply ingrained. My first thought was to get the sun behind me to saturate the missiles' seeker heads. But the angles were all wrong.

Once again, time seemed to slow down. I retarded the throttles to idle to reduce my heat source and saw my left hand pull the handles aft. I read the time on my watch. 14:02. Then, I banked to the right and pulled the nose to the right to put the missiles' incoming flight path exactly at my left wing. The course I rolled out on was exactly 120 degrees. Finally, I pushed the stick forward to descend and build some airspeed. The T-38 plunged to the surface of the ocean.

I didn't know how far from the yacht I was so I didn't know how much energy the missiles would have to work with. I didn't even know what kind of missiles they were and whether they were tracking hot metal, my fuel plume, or my jet's ultraviolet silhouette. What I did know is how these missiles typically flew the end game of their intercept. Initially, they would follow the heat source of the target they were tracking, but then, as their target stabilized in course, they would bias forward in their flight profile so that when the warhead detonated it would do so further forward on the target and damage more crucial components – like the pilot.

The two missiles, the second in close trail of the first, were now aimed directly behind me; and as I looked at the small fireballs which revealed their positions, they were moving aft on my canopy. They were settling into a tail chase. But no sooner had my eyes detected that movement then the aft movement stopped and now the small flames began moving forward.

It was time.

I pulled the control stick into my lap and commanded

the jet into the vertical, a path that was perpendicular to the missiles' course. The first missile corrected to my vertical movement and I banked toward it slightly to keep my course perpendicular to it. The first fireball went underneath my jet and I felt a mild bump as it detonated harmlessly behind and under me.

I wasn't as lucky with the second.

It was déjà vu all over again. The second missile went under my jet too—but since it had more time to correct for my movement, it detonated much closer to the aircraft.

The T-38's left engine FIRE light came on almost immediately. With the jet's fuel tanks located in the fuselage just above the engines, an engine fire warning means there's a lot of heat and maybe a flame near the fuel. I had no choice but to shut down the number one engine and hope the light went out. I pulled the left throttle over the detent and into the off position.

The light didn't go out.

The next line in the procedure was something like, "If Fire Light Remains On—Eject."

But that assumed that the pilot cared about whether he lived or died. And at that moment, I didn't give a shit.

Instead, I rolled out of my evasive maneuver nearly over the yacht and pushed the right throttle into full afterburner, forcing the crippled jet into a climb. I could see the harbor at Avalon under me now as I coaxed the jet higher into the clear, California sky and the drama unfolded on the sea below. The large boat that lay all by itself, the Presidential yacht, was teaming with activity as a contingent of men in suits brought weapons to the side rails and trained them on their attacker. *Viva Mexico* was ready for them, though, and had some sort of heavy weapon mounted on its foredeck. The heavy weapon belched flame and smoke and began raking the Presidential yacht with direct fire. Small explosions and pieces of debris torn loose by the fusillade of projectiles were visible from the Presidential yacht as I climbed. The left fire light stubbornly remained illuminated and I could feel the controls becoming sluggish under my gloved hand.

"Not too much longer, baby," I coaxed it. "Not too much longer."

$KE=MV^2$. $KE=MV^2$.

At 10,000 feet, the RPM on the right engine started to become erratic as the right fuel tank became too low to feed the afternurner's insatiable fuel flow. I retarded that throttle to idle just to keep the engine running so the electrical generator and hydraulic pump would both stay online, and I rolled the T-38 inverted.

Below me, a tranquil day in Avalon's harbor had turned into a firefight that would have been more at home in a warzone. The few survivors from the Presidential yacht were spraying Viva Mexico with automatic weapons fire and the men on *Viva Mexico* returned the fire in kind. The hostile crew serving the larger deck-mounted weapon—it seemed to be a rapid-fire cannon of some sort—were dead at their posts but others were attempting to replace them, only to be picked off by highly-accurate sniper fire from the Presidential yacht. But even from my altitude, it was apparent that *Viva Mexico* had more men. Many more men. And it was only a question of time before the heavy weapon was active again and the Presidential yacht was destroyed.

"Not today," I said.

Even as the T-38 began to fall toward the earth with just under 200 knots, I gently applied back pressure to the stick and tracked the nose across the water toward the hostile yacht. The vertical velocity increased and the airspeed climbed.

$KE=MV^2$. $KE=MV^2$.

The mass of the aircraft was not going to change at this point, but the velocity was going to increase. For every 1,000 feet of altitude I lost, the jet would gain about 50 knots.

"Should just break the Mach before impact," I said to myself with a satisfied smile. "That ought to do it."

The nose continued to track toward the hostile yacht. The two craft were visible through the upper portion of the windscreen and the airspeed was accelerating through 350 knots.

About 6,000 feet to go.

As the nose continued to track, the airspeed continued to build and the altitude continued to decrease, I realized that I was going to be responsible for my own death. The standard ejection seat installed on the T-38 was good enough for the maneuvers that pilot-training students normally performed, but it wouldn't get me out of this. The sink rate was too high and the altitude was too low. If I ejected, I'd end up a bloody bag of broken bones, just a few thousand feet from the impact of the aircraft.

That was no way to meet one's end.

No, I would stay with the aircraft and ride it in.

I found I was at peace with that outcome.

The nose reached the hostile yacht and I placed the end of the pitot tube directly on the foredeck, right on top of the heavy cannon and the crew that was just about to restore its operation. Then I trimmed the nose down to hold it on target.

4,000 feet to go. 450 knots.

I wasn't sure if the jet would break the Mach before impact now, but it would be close and certainly it would generate substantial damage. I smiled to myself as I watched the deck grow larger. One of the men below suddenly noticed that there was six tons of aircraft accelerating toward them at high speed, and he pointed upwards and shouted something. There were a few muzzle flashes as weapons were raised and fired at me. I welcomed them. At this point, I didn't care how the end came.

2,000 feet. Just about 600 knots. Plenty of smash.

"I'll be with you soon, sweet Sarah," I whispered. "Very soon."

"I love you, Colin Pearce," she said. *"Don't forget that."*

"I love you too, Sarah," I replied. "I have since I first saw you."

"Then pull the fucking handle, Colin," her voice said sternly in my ear, *"and get the hell out of there."*

And that's what I did without ever knowing why I did it or how my hands found the handle between my legs.

The few seconds that followed were like a surreal dream. I heard the blast and felt the rush of air as the canopy separated from the aircraft. Then, I felt the incredible acceleration of the ejection seat as the rocket motor ignited and pushed me clear of the T-38 even as the deck of the huge yacht below me seemed impossibly close.

My neck was yanked sideways as the helmet was ripped from my head by the relentless airstream.

I heard a terrible, ear-piercing scream that sounded like someone was experiencing unbearable pain and I looked around me and saw my legs and arms turned in terrible and unimaginable angles.

Then, I realized, I was the one who was screaming.

Initially, the ejection seat propelled me horizontally to the water, which was what I expected; and as the water got closer to me, I closed my eyes so that I wouldn't know exactly when the impact came. But then the seat changed its direction and I was propelled upward, away from the water.

Gyro-stabilized seat, I thought to myself. *Oh yeah, Aces II?*

WHUMP! There was a massive explosion somewhere nearby. I felt the wave of overpressure pass through my body and the surge of heat that followed.

Then, there was the pull of the parachute and the deceleration from the drag it created. I screamed again as the hard yank of the parachute aggravated the multiple bone breaks and fractures all over my body. Even as the parachute finished its deployment, I hit the water with a heavy smack and plunged far beneath the surface of the cool Pacific Ocean. The water surrounded me and I welcomed its embrace. I wondered what it would feel like to drown.

But then I was back on the surface, facing upwards with pillows of air under my neck and under my head and the parachute was gone.

"Naval horsecollar and SEAWARS," I muttered, not even sure if I was really talking. "Of course. They thought of fucking everything."

I could hear the loud whine of familiar jet engines overhead. I opened my eyes to find that I could barely see, despite the bright sunlight around me. I saw a large, gray shadow go over me and then saw an A-10 fly over and bank hard to the right with small vapor trails coming from its wingtips.

"They made it," I muttered. "They finally made it."

And then the world went dark.

TOP SECRET/SPECIAL
COMPARTMENTALIZED INFORMATION
CLASSIFIED BY: US Central Intelligence Agency
DECLASSIFY ON: OADR

From: Special Projects Group [NCS]
Sent: Friday, 27 November 2009, 1700 PST (28 November 2009, 0100Z)
To: Director, NCS
Cc: Special Projects Group [NCS]; damrine@cmail.cia.gov; dsmith3@cmail.cia.gov

SUBJECT: Preliminary After-Action Report – Operation Baja Sunrise

(TS) Narrative:

1. (TS) Yesterday, 26 November 2009, two separate operations were conducted against the senior leadership of the United States.

2. (TS) A biological weapon attack was attempted against San Francisco, California using Candlestick Park, where the Vice-President of the United States was attending a football game, as ground zero. The aerial platform used in the attack was intercepted well prior to its arrival in the target area and the Vice President was not threatened or evacuated.

3. (TS) A waterborne assault was attempted against the President of the United States while he attended a secret meeting at Santa Catalina, California with the President of Mexico in order to sign the US/Mexico Border Treaty. The assault terminated in a battle in the harbor of the town of Avalon, California. While an exact casualty count is still being compiled, initial estimates are at least 23 Secret Service agents and local law

enforcement personnel either dead or severely wounded. No civilians were wounded. Enemy casualties cannot be assessed due to the explosion which destroyed the attacking vessel. No hostile personnel survived and bodies or identifiable body parts have been difficult to recover. The President and the President of Mexico were both lightly wounded and evacuated safely. The treaty was not signed.

4. (TS) While no person or entity has claimed responsibility for either of these operations, intelligence has confirmed that both operations were planned and funded through a partnership between Mohammed bin Rashid al Qudamah, his brother Abdullah bin Rashid al Qudamah and the Mexican Drug Lord who calls himself Miguel Hidalgo. All three remain at large.

5. (TS) The security implications these operations have generated are of extreme significance. First, regardless of standard Secret Service security protocols, the attackers knew the timeline for the Vice President's entire visit to the west coast for several weeks in advance, well prior to even the intergovernmental release of this information. Second, in spite of enhanced Secret Service security protocols, the location of the President's "secret" meeting was known to the attackers for several weeks in advance of their attack.

6. (TS) Contractor 09-017 (Pearce, Colin M.), flying a Northrop T-38 Talon, N5494D, intercepted Gulfstream G-IV N36WMS over Monterey Bay on the coast of California. After positively identifying the aircraft for air defense fighters (Bear 01 Flight, two F-16s from March AFB, CA), Pearce flew to Santa Catalina Island, positively identified the attacking vessel and with no other assets available and with the President's vessel in severe peril, Pearce crashed his aircraft into the attacking vessel and destroyed it. He ejected just prior to impact and was severely wounded. He has been placed in a drug-induced coma to allow

his body to recover.

(TS) CONCLUSIONS:

1. (TS) Mohammed bin Rashid al Qudamah and Abdullah bin Rashid al Qudamah remain a threat and require dedicated surveillance and analysis.

2. (TS) The Drug Lord calling himself Miguel Hidalgo also remains a threat. The extent of his infiltration of and his determination to overthrow the legitimate government of Mexico significantly increases the threat he constitutes to US National Security. He also requires dedicated surveillance and analysis.

3. (TS) The Secret Service's lack of effective communication with other US Security agencies requires examination and investigation.

(TS) ACTIONS: None. Information only.

(TS) RECOMMENDATIONS:

1. (TS) Form dedicated surveillance and analysis teams to monitor activities of Mohammed bin Rashid al Qudamah, Abdullah bin Rashid al Qudamah and the Drug Lord calling himself Miguel Hidalgo.

2. (TS) Initiate bureau-level investigation of Secret Service communication protocols.

TOP SECRET / SPECIAL
COMPARTMENTALIZED INFORMATION
CLASSIFIED BY: US Central Intelligence Agency
DECLASSIFY ON: OADR

CHAPTER TWENTY-FIVE

Thursday, February 4
1155 Local Time
UCLA Medical Center
Los Angeles, California, United States

The first thing I became aware of was the pressure of a hand on mine. It was a smaller hand, and it was soft and warm and very comforting. I think I would have probably panicked if it hadn't been there to steady me. Somehow, a part of me knew whose hand it was but refused to believe it could be so.

Awareness is an odd thing. One moment you don't possess it at all and the next moment, suddenly, you do. Just seconds ago, I was somewhere far away and now I was here. And I had no idea where I had been and no idea where I was.

But I was grateful for the hand. It gave me something to hang on to. And it had been there for a long time, I realized. It had always been there. Occasionally, a different hand would replace it but the regular hand, the familiar hand, would always come back.

My state of awareness was peculiar; I couldn't see, but I knew I wasn't blind. I don't know how I knew that. I felt disembodied. Weightless. Like I was swimming inside myself. But I could hear things and I could feel and I could smell.

I knew there were people nearby. People talking. I wanted

to talk back. But I couldn't. I was separated from those people by a barrier that I couldn't find. And that terrified me.

But the warm pressure on my hand made it all right somehow.

"*How is he?*"

It was a male voice nearby, but not next to me. It was a voice I recognized. A voice that sounded concerned and responsible. *Smith?*

"About the same."

This was a female voice. It was next to me. It was a familiar voice. The voice that belonged to the hand. I knew who it was but my brain prevented me from identifying it. *It can't be,* my brain insisted. *It will hurt you to think about it. It just can't be.*

The male voice: "Why don't you walk down to the cafeteria and get something to eat?"

There was a pause. I could feel the woman thinking. She didn't want to go but knew she should. *How did I know that?*

The male voice again: "I'll let you know the moment he comes out of it. Go on. Take your daughter and get some air. You deserve it."

The female voice now: "Well, maybe just a few minutes."

Another female voice chimed in. "I'll take over for you. He's right. You do need a break."

The pressure on my hand was suddenly gone and I felt like a part of me was ripped away. I wanted to scream and protest but I couldn't. I couldn't do anything.

But then another hand was there, holding mine. This had happened a lot, I realized. I felt comforted, but I wanted the other hand to return.

Then there were barely audible cooing noises. These were familiar. I had heard them before. I liked them.

The familiar female voice again. "C'mon little girl. Let's take a little stroll. Let me get you strapped in. Here we go, sweetie."

A few moments later, there were footsteps. The sound of a door opening. A new male voice.

"What did the doctor say?" asked the male voice I had heard before.

"Nothing new. The drugs have been out of his system for over a week. It's up to him to want to wake up." This was a new male voice. *Amrine?*

"He was pretty messed up," said the first male voice. "They kept him under for two months. That's a long time. I knew a guy in the first Gulf War who was under for like six months. They didn't give him drugs to put him down but he had a hard time finding his way back. If it wasn't for his wife, he never would have."

"Well, he's lucky that she has been here."

"Yes, he is."

Yes, I am lucky, I thought. *I've always been lucky.*

I drifted away again. It wasn't so bad in here. I was warm, I was comfortable and best of all, nothing hurt. Nothing hurt at all. My body felt whole and relaxed. My mind didn't have to struggle with memories or thoughts or dreams. It could just rest.

I became aware again when I heard a baby crying. And I felt the pressure on my hand go away. But I didn't panic this time. I knew it would be back.

"She's hungry," said a new female voice.

"She's always hungry," said the familiar female voice that didn't make sense.

"Just like her mother," said the new female voice and the two shared a laugh. "So if he wakes up are you going to tell him?"

"You mean when he wakes up?"

"Yes. Of course. Sorry."

"I don't know. He's got this duty thing. He wants people to believe that he has no conscience, but underneath it all he's about duty and loyalty. I don't want him to feel compelled in any way. He has to want to be with us."

"I think I understand. By the way, that was a stroke of genius on your part."

"Well, you were the one who made it happen. If you hadn't been working at that fertility clinic it wouldn't have been possible."

It was silent for a while and I thought I could hear a sound like humming coming from the familiar voice.

"So I have to know." The new female voice asked. "Why him?"

There was a pause and I was impatient to hear the answer even though I had absolutely no idea who or what they were talking about.

"Because it seemed right. He was the only man I ever knew who wanted me for me and all of me. He didn't make any demands. He just let me be me. It was the best three weeks of my life. When that idiot I married insisted I get pregnant, I knew I didn't want to have his baby so the choice was obvious."

I could hear murmurs of agreement. There were other people around me.

"I think she's done. I'll burp her for you."

"Thanks."

I felt the pressure on my hand resume. And I smiled.

"Oh my God, Sarah! He smiled when you held his hand again. I just saw it! I saw it! I'm going to get Gwen."

The hand gripped me tighter and I felt the brush of familiar lips on mine and the familiar scent that went with them.

"Come back to me, Colin," the familiar voice said. "Come back to me."

I was now impatient with my comfortable place and I wanted out. The blackness around me felt like tar that was binding me to it. It was sticky and viscous and unyielding. Up above me I could sense that there was a light, just above the surface of the water. I wanted to pull myself upward toward it but I couldn't move. I willed every muscle in my body to move. Nothing. I was frozen.

I wanted to scream in frustration but I couldn't even do that.

"He's trying to come out of it. Keep talking to him." A different female voice.

"Wake up, Colin. Wake up. You've got to come out of this. I've got someone for you to meet. Just open your eyes."

Open my eyes? Was it that easy? It couldn't be. My eyes were already open. Weren't they? I pushed against my eyelids with every fiber of concentration I could muster. To my considerable surprise, I could suddenly see a small slit of light.

"You can do it, Colin. Open your eyes. We're here. Open your eyes."

I concentrated even harder. I pushed inside my brain. I willed my eyes to move upward. I could feel a bead of sweat on the side of my face. Slowly, excruciatingly slowly, my eyelids moved upward until they were wide open and the brightness of the light was overwhelming.

There were people all around me. They were dressed in white. The light seemed to make their features indiscernible. But there was one face I could see clearly. The one face that was right in front of me. The hair was a mixture of red and blonde, and the eyes were hazel and absolutely bottomless. And they were also filled with tears.

"Oh, Colin," Sarah said to me, as the tears streamed down her cheeks. "You came back to me. I'm so happy you came back."

"Sarah," I whispered hoarsely, "what are you doing here? Are we in heaven?"

There was a chorus of feminine laughter. My eyes began to focus and I could see several beautiful female faces surrounding my bed. They were all looking down at me and they were all smiling through glistening eyes.

"This has to be heaven," I said, sleepily. "And I like it."

More laughter.

A different female face came into view from the other side of my bed. This one was framed by blonde hair pulled behind her head and it sported a pair of stylish, black-framed glasses.

"Let me have a quick look at him, Sarah," she said.

"Sure, Gwen."

A bright penlight was shined in my eyes and I squinted. The face looked me over very carefully.

"Can you remember your name?" Gwen asked, at last.

I had to think for just a second but the answer came to me clearly. "Colin Pearce," I said carefully, concentrating on the words.

There were squeals of excited delight all around me and I had idea what the excitement was about.

"How do you feel?"

That was a good question. I didn't know what sort of answer she expected. I assessed the way my body felt. It seemed to be slowly waking up now, joint-by-joint and limb-by-limb, and the messages it was sending my brain communicated a pain beyond reason that had been replaced by achiness, soreness, and fatigue.

"Beaten up," I said, after a long moment. "Broken up."

"Do you remember what happened?"

A series of rapid-fire images filled my brain. There was the image of the blue water of Monterey Bay below me as I circled a G-IV; then, the clear-blue sky as I climbed to altitude for the flight to the south; the sleek lines of the yacht traveling at high speed and churning up the wake behind it; the thumps on the side of my jet and bullet holes in the canopy as I was fired upon; the wall of dark blue water next to me as I made the low-altitude turn to escape; the quickly-moving fireballs of the surface-air-missiles reaching up for me; the red FIRE light in the T-38's cockpit; and the image of the deck of the yacht getting bigger and bigger and bigger.

Then the images slowed down. The canopy departing the airplane; the impossible angles of my arms and legs; rising above the sea below; the orange, white, and green parachute above me, and then the ocean rising to meet me again.

And then the pain. The overwhelming pain. I leaned back against the pillow and nodded slowly.

"How bad was it?" I gasped.

"You ejected at over 600 knots," Sarah said quietly. "You're lucky to be..." Her voice cracked and then she squeezed my hand tightly and kissed it.

"Your arms and legs were basically shattered," Gwen continued, softly but authoritatively. "Broken in too many places to count. Your arms were ripped out of your shoulder sockets and your legs were ripped out of their hip sockets. Your spine was actually bent. Your ejection seat did a pretty decent job but you still hit the water at about fifty miles an hour." Then she smiled at me. "You were a mess, Mr. Pearce. We didn't know if you'd make it or not, but here you are."

"But I'm not in casts or anything," I protested weakly.

"We stitched your bones back together with a lot of titanium rods and screws and put you into a drug-induced coma so that you could heal more quickly, and because the pain would have been unbearable. We took you off the medication about a week ago. We've just been waiting for you to wake up so we can start your physical therapy."

My mind reeled with the information. There were so many questions I wanted to ask, but one came out of my mouth without my even willing it.

"How long?" I asked.

"Exactly ten weeks," Gwen said. "Today is February the fourth, 2010."

I exhaled loudly as I took in the revelation.

Ten weeks. Ten weeks of my life gone. It just didn't seem

real.

I wanted to question Gwen's credibility, but she had a stethoscope around her neck and as I looked down to search for her name tag, the words *Gwen Brower, M.D.* were clearly visible. I nodded in acceptance. Of course, then my eyes looked to the left of her name tag and down the v-neck of the surgical scrubs she was wearing. I was rewarded with a glimpse of well-formed breasts inside of something white and lacy. As I raised my eyes back to hers, I noticed she had a smirk on her face.

"I think you're well on the way to recovery, Mr. Pearce," she said, as she rose. "Go easy on him, girls. He still needs to get his rest." She picked up her clipboard from the table across my bed, winked at me, and then left the room.

Girls? Oh yeah.

I looked around my bed to see that I was surrounded by what my eyes first beheld. The room was filled with beautiful women. Some of the faces were familiar, and I remembered them from my dinner at the mansion many weeks ago.

"I'd love to believe you all came here to see me," I said in a lame attempt at humor, "but I assume you're here for other reasons."

Sarah smiled at me and released my hand. She motioned to the women standing near around us. "Every one of them has held your hand when I've been away from your side over these last several weeks, so they've all been here multiple times. But today," she leaned over to a bassinette that was next to the bed and reached inside, "they're here because somebody is exactly two months old." From the inside of the bassinette came a very small bundle, tightly wrapped in a pink blanket.

"Hey, little girl," she said in a tender voice. "Somebody's finally awake to see you."

She tucked the bundle into the crook of her arm up against her breasts, which I noticed for the first time were larger than

I remembered them. Then she leaned in close to me and bent over so that I could see the baby's face.

"I wanted to name the baby after you, but it turned out to be a girl," she said apologetically. "So, I named her Colleen. I thought that was pretty close."

I don't know what I was expecting when I saw the child for the first time. I had seen my fair share of babies and small children throughout the course of my life. But there was something very special about this little girl. Her eyes were wide open and she regarded me with open curiosity. There was a wisp of red hair visible on her tiny head and her face was positively angelic. But it was her eyes that caught my attention. They looked disturbingly familiar but I just couldn't place them. One thing I did notice, however. The little eyes were hazel, not the deep-brown hue of an Arab.

I looked up at Sarah.

"She's not Damian's, is she?"

#

Later, after the girls left and Gwen had looked me over again, it was just Sarah, Colleen, and me. Sarah was sitting on the chair next to my bed, a gliding chair which had a rocking motion built into it, and she had Colleen to her breast. I had never seen a woman breastfeeding in real life before. My mouth was open as I watched and Sarah lifted her eyes to find me looking. She didn't even twitch.

"What are you thinking?" she asked softly.

I couldn't talk for a moment because of the huge lump that seemed to have taken residence in my throat. "Just how amazing this is," I said, when I could trust my voice. "I can't believe how perfect you are at this and how perfect she is. I knew you'd be a great mother."

Sarah smiled at me. "You always know the right thing to say," she said. "But I've been lucky. With all the girls at the mansion, I've always got someone to watch her or change her or do whatever if I need it. I can even pump breast milk and they can feed her. She sleeps through the night already and hardly ever cries unless she's really upset. She's a great baby."

"Thanks for being here," I said, trying to keep my voice under control. "I know it couldn't have been easy with your responsibilities where Colleen is concerned."

Sarah was looking down at her daughter and pulling her breast back a little from Colleen's mouth as she nursed.

"We just kind of moved in," Sarah said. She motioned to a suitcase in the corner of the room. "Gwen took your case. She's the lead orthopedic surgeon here. And she is a former Monthly Mistress. Actually, Mistress of the Year. 1998, I think. She let me pretty much live here. I wanted to be with you." She paused for a moment and I could tell that she was trying to control her own voice. "I needed to be here with you."

"I knew you were there," I said. "I can't tell you how I knew. I just did. That feeling of your hand holding mine, it meant everything to me."

"I'm glad," she said. "But it wasn't always me. The other girls were there too, like I said earlier. When I needed to eat or sleep or go to the bathroom or something, one of them held your hand."

"I know," I said truthfully, totally baffled by how I remembered. "I could tell when it was you and when it wasn't. I can't tell you how I knew that. I was always grateful there was someone there. But I always felt the best when it was you." I paused for a moment again as a wave of emotion passed over me. "Having something, having someone to hold on to while I was out there floating in the blackness was everything. It gave me focus. It gave me a reason to come back."

She nodded. I could see another tear roll down her cheek as she removed Colleen from her breast. The little eyes were closed. Sarah buttoned her blouse and let Colleen sleep where she was.

"I had to be here for you," she said, after a moment. "I owed you that."

After I handed you off to die? I don't think so.

I turned my head away from her and looked out the window on the far side of the hospital room. It was a tremendous view of the mountains ringing the San Fernando Valley.

"Sarah," I said, "you need to know something. You didn't owe me anything. I thought you were..."

"You thought I was dead," she said matter-of-factly. "You found the G-IV and you guided those air defense F-16s to it. And you expected them to destroy it."

"Yes," I whispered, barely able to get the word out. "And I wanted to die afterwards. I almost didn't bail out of that damn T-38 before it hit the damn ship. I almost rode it in. I didn't want to live."

"Until I told you to get out," she said simply.

My head pivoted around to her and my jaw dropped open. "How did you know...?"

"How did I know you were about to kill yourself? I was watching the whole thing on CNN. It was all over the news. I saw the jet headed for the ship and I could see you weren't ejecting so I told you to get out."

"But... how... I heard you. I heard you!"

She nodded.

"I know you did. I knew you would." She watched me struggle with the lack of logic I had assigned to her statement. Then she stood up and gently placed Colleen in her bassinette and made sure the little girl was all bundled up. She returned to her chair and took my hand in hers again. "I knew that the same way you knew when I was holding your hand. We're *connected*, you and me."

I nodded dumbly. The logical part of me refused to accept her explanation—but deep inside me, I was certain of its truth.

"But how were you ali..."

"How was I alive to see it?"

411

I nodded again.

"For two reasons. First, Adam can't tie knots for shit. And second, there's this certain former Air Force fighter jock I know who told me what the universal sign for aerial surrender is."

My mouth fell open and my eyes filled with wonder.

"You lowered your gear!"

She nodded.

"I actually saw you circling the G-IV. Adam had me tied to the seat in the corner of the conference table on the jet, up against the bulkhead. When you left, I knew fighters had to be on the way. I had worked the knot free by that point and I ran to the cockpit and threw the gear handle down. I probably over-sped the gear. I think the jet was accelerating through about 250 knots at the time."

"You lowered the gear. I actually taught you something useful. You lowered your gear."

She smiled at me and shook her head, clearly unimpressed with herself.

"It wasn't *that* big a deal. Once I got the airplane slowed down with the gear extended, I turned out over the water to show the fighters I wasn't going to allow it to proceed northbound. Then, it was a simple matter of landing at Monterey Airport. They had the guys in HAZMAT suits waiting for me. They disarmed the device and that was that. When I walked into the FBO there, CNN was reporting live from Avalon Harbor. They had a news crew there for some reason and they were covering the gun battle between those two ships. And then you arrived."

She looked deeply into my eyes.

"It was like I was inside your head. I totally knew what you were thinking."

I just looked back at her.

"Do you know what I kept thinking about?"

She nodded back at me.

"The last words I said to you," she said. She cocked her head as if straining to remember. "Something like, 'I love you, Colin Pearce. Don't forget that.'"

I nodded back at her, unable to speak.

"It's true and I do."

I shook my head in wonder at how it could possibly be true. "I know," I said, after a moment. "And I so don't get it."

She laughed. "Love doesn't have to make sense, Colin. It's unpredictable. And it just happens. I loved you since we were together those years ago. I just didn't know what to do about it." She looked away. "It's the main reason I called you to come out here. I wanted you to save me."

As I regarded her beautiful profile, I could see the tears form in her eyes and her face began to crumple. "And I almost got you killed," she said quietly. And then she began to sob, very softly.

I could feel the emotion wrack her body and it broke my heart. I summoned all the energy I could find and reached out to her and lifted her chin. "I came because you called and I couldn't stay away," I said to her quietly. "I meant what I told you in the mansion weeks ago. All you ever had to do was call. I was always yours. I've never stopped thinking about you. I've always wanted to come back to you." I paused for a second because I wanted to relish saying the words. "I love you too, Sarah. And if I had to go back and do this all over again, I wouldn't change a damn thing."

She clung to me then and we both cried in each other's arms for a while. It was good for both of us.

"You know," I said after a few moments, "this bed is pretty big. I think you might be able to sleep up here with me."

Her eyes lit up. "Really?"

I nodded. "Unfortunately though, you'll going to have to wear pajamas or something."

"No problem!"

She leapt off the bed, disappeared into the bathroom and

reappeared in loose gym shorts and a t-shirt a few moments later. Working together, we moved me over to one side of the bed and she crawled in next to me.

"I hope I don't stink," I said apprehensively.

She nestled against me. "You don't. Two of the girls and I bathed you yesterday."

"Oh, really?" I said, laughing. "Can't imagine how much fun that must have been."

"Are you kidding? It was great! There was a certain part of you that needed a little extra attention, though."

I could feel my face reddening and I tensed slightly.

"Your leg," she said, raising her head to look at me and smiling. "The one with all the gunshot wounds? What part were you thinking about?"

CHAPTER TWENTY-SIX

Friday, March 5
1115 Local Time
UCLA Medical Center
Los Angeles, California, United States

It was a smoggy, dreary day in Southern California, but it seemed beautiful to me. I was finally leaving the hospital. Dr. Gwen had pushed me to the door in a wheelchair, even though I didn't need it. She was effusively telling me all about the medical journal article she was going to write about me, and how my case would be the key example in her research as she propelled me through the lobby. When we reached the front door and Sarah brought the car around, Gwen surprised me by giving me a warm hug, and a no-flinch kiss right on the lips that lasted a second or two more than the requisite good-bye kiss. Then, she disappeared back into the hospital.

As I stood there shaking my head in amazement, Sarah good-naturedly called to me from the car, a sporty black Cadillac CTS-V.

"Are you planning to join us, Casanova? Or maybe see if you can find more doctors you can make out with?"

I turned to her with my mouth agape, trying to come up with a suitable excuse and found her laughing at me.

"Relax, Colin," she said. "We're like a sisterhood. Gwen

told me all about how grateful she was to be your physician with this research she's doing, and she thought you were a model patient. I knew she'd probably kiss you when she dropped you off. All the girls want to kiss you."

I was at a complete loss. "That doesn't make any sense," I muttered, as I reached for the passenger's side door.

"Would you mind sitting in the back with Colleen?" she asked. "She gets lonely back there and she really likes to be with you."

"It seems I have that effect on women," I said, as I opened the door and slid onto the comfortable leather seats. I looked over at the little red-haired baby strapped into the rear-facing car seat. The familiar green eyes looked up at me. I made a face and she laughed that contagious baby laugh. I fastened my seat belt as I made several more faces at her, reveling in the innocent sound of her laughter.

"Looks like you've got women swooning all over you," Sarah commented from the driver's seat.

"That may be true," I said, as I rested my left hand on Colleen's car seat. "But there's only one who is going to be stuck with me."

"Well two, actually," Sarah said, as she put the car into gear. "Colleen *and* me."

"Good point!" I said. Then looking down at the infant next to me, I tickled her little belly. "You're stuck with me too! You are!"

More baby laughter filled the Cadillac's interior as we drove out of the parking lot. We had a stop to make and then we'd drive to the mansion; the place Sarah and I planned to live together until we could find a place of our own. That would be after the wedding, of course.

"You still feel like you need to do this?" Sarah asked.

I nodded from the back seat as I continued to tickle some baby belly.

"It was her last request. And regardless what she did or

didn't do, she helped me deal with Saif-al Din, and what she told us about the boat helped us to get our heads in the right place about what was really going on. Besides, I gave my word."

"I know how you are about that."

"We won't be late for the engagement party, I promise."

"We can't be! Bill and Shelly are going to throw us quite the soiree! I think they even invited some celebs to join us."

"The CIA won't be happy about that," I said solemnly. "Even though their agents did rescue both of them."

"Well, you're not working for them anymore, remember?"

"Yes, I do," I said.

"Are you regretting your decision, Mr. Pearce?"

"Let me think," I said, stroking my imaginary beard. "Wander around the world getting shot on a regular basis or fly a G-IV with the girl of my dreams who just happens to be crazy enough to actually want to marry me? What a tough decision..."

It really wasn't a tough decision at all. Sarah and I had spent nearly every waking moment and some sleeping moments together over the last four weeks as I had endured the exhaustive process of teaching my arms and legs how to work again. After a particularly strenuous session about two weeks ago, I was recuperating in my room and she was going through some of her mail that the girls from the mansion had brought her. One envelope contained an official notice from the county government informing her that her marriage to Mohammed/Damian wasn't valid because he had used a false identity.

"Looks like I'm single again," she said sardonically. "In fact, it looks like I was never really even married. Looks like you're hanging out with a tainted woman."

My mouth was moving before my brain could even engage.

"We could fix that," I said softly.

She looked at me cautiously.

"What do you mean?" she asked, her eyes intently watching mine.

"We could fix that," I said, again with a wry smile on my face. "The single part, I mean. As far as the tainted thing goes, that ship has sailed."

She threw a towel at me from her chair.

"I didn't think you were serious," she said, returning her gaze to the mail on her lap. But I could see that her face was slightly flushed.

My body had a will of its own and all the defense mechanisms that had been in place for my whole life were, for the first time, idle on the sidelines. I rose from my bed, walked over to her chair, and then lowered myself to my knees in front of her. I took her hands in mine and looked up at her. Her hair, now almost completely back to its original red hue, shone in the brightly-lit room. The beautiful face which had never been more than a few feet away from me over these many weeks and months looked back at me. The bottomless hazel eyes were frightened, but hopeful, and the rich lips were slightly parted.

"That was a poor attempt at humor," I said, pausing for a moment to get the right words together. I looked directly into her eyes. "Some things that have happened to me over the last several months, even before you called me, have made me realize that you need to seize the good things in life and enjoy them while you have them—because you might not have them tomorrow. The time you and I had together those few years ago was one of the very best things that has ever happened to me and I didn't seize it. Hell, I didn't know what to do about it."

"Me neither," she said quietly.

"But now I've been given a second chance. We've been given a second chance. And it's been my experience that second chances are rare."

I interlaced her fingers with mine.

"Sarah, I'm no bargain. I'm at least fifteen years older than you and I have probably more than my share of mileage on me for my time on Earth. But if you'll have me, I'll be yours. Now and always."

"Exactly what are you trying to say, Colin?" she asked me, eyes wary.

"Well, you caught me off guard, so I don't have a ring handy. But I figure I need to act fast before some guy who is lot younger and a lot better looking with a lot less baggage asks you to marry him."

Her jaw was open and she was staring at me.

"Are you serious? Are you asking me to marry you?"

I nodded, feeling slightly ridiculous.

She sat there and looked into my eyes. "Please tell me that you're not doing this out of some sense of duty," she said, solemnly. "I know how you are."

"No ma'am," I said evenly, looking right back at her. "I'm doing it for one reason and one reason only. Because I love you."

She nodded slowly as she leaned forward and wrapped her arms around my neck. Then, she put her head on my shoulder and pulled herself to me as tightly as she could manage. For a moment, I thought she was just taking the moment to decide how to gracefully turn me down. But then I felt her tears on my neck.

"Are you okay?" I asked. "I didn't mean to upset you. If you're not interested, just say the word and I won't bug you about it again. I probably was just assuming too much. All this togetherness over the last several weeks. I know I'm not the best catch out there. You know how we old guys are. We always want to believe..."

"Oh, Colin, just be quiet," she said through her tears. "Of course, I'll marry you. I'm just in shock. I can't believe you asked me. I hoped that you would at some point, but I never wanted to put any pressure on you and press that damn 'duty button' of yours." She paused a moment and rubbed her eyes on my shirt. Then she spoke in a voice so soft that it was almost like I was hearing her thoughts. "I was prepared to wait a long time," she said, caressing my neck with her fingers. "A very long time."

She raised her head to look at me. I looked into her eyes and was awestruck by all the things I saw there.

"Why?" I whispered, without thinking. "Why would you wait for me? You could have anyone. I'm just some old..."

She put her finger on my lips.

"Because you're worth it, Colin Pearce," she said simply. "Because you don't have any other agenda than to love me and to be with me. Because you accept me as I am with all my neuroses and flaws and don't criticize me, judge me, or try to talk me out of them. Because you're the only man I've ever met who is totally comfortable in his own skin and doesn't have any ego issues he needs to work out in a relationship. Because you say what you mean with no bullshit. But mostly," she paused for a moment to regard me, "mostly because I love you."

"Wow," I said, delightfully stunned and surprised by her candor. Of course, the smart ass in me couldn't resist running with her words a little. "So, I guess I am a catch after all. I never knew I was so appealing. Maybe I should spread myself around a little more so that others can get some of this."

"Are you done?" Sarah asked me, with quite the bemused expression on her face.

I nodded. "Yeah, I guess I am."

"So, are you going to kiss me at some point and make this official?"

"Well, I was, but then we started having this discussion about..."

"Colin?"

"Yes, Sarah,"

"Would you shut up and kiss me?"

"Yes, ma'am."

A little later, she extricated herself from my arms, stood up, and walked over to the window. It was a beautiful day in the L.A. Basin and the mountains separating the basin from the San Fernando Valley were clearly visible in the distance. After appearing to take in the view for a moment or two, she turned around and looked at me with a stern expression on her face.

"There's only one thing we need to discuss," she said. "I like your two buddies, Smith and Amrine, a lot. But they do get you into some shit."

"Well, actually, I seem to get myself into the shit," I said. "They just kind of help."

Sarah lowered her eyes to the floor, and then she swallowed hard. I could tell she was struggling with something but she was determined not to let me see what it was. Finally, she raised her eyes to mine and spoke through defiant tears.

"You almost died, Colin!" she said, her voice wavering. "You were so close that the organ-donation scavengers had begun to hover. They talked about disconnecting you from life support three times! I almost lost you! I can't go through that again!"

I walked over to her and she pushed me away.

"Do you see what you've done to me?" she said, turning her back to me. "I used to never cry. You've turned me into one of those blubbery chicks I used to make fun of."

I slid my arms around her and pulled her to me. She wrapped her arms around mine.

"I can't lose you again," she said, quietly.

"Sarah," I said. "I never wanted to work for the CIA in the first place. If I have to choose between being with you and working for them, that's about as easy as it gets."

Smith and Amrine weren't terribly thrilled when I told them I was out of the independent contractor business the next day in the last debriefing we had together. Apparently, I had become a valuable asset and with the al Qudamah brothers still at large, they had wanted to use me to track them down. I also seemed to be one of the leading authorities on Miguel Hidalgo, aka Santa Anna, who was now identified as a major threat to the stability of US-Mexico relations. But when I brought Sarah in and told them about our engagement, they acted appropriately enthusiastic and the handshakes and hugs seemed genuine. They also promised to attend both the engagement party and the wedding.

And now, with our whole lives in front of us, we made our way to our rendezvous, a nice beach house in Malibu that was about forty-five minutes away. The traffic wasn't terribly heavy and, through a combination of Sarah's skillful driving and some great luck with the traffic signals, we were pulling up to the house just prior to the time I had agreed upon with Susan's family.

The house was done in Mediterranean style with tan stucco walls and terra cotta tiles on the roof. The view behind, what little I could see between the closely-spaced houses, was magnificent. I could see several cars parked in the driveway and at the curb, and every one of them was manufactured in Germany or Italy. Apparently, quite the gathering was underway and my attendance was expected.

I exited the car, straightened my suit jacket, and grabbed my cane which was lying on the floor of the back seat.

"You don't need that thing," Sarah said. "Why are you bringing it?"

"I don't know," I answered honestly. "Security blanket I guess. Plus it was the weapon I used to kill Saif-al Din and she helped me with that. It seems appropriate."

I walked around to the driver's side of the car, leaned in,

and kissed Sarah lightly on the lips.

"Are you sure you don't want to come in?" I asked.

She nodded. "I'd feel awkward," she said. "How long do you think you'll be?"

"Half-an-hour maybe," I said. "What are you going to do to kill the time?"

"There's a park nearby. I'll take Colleen out for a little stroll."

"Sounds good," I said. "See you in a little while."

Sarah winked at me and slowly drove off. I watched her go, and then I turned around, squared my shoulders, walked up to the house, and knocked on the door.

##

Thirty minutes later, I was back on the roadside, waiting for Sarah to return and reflecting on the last few minutes.

The house belonged to Susan's parents and they had invited the entire family, including the children, to hear what I had to say. I had previously cleared a script with Smith and Amrine and I stuck to it. I told the kids that their mom had died a hero, and I didn't feel I had lied. When I left the house, there wasn't a dry eye in the place and the faces reflected acceptance and gratitude. I was glad I had been there.

I looked up the road and was glad to see the Cadillac coming my way. I walked to the side of the road where I'd be on the passenger side and leaned on my cane, contemplating the promise of the evening. I was anxious to get to the mansion and to attend the party, but more than that, I was just anxious to be with Sarah. As the car rolled closer, I saw something that gave me pause. Sarah didn't seem to be driving it. There were two men in the front seat. Both wearing dark suits and sunglasses. Maybe I had the wrong car? I stepped back from the edge of the street, resigned to wait for a few minutes longer.

Then the car stopped in front of me and the man in the

front passenger seat turned toward me with a gun in his hand.

"Get in the car, Pearce," said Adam/Abdullah. "Or your precious little slut will die."

I had the oddest sensation just then. It was like my mind had been in a daze somewhere and was forced to suddenly focus; like a beautiful impressionist picture had morphed into hard-core realism; like my dream life had instantaneously transitioned into my real life.

And make no mistake, Pearce, a voice inside me said, *this is your real life.*

My mind immediately went into tactical overdrive. A glance in the back seat told me that Sarah wasn't there and I assumed Colleen wasn't there either. They were somewhere else and I needed Adam/Abdullah to take me there. I regretted resigning my status as an asset because the federal concealed-carry permit, with its associated weapon, would have come in very handy right about now.

I limped over to the car, making a show of leaning on my cane.

"I see the leg is still bothering you," Adam said, mockingly. "Saif was a good shot."

You should see how he died, I thought.

And then, for the first time in months, I felt the rage rise in my blood again. I had hoped Sarah's love had killed it inside of me, but it was still there and very much alive. It came out of its apparent hibernation and coursed warmly through my veins. It was patient, but it would get hotter. It wanted to be fed.

"He fought like a woman," I said, imparting the greatest insult I could think of to a Muslim man. "I'm limping because I ejected from an airplane at six-hundred knots."

Adam motioned toward the back seat with his gun. "Get in the back seat," he commanded. "And slide over behind the driver."

I did as I was told and noted that the driver covered me

with a pistol of his own as I passed behind Adam's seat. He was the same driver Adam had used when I first arrived; and he held his weapon in a much more no-nonsense manner than his boss did. I made a mental note of that.

"Hands," Adam commanded, as I reached the center part of the rear seat.

I let the cane fall to my lap and offered my hands to him under the coverage of the driver's weapon. Adam used a plastic zip tie to bind my wrists, and then instructed me to slide over further, completely behind the driver so Adam could cover me more easily with his own weapon. Adam nodded to the driver and spoke a command in Arabic. The driver holstered his weapon beneath his jacket and put the car into gear.

"We're going to the park," Adam said gaily. "You can meet your slut's true husband and her baby's true father. And then," he looked at me with a hint of manic anticipation in his eyes, "we're going to kill all of you."

I should have been frightened. Or angry. But instead I felt oddly at peace. This was my fate. It had always been my fate. Happy endings weren't for people like me. I just hoped I had time to save Sarah and Colleen and spare them from the collateral damage that seemed to come with my life.

As Adam shifted his attention from watching me and watching the road, I managed to unlock the blade from its cane-scabbard and slide about half-an-inch of it out. Then I went to work on the plastic tie binding my hands. The blade was still razor sharp and the work was done in less than fifteen seconds. Then I closed the scabbard, reset the lock, and waited for my chance.

The driver went to the end of the street, carefully signaled, and then made a left turn onto a busier street. After two blocks on the busy street, he turned left again down a more residential street, and followed it past the last few houses and around a curve where it ended in a small park. There, underneath a concrete pavilion in the center of the park, sat

Sarah on a concrete bench at a concrete picnic table, with her hands bound in front of her. A man, about the same size and shape as Adam, stood next to her with his back to me and another large Arab-looking man, obviously a bodyguard, stood nearby. It was just after lunchtime on a school day. There was no one in the park but us.

The car stopped in a parking space about twenty feet from the table and Adam motioned me out of the car. As I exited, I noticed that neither Adam nor the driver held their guns so much in the open. Instead, they kept them shielded behind their coats. I nodded to myself, hoping that would buy me a few milliseconds of time.

We walked over to the picnic table where the one guy still had his back to me. Adam grabbed my shoulder to stop me when I was about two feet from the guy, and I halted and stood. I turned my head slightly to the right and in my peripheral vision, I could see Adam standing directly behind me, at my 6:00 position, maybe two feet away. His driver was two feet to left of him, at my left 7:30 position, about four feet away. The new guy was at 12:00 with his back still turned and apparently, holding Colleen in front of him. His bodyguard was at my left 11:00, about four feet away, leaning against one of the pavilion's posts.

I was never going to get all of them. There just wouldn't be time. But there was enough cover nearby that I might be able to create sufficient confusion to let Sarah and Colleen get away. That was all that mattered.

I was leaning on my cane and had unlocked it so the only thing holding the blade in the scabbard was the pressure of my weight. Sarah was seated just beyond the guy with his back to me, facing outward on the bench. Her beautiful face was bruised and her hair and dress were disheveled.

The sight of her made me smile because it fueled the rage even more. As she raised her eyes to me, full of fear, despair, and dread, I winked at her with my right eye. She looked at me questioningly and I glanced down at my hands. I pointed briefly at the guy in front of me and made a catching motion with my hands. She cocked her head ever-so-slightly, then her eyes showed understanding and she nodded her chin a fraction of an inch.

Good girl.

The guy in front of me turned around, holding Colleen in front of him at arm's length with his hands under her little arm pits. It was obvious he had no experience with children at all. The baby's face was red on each cheek and it was obvious she had been slapped several times. Her eyes were wild with fear and she was whimpering pitifully, clearly terrified.

I smiled again. And the rage rose to boiling.

"Hello, Mr. Pearce," the guy in front of me said before his eyes had even met mine, "I'm Mohammed bin Rashid al Qudamah. Imam Mohammed bin Rashid al Qudamah."

He looked as he had in the picture I had seen at the suite in the Marriott, months ago—a younger version of Adam. Same build, although maybe a little shorter and a little wider. Same hair, and a face like Adam's with the attitude to match.

"I know who you are," I said.

"I've been anxious to meet you," he continued, ignoring me. "To make you suffer. You have stolen my wife, you were responsible for the failure of a great campaign against your evil nation, and your actions have disgraced both my brother and me. It is time to have our vengeance."

I laughed out loud. How much of it was acting and how much was hysteria was open to debate. "First of all, she never was your wife because you're Muslim and how does that passage from the Qur'an go? Something like 'Do not marry unbelieving women until they believe?' She didn't believe and you married her anyway. As far as your campaign is concerned, I'm confused. Are we talking about the half-assed aerial strike against San Francisco that a woman foiled or the half-assed attempt to kill our President which I stopped without firing a shot? Oh yes, and these would be the same operations in which you teamed with a mad Mexican who thinks he's going to take over the whole country? No wonder the CIA thinks you guys are a joke. Was that really the best you could do?"

Mohammed's eyes blazed. "You are as arrogant as my brother told me you were."

"This would be the same brother who spent the whole operation fucking a CIA undercover operative, another non-Muslim, right? Just like you spent a good portion of the set-up fucking a non-Muslim? You radical types sure like to spout the 'Great Satan' shit where American morality is concerned, but I'm just not seeing you on the moral high ground here. Maybe you can explain it to me."

He began to quiver with anger. I tightened my grip on the handle of the blade.

"It is time for you to see all you love die," he said. "For you to see the consequences of your acts against Allah."

"Well, I sure hope Allah's got better players on his team than you two or he's in deep shit."

He wanted to stay calm. He tried to stay calm. And he almost managed to do it. But then he did something I didn't expect. As his face clouded with fury, something suddenly occurred to him that surprised him. He looked at me with an expression of recognition. Then he looked at Colleen and looked back at me. He saw something in those few glances that drove him into pure, unbridled wrath—and I knew it was time.

He tried to throw Colleen to his left side so he could reach for the gun that was undoubtedly somewhere on the right side of his waist, but I was ready for him. The plastic tie around my wrists, which I had severed in the car, fell to the ground and I caught Colleen with my right hand and pulled the blade free of its scabbard with my left. My left hand was upside down, with my thumb and index finger nearest the blade, so the angle was awkward, but the blade was sharp and the adrenaline pumping through my body made the stroke savage and sure. In one motion, as I drove the blade from scabbard to sky, I ripped Mohammed bin Rashid al Qudamah's body open from groin to throat.

The rage was singing in my veins now. I could feel the endorphins rushing through my blood and the familiar euphoria possessing me. The scene around me dissolved into the odd, ultra-slow pace of events generated by temporal distortion.

I gently tossed Colleen to Sarah, who by now was poised to catch her with bound hands.

"Run," I commanded her.

Colleen flew through the air in a very small arc and landed neatly in Sarah's arms. Sarah started to pivot and run for the nearest house.

Mohammed's body guard was under orders and he was fast. He was very fast. Ignoring his master's fate, he pulled his pistol from his jacket and trained it on Sarah's back more quickly than I would have believed possible. I didn't even have time to scream a warning at her as I saw his finger tighten on the trigger.

And then his head exploded.

The dull crack of the suppressed rifle shot was audible a fraction of a second later.

Miguel! I thought.

There were still two more of them.

I twirled the blade around my left hand like a baton and I reversed its direction so that it was pointed down and to the rear. Then I stepped backward into Adam, just as he was trying to extract his pistol from his coat and raise it. I deflected his right arm with my right shoulder and locked his right arm with mine as I drove the blade rearward and into his stomach, all the way to the hilt. The resulting grunt that emanated from his once-arrogant mouth was most satisfying.

I looked to my left, only to see Adam's driver raising his pistol and bringing the weapon to bear. He wasn't aiming at me, so I knew he was preparing to fire at Sarah, who by now was only about fifteen-to-twenty yards away. I threw myself at him to spoil his aim and braced myself for the impact of the bullets, but I never reached him. His head snapped back and a cloud of blood and gore sprayed all over the tree behind him. He crumpled to the ground like a sack of potatoes. The dull crack of a suppressed rifle was audible once again.

About five seconds of time had elapsed.

For a moment, all was quiet. I could hear wind rustling the leaves of the trees around me and the gentle chirping of the birds in the nearby branches.

Peace was returning to the scene.

I felt a stirring from somewhere behind me and I turned to see Joe Sanchez step from a small grove of nearby trees. He had an AR-15 rifle in his hands, fully equipped with a bipod, telescopic site, and sound suppressor. He nodded at me and I nodded back. The message was clear. Miguel's debt was paid.

And then he was gone.

But there was still work to be done. For while the rage had been fed, it wasn't sated.

Adam had somehow landed in a sitting position and had his hands on the handle of the blade as if he could lessen the damage to himself by holding on to it. I brushed his hands aside and then extracted it, eagerly watching the dark red blood flow from the damaged organs in his lower body. His eyes were open and I could tell he was still conscious. His eyes were watching me closely, but tiredly, and he didn't seem to even have enough strength for his facial muscles to form their usual sneer.

"So, you wanted to know what T.C. stood for, remember?' I asked him. "It's actually easier for me to show you than to tell you."

I walked over to Mohammed, who was still breathing with a slight whistle through his perforated lungs. I walked behind him, grabbed a handful of the thick, dark hair, and pulled him up to a sitting position from the pile of entrails that surrounded him.

"Let me give you a hint. The 'T' stands for throat."

Then, looking directly into Adam's eyes, I cut his brother's throat slowly and completely, from ear to ear, slicing so deeply that I could feel the blade in contact with the bones in Mohammed's neck as it carved his flesh. Then, I extricated the blade and cast his body aside like I was tossing garbage to the ground.

I walked over to Adam and laid the edge of the blade against his neck.

"The guy who sold me this told me it was sharp enough to decapitate a human being with a single stroke," I said, thoughtfully. "Maybe it's time to see if he was telling the truth."

Adam looked at me, barely conscious but still mentally present enough to register the words. I could see fear in the depths of the dark brown eyes.

I smiled at him.

"And what's the penalty for murder in your country?" I asked. "The penalty all the low-lifes and criminals must suffer?" I paused for a moment, letting him consider the words. "Oh yes, I remember. It's beheading. We'll, you're a criminal, so I guess this is apropos."

I raised the sword.

"When you see Allah," I said, "Tell him Colin Pearce says hello."

The guy who sold me the sword exaggerated a little. It took me two strokes to take Adam's head. And the rage loved it.

EPILOGUE

1000 Hours Local Time
Sunday, March 7
Bob Hope Airport (KBUR)
Burbank, California, United States

The three of us drove in silence to the Burbank Airport, Sarah and I up front and Colleen sleeping peacefully in the back. The journey seemed eerily familiar, but the sense of loss I felt was an order of magnitude greater than the last time three or so years ago. My wonderful future had been taken away from me with a single phone call.

The morning after our engagement party—our fabulous engagement party—where Sarah and I had danced the night away and kissed each other more times than I could count, my new BlackBerry rang.

"You did well yesterday, amigo," Miguel Hidalgo's voice intoned. "Very well, indeed. You are indeed a true warrior. A man after my own heart. I had wanted to deal with the al Qudamahs myself, particularly after Abdullah disobeyed my orders where your woman was concerned, but you took care of that for me. The least I could do was take care of his henchmen before they could do your lady friend and her baby harm. The fact that it kept you from harm, as well, is my gift."

I had felt a chill go up my spine. I remembered Joe Sanchez

being there, but what hadn't occurred to me until just then, was that he, or another one of Miguel's men, had always been there. For the three months after my crash. Miguel had someone there. And I never knew it.

"It is good to see that you are back in action. Have you given my offer any further thought?" he asked evenly.

"No," I answered. "Respectfully, sir, I'm out of this. I want to get married and raise some kids and have a nice, normal life."

"That is not possible for you, amigo. You killed too many of my men at Catalina. You damaged our cause. Were you to come to our side and admit the error of your ways, I would be able to accept you as an ally and overlook that transgression. But now my men, they want your head. And every day you remain alive makes them believe I no longer have the power or the resolve to do anything about it. My honor has been damaged. I may have to rectify that personally."

I shut my eyes and shook my head in despair.

"What about your debt of honor, Miguel?" I asked. "What about your word?"

"My word stands. Your woman is a non-combatant and she will not be harmed. Nor will her child."

"Your word didn't do her much good last November," I said.

"My apologies," Miguel said in a surprisingly sincere tone. "At that time, I believed Abdullah al Qudamah to be a man of integrity. A man who could take orders. Obviously, I was wrong. But, thanks to you, he is no longer an issue. Now your woman's safety is entirely in your hands. She will remain a non-combatant in my view, but if the two of you were together when someone came after *you*..."

"But what about your policy on collateral damage?" I blurted out, silently cursing the pleading tone that had entered my voice.

"Oh, I would not tolerate that from my own men," he said.

"But I plan to put a price on your head so large that I expect many who are less scrupulous and less precise may engage you. Of course, they will be publically penalized and may even pay with their lives, but that won't help you or your woman or her child. But if you are alone, then I may come after you myself. So, we can finish this in person, man-to-man. Do you understand?"

"I understand," I said, feeling my heart sink. "I understand perfectly."

But Sarah didn't understand after I told her about the phone call. For the rest of the day, she pleaded with me to stay, but I remained firm. Leaving was the only option.

And that night, in spite of our agreement to remain celibate until our wedding, she came to my room and we made love for the many hours until morning. It was slow and sweet, utterly fulfilling, and completely heartbreaking.

Sarah stopped the car at the airport curb. She had been stoic as she drove me to the airport; but now, as she put car into park and it was time say our farewells, her façade was failing. She sat in her seat with one hand on the Cadillac's steering wheel and the other still on the gear shift, shaking her head and looking through the windshield of the car while the tears began to stream down her cheeks.

"We could have been so happy together," she said, her words heavy with emotion. "It's just not fucking fair."

I turned to her and looked at her beautiful profile a final time, resolving to keep my voice steady and make my exit before I failed in that attempt. "You're right, Sarah," I said. "It's not fair. But people have had a nasty habit of getting dead around me recently and if something happened to you or little Colleen because of me, I'd never forgive myself."

At the mention of her daughter's name, Sarah lowered

her eyes to the dashboard in front of her. "There's something you need to know," she said as the tears fell unheeded onto the soft cotton of her skirt. "I may never... we may never see you again."

I opened my mouth to comfort her but she continued before I could speak.

"Colleen's yours," she said without preamble. "I've been meaning to tell you but I just didn't know how. I planned to tell you on our wedding day if you hadn't figured it out by then."

I felt my lower jaw open in astonishment as my eyes moved to Colleen without my commanding them to, settling on her face which was reflected in the mirror mounted above the rear-facing seat. Almost on cue, the child opened her eyes and it was like a disguise was lifted from the little face. I saw my own image in the shape of her face, the curve of her jaw, and the gleam in her eyes. And I wondered how I had not seen before now.

Suddenly, I became very aware of the sensation of my heart pounding inside my chest and a rapid increase in my breathing. My brain was in a full-fledged compressor stall, like a jet engine unable to take air in and produce thrust, my mind was unable to take in what it was seeing and process it.

"But... how?" I said in a barely audible whisper.

"Remember your contribution to the fertility clinic years ago?" she asked in matter-of-fact voice. "When Damian or Mohammed or whoever wanted me to get pregnant, I decided that if I was going to have someone's baby it was going to be yours."

There it was. It made sense and I knew it was the truth. My eyes remained locked on to Colleen's and I felt her looking back at me innocently, but expectantly.

"Well, daddy?" She seemed to be saying. *"What's it going to be?"*

I could feel myself becoming light-headed. The implications

here were too much for me to grasp. All my life I had been alone and concerned only for myself. My mother's words from one of her many alcoholic tirades still rung in my ears all these years later: *"You're a selfish little shit."* I had lived as a testimony to her characterization of me, never caring about anything else or anyone else.

But that was all changed. Now I had someone who depended on me. Someone who was a part of me. Someone who had my blood in her veins.

God help her.

"I'm a... father," I said, the words leaving my mouth without my willing them. "*I*... am a father."

"You are," Sarah said simply as she wiped some of her tears away. "And I didn't want you to find out this way, but if you're determined to leave, I thought the least I could do is tell you to your face."

I'm a father. As the stall cleared and my brain began processing again, I could feel the emotions slowly settling inside of me.

I wasn't scared, or angry, or even apprehensive. I wasn't resentful at Sarah for impregnating herself with my child or frustrated because I hadn't been asked.

Instead, I found I was grateful. But more than that, I was awestruck. Something good had actually come from me.

Jesus. How is that even possible?

"I don't know what to say, Sarah," I began, struggling to express what I was feeling.

She shook her head as if I had disappointed her and leaned away from me, raising her hands defensively. "I'm not looking for financial support, if you're worried about that. I decided a long time ago that Colleen and I weren't going to be a burden..."

I didn't let her finish. I captured her hands with mine and kissed each one of them as tenderly as I could. I could feel the tears welling in my own eyes but I fought to keep them under control.

"It's a lot to take in, Sarah," I said, softly. "But the thing that's occurring to me is that you've given me something priceless. Something I've looked for my entire life."

Her eyes cleared and she cocked her head, looking me straight in the eyes. "And what would that be?"

I looked back at her evenly. "You've given me something to believe in," I said. "You've given me something to live for."

"Then come back to us." she said. "Promise you'll come back to us."

"I will," I said resolutely, looking directly back at her. "When this is over. I promise."

She regarded my eyes carefully and found something there she could believe in. I pulled her to me and I lost myself in her arms and her lips, pouring as much of myself into her as I could; wanting her to feel what I felt about everything.

"I'll be brave," she said, as our lips parted.

"I would never doubt that," I replied. "You're made that way."

"You know why I believe you, right?" she asked.

I looked back at her questioningly.

"I know how you are about your word. You never go back on it."

I nodded. "And I'm not just giving it to you. I'm giving it to her too."

I slid out of the front seat and into the back. Colleen looked up at me, delighted I had joined her and reached for me, squirming to get out of the restraints of the car seat. I ran my left hand down her perfect little cheek, and then bent forward and kissed the smooth skin of her forehead.

"Be good, little one," I whispered to her. "I'll be back as soon as I can."

And with that, I left the car and Sarah drove away, waving and smiling at me. I waved and smiled back, storing the joy of the news I had just received deep inside of me and placing my own personal "happily ever after" on an indefinite pause.

So I focused on my near-term goals. I had to get faster, better, and more lethal. And then I'd find a place to hole up and I'd wait for Miguel Hidalgo to come and get me. I knew he'd want to do it himself. I knew he'd want to settle the debt personally.

Sarah was right about me keeping my word. I had every intention of coming back to her and coming back to my newly found daughter.

There was just one problem with that plan.

I was pretty sure I wouldn't live that long.

TOP SECRET/SPECIAL
COMPARTMENTALIZED INFORMATION
CLASSIFIED BY: US Central Intelligence Agency
DECLASSIFY ON: OADR

From: Special Projects Group [NCS]
Sent: Sunday, 7 March 2010, 1000 PST (7 November 2010, 1800Z)
To: Director, NCS
Cc: Special Projects Group [NCS]; damrine@cmail.cia.gov; dsmith3@cmail.cia.gov

SUBJECT: Reassignment of Contractor 09-017 (Pearce, Colin M.) to Asset Status

(TS) Narrative:

1. (TS) Today, at 0730 hours PST, Contractor 09-017 (Pearce, Colin M.) contacted us and asked to resume his asset status with the agency. As you recall, he requested deactivation approximately two weeks ago. We did not inform him at that time that deactivations are not possible.

2. (TS) As we reported previously, on Friday 5 March, Pearce's fiancé, Sarah Morton and her child, were briefly abducted by Mohammed and Abdullah bin Rashid al Qudamah while Pearce was conducting an authorized debriefing with the family of Susan Turner. While we had a crew in place to intervene if necessary, Pearce killed both of the al Qudamah brothers. Miguel Hidalgo also had a team in place and one of his men killed two of the al Qudamahs' henchmen. Apparently, this was the outcome of a promise Hidalgo made to Pearce concerning Sarah Morton's welfare. This was a highly desirable occurrence and neatly closes the file on the al Qudamah brothers.

3. (TS) Yesterday, we monitored a phone call Pearce received from Hidalgo in which Hidalgo threatened his life if he did not come to work for him. While Hidalgo didn't threaten Sarah Morton or her child directly, he did make it clear that if Pearce remained with them, Hidalgo would not guarantee that they wouldn't be hurt. (NOTE: Colleen Morton is actually Pearce's daughter and we know Sarah Morton has informed him of that fact.)

4. (TS) Pearce has offered to return to our service to act as bait to bring Hidalgo out of hiding. Pearce is convinced that Hidalgo's code of honor will force Hidalgo to engage Pearce personally or at least be present when he is killed. (Note: Intel confirms that Hidalgo suffered an extreme loss of prestige among his followers after Pearce's refusal of his offer to command his revolutionary Air Force and Pearce's subsequent actions which thwarted his operation against the Presidents of the United States and Mexico.) Our knowledge of Hidalgo's capabilities has grown significantly since the attack last fall. We know of his financial holdings, his government influence and his power within the Mexican Federal Police and the Mexican Military. We briefed Pearce on Hidalgo's capabilities and he seemed unconcerned and reiterated his offer. He did, however, demand specialized weapons and hand-to-hard combat training to prepare for further operations.

(TS) CONCLUSIONS:

1. (TS) DEA uncover operative, Joseph Sanchez, remains in place but his opportunities for contact are limited. We have reason to believe that Hidalgo will monitor Pearce's movements and will lead a team to kill him.

2. (TS) We will assume custody of Sarah and Colleen Morton

and move them to a safe location where they will be impossible to discover.

(TS) ACTIONS:

1. (TS) Provide Pearce weapons and hand-to-hand combat training through approved commercial vendors;

2. (TS) Implement operation using Pearce to lure Hidalgo into action.

(TS) RECOMMENDATION:

Approve the suggested operation. Miguel Hidalgo represents a significant threat to US National Security. This operation presents an extremely high risk level, but it also presents the best opportunity to engage and eliminate Miguel Hidalgo. While the personal danger to Pearce is high and his behavior may be unpredictable, he has proven himself a reliable operator and has shown surprising resilience, ingenuity, and aggressiveness. We are confident he will prevail.

COLIN PEARCE WILL RETURN
IN
THE SATAN CONTRACT

ABOUT THE AUTHOR

Chris Broyhill is a retired U.S. Air Force fighter pilot who flew the OV-10, A-10, and F-16 while on active duty. He holds a bachelor's degree in computer science from the U.S. Air Force Academy, a master's degree in national security studies from California State University at San Bernardino and a Ph.D. in aviation from Embry-Riddle Aeronautical University. Chris is an outstanding graduate of the U.S. Air Force Fighter Weapons School and is a National Business Aviation Association Certified Aviation Manager. Chris has flown in and led aviation organizations for over 30 years.